GODS OF EGYPT

a novel

by

Orlando Smart-Powell

CHAPTER 1

What Tamen saw not only disgusted him, but also brought back a sense of excitement he hadn't felt in centuries. The voices of men, and the cries of one in particular had drawn him off the country road he walked and onto a dirt trail leading to nowhere in a dense forest. And nowhere—Nuxta, Mississippi—was exactly where he felt he was.

The screams from a man right before the blast of a shotgun silenced him, was all it took to finally peak Tamen's curiosity. Occasionally, after having lived for more than three thousand years, there were times when humans were apt to do things that actually surprised him. It was not as though he would be wasting time if he detoured to see what was happening. He was an eternal being—a god at one time—after all. And time—well, at least for now—was something he had plenty of.

He stood not even a hundred yards from the men and a boy who was with them. In the middle of the path, the glow of a full moon at his back, he was invisible to them, for he willed their minds not to see or hear him.

Just a boy, Tamen thought, as he searched for the source of the urine that was permeating the humid night air. *Fifteen years old,* he discovered from reading the boy's thoughts. *Afraid...afraid of what he almost did. Hmm? What his father wanted him to do to the Negroe. But....* As Tamen looked closer, he discovered exactly what it was that had caused the boy to wet his blue jeans. It was a black man—a dead one whose chest was still smoking from the shot fired into it—propped up at the base of a hearty oak tree. Not more than a few feet away from the body were two other white men playfully shoving each other toward the corpse.

The other white man, the father of the boy, were in a far less jovial mood than his counterparts were, who were now daring each other to touch the dead man. "What da hell wrong wit you boy?" The father barked in a thick drawl. The boy quickly lowered his head. "Henry? Junior! Ya hear me talkin'?" Henry closed in on his son. His naked, pregnant size belly butted at the boy's chest. "You gonna stand there a grown-tail man and piss yo' pants? Dammit-all, boy! All you had to do is point the thing and pull the triggah."

"Like coon hunting, ain't it, Jackson?" the thinner of the other two white men added.

Jackson, who was holding the shotgun, wiped his beak of a nose and chuckled. "Hell yeah, Timmy-boy! We sho' got us a coon, too!"

"A lying coon is what he be," Henry corrected. "You don't pay for your goods at Ms. Emma's store, this be what happen to ya."

"See Junior," Jackson said, "it don't pay for blackies to be going around being mouthy neither."

"But...but...," Henry Jr. sputtered.

"But what?" Henry demanded.

"He...he sa—sa—said he was gonna pay."

Henry swung and smacked the boy in the face. Henry Jr. yelped as he tumbled to the ground. To Tamen's immortal eyes, Henry's swing of his arm seemed as though he was moving in molasses instead of air. But to the boy, Tamen knew, the blow to his cheek had been dealt swiftly, with nary a chance to avoid it.

Despite seeing the corpse, and now the boy being struck to the ground for his failure in inflicting the fatal blow, Tamen had yet to wince. For thousands of years, he too had killed and denied mercy to those who might otherwise have deserved it. But when Henry Jr. looked up, Tamen paused when he saw tears—innocent ones—seeping from the boy's dark brown eyes.

He dropped the illusion of invisibility he'd been casting into the men's minds and began walking toward them. The first to notice him was Henry Jr., who immediately stopped crying and stared at him with mouth wide open. It pleased Tamen that Henry Jr. grew even more frightened at his approach. He sensed the boy fearing not for himself, but for this obviously insane Negroe man dressed in white linen pants, a stark-white shirt complete with a black tie, who was foolishly approaching a group of white men still basking in the afterglow of a murder. Though Henry Jr.'s concern for him was thoughtful indeed, Tamen thought, it was completely unwarranted and misplaced.

"Get up, you little yella-back!" Henry Sr. growled at his son. "Ya barely even worth your...boy? Junior! You listening? I said get uhhh...." He stopped in mid-sentence as he followed Henry Jr.'s gaze down the path where Tamen was walking toward them. With perfection, he mimicked Henry Jr.'s same slack jaw expression. "You gotta be jokin'."

"Holy hell!" Jackson blurted and nearly choked on his chewing tobacco when he saw Tamen. "Timmy, look!"

Timmy did just that and then eyed Tamen from his bald head to his shiny white shoes. He snorted and then spat on the ground. "Jackson, you got some rope for this dumb boy?"

Jackson cocked his head. "For a boy as tall as him? I right reckon I do. I still got some more shells, too."

None of their bravado or threats bothered Tamen. They were of flesh, bone, blood and organs. They were everything he was not. There was nothing they could do to harm him unless they could command the sacred chant, which of course he knew they knew nothing about.

No...they were simply dead men.

"Boy...you done come just in time," Timmy teased.

Tamen kept his eyes on Henry Sr., and it was to him that Tamen spoke. "What was this man's crime that he has deserved such a death?" His voice was hearty and smooth as it was at the age of twenty-six when he became, Horus, god of Egypt.

"Where the hell you from, boy?" Henry Sr. asked, but didn't wait for an answer. "Ya ain't from here, I know that much. You may be all dressed up fancy there and talkin' educated, but ain't smart enough to know you done walked into a world of mess—do ya? You ain't walking outta here, ya know that? I kinda feel sorry 'bout it, seeing that you just a boy and all. But...tough shit, dumb-ass."

Tamen didn't need to read Henry Sr.'s mind to know that he wasn't sorry in the least. Excitement was the true emotion he gleaned from the man's thoughts. And Henry Sr. was wrong about one thing, Tamen knew. Though he possessed the face and lean body of a young black man, in simple terms, he was ancient. And in so many of those long years, such as now, Tamen realized once again that mankind had not evolved much, but quite the opposite.

"Will you answer me?" Tamen asked softly. "What cause? What reason can you give me that can justify what you have done to that man?"

"I don't owe you nothin'!" Henry Sr. retorted.

"What can you tell me that will make me even consider sparing your lives?"

Henry Sr. crossed his arms and glared at Tamen. "You ain't for real, boy. Timmy! Rattle this boy's cage...*hard!* Jackson...you go get that rope off the tail of the truck there. I'm gonna show you boys here how we really used to treat blackies in Nuxta, Mississippi." He smiled and winked at Tamen.

Tamen winked back at him.

Quicker than their mortal sight could see, let alone follow, Tamen sidestepped Timmy and pounced on Jackson. To them, Tamen knew he had moved so quick it seemed as if he had all but disappeared from sight and suddenly reappeared in front of Jackson. Jackson, bewildered and startled, raised the shotgun he had and fired directly at Tamen's chest.

In the time it took for Jackson to blink, yelp in fright and fire the shotgun, Tamen figured he could have taken the man's life several times over and been on to his friend, Timmy. But there was something he wanted them all to see before they died... *which was that he had no fear of them.* "Shoot again," Tamen dared him. "Two, three or twenty times will make no difference. Your metal pellets cannot end my life and certainly will not save yours tonight."

Tamen grabbed hold of Jackson by the throat and lifted him from his feet as though he weighed two pounds instead of almost two hundred. He then began to literally squeeze the life out of him. He sensed Timmy coming from the side and about to attack, even as Timmy produced the very thought in his mind to do just that. Tamen simply turned and grasped Timmy by the throat also, halting him in mid-stride and raising him in the air along with Jackson.

"*Oh my dear God!*" Henry Sr. gasped.

"Indeed," Tamen replied, holding both flailing men aloft. He squeezed their throats until their lungs were completely deprived of oxygen. Their hearts pounded crazily for a short moment and jerked to a stop. Both men drooped like marionettes whose strings had been cut. Tamen dropped them at his feet, never once taking his eyes off of Henry Sr.. The boy, Henry Jr., scrambled to his feet and ran off into woods without so much as a look back at his father.

"Goddamn you, boy!" Henry Sr. yelled at his son, who had already disappeared into the darkness of trees and thick brush. He turned back and looked at Tamen.

Tamen saw Henry Sr.'s eyes darting around frantically. He knew what the man searched for. Tamen picked up the shotgun lying next to Jackson's body and threw it at Henry Sr., who caught it and clumsily tried to orient it. "Think now. I have already been shot in the chest once, yet I still walk and talk, but your comrades are dead. You have no idea of the power you have unleashed. I see all of your sins and they are many. I think you shall pay for them all tonight." Tamen pulled his shirt open, ripping the buttons away as he revealed a smooth, ebony-skinned chest that was slightly indented with shotgun pellets.

Henry Sr. dropped the shotgun. "You...you-you ain't bleedin'. You ain't *human!*"

"Of course not. But you, my friend, *are*," Tamen replied. He ran forward—barely touching the ground as he did—and wrapped his arm around Henry Sr.'s shoulder and placed his other hand on his chest. Henry Sr.'s quickly formed pleas for mercy were only half-formed words bubbling through a mouth full of slobber.

"Sshhhhh," Tamen whispered to him as he started patting Henry Sr.'s chest...slowly at first. "It is too late to ask forgiveness from me." He tapped harder—with his granite hard hand—causing Henry Sr. to pant and gasp for air. "May God have mercy on your soul, for I do not." With one firm slap of his open hand to Henry Sr. chest, he stopped the man's heart once and for all.

* * *

Tamen set out after the boy, Henry. His urine-soaked pants and the scent of adrenalin oozing out of his skin were like flashing beacons to Tamen. In Henry's thoughts he sensed fear, disbelief and a feeling of the 'black man' in the woods somewhere about to pounce on him and snap his throat like he had the others.

The ability to read thoughts and cast his own into the minds of others had always come easily to Tamen. Years before becoming the thing that he was now—neither man nor the god, Horus, he was worshipped as—he'd honed the skill better than any other priest in Egypt, save one. But after the transmutation of his mortal flesh and blood into nearly indestructible flesh and bone with the power of a god only a chant-spell away, not only had his mind-reading ability been heightened a hundredfold, but his hearing, sight and strength were as well. Moving swifter than the wind, as he did now, was as simple as willing his legs to do so.

Within moments, Tamen was a mere step behind Henry and listening to the thudding of his young heart against his ribcage. Tamen began projecting the sound of his voice as a whisper into Henry's mind. *Slow down, young one.* Upon Henry's senses, he conjured the scent of musky-myrrh, a calming aroma for the sick he'd used many times before. *Despite what you have seen me do, you have nothing to fear from me.*

Henry began to slow down and eventually came to a stop. Tamen slowly dropped his illusion that hid his figure from Henry's sight and materialized behind him. He placed a hand on Henry's shoulder and turned him around so that they were face-to-face. He stroked Henry's tear-soaked cheek. "The deeds of thy father have died with him. You, child, are sinless in my eyes."

He peered into Henry's mind and searched for memories. In them, Tamen saw the regular beatings with switches and fists to Henry's slender face that were doled out by his father. He sensed that hopelessness and despair were the only true emotions Henry thought existed. There seemed to be not one ounce of happiness or joy that Tamen could find anywhere in Henry's short fifteen years of life. While sharing in Henry's thoughts, for the first time in thousands of years, Tamen remembered what it was like to be human for a moment.

"You gonna kill me?" Henry uttered. "I didn't wanna do it. I knew him...that Negroe—Mr. Tripkin. I didn't want to but...."

"I know of all that. And no, dear child, I will not take your life."

He moved closer to Henry and intensified the sense of myrrh in the boy's mind. Now, he mingled it with a hint of lavender and peppermint to relax him further. But Henry moved backward and began to stumble. Tamen took hold of him and pulled him close to his chest and held tight. Henry struggled momentarily and then went limp. He collapsed into Tamen's granite-hard chest and began sobbing. The more he wept, the more Tamen began to feel a need to protect such a tortured child. In that moment, he thought of an idea that would be beneficial to both himself and Henry, and another who was most dear to him.

Tamen looked down at Henry. "Tell me...if you were given a chance to start anew and reclaim your life as it should have been, would you take it?"

"I don't understand," he mumbled.

Tamen cocked his head to the side and smiled. "Of course you do not. You have no mother, no father now, or even a brother or sister for that matter. All I see is loneliness within you."

"How—how did you know?" Henry asked in astonishment. His eyes suddenly doubled in size. "You were shot!" he blurted, as though having just realized it. "And—and—you killed Mr. Timmy with your hands. Just your hands! You ain't a real person."

"No, I am not."

"But—but...."

"I am something you have never known before," Tamen told him. "I am a creature that is part man and part god. I know I look as though I am only a few years older than yourself, but I assure you, I am far older than anything you know of. And know this

Henry...it is within my power to give you a new life. One far away from harm, if you can serve me."

"Serve?"

"You can live the rest of your short, mortal years and become a man of dignity and honor. All I ask is that you answer my call if ever I have need of you," Tamen explained. "Vow upon your life that I have graciously spared, and these things I promise will be fulfilled."

"And if—"

"Then you may go back to your home that has nothing left for you," Tamen said, already having heard the question formed in Henry's mind before he could speak it. "But do you really wish to spend your life fending for yourself and praying to survive each and every day?"

Henry was on the verge of tears again. "I—I don't know what I want."

"Then listen to my words and choose," Tamen said. "I will show you the way to a woman who lives deep in the bayou near the city of New Orleans. She is my daughter, and she is barren, though craves a child of her own. She can attend to your every need. Do so, and in the years to come, all the sorrow you have known shall become just a distant memory, like a nightmare you once had as a child long ago."

Henry Jr. closed his eyes and shook his head. "Am I dreaming now?"

Tamen sighed. He knew there was only so much a mortal mind could comprehend. Things that mortals always wanted to believe in—gods and spirits and heaven and hell—were always doubted when confronted with proof. Tamen reached into his back pocket and pulled out a roll of twenty-dollar bills and put it in Henry's hand.

"I will cause a great sleep to come over you and show you the truth of myself to help you comprehend this thing that I am, and the truthfulness of my offer to you," Tamen said. "When you wake, I will not be here. The bodies of the dead and all traces of what occurred tonight will be gone. You may then go to my daughter, following the way to her that I shall set in your mind. If you choose wisely, Henry, you can be free of all of this. You may also follow your own path and believe all of this is just a dream if you wish. The choice will be yours. Do you understand, child?"

Henry nodded.

"Then sleep!" Tamen commanded, as he forced Henry's mind to shut down and reawaken within his control. As Henry lost consciousness, Tamen swept him up into his arms. "See now what few other mortals have ever seen. Great sights I will now reveal to you."

* * *

Tamen stood over the corpses of Henry's father and the other men and admired his handiwork. He'd already placed Henry in the driver's seat of the truck and induced a deeper sleep over him so that he would have time to dispose of the bodies. Whether Henry would believe the visions he had shown him and then go to his daughter, Aria, he wasn't sure. He hoped so. But at the moment, he had more pressing things to attend to.

With a simple spell, he conjured flames to arise beneath the men's corpses. Once they had, he commanded them to grow and burn hotter, until the red-yellow flames turned an unnatural blue hue. He wanted their bones to bake until they were brittle enough to grind into dust between his hands.

He didn't even consider using the sacred chant to create the fire. It would have made the process so much quicker if he had, as the power of the chant would have reduced every piece of flesh and bone to ashes in moments. But he knew he couldn't. He hadn't uttered a single chant since fleeing almost two thousand years ago from the two who sought to kill him. Even giving voice to one sound of the chant and they could follow the power it exuded and find him. He was confident he could easily best Lord Yikan. But Shazadeh, the female at Lord Yikan's side, was vastly more powerful. There was only one who could face Shazadeh, but he had yet to find *that one* who could, and would, be her counter-balance. *And if I'm killed before I do find that one, then all is lost,* he thought, recalling the charge given to him by the Christ.

The reflection of the blue fire danced crazily on his brown skin and hairless head as he watched the bonfire of bodies roast. He looked over at the dead black man and felt a hint of pity for him. *Another victim of bizarre circumstances,* he thought. At least his death seemed bizarre to Tamen.

The southern states of America and their preoccupation with race astounded him when he first arrived right after the Civil War. It was nothing like his beloved Egypt, where when he was mortal, the only thing that had ever set him apart was his towering height of six feet and four inches to boot. That he had full lips, high rounded cheekbones like his Nubian-born mother and a broad nose from his equally dark Egyptian father didn't matter. All that mattered to Egyptians was whether one was a citizen of Egypt or not, not what one looked like.

In all of his travels, across the world and back, and through long, weary years, he could think of no civilization yet that rivaled the past glory of his own Egypt. But he hated remembering Egypt just as much as he loved reminiscing about it. To him, it was the only true land of 'milk and honey' despite what the prophet Moses proclaimed to him.

"And what of you now, my Egypt?" he muttered. "A few crumbling pyramids and excavated temples for archeologists to plunder?"

He quelled the fire and set to grinding the charred bones of Henry Sr. and his cohorts into dust. Soon after, all that remained of what happened was a circle of scorched earth and the still warm body of the black man not far from it. Out of a sense of ancient tradition, he decided to take the black man's body to the family for a proper burial instead of leaving it to rot in the woods. He gently slung the body over his shoulder and began walking toward the road. Tamen knew someone—somewhere—had to be thinking about the dead man. So he listened.

Tamen picked at the wayward thoughts of Nuxta's townsfolk hovering in the air. He grabbed at them. He listened. But as he searched the thoughts of nearby mortals, a presence that was not human suddenly pricked at his senses.

Tamen knew he was not alone.

He stopped in the middle of the road. The skin on his arms now truly began coming alive with electric pinpricks that traveled up his shoulders and spread throughout his body in an undulating wave. At first it tickled, and then began burning. It was the same feeling he had experienced at the Red Sea when Moses parted it into two.

"Show yourself!" Tamen demanded, turning around with the body still hanging over his shoulder. "I know you are there creature...*angel*. I can sense you! Feel you! Why are you here?"

But it was simply a dark road lined with trees that he saw, though he knew without a doubt an angel was near. Save for those who hunted him, the angels and its kind were all that he knew that could cause him harm. They had before in Egypt.

Tamen knew one was watching him right now, but refused to allow itself to be seen. But was its presence a sign or a warning? He wondered. The first time he'd seen any of the glowing blue skinned angels was in Egypt when he and the other gods fought and were bested by them. The last time was in Germany just as the Nazis were advancing on Poland.

Turn from this path Egyptian, Tamen remembered the angel commanding him. *We know thou hath plans to kill the evil one...he who is called Adolf Hitler. But you are forbidden to harm him. At-*

tempt to harm this mortal, and from the nether-realm the demons will arise to strike thee down mightily. Thou knowest the balance of all things must be kept. Three of light and three of dark shall always roam the Earth unmolested until their duty is done. That is the sacred covenant! It shall not be broken by thee!

"And what of the demoness, Shazadeh, who was once a mortal woman?" Tamen had asked.

Keep thy agreement with the Lamb of God and find the one—the light—to balance the dark Shazadeh has become and brought upon this world. Without balance upon this earth, she will rule it forever and ever, it replied.

Tamen looked down the road, which was empty, save for the moonlight beaming off the oil laden black asphalt. He called for it once more, but to no avail. It was not going to show itself. But that it had come at this moment made him wonder if Nuxta, Mississippi was where he was supposed to be after all.

* * *

It was minutes shy of one in the morning when Tamen entered Nuxta. 'Gem of the South' the welcome sign boasted, which made him smile as he saw that the population was a whopping three thousand. He could tell he had entered on the side of town where blacks lived just by the abysmal state of the homes he saw. Such was the way of the south, he knew. Negroes were always on one side and whites on the other, with no middle ground between them. It was the same with their restaurants, bathrooms, schools, drinking fountains and every other gathering spot whites could think of to place their signs of segregation.

Most of the small homes had cucumber-shaped drain ditches in front and stood on cinder blocks. Screen doors, if they had them, were mottled with holes or ripped open. Occasionally, he would happen upon a home that actually appeared decent—one with a gravel driveway—or one whose paint had not been completely stripped by the elements.

He was only a few blocks into Nuxta when he heard a voice of desperation and sorrow call onto the wind in thought. He followed the pain-wrought voice—a woman's. At first, it was only a whisper, but it began to grow stronger as he walked farther into town.

Walter..." he heard a female think.

Damn them! another woman thought.

The house where the thoughts were coming from was at the end of the road from where Tamen was walking. The lights were on inside. He could almost taste the raw anguish emanating from it. He stopped and stole a few bed sheets that had been hung to dry in the back of one of the neighboring homes. After gently wrapping the body in them, he recited the ancient Egyptian *'Prayer of the Dead'* over the body before proceeding on to the house.

He stepped up on the porch and dissolved the illusion that had hidden him from sight while walking through town. From the window to the right side of the door he saw movement—a black woman with grey hair. She was tall, and wide about the shoulders and hips. She sat down in a wood chair and was quickly joined by a small girl with puffy pigtails, who then sat on the floor between her legs. The old woman's face was ashen and her wrinkles set deep with worry.

Tamen turned the doorknob and crushed the inner lock and walked into the first room of the house, which was completely dark. All movement ceased in the other room as he approached. When he stepped into the room they were in, they all stared at him incredulously, and for good reason, he thought. After all, he was a stranger who had just entered their home and was carrying a body across his shoulder.

He quickly stole each of their names from their thoughts. To Tamen's left, wearing a black derby cocked sideways, was Tobias. In addition to his mouth hanging open, he was short, very round and light-skinned. In front of Tobias sitting down was Hazel, the old woman he had initially seen. The child snuggled between her legs was Maymee. To Tamen's right holding on to each other were two middle aged black women, Althea and Lilly. Lilly was the shorter and older of the two and barefoot. When Althea looked at what Tamen was carrying, she dropped to her knees, flung her hands in the air and began screaming.

Hazel sprang from her chair. She grabbed hold of the young girl who had been sitting between her legs and whisked past Tamen toward the hallway behind her. But even as she did so, an even younger girl than the first—one with warm chestnut eyes—came running out of the door Hazel was headed toward.

"Dotty, get your tail back in there!" Hazel snapped. She spun young Dotty around by the shoulder while still dragging Maymee behind her. She shooed both girls inside the room and slammed the door shut. "Maymee, you keep your baby sister in there. Hear me?"

"Yes'm," a voiced squeaked from the other side of the door.

Hazel put her hands on her hips and took a deep breath. She sighed and slowly turned around. "Go on and set my chile down," she said to Tamen. "I knew they was gonna get Walter. I told him and told him, don't be takin' credit from no white folk when you ain't got no way to pay folks back."

Althea was still on the floor and wrapped in Lilly's arms. She reached for the sheets the body was wrapped in, but quickly pulled away as though she suddenly couldn't bear to touch it. "They done killed my Walter," she cried. She shook her head from side to side. "Lord Jesus no! No Lord!"

Tamen laid the body on the floor next to the women. But as he began reading their thoughts further, he felt resistance from Lilly. He was utterly amazed, especially when she then looked directly in his eyes and raised her brow. It had been thousands of years since anyone had been able to block their thoughts from him.

"I found him in the woods not far from here," Tamen told them all.

"We know where he was," Hazel replied curtly. She walked back to her chair and sat. "That's where they always take black folks to lynch'em. Everybody know that."

"That ain't him momma!" Althea protested to Hazel. She scrambled free of Lilly's grasp and crawled over to Hazel. "That ain't my Walter in there. Say it momma. Say it ain't him!"

Hazel put her hand on Althea's head and shook her own. "Now, now baby. Shush now," she whispered. She motioned with her other hand for Tobias. "Come get her. You and Lilly take her on in with her children."

"Just say it, Momma! Aunt Lilly, you say it too...*please*," she begged.

But no one seemed ready to commit to a lie.

Aunt Lilly and Tobias lifted Althea to her feet, one on each side of her. They walked her into the hallway, and then into the room where her daughters were. When they returned, Tobias plopped down on the sofa next to Hazel's chair and planted his head in his hands. Aunt Lilly, however, focused her pea-sized eyes on Tamen. Tamen knew she was sensing that something was not quite right about him, just as he was sensing the same about her.

Tobias looked up and wiped his oily brown face. "Who you be anyway, boy?"

"No one of any importance," Tamen replied.

"Well you ain't from 'round here. I can tell by the way you talkin', that's for sure." Tobias looked at Aunt Lilly and Hazel and raised his brows. "You from up north, huh? Who your people be?"

"Shut up, Toby! You ol' fool," Aunt Lilly growled.

Tobias hopped his rear to the edge of the sofa and glared at her. "Old? Look here, you witch. Ain't—"

"It ain't where he be from that need answering," Aunt Lilly said to everyone. "It what he doin' here in the first doggone place."

"You right, sister," Hazel said.

"Uh yeah!" Tobias sputtered. "Boy—what you doin' out here this time of night anyway? You best thank God they didn't get you too!"

"Yeah...*boy*," Aunt Lilly added. "How you come upon Walter out in some woods? And how you know where to bring him? Hmm?"

"His body is returned to you. That is all that is of any matter now," Tamen replied. "Those white men you speak of—"

"Murderin' crackers!" Tobias corrected him.

"Those men are no more."

"What you mean?" Hazel asked.

"Yeah...*boy! If* that's what you be. Tell us!" Aunt Lilly demanded.

Tamen replied directly to Aunt Lilly. "It is just like I said. They are dead."

Hazel moved to the edge of her seat. "You kill them?"

Tamen knew the questions wouldn't cease until they knew everything. Even if he did tell them he used to be a god of Egypt, they would never comprehend it, except maybe the short woman, Lilly, who continued to eye him devilishly. He was about to leave when Aunt Lilly stepped toward him. This time he pushed past her weak mental defenses and stole into her mind. Now he could hear her clearly as she eyed him from head to toe and then back again. *Boy got bullet holes in him...shirt ripped up...but ain't no blood on him except Walter's!* He looked down at the same spot on his chest that Aunt Lilly was now eyeing.

Aunt Lilly edged back from Tamen. "Oh, he done did somethin' to ol' Henry and those redneck boys alright! Aint'cha?"

"They damn well deserved it then," Tobias seethed.

Aunt Lilly jabbed a finger at Tobias. "You shush up! What you gonna do when white folks find those boys dead?"

"No one will come looking for anyone. I assure you," Tamen said.

"You never said who you be," Hazel interrupted.

"I am not from here."

Aunt Lilly took another step back. "You sho' ain't!"

Tamen had had enough. "Peace onto this house," he announced and was about to leave when he felt a nudge at his chest. It was barely a touch really, but one nevertheless, and one that was not physically made by skin-to-skin contact.

Tamen spun around. His focus was now upon Aunt Lilly and her alone. He delved even farther into her mind and could now see her for what she truly was. What he saw was that Tobias had not been far off when he called her a witch. And this old woman...*this witch*...knew some remnants of Egyptian sorcery which he himself had infused into the women of Nubia. But the powerful magic they once possessed had grown weaker with each generation. He hadn't sensed it so strong since encountering and for a while, loving, Madame Laveau—the witch-sorceress of New Orleans. Tamen didn't know whether to be pleased at his own handiwork or be furious that a mortal woman had dared to use his own magic against him.

"You can hear me thinking in here can't you?" Aunt Lilly asked, tapping her head full of fuzzy and frayed cornrows. She slammed her barefoot on the floor. "Speak up you haint! I knew something wasn't right about you the moment you walked in."

Tamen didn't respond. Instead, he listened to her thoughts as she exhausted everything that he could possibly be...*a ghost...a zombie...a demon!* He nearly laughed at her last guess.

Aunt Lilly raised her arms, flapped her hands and began mumbling. Tamen heard more jibber-jabber than anything, except for one set of ancient sounds that was spoken perfectly. He felt another nudge to his chest, like someone had poked him with a finger.

"Enough!" Tamen demanded.

"I knew it, knew it, knew it," Aunt Lilly sputtered victoriously. "Get from here, haint, before I do more than that to ya!"

"Lilly!" Hazel snapped.

"I told ya'll that woman nutty!" Tobias said, rolling his eyes at her. "Boy, don't pay—"

"That ain't no boy and it ain't alive neither," Aunt Lilly warned. She raised her hands and began jabbering again.

"Submit mortal!" Tamen bellowed as he pointed at her. The force of his voice—a deep echoing timbre—rattled the walls and every picture hung on them. He seized control of her mind, as well as every inch of her body. With the skill of a master puppeteer, he brought her to her knees, and then completely prone on the floor. And as simple as one flicks a switch to turn off the lights, he sent her into unconsciousness.

Hazel slid out of her chair and onto the floor next to Aunt Lilly. She shook her and called her name repeatedly, which had absolutely no effect. She looked up at Tamen with wide eyes. "Oh my Lord! Lilly was right."

"She was...was...*oh shit!*" Tobias spat. He knocked the derby hat from his head as he jumped from the sofa and ran toward the patio doors to his left. He pointed at Tamen and screamed. "Haint! Haint!"

"Leave us be now, ya ghost, or whatever you are—*please*," Hazel begged. She put one hand on Aunt Lilly and another upon Walter's sheet-wrapped body.

"You have no reason to fear me," Tamen replied. "But I will leave you all to your suffering now. I feel I have caused more harm than good." He looked to the hallway as the bedroom door opened where Althea, the grieving wife, and her children were. Inside he saw Althea skittering off the bed and racing to catch Dotty, the one who had opened the door and was now walking toward him. Her large brown, and so very sad eyes gave him pause just as the young white boy Henry's had. Dotty and Henry...so very different...now so very similar, Tamen thought.

Tamen knew Henry would be taken care of were he brave enough to journey to New Orleans and seek out Aria. But it would not be so easy for this girl, he figured. The segregated south was filled with a foreboding uncertainty for blacks, but especially for black girls. The family was already poor. What furniture they had, he saw, was already near their end of usefulness. Just giving this child a handful of money like Henry would do nothing to fix her troubles. But the difference with Dotty was that here she was loved. Henry had never even known what love felt like.

"Is that my Papa?" Dotty asked Tamen, as she pointed to the shrouded corpse. He replied with a nod. "Mama said he's sleeping. But why she cryin' if he just sleeping then? You know?"

"Dotty get away from him!" Hazel hollered, as she grabbed Dotty by her threadbare nightgown and pulled her close.

"He is sleeping, sweet one," Tamen replied softly.

"He sick?" Dotty asked.

"No sweet one. He is with God now."

"But God lives up in the sky," she insisted as she pointed up.

Hazel pulled Dotty's arm down. "Shush, gal."

"In time you will understand these things," Tamen explained. "But not now."

Tamen turned and left. Once on the porch he quickly made himself invisible once again. A few moments later, Hazel with Dotty in hand, and a still shaking Tobias several steps behind, came walking out the door and onto the porch in search of him. Tamen was actually standing literally a breath away from Hazel. He kneeled next to Dotty. He wished he could comfort her and erase the grief she was sure to endure in the years to come when she truly understood what had happened to her father.

The small town would awaken in a few hours, and news of the murder of Walter Tripkin was bound to spread quickly. And soon thereafter, Tamen figured word of the missing white men and Henry Jr. would follow. Perhaps even tales of a wandering, young black man who brought back the body would be whispered about amongst other blacks. He was certain Aunt Lilly would spread the word as quick as her mouth would let her.

He had left New Orleans only a few days ago, but now would have to go back to see if Henry had gone to Aria. He actually preferred not to see his adopted daughter again. After all, it was because of her that he'd left in the first place. Watching Aria whither and die of old age while he stayed forever young was something he didn't want to face. And Aria had only fifteen, maybe twenty more years of life left if she were fortunate. But going back and witnessing her body slowly decay, at least in spirit form, was worth it to him if it meant being able to see young Henry grow into man.

He mused for only a short while before deciding to stay in Nuxta to watch little Dotty grow into adulthood. Dotty's short years from girl to woman to the grave would be but a whisper time would not even remember, he figured. But not only was the child, Dotty, reason enough to stay, but an angel making its presence known so close to the town intrigued him.

He began walking down the road plotting his next move. Of course staying in Nuxta appearing as he did would never work. He would have to assume a new life, as well as a new face and body, and maintain absolute concentration to cast that illusion for all to see.

So, Tamen—who shall you be this lifetime? he wondered.

CHAPTER 2

During the last few weeks of summer, Tamen made a home in the small town of Nuxta, Mississippi. Word of Walter's murder had indeed circulated quickly and quietly among the black populace. And for a few weeks after, the sheriff questioned many of them about the disappearance of Henry Sr., his son and the other white men that everyone knew had committed the murder.

At first, rumors swirled that black folks had taken revenge upon Henry Sr. and his friends and disposed of their bodies. But all of this was put to rest when Tamen cast himself in the illusion of Henry Sr. and the other white men, and then went to speak to the sheriff and denied any part of murdering Walter Tripkin and also their intention of leaving Nuxta for good. The sheriff, who had no intention of prosecuting them over Walter's death anyway, simply closed the case. Slowly, Nuxta returned to the same sleepy, forgotten dustbowl of a town that it had always been, just as Tamen had planned.

In his spirit form that could transverse great distances at the speed of thought, Tamen traveled to New Orleans and paid Aria a visit. She was still glowing over the boy-child, Henry, he'd sent to her. "He a bit of a scrawny thing, Papà," she said, in French-ac-cented English. "Scared of his own shadow—and the shadows too! You told him what I am, didn't you? You know white children don't know about such *tings* like us."

"Of course I told him," Tamen replied. He manifested his spirit in the illusion of a physical form so that she could see him. "I showed him almost everything I have shown you."

"Does he believe that you are really a god? Well, a god-like thing?"

"I do not know, my child. How can I expect him to believe it when I do not at times? I still look in the mirror and see that young, black Egyptian boy staring back at me, not a god nearly three thousand years old. Regardless, the boy's father was an evil man. I simply wanted Henry away from such a vile creature."

"I read Henry's mind while he was sleeping, Papà. His father *was* a bastard," she agreed. "But you don't worry a bit about Henry, I'll see to him for you. I make him forget that past. Make him for-get that bastard."

"Be gentle, Aria. He is fragile right now," Tamen warned. "Two weeks is not enough time to digest this new world he has walked into."

"I could...show him a *ting* or two," she offered. "It make him un-derstand what you and me really are."

"One or two things?"

"You never know, Papà."

"I know what you are thinking, Aria. You are far too much like your voodooiene-mama, Marie! Always dabbling in people's heads."

"He never be good at it anyway. He just a white child after all."

"So are you, my sweet."

"Only half, Papà!" she retorted. "Just half!"

"But you look white," he teased.

"My magic is in my African blood. The magic you gave all of us African women!"

"Fine then, child. You have my permission. Though not having my permission would not have stopped one as sly as you."

"No—you're right."

"I know. I did not expect you *not* to teach him," Tamen added, before whisking his spirit form back to Nuxta.

* * *

While continuing to block mortal's ability to see him, Tamen began putting his own plans into action. Obtaining the money he required was the easiest. In the next town over, he waited until the local bank closed, walked in and took what he needed. Though what would require the most work would be to cloak himself in an illusion as someone else.

The following Sunday, instead of following the Tripkins to church as he had for the past four weeks, he slipped into their home after they'd left. He went into the bathroom and stared into the mirror, and then began shaping the illusion he would wear. He kept the chestnut hue of his skin, but added fat to his narrow face, arms and legs, and then distended his belly so that it would hang over his belt. On his bald head, he placed a half inch of tightly curled black and gray hairs all over, but kept it sparse so that it appeared to be thinning. He was more generous with hair when he added a neatly trimmed salt and pepper beard. Around his mouth and eyes, he carved a small network of wrinkles. On his arms and hands, he sprinkled a few keloid scars to tell everyone who glimpsed them that he was no stranger to a hard day's work. And finally, he withered away six inches from his towering, six foot-four frame.

"Mornin'," he said, to the fifty-five year old*ish* black man now staring back at him in the mirror. "I'm Mr. William Bell, but just call me Willie—everybody does. Just come down from the north—

Chicago see? But I was born and raised in the south. Thought I come on back and get myself a little store and see if I can make a go of it." With money in hand and the illusion of Willie Bell projecting to all he looked upon him, he travelled uptown and bought a small farm on the outskirts of Nuxta he'd spotted earlier. And after becoming a new homeowner, he purchased a small wood shack to turn into a fruit and vegetable stand not far from the Laundromat where Althea worked.

He then set about ensconcing himself into Nuxta's black community. His persona, Willie Bell, became quite the talk very quickly. He heard from eavesdropping on conversations and thoughts that he was often referred to as *that rich Negroe from the North.* He also began attending the sole black church in town—Mount Zion Baptist Church—as the Tripkins were devout Christians and never missed a Sunday.

But it was at his small fruit and vegetable stand where he enjoyed being the most, and almost as much when he presided in pharaoh's court as high priest. Besides being able to be close to them during the day, each night Althea and the children would walk past his stand on their way home. He would always listen for Dotty's thoughts in particular and could sense her coming blocks away.

In her thoughts, he saw Dotty's dreams of one day getting a real dolly, not one stitched together by her grandmother...or being able to double-dutch with the speed and flair of the older girls...and possibly getting new clothes, not hand-me-downs from her sister Maymee. But there was always sadness hiding in the shadows of her mind. Hazy images of her murdered father often became vivid ones of him hugging her, playing and rocking her to sleep at night, as if he still lived. In her father's arms she felt safe. She felt wanted. She felt loved.

* * *

It was a Saturday afternoon when Althea finally stopped by the market with the girls in tow. Tamen was beginning to think that they never would. Other blacks had already come by, if not to buy the fresh vegetables he'd grown—unnaturally—so late in the season, but to snoop for more gossip about the 'rich Negroe', Mr. Willie Bell.

The sight of Dottie with her five pigtails all prettied with blue ribbons in each warmed his bloodless flesh. She clung to her mother's dress, and without being told, didn't touch one single object in the store. He rounded the counter and approached them. Both Althea and Maymee quickly locked eyes with him. Dotty studied the floor.

"Alright now, alright!" He smiled broadly. "Afternoon ladies."

"Afternoon, suh," Althea replied.

"Suh," both girls replied in unison. Dotty was still hiding behind her mother's skirt. Maymee generously returned his smile, sans her front teeth.

"I done seen you at church a time or two, haven't I? Ms...?" He cocked his head to the side.

"Althea Tripkin," she answered, "my momma, Ms. Hazel Tripkin?"

"Oh yeah—yeah! I done heard tell of the Tripkins. All good from what folks say. Real good folk. Mmm—hmm. And who in heaven are these two lovely angels wit ya?"

"I'm Maymee!" she volunteered proudly before her mother had a chance.

"And what a pretty name for a pretty girl in a pretty dress, too!" His flattery was rewarded with an even wider smile. He bent down onto one knee and grunted with effort for effect. "And who this one here hiding around your momma skirt-tail?" Dotty scurried even further around the back of her mother.

"That's Dotty," Maymee volunteered. "She shy. But I ain't."

"Dorthea...but we just call her Dotty," Althea corrected.

"And ya'll can just call me Willie, too." He grabbed the counter to sturdy himself as he stood back up. "So what can I help ya'll find? I got collard and mustard greens—black-eye peas and purple hub, too! Got some squash and tomatoes—red and green *'pendin'* on if you like'em fried up or not. And I just picked up a load of fruit—sweet to look at and even sweeter when it hit your mouth."

Althea waved her hand. "No, suh, thank you. I thought we would just stop in and say hello seeing that we pass by here twice a day and all."

"Well, I'm sure glad you did. Always nice to see a smiling face." He looked down at Dotty who was now peeking around the other side of Althea. "Well, maybe next time I can interest you in some good ol' greens. You do like greens, don't you?"

"I do!" Maymee peeped.

Althea closed her eyes and smiled. "I guess we all do. But maybe another time, Mr. Bell."

"Wait—wait—wait now," Tamen told them, holding up his hands. He walked around the counter and grabbed two small baskets. He handed one to Maymee, who snatched it out of his hand before he could let go.

"Mr. Bell, no," Althea protested. She took the basket from Maymee, who groaned her displeasure. "Shush, gal!"

"Now, Ms. Althea," Tamen said, summoning an old and genteel southern drawl. He pushed his chubby lower lip out. "You trying to stop this old man from getting into heaven?"

"Wha?"

He handed the other basket to Maymee which renewed her smile. "Lord Jesus himself said, *suffer the little children,* now am I right sister?"

"Ye—yes, but..."

"And *bless* the children—hmm?"

"Yes, Mr. Bell...but we don't..."

"Amen then, sister," he proclaimed. "Mr. Willie done made a rule. Every chile that walk up in this here store gonna get a bit of something sweet for free. Now that's the Christian thang to do. It say so right in the good book itself."

Maymee looked up at Althea with wide, pleading brown eyes. Even Dotty had poked her head around to look up at her. Althea sighed before giving in. And now with baskets in hands, both girls squealed as they ran toward the rear of the store where the fruit was. "Just one piece now! Hear me?" Althea called out.

"Or three or four now," Tamen uttered, and then cleared his throat.

"Mr. Bell, please. That's money out of your pocket and I ain't—"

"I ain't got a child of my own, Ms. Althea," he interrupted, and then looked away as though he couldn't bear for her to see him. "Good Lord done seen fit to give me enough money to see me to the end of my days...*thank you, Jesus!* But my dear wife—God rest her soul—just never could carry a child. I figure what God done blessed me with is meant to be shared. It's all an old man got nowadays."

Althea glanced down and then looked back at him. He could almost taste the empathy emanating from her, especially when he made his dark brown eyes gleam as though he was holding back tears. *Nothing like a sad story to soften the hardest stone,* he thought.

"I'm sorry about your wife and...the..."

"Thank you," he choked out.

Althea and the children were semi-regular visitors to his store after that day. And once word got out, Nuxta's other black children began visiting for their complimentary crisp apple or pear. Even white children, who had been forbidden to patronize Negroe stores, snuck by to see portly old Mr. Willie to obtain their free goodies, too. But for Tamen, what was more important was that with each visit from Dotty, she became less apprehensive of him.

Soon she was looking him in the eye and smiling, especially when he jiggled his illusionary double-chin and crossed his eyes at her. At church, Althea started going out of her way to speak to him, as did Hazel, Tobias and his wife Loretta Ann and their three teenage boys who all took up an entire row at church. Aunt Lilly, however, never attended church, they told him.

At church, he was always the first to give witness to the reverend Michael Boremon or his son Phineas—who was twenty years of age and following in his father's footsteps. Gifted, he heard people referring to Phineas as being. "Sure to give you the Holy Ghost," Negroe folk told him. Tamen was not so easily impressed with the quick-tongued young man who had a penchant for custom suits and shiny gold watches. Regardless of his disdain for Phineas, he played along. "All right now! Preach rev'ren!" he'd bellow with the other men and then grit his teeth.

When cloudy autumn skies came rolling in, bringing all day porch sitting weather along with it, an invitation for dinner after church was extended by the Tripkin matriarch, Hazel. He arrived retaining the illusion of still wearing his Sunday finest—a tan linen suit with a stark white shirt and a dark-blue tie. Tucked under his arms was a paper bag of collard and turnip greens, two thick hunks of smoked ham-hocks to boil them with and surprises for the girls.

Tobias opened the door. Before even greeting Tamen, he pulled the corner of the bag down and spied its contents. "Hey Hazel! Mr. Willie here done brought some good grubbin' to fix up." He waved Tamen inside and then tilted his camel-brown derby to the side. "Man—I hope you got some collards up in that bag. I ain't too keen on those mustards—they bitter."

"It must be your lucky day then," Tamen replied. "I got a whole mess of them."

"Alright then, brother," Tobias said, with a smile short of three teeth on the right. "That's what I'm talking about!"

Tamen searched for Althea and the girls, but didn't sense them anywhere near. Aunt Lilly was absent, too. Outside in back, though he couldn't see them, he heard all three of Tobias' sons and could tell at what stage of puberty each was at by the tenor of their voices. He walked through the small living room and into the larger den and shared dining room, resisting all the while looking down at the spot where he'd laid the body of Walter Tripkin months ago.

Loretta Ann, Tobias' wife, was sitting in a chair facing the sofa. She was wearing far too much foundation that was too dark for her honey-hued complexion. She looked waxen as sweat beaded about her forehead. She displayed her dentures in a broad smile at Tamen. "Fine Lord's day ain't it, Mr. Bell," she said.

"Sho' nuff," he replied. "Got right so better when Ms. Tripkin invited me over for dinner. I done heard some good tales about her cooking."

"Well I tell you now, Willie, ain't a woman around here can cook like my cousin Hazel here," Tobias said.

"Well, *thank you*," Loretta Ann snipped.

"Now, Loretta," Tobias cooed. "You know you can cook, too. I was just saying—"

"All right now," Hazel interrupted, as she came through the kitchen door. She had a white apron tied around her dark, purpled-flowered dress with hints of red throughout.

"Thank you for having me, Ms. Hazel," Tamen said. "It sure been a while since I done had a real southern cooked meal. I ain't much of a cook, you see. I can grow it, but I can't cook it."

"You didn't have to bring anything, Mr. Bell," Hazel replied, nodding at the bag in his arm.

"Willie is fine, ma'am."

"Well you didn't now, ok? I invited you over to eat *my* food, you hear?"

"Ma'am," he acknowledged.

"But, since you done brought some anyways, I can't just let it go to waste."

Tobias clapped his hands, startling Loretta Ann. "Now you talkin', gal!"

Hazel gave him a wicked smile. "Toby, hush up!"

"Alright with that *Toby* mess. Toby this and Toby that...its Tobias!" he demanded. *"Toe—bye—us!"*

"Well grandpappy called you Toby," Hazel stated.

"Well that was grandpappy," he retorted. "Ain't nobody call me Toby but that old crazy-tail Lilly, and that's where you getting this *Toby* mess from. And speaking of that ol' witch, she ain't coming is she?"

"Tobias," Loretta Ann chided him.

"She is!" Tobias leaned into Tamen. "You watch yourself around Lilly. She an ol' voodoo woman or something or another."

Hazel took the bags from Tamen and gave Tobias a glare. "Don't pay him no heed about my sister Lilly. First of all, she ain't coming."

"Good," Tobias croaked.

"And second, he just tellin' tales, ain't ya...*Toe—bye—us?*"

"Nope!" Tobias turned around and plopped down on the sofa. "I wouldn't lie on a witch. It's bad luck they say."

Hazel departed into the kitchen, but not before offering up a desperate prayer. "Lord help."

Tobias waited for the kitchen door to close, and then waved Tamen over to sit. "Let me tell you about that ol' crazy woman... Lilly."

"Tobias...Mr. Bell don't wanna hear that mess," Loretta Ann said.

"Lord can strike me down if I lie on that ol' thang."

"Well I ain't gonna listen to you talk ill of poor Aunt Lilly. She just as sweet as she wanna be."

Tobias feigned choking and tapped his chest. "Now the Lord gonna strike you dead-as-a-doornail for telling *that* lie!" He grabbed Tamen by the arm and playfully pulled at him. "Brother we best run before we get struck, too! Heh! Heh!"

Loretta Ann rose from her chair and fast-walked into the kitchen.

"Now, boy," Tobias whispered, "I ain't lying about ol' Lilly. Hazel don't want nobody saying nothing about that witch, 'cause she embarrassed—you see?" Tobias continued. "You know she live up there in the sticks—the swamp—all by herself. And she like it there, too."

"A witch?" Tamen asked.

"Well, she ain't gonna go flying on no broomstick," Tobias offered reluctantly. "She into all that voodoo-hoodoo mess...chicken heads and gris-gris. I tell you what, Willie, when we were children and played hide and seek, you know?"

Tamen nodded.

"We couldn't ever play with her." He leaned back on the sofa and folded his arms on top of his inflated belly. "She always knew where you be! She just come straight on over and find you. Hell—you could've been in the outhouse covered in mess and she know just where you was."

Tamen resisted smiling. He found it amusing how easily mortals like Tobias were impressed by mind reading. With a bit of innate skill, which obviously Aunt Lilly possessed, and a bit of practice, it wasn't that hard at all, he thought. "Sho' nuff?"

"Mmm-hmm! I'm telling you, man," he continued. "Grandpappy was always taking a switch to my backside 'cause she go and tell him something I did, but she never seen me do it with her eyes.

Tamen shook his head. "My—my—my."

"And I tell you something else too. Don't let Hazel fool you neither. She got a touch of that mess up in her, too! Sometimes she slips and say things that nobody 'spose to know but just you. Uh-huh." He looked over at the kitchen door, and then back at Tamen and whispered. "They witch sisters."

Loretta Ann stuck her head out of the kitchen door. "Ms. Hazel said that enough of your yappin', Tobias," she said, and then disappeared just as quickly.

Tobias raised both of his brows and puckered his brown lips. "See man? What I tell ya."

* * *

Althea and the children arrived just before Hazel announced that dinner was ready. Though to Tobias' disappointment, Aunt Lilly arrived with them. "Aw hell," Tobias sputtered, as Aunt Lilly came walking in directly behind the children.

"And aw hell back at ya!" Aunt Lilly replied in kind with hands on hips. Her slip over dress hung nearly to the floor, but not long enough to hide her bare dusty feet.

"Don't you got some chickens needing their heads cut-off?" Tobias jabbed.

She squinted at him. "Why you think I here, Toby?"

"I done told you 'bout calling me that. It Toe—bye—us!"

Aunt Lilly snorted. "Hell...all I hear is dumb—dumb—dumb."

"That's 'cause you a witch," Tobias spat.

"Naw...it 'cause you dumb, Toby. Dumb as a doornail."

Aunt Lilly and Tobias bantered just long and loud enough to draw Hazel out of the kitchen with a reprimand for both of them. Even though she was younger than Aunt Lilly and just a few months older than Tobias, both listened to her as though she were years older than both. Aunt Lilly and Tobias retreated to separate corners, but not before exchanging glances, as though saying to each other...to be continued.

Dotty and Maymee had already surrounded Mr. Bell and were pulling at his thick, illusionary arms. It warmed Tamen that both children had taken a liking to him, especially Dotty, who had for so long been quiet and guarded.

"You got us some apples, Mr. Bell?" Maymee asked.

"Girl shush," Althea said. "You don't be asking guests if they brought you things, chile." She reached for both girls but Tamen was quicker. He pulled Dotty up and onto his knee and Maymee closer to his other leg.

"I sho' nuff did!" he answered. "Something for both you pretty gals in the bottom of that bag your granny got up in the kitchen. But you gotta eat some dinner first."

Althea was eventually successful in shooing both girls away from Tamen and into the kitchen. Shortly after, Hazel could be heard calling Tobias' boys in from outside to get their supper and then directing them back out to eat on the back porch along side Dotty and Maymee.

The meal was accompanied by a good deal of talk around the table. Tamen had already prepared a deeper back-story for Mr. Willie Bell if he was questioned more, but never got a chance to use it since Tobias dominated every topic of conversation. Whether Tobias knew a little or nothing at all about something, he always jumped in to give his say. "*Well, I hear folk say that...,*" Tobias prefaced his every opinion, but never actually said who these *folks* were.

After supper, Hazel and Althea began clearing the table, while Tobias and Aunt Lilly reignited their teasing of each other. Tamen grabbed his plate to dispose of the food he hadn't even touched, but had made it look as though he had eaten it all. Once in the kitchen, he hid the food from his plate in the garbage can under the other refuse. He then glanced out the window above the sink and saw Tobias' two younger boys swinging a laundry-line rope for Maymee and Dotty to double-dutch with. Althea came up behind Tamen, stood on her toes and peered out also. "I best go out and check on these children," she said, as much to herself as she did to him.

"Whiff of fresh air won't kill me neither," he said. "I been done sat on that couch and fell asleep. You know how it be when you got a belly full of somethin' good."

Tamen divided his attention between the girls and Althea. His eyes, made keen by the chant-spell that made him immortal, allowed him to perceive what was invisible to the human eye. When he looked at humans, sometimes all he saw were cells mashed together, some living and others in the midst of dying. He could see wrinkles forming upon their skin years before they would ever show. Even blemishes and old scars from their youth were not hidden from his eyes. But he focused on seeing Althea as another mortal would—smooth, dark brown skin and large almond eyes that she'd passed on to both Maymee and Dotty. Her yellow flower-print dress hugged her curves and showcased a tiny waist that he knew men would eye lustily.

"You been the talk of the town," Althea said, interrupting the silence between them. "You done made a whole lot of black folk happy with those low prices you charging. If white folk weren't so ignorant, they'd be scrambling over to your place to shop."

"That's Jim Crow for ya," he told her.

"You're right," she said. "'Don't drink outta my fountain...and you come in through the back, if I let you in at all. Humpf!'"

"Well sister, it might not be like that for too long."

"White folk ain't gonna change, Mr. Bell," she professed.

"Change is coming one day, sister, whether we or white folk want it to or not—Lord willing. Ain't nothing ever stays the same." Of this, Tamen knew his words were undeniable. In just one mortal's lifetime, he'd witnessed entire landscapes of values and morals and laws and powers change hands. In three thousand years, he had seen the entire earth become nothing as it was before, except more violent.

"I for one don't like change a bit," Althea admitted, with a cock of her head. "It sure would be nice to just rest a while and not have to think about what's gonna happen in a month or two." She sighed and then bit her lower lip that was painted a dull church-going red. "I just wanna know the next day I wake up, mama and Aunt Lilly and the girls are gonna be ok, but...I—I—I shouldn't even been saying nothing about it."

Tamen smiled even though he sensed ominous thoughts forming in her mind. He could have forced her to speak them, but he knew it wasn't right to do so. He wanted his trust from the family to be earned, like it was now with Henry whom he visited and in-structed at least once a week in spirit form. In the last few weeks, he had begun to crave their company like an addict. For it, this warmth and love from Henry and the Tripkin family made him feel human again.

"Mama's sick," Althea uttered. She sighed heavily and hung her head. "She's failing more each day, and now it's starting to ache in her bones. That's why I take the children with me to work. She don't need to be running after children all day."

Sickness—he had sensed that within Hazel, but not the true depth of her illness. He looked over to Dotty. He wondered just how much more grief her tiny soul could bear so soon after the loss of her father.

"I shouldn't have said nothing about it. But...mama thinks you just as good as butter," Althea added. "So don't go around saying it to folks—please. I'll know where it come from if I hear folks talk-ing."

"Ain't no way, Ms. Althea. I'll pray about it though," he promised.

"I do thank you for that." Althea smiled weakly at him, and then looked over at the children. "Ya'll get in here in a bit. And don't even think about getting on the ground in those dresses—hear? They already dusty right up to the collar."

Althea went inside, but Tamen remained and watched the chil-dren play. More death coming to the Tripkins and the effect it would have on Dotty induced a sense of dread in him. He walked toward the children hoping their light would dispel the darkness shadowing him.

"Mr. Bell, look-it!" Maymee called. She jumped into the midst of the swinging ropes and displayed her skill at double-dutch.

Dotty, who was still on the outside of the ropes, swayed, but not in rhythm to the rope's cadence. She stiffened when Tamen came and stood next to her. "You plan on getting in there?" Tamen asked her.

"Uh-uh."

"Why ain't cha?"

"'Cause Sam and Isaac swinging the ropes too fast, and I don't like it fast."

"Well then," he said, "I guess I just gotta take your place."

Dotty's head snapped up, causing her four hot-pressed and braided pigtails to swing about her head. "You can't double-dutch. You old!" she reminded him.

"Gal, I been double-dutchin' before you was born," he bragged. "Don't think these old bones can't jump a step or two."

He pulled Dotty back a few feet and then asked Maymee to step out. He had the boys—Sam the oldest, and Isaac—to move in closer to increase the height of the rope's swing. Though he'd never jumped rope or double-dutched for that matter, his mind effortlessly mapped the patterns in which the ropes swung. He leapt in and instantly found his groove. The girls squealed! The boys howled their excitement and swung the ropes faster.

Tamen didn't have to think about moving his feet in time with the ropes as a mortal would. He even twirled around as he'd seen Maymee do earlier. He exited and crouched, and then pretended to be short of breath. But the children were having none of that. They grabbed at his arms and begged for a repeat performance.

"Alright—alright," he said to the toothy smiles around him. "But only if Dotty jumps too."

Only after Maymee promised Dotty half of her ice cream—whenever they got a chance to have it again—did she agree. Samuel and Isaac started up the ropes again. Maymee swished her tiny hips from side-to-side and started chanting and quickly infected everyone else. "Mr. Bell! Mr. Bell! Mr. Bell!"

"Ready?" he asked Dotty.

She nodded.

Just as she was about to jump in, Tamen scooped her up, cradled her and deftly entered the swinging ropes. Dotty dug her fingers into his arms, but not out of fright, for she let loose a deafening peal of utter joy. And her laugh...the precious, untainted purity of it was, at the moment to him, worth more than all of the gold he'd buried in the tomb of his dearest friend and brother, Amenhotep.

"Faster?" Tamen asked her. She flipped her head back and squealed, which he knew in child language meant, *oh yes!*

His feet skirted the ropes as quickly as the boys could turn them. He spun, jumped and kicked his feet in ways he knew would cause them to wonder later if it were truly possible to even do so. The chorus of "Mr. Bell!" rose to a frenzy, with Dotty's squeaky voice the loudest by far. "Mr. Bell! Mr. Bell! Mr. Bell!"

And then...

"Mr. Bell?" Althea called out.

Tamen stopped abruptly. He allowed one of the ropes to become entangled around his feet and even stumbled a bit. "Ow!" he grumbled. He panted as he hobbled over to Althea and Hazel who were on the back porch. Both women looked at him as though they were in a contest to see whose eyes could open the widest.

"Haven't did that in a while. Whoo!" He created the illusion of sweat upon his forehead and wiped at it.

"I wouldn't have figured you could've in the first place, Mr. Bell," Althea remarked. "How'd you learn to do that when I can barely jump one rope without breakin' my fool-neck?"

Tamen shrugged. "Just takes a bit of practice I 'spose."

"I wanna rope some more," Dotty said. "Please?"

"Ain't no more *rippa-ropin'* tonight," Althea replied.

"Ya mammy's right," Hazel added. "Tobias and Loretta Ann about to leave, and ya'll girls gotta get cleaned up for bed. Every one of you dirty as a billy-goat."

The children grudgingly marched toward the house. Althea shooed Maymee inside first, but had to raise an eyebrow at Dotty to follow suit. Tamen then took his chance and stopped Hazel before she had a chance to go in.

"I'm about to get going myself, ya'll," Tamen said, as he waved goodbye to Althea as she went inside. "Ms. Hazel...thank you again for asking me over. I sure did enjoy every bit of it." He extended his hand, but not only to thank her, but to *see within her. Just a touch,* he thought.

It was a gift and a curse that he possessed which allowed him to detect sickness within another. As a Lector priest, his unparalleled ability had made him the most famous priest in the temple of Amon-Ra. And now as a god-like being, those same senses were amplified a thousand fold.

As his skin touched hers he could sense the sickness in her blood and hear it squeezing through her hardened veins. As he traced the source of the sickness backward—from lungs and liver, and now just starting to grow in her pancreas—he found that the strongest concentration of cancerous cells had originated from one single point of origin...her right breast. And in Hazel's eyes he saw death. And he saw that she knew that specter was travelling her way.

He smiled and waved farewell. Though at the moment, he didn't felt good about anything. It wasn't just that Hazel was dying. It was that with a simple chant-spell he could easily cure the old woman. But in doing so, he knew the power of the chant would draw Shazadeh and Lord Yikan right to him.

"How low the mighty hath fallen," he grumbled. *What of you now, Tamen? Not such the great and almighty Horus—god in the horizon—now, hmm?* he thought. Why his powers were castrated made him remember what had governed his immortal life for so long. The tale the Christ had told him, as he kneeled before him at the cross, had changed everything he thought he knew about the world and himself as the god Horus.

'For there to be a new earth, first there must be darkness,' he recalled the Christ saying in a voice imperceptible to all but him and his guards—three angels—who were the height of two-and-a-half men. *'Before my return as king of kings, this must all come to pass,'* the Christ continued. *'There must be a balance in all things. Those are the words of the Father, who is great and almighty.*

'And when the balance hath been forged and the Great Deceiver awoken from his sleep to ravage the world, I will return with glory in my left hand and the Father's almighty righteousness in my right. And even Lucifer—the beautiful fallen one, shall proclaim, 'Woe to ye inhabitants of the earth! Thy time of reckoning hath come!

'Find the balance, Egyptian,' the Christ commanded. *'Do this, and thou shall atone for thy many sins against my children who were thy slaves when Egypt was great and mighty. Fail, and bow your knee to the demon, Shazadeh, for all thy immortal life.'*

Without balance in the world there could be no Rapture or Armageddon and a rising of the dead, he remembered the Christ saying. And without those end time events ever occurring, Shazadeh and her demon ilk would be free to rule the Earth, with she as it's goddess. Shazadeh's false churches were recruiting mortals by the thousands, Tamen knew. But it was that one mortal who could be her balance that she desperately wanted to find above all. And that mortal she wanted dead, along with himself, who was the only one who could find that mortal.

CHAPTER 3

Hazel Tripkin passed away a week before Christmas and was buried on a cloudy Saturday morning. It had been an unusually cold day, with most people thinking that if it were to ever snow in Nuxta, it was going to be that day. But it never did.

By the time Hazel was laid to rest, Tamen—masquerading as Willie Bell—had become an integral part of the Tripkin Family. After the first visit that Sunday, his presence at dinner after church was expected and his absence—the time he spent with Henry in New Orleans—was met with worry about his well-being. Those Sundays had become *some* of the best days he could recall in hundreds of years.

Whether he and the girls, Dotty and Maymee, double-dutched or hop scotched, he always drew a gaggle of neighborhood children to the Tripkin home. Older folk of course thought it queer that a gray-haired man would behave in such a childish manner. Tamen wondered what they would say if they knew he was actually three thousand years old...give or take a decade?

His favorite pastime above all was storytelling. To the children, they were just that—stories. Though to him, they were memories of his many lives lived long ago.

With Dotty on his lap and Maymee on the step below with the other children, he recalled his travels through Africa and Asia and Europe. He enthralled them with tales of ancient kings and queens, and how their greatness or failures changed the world they lived in now. He loved to see the children's eyes widen in amazement and delight. And some nights after storytelling and returning to his home on the outskirts of Nuxta, he sat for hours—which were but seconds to him—remembering the faces of people he once loved but had now been dead for centuries. But it was in the most un-likely of persons that he'd found solace for his ache. Being in New Orleans with Henry made his immortal life bearable.

Although with virtually no skill in the unseen arts, despite Aria's instruction, the boy she renamed as Henrì Bedeau had be-come quite aware that there were things that lived outside the vi-sion of human eyes...shadows within shadows...Tamen being one of them.

In only ten years, under Aria's guidance and love, Henrì trans-formed from an abused and scarred boy, to a bright college gradu-ate. It was also during that time that Tamen knew he loved the boy as his own son, as much as he loved Dotty and Maymee as daugh-ters. Those beautiful years with his adopted children were almost enough to outweigh the dark ones he sensed coming. More and more, he detected sacred chants being spoken upon the wind, as sure as if it were a frigid winter gust whipping at his face. Without the demoness Shazadeh's balance in place, the more demons, Tamen sensed, were escaping from Hell and into the mortal realm.

The strength of the sacred chants he heard assured him that Shazadeh and Lord Yikan were now in the Americas. Their new-age churches were drawing multitudes of worshippers they could turn into spies to help find the one that would balance Shazadeh.

Promises of wealth, acceptance, salvation and most importantly, outward physical perfection were used to entice the mortals. And it was working beautifully. Their following was growing larger with each passing day.

But there was a steep price to Shazadeh's offer—Tamen had seen it countless times. Mortals that chose to follow their heart's dark desire, but refused to worship Shazadeh as a goddess, paid with their lives. In the old days, they would burn what was left of the mortals—brittle husks of skin—after draining them of their essence. In this new age, they were far less concerned about being discovered amidst all of the other cults and pseudo-religions abound.

And in their possession was Lucifer's great golden book—a tome of dark magic—that had created Lord Yikan and Shazadeh. But it was the other gold tome, written by the angel Metatron that contained the spell to transform *the chosen child* into a being who could balance Shazadeh's darkness with light. And for now, it having been hidden with Tamen's own hands, it was safe, but ceaselessly searched for by Shazadeh's followers she called *watchers*.

And all of these events, it seemed to Tamen, were being heralded like times of old by the almost constant presence of an angel near him—the same one he sensed on the road leading into Nuxta that first night. Though it never showed itself, its proximity was near enough to excite his skin with its electricity. Not only was the angel's electrical charge ever present, but it grew in intensity whenever he was near the young reverend, Phineas Boremon, who now lead the church the Tripkins attended. But even more disturbing to him than that, was that he couldn't read Phineas' thoughts. The harder he probed, the more static he encountered from Phineas.

* * *

After Hazel's death, Dotty had withdrawn into herself as she did when her father was killed, Tamen noticed. But this time, instead of scampering back into the light, she stayed and caroused in the darkness of her sorrow. Story-time in the evenings, and her frequent visits to his market stand became occasional, and then stopped abruptly once she started puberty. As she grew older, her already too short skirts and too tight tops became shorter and tighter when her sister, Maymee, was successfully wooed and married deacon Larry Caruthers. Her sister marrying and then moving north to Illinois was a joyous event for all except Dotty. Tamen saw in her thoughts that she felt it was just one more person being stolen from her life.

With Althea getting older and unable to keep up with her work at the cleaners, Dotty took over at Jacob's Press and Laundry. But Dotty's insistence of working only in the evening was odd to all, except Tamen. Having spied her thoughts, he learned that Dotty had more than cleaning and pressing clothes on her mind while at work, especially when the reverend Phineas Boremon stopped by. And knowing exactly what they were up to, Tamen wanted him dead.

Phineas was slightly darker in complexion than Dotty's cocoa hue, but just as tall and slender as she. A prominent square jaw and wide shoulders that framed his custom-made suits did make him something of an attraction, Tamen admitted grudgingly. But Dotty was far from being the only sixteen-year old deflowered flower in his church garden. It was only weeks into their affair that the Tripkins family began hearing rumors of what Dotty and the reverend were up to.

Late Friday evening, after closing down his fruit stand, Tamen slipped into the alley behind the cleaners and willed himself invisible to mortal eyes. If the reverend stayed true to the schedule he'd been keeping the last few weeks, he would be arriving soon to see Dotty. And fail to do so Phineas did not.

Tamen caught sight of Phineas, and watched as he casually glance up one side of the road and then down the other before slipping into the alley. Tamen was prepared to strike when the air around him came alive with a telltale electrical charge. The closer the reverend approached, the more the air sizzled around him. At first it tingled, then grew ferociously hot. It was pain he'd not felt since the *Chant of Making* burned off his mortal shell and replaced it with one of a god.

The angel was near, Tamen knew. It was closer than it had ever been since he came to Nuxta. But why?

Tamen backed away from Phineas and the electrical-fire scalding his immortal skin immediately lessened. The more Tamen retreated, the less the pain became. Realizing the angel was protecting the reverend, Tamen watched helplessly as Phineas—with a smirk on his face—walked through the backdoor of the cleaners.

Damn you creature! Tamen knew the angel could hear his thoughts as easily as he heard that of human's. *You protect this one? This—this adulterous piece of rotting flesh?* Tamen waited for a moment but was rewarded only with silence. *'Keep your secrets then. I may have never been a real god, but at least when I pretended to be one, I ruled with love and justice, and protected the weak and innocent, like Dotty.*

Again, there was no reply.

* * *

Undeterred from his quest to put an end to the affair, Tamen decided to try and drive some sense into Dorthea, since he wasn't allowed to kill Phineas. The following Friday night, he waited until Phineas had come and gone, and then surprised Dotty as she exited from the same door moments later. Momentarily, her brown face softened into the same, young innocent Dotty that he hoped would return one day. But she quickly composed herself and pursed her lips.

"What you doing here, Mr. Bell? Momma told you to come check on me?"

"Something wrong with me just wanting to see you?" he asked, ignoring her sass.

She raised her arms and then spun around on her three-inch heeled, pink and black pumps. "Here I am!" she sang. "Ready for my Friday night."

"Come on, Dotty-girl, don't—"

"My name ain't Dotty," she fumed. "Dorthea, alright? And I ain't your girl neither!" she snapped. *"Damn!"*

"Dorthea...I know about you and the reverend. I see him coming around almost every Friday," Tamen volunteered.

She put her hands on her hips. "And...?"

"And...." His voice rose. "You know it ain't right. He's just using you, Dot...Dorthea. Using you and all those other gals he sneaking around with, too."

"Well one—he ain't sneaking around with no other girls. And two...how you know I ain't the one using him?" she asked, tapping her heeled foot. "Like I told you before—Mr. Bell needs to take care of Mr. Bell, and Dorthea will take care of Dorthea." She wiggled her head, making her freshly pressed curls dance on her forehead before walking away.

Tamen reached and touched her shoulder. She spun back around and spat a string of venomous words at him. He released her, but not because of any of the curses she hurled his way, but because he suddenly realized they were not alone.

"...and keep your damn hands off me, old man," she added to the end of her barrage of tell-off's.

Tamen looked down at her belly. The blue dress she wore lay flat against it with nary any room for her to inhale without ripping a seam loose. But it wouldn't be like that for long, he realized. Out of impulse, he decided to tell her now. He figured when her next period failed to show, she would discover sleeping with Phineas Boremon came with unexpected consequences.

"What?" Dorthea asked.

He said it again. "You pregnant, Dorthea."

"I ain't pregnant? You an old fool, Mr. Bell," she grumbled while walking away, swinging her hips left and right.

After she walked out of the alley, Tamen made himself invisible and caught up to her. He had to know more, for something about the embryo was greatly amiss. When he touched Dorthea, he felt its presence within her. Though even stranger than that, it seemed to feel him, too. Tamen stopped and watched as Dorthea continue to sashay down the sidewalk.

It was then that the air around him began to grow dense, though those out for a Friday stroll walking past him were completely oblivious to it. Like an illusion of being invisible in one moment and being visible the next—a trick he'd performed thousands of times—the outline...a shape of a being started to form before his immortal eyes.

The naked being that coalesced out of nothingness was well over twelve feet tall. Like his own true form, Tamen observed that it too was completely hairless. But unlike him, its skin glowed with a subdued, white luminosity—like fresh-combed cotton in the face of the morning sun. It looked down at Tamen with lidless, ever-watching eyes that glowed blue white.

"Why have you come, angel? Speak!" He thought his demand, knowing the angel could read his mind.

The angel remained silent, but slowly raised its hand and then pointed a finger in the direction that Dorthea had gone.

As an immortal, Tamen could only describe that so human emotion sweeping over him, as being dizzy. Flashes of what was and had been all came tumbling down hill at him...arriving in Nuxta that night...finding Walter Tripkin and then befriending the Tripkin family...Dorthea, who was now pregnant by...the reverend

Phineas who was protected from harm by the angelic being. *The child...the one he'd searched two thousand years for, and who could counter Shazadeh was now growing in Dorthea's womb.*

"*Wait!*" he thought, as the being began fading back into nothing. "*You—angel with no name...what am I to do now?*"

The being grew even fainter, but its voice slipped into Tamen's mind.

"*Tamen—the Egyptian, must protect it. For the demoness now hunts this child, and you as well. Oriziel—of the celestial order of Virtues, I am. That is what the Father, Son and Spirit call me. And I leave thee now to thy holy task.*" Oriziel glimmered as he vanished completely.

* * *

Eight months and a few weeks later, Tamen, as Mr. Bell, waited along with Tobias, Loretta Ann and Aunt Lilly, for Althea to bring Dorthea and her new son home from the hospital. The pregnancy had drowned Dorthea's 'I-know-it-all' attitude, especially after Phineas refused to see her and married a woman who sang along with Dorthea in the choir. With the father of her baby gone, Dorthea sought solace from those who had always remained close to her.

Now a newly crowned grandmother, Althea stepped into the living room where the rest of the family waited for Dorthea to follow along with her son. "Where he be now?" Aunt Lilly asked. She smiled, displaying a mouth of nothing but gums. She rose from her chair and toddled barefoot over to Althea. "Why you got your face all mushed-up? At least wipe that ol' frown from your face and smile a bit. You a granny now."

Althea sighed.

Tamen heard the baby squirming in his carrier. Though he'd already seen the baby being born—having traveled in spirit and slipping into the delivery room—it was just as exciting to see the little one now along with everybody else.

"What this make me? Huh, Loretta?" Tobias asked. "I be second or third cousin to this chile?"

"Second monkey," Aunt Lilly answered instead. Tobias turned and glared at her. Aunt Lilly ignored him. "Come on gal, get in here with that baby so I can get some sugah of them sweet baby-cheeks!"

Dorthea did just that. She walked in and handed the baby to Aunt Lilly, who kept her promise and kissed his mouth repeatedly. "Give your auntie some sugah!" she told him, before smothering him again with kisses. "What you name this youngin' anyway?"

Althea looked down, but not as quickly as Dorthea.

"Jared," Dorthea whispered.

Aunt Lilly furrowed her brow and smacked her toothless gums. "Well...sound like a white-chile name to me." Althea and Dorthea remained mute.

Tamen slipped into both Althea and Dorthea's minds, but jumped out quickly. What he discovered made him nearly lose his focus on maintaining the illusion of Willie Bell. He'd only stayed briefly in the hospital after Jared was born, and realized now that he'd missed a very important detail. Now, he had to concentrate to make Willie Bell appear as clueless as the others.

"What be a matter?" Loretta Ann asked, as she adjusted the elastic waist of her burgundy pantsuit she'd sewn and looked as such.

Althea began muttering. "Um...well? I tried to get her to give the child our last name."

Tobias, who was waiting to hold the child, suddenly sat down. "Awww hell!" he uttered, and then looked away and stared at the wall next to him.

It took Aunt Lilly a moment to catch up to speed. "You didn't, Dorthea. You better say right now you ain't gave that chile that preacher's last name, gal!"

Althea looked over at Dorthea and raised her brows. "Tell'em, gal—all of it."

Dorthea peeked at Aunt Lilly and quickly looked down. "His name is Jared..."

"Tripkin," Aunt Lilly said resolutely. "Jared Tripkin, right?"

"Boremon," Dorthea corrected her.

Tobias sprang from his seat. He grabbed Loretta Ann's arm and began pulling her toward the patio doors. "Well ya'll...we gonna swing by early tomorrow. I done forgot Loretta Ann done left some peas simmerin' on the stove. We talk to ya'll later."

Loretta Ann batted his hands away. "Sit your fool-tail down, Tobias."

Aunt Lilly had yet to take her eyes off of Dorthea. "You done lost your mind?"

"Tell'em the rest," Althea said.

Dorthea took a step back before speaking. "His name is Jared... *Phineas...Boremon.*"

Loretta Ann was now grabbing at Tobias. "Come to think of it, I did leave some peas cooking. Chile...I can smell them scorchin' the pot right now. We gotta go, ya'll."

"And I think I left the door to my fruit stand open," Tamen announced. "I best go check on it."

"I couldn't talk her out of it, Aunt Lilly" Althea explained. "Dorthea said the baby gonna have Phineas' name since it's his."

"Well ain't that just smart of you, Dotty," Aunt Lilly sassed. "I 'spose you wanna bring the baby to church just in case there be one or two people in Nuxta that *don't* know yet."

"She ain't staying," Althea said. "She's going up north to live with Maymee."

"What?" Tobias and Loretta Ann asked in unison.

"You is?" Aunt Lilly asked.

"I spoke with Maymee this morning," Dorthea said. "I'm gonna raise my boy up north and get myself going in college."

Good choice, Dotty, Tamen thought. He followed Loretta Ann and Tobias out, leaving the Tripkin women to finish plotting their next course of action, as he now needed to do also. There weren't many useful years left on the persona of Willie Bell anyway, which would make it easier to retire him without much fuss, he figured.

He decided at least three months should pass before letting Willie Bell suffer a heart attack in his sleep. But before that, he would arrange for Althea, Maymee and Dorthea to be the beneficiary of all that he possessed. They would not only inherit the market and his house, but also the thousands of dollars he'd saved over the years and had no need of.

He planned on meeting Dorthea and the child, Jared, in a few days time, and once then, never leaving Jared's side until all was said and done. Even now, he realized it was a risk to leave Jared unattended, for the child would forever be in danger until he became what he was born to become. But a most important visit was in order, he thought. There was a young man in New Orleans he had great need of.

CHAPTER 4

"I know you're here, Papà," Henrì called out, as he walked into the foyer of his home. The shadows, his ever companions for the last twelve years, swooped in and flittered around him. "I may not have Aria's senses, but I know when you're near. Besides...they just told me you were here," he added, glancing at the two shadows whispering in the hallway straight ahead.

He proceeded down the narrow hallway and into the first parlor. After pouring two shots worth of brandy into a glass and immediately downing one of them, he scanned the room. "So—are you going to say something? Or did you just come to check on me again?" He knew Tamen could be anywhere unseen...by the bookshelves, the red velvet sofa or standing against the blue fabric covered walls. After no reply, Henrì shrugged and sat in a chair by the window facing the flower garden.

"What would you like me to say?" Tamen asked, as he walked into the room through the same door Henrì had moments before.

"Hello for starters," Henrì replied, unfazed that Tamen hadn't produce a single sound as he entered. Rather, he took a sip of brandy and motioned for Tamen to sit in the chair next to his.

While he had aged into adulthood, Tamen was still that young black man he had encountered that night in Nuxta. Each time Henrì saw him it reminded him what Tamen *was not*...and that was human.

"I have come to ask a favor actually," Tamen said.

"Wait a minute." Henrì scooted to the edge of his seat. "You're here? In the flesh?"

"What flesh?" Tamen replied, and then smiled. "Yes—I am truly here. No illusion whatsoever this time."

"No wonder the shadows were so excited when I arrived home. *He's here! He's here!*" Henrì exclaimed. "You know, this is the first time I've seen you in the flesh since...that night. So that must mean...."

"It is time to plan Willie Bell's demise. Perhaps in the next year he will go on vacation and pass away in his sleep," Tamen said. "I will make it peaceful for him, which will make him easier to mourn for."

"You liked being him didn't you?"

Tamen waved his hand as if brushing away a fly. "No more than all the other people I have masqueraded as."

"But you liked the people Willie Bell knew."

"That *I* knew," Tamen corrected him.

"Of course. You know what I'm getting at Papà. Every time you flew down in spirit form for my weekly lessons, you always gushed about what Dotty was doing and growling about what she shouldn't be doing." He lowered his head and smirked, but kept his brown eyes on Tamen's. "She must have had the baby—hmmm?"

"A day ago. She named him Jared."

"Well good for her...in a way I guess." Henrì shrugged. "I know you're not thrilled about her being a teenage mother and about who the father is."

"Please do not speak that man's name. It is a curse to me now," Tamen uttered.

"A baby is a baby, Papà. And not just any baby...it's your Dotty's baby."

"To her it may be, but not to me," he replied. "That is why I am here actually."

Henrì sat back and sipped at his brandy. "Am I going to need another drink before you spring whatever it is on me?

"If I were mortal like you—yes. Perhaps it would be a wise thing to do."

Henrì took Tamen's advice and then returned to his chair. "I can tell when something is bothering you," Henrì said. "I can hear your voice with my ears and my mind all at once. It's like being in an amphitheater. The last time I remember you acting like this was almost twelve years ago. You told me to close my eyes and relax. And one minute I'm upstairs in my room, and the next, I'm wearing a loincloth in an illusion you created in my mind of Pharaonic Egypt...Karnak, Egypt to be exact. Besides, your left eye twitches when you're up to something."

"It does not," Tamen protested.

"I know." Henrì smirked. "But let's just say it does and it's telling me you're about to lay something really heavy right in my lap."

"Fine." Tamen twitched his left eye. "Feel better about it now?"

"Absolutely."

"Good," Tamen said. "And how goes the tracking of Shazadeh and Lord Yikan?"

"They're ramping things up," Henry answered. "They have churches and ministries...seminars and what have you all over the Midwest and east coast, but under different names of course."

"Well done, my son," Tamen said. "If we know the child who can balance her has been born, then so do they. Lucifer is bound by the covenant he struck with God and must sleep until the final battle, which will occur once there is balance again. But in his absence, the demon, Duke Astaroth, is regent of hell and has no plans of giving up power. That is why he created Shazadeh in the first place. If Shazadeh can kill the child and keep the world unbalanced, she will rule earth as a goddess and Duke Astaroth, with Lucifer bound in an eternal sleep, gets to keep hell in his grip. But do not think for a moment that the Duke will stop there. He covets the earth for his own. Shazadeh is but a puppet, but she is too drunk with power to realize it. The world as we know it has shifted, Henrì. We are upon a new age...perhaps the final one if we are lucky."

"Where's the fairness in that?" Henrì snipped. "I'm not even thirty yet and you're eager to see the world end in fire. You've already lived for thousands of years, but I only get a few?"

"Be calm, child. You will have many more years to come even after the balance has been made," Tamen assured him. "But you forget about what comes after the world ending. You heard the words of the Christ just as I did...at least in the illusion of my past that I showed you."

Henrì sipped his brandy. "A new world full of peace and love."

"Those upon the new earth will bask in the everlasting light of the Lamb," Tamen professed reverently. "You are human, Henrì—my son. Evil, sickness and death is what you are accustomed to. I know it is hard for you to imagine an eternal realm seeped in love."

Henrì swirled the ice in his brandy. "Papà," he said slightly above a whisper, "you saved my life that night and gave me a new one that I could never have dreamed of before. You know I'll do anything for you."

"And I made you a promise not to put you in harms way," Tamen countered. "Do not do this because you feel you owe me something...you do not. You never have, except to grow into the handsome young man you are now."

"Then I break you from it...or—or...release you from it, or whatever," he sputtered. He leaned forward and grasped Tamen's hands. "I promise to do whatever it is. Just say it, Papà, and I will."

Tamen leaned back in his chair. "First you must ponder the proposal. If you are still willing, I will accept your pledge. But remember, I did not complete the spell out of the angel Metatron's tome that changed me into the being that I am now. I am a hybrid. The path I must take will likely bring me face-to-face with Shazadeh. She completed the Spell of Changing from Lucifer's tome—with Astaroth's assistance. I cannot defeat her, or protect you from her. If you come with me, know that you may well be joining me in the hereafter."

"If you go, then I go, dammit!" Henrì swore. "You're my father. And Aria was the mother I always dreamed a mother should be— *and she was a witch!* This is my family. If Shazadeh tries to kill you, then she'll have to obliterate me first."

"She will stop at nothing to have this earth for her own," Tamen pressed.

"My answer won't change, Papà," Henrì said resolutely.

"Regardless, you must listen and then decide."

* * *

When Tamen finished speaking, Henrì saw that his body had gone stiff. Tamen's eyes were still open, but stared off into nothing. His hands still grasped the leather arms of his chair and his feet were still planted firmly on the ground, but his spirit was elsewhere.

"It's still yes, Papà," he said, not sure if Tamen could still hear him or not.

He poured himself another shot of brandy before deciding to just take the decanter with him. Once in his room, the same one he'd slept in ever since arriving at Aria's doorstep, he turned on the TV and flipped over to the all hour news channel like Aria had always done.

He drifted in and out of sleep as his thoughts shifted to the night he came to see Aria—the one-eyed witch. From then on, his world, already topsy-turvy from his first encounter with Tamen, was once again flipped upside down.

* * *

"Of course you're scared, mon ange," Aria told him, flinging her stark white hair behind her. Her alabaster skin glowed in the light of the moon. "I would be too if I had seen such awful tings as you have."

Henry looked up at her as she stood in the doorway of her old, bayou mansion. "How do—do you know that?"

"Him," she said simply.

"Tamen?"

"Papà," she said with a thick, French accent. "Only one I ever knew."

It was hard to believe that the one called Tamen was the foster father to Aria, who seemed old enough to be his grandmother. He shook his head as he realized that he had stepped off the road of reality and onto the one called fantasy. She backed up, allowing him room to step inside, which he did. But when the door promptly closed behind him, he realized he hadn't touched it...and neither did she.

"You'll be *mon ange*—my angel," she said with a firm nod of her head. "You'll learn to speak and write French here and at school as soon as we get you enrolled in one. Spanish and Italian I'll teach you myself. When Papà comes round he'll teach you the old languages too, hmm?"

"What an old language be?"

"*And dear God*...we will rid you of that guttural English. It'll make you sound simple if you walk around talking like that, boy. And old languages are the ones Papà spoke when he was still young like you—but a long, long time ago."

"You believe him? That he be what he say he be?"

"Like I told you—I've never known anything other than what he is. But I tell you *dis*, he taught me to see and do things that no man or woman *I* know can do."

"Like how he know what I thinkin'?"

She winked her grey eye. "That and more. I used to just see people and plants and rivers and *tings* how you're supposed to. But now," she gasped, "I see life everywhere I look! I see it *in* the plants and *in* the trees and *in* the grass at their feet. I never knew that air and water had a life of its own until he showed me. You coming here makes you a very fortunate boy indeed," she told him. "I will teach you the art of the unseen, mon ange. You will see harm coming your way before you see it—with those pretty brown eyes of yours. Papá said he told you that no harm will ever come to you again, but I will see to that myself."

She led him upstairs and into a bedroom that was twice the size of the trailer he used to call home. The room smelled and felt wet, but was tidy. The oak poster bed with a sheer netting draped over it was large enough for three adults with room to spare. The bed had been made and its covers pulled back, as if expecting him.

Aria hummed as she moved him toward the bed, where she undressed him down to his pee-stained underwear. "Up and in now," she'd directly gently, and then snuggled the sheets up to his neck. "I soak you in a hot bath tomorrow and wash that skin of yours back white, hmm?" She kissed the top of his head and began stroking his face—temple to chin. Over and over her soft white hands caressed his face until he drifted asleep for a while. But he startled awake by the sound of whispers in the room and Aria nowhere to be found.

Like a child, he shut his eyes and went still, though the whispers only grew louder. He heard men and women...children's voices were all around him. Some began calling his name as if they knew him. He dared a peek, but when he saw the shadows in the room peel away from the wall and ceiling and move toward him, he squeezed his eyelids together as tight as he could. Too afraid to scream for help, he bit down on his tongue until he tasted blood.

Then came footsteps patting outside of his door. When he heard it open and the creaking from the hinges echo in the room, Aria's voice followed right after. "*Alle-vous en!* Go away, I say! I told all of you not tonight, didn't I? You wait until I say come see him." The shadows moaned in reply.

Even with Aria leaning over him and again stroking his face, it took some convincing for him to open his eyes again. When he did, he caught the last vestige of a fleeing shadow slip between a crack in the coffered ceiling, as if it had been sucked into it.

"They're nothing to be afraid of, mon ange," she promised. "Just some old shadows that can't even touch you. They just got too excited seeing you here."

"What...what are they? Ghosts?"

"Yes," she whispered. "They used to be alive like you and me. But they're harmless as moths. They keep me company, and I them. But they scare other people, like they did you, no?"

He shuddered. "Ghosts!"

"Mon cochon—my piggy," she cooed. "It take some time for you to understand all of this. You don't know about these tings yet, but you will. You going to discover that it's what's outside this house—not in it—that should be feared."

In the years that followed, Tamen and Aria had kept their promise. As now, he didn't want for a single thing. He had more money than he could ever spend in three lifetimes thanks to Tamen. He attended the best private school in the city, and as told he would, he learned to speak French, Spanish, Italian and his own native English with utter fluency. The first two years, Aria refused to converse with him in anything but French. The next two were in Spanish and Italian followed. During weekly visits from Tamen, who would take control of his mind, he learned Latin, ancient Egyptian and modern day Arabic.

Though the most important lesson he ever learned from Tamen was about Tamen himself. In 1425 B.C. he was born a mortal... years later he became a god...and then discovered it was all a lie. "Now the story, Henrì. My story," Tamen had said. "The illusions I am going to create in your mind will feel so real to you; you will not know the difference, my son. Cold will feel cold. Hot will be just that...hot. Just know that none of it is real. Now close your eyes and journey with me."

* * *

The next morning, Henrì returned to the study. He bent down and positioned his face right in front of Tamen's, whose brown eyes were like gleaming stones and just as inanimate. He'd seen Tamen separate his spirit from his body before, leaving only his granite hard shell of skin behind.

"Where are you, Papà?" he asked, and then studied Tamen's brown face for any hint of life. "Take your time, wherever you are. I'll just go down to the kitchen and get a cup of coffee, all right? Don't go anywhere now—hah hah! Just kidding." He paused and looked back before walking out and closing the door.

With a cup of coffee in hand, he walked over to the library on the other side of the mansion. He stoked up a fire in the marble fireplace, and then settled down in front of his desk that was nearly all covered with stacks of newspapers and magazines. "Let's see—let's see—let's see. Where did I leave off last time?" He looked up at the white and gold-coffered ceiling for guidance. "How about...?" He pointed at each of the stacks. "West Coast papers to-day." He picked up the top newspaper and began flipping through it.

In his mind, he pulled up a list of keywords to look for as he scanned the news stories...religion...cult...suicides...new age...spirituality.... Shazadeh and Lord Yikan were wily beings, he knew. So he kept an eye out for key phrases...skin rejuvenation...perfect body secrets...eternal youth...or anything that might attract humans willing to pay any price to be beautiful, just like the angels did when they revolted in heaven, and thus became demons.

For the greater part of the morning and afternoon, he compiled lists of groups and organizations that fit the mold. Later, he planned on heading over to the library and cross-referencing what he found with other organizations Shazadeh and Lord Yikan had created over the centuries. But for now, he wanted to give his weary eyes a rest, and his tongue something to savor.

He returned to the parlor where Tamen was and poured a shot of whiskey. The liquor hadn't time to even stop swishing about the shot glass before he dumped it down his throat. Next, he poured some brandy into a snifter and sat in the chair across from Tamen. Henrì looked directly into his eyes. "Hey, Papà." Tamen seemed to just stare back and through him.

"Alright then," Henrì said. "Let's try this then."

Henrì sat back in the chair and closed his eyes. He placed his hands on his knees and exhaled slowly. He concentrated on eliminating every sound around him...the wind whistling through a crack in the window...a cricket chirping outside...even the sound of his own breathing, which he slowed. And then, as Aria and Tamen had taught him, he opened his eyes and tried to see what was in front of him for what it truly was...*life*.

He tried not to see Tamen's physical form, but the millions times billions of particles of energy—his essence—bound together to give his body shape and substance. It was then that Tamen's image began pulsing from white light to dark—like a beacon trying to jump-start itself. It flashed slowly at first, and then without warning, it took on a strobe-like effect. Finally, it appeared as though every inch of Tamen's being was made of white light. The only problem was, Henrì realized he was looking down at Tamen...and himself.

Papá? He pushed his thought at Tamen, realizing that some part of him was now floating up by the ceiling. He could see and hear with his new form, but when he touched the plaster ceiling, his hand passed right through it. *Papá? Help? I think I did something wrong.*

"Yes, I think you have," Tamen replied.

Henrì's ethereal form began to lower toward his body. Once they were reconnected, he saw that the light that had exuded from Tamen was gone. He rubbed his temples. "Whooo!"

"Take your time," Tamen told him. "You were releasing your spirit form...your *ba.*"

"I was trying to contact you, not go floating off into space."

Tamen smiled. "I would not have let you get very far."

"You heard me," Henrì stated, not asked.

"I always hear you. Even when I am far away, I know when you need me. I made sure of that when you were just a boy—when I was in here," Tamen said, as he tapped his head. I did the same with those who worshipped me. I could hear their prayers day and night. I was Horus—he who resides in the horizon, remember?" Tamen held up his hands—palms facing inward—and stared at them. "I was a god, my son. Now I am just prey."

Henrì smiled and took hold of Tamen's hands. "You're my father," he stated. "You were Aria's father too. And you already know my answer, right?"

"Yes."

"It's always and will forever be yes!" Henrì demanded. "Alright, Papà?"

Tamen rubbed the top of Henrì's head and caressed his cheek. He then nodded slowly.

"Good then," Henrì said. "So now—just exactly *how* are we going to pull off this plan of yours?"

CHAPTER 5

"So if you were me then, young man, what would you do? Hmm?" Principal Allen asked.

Jared slouched even further in the chair next to his mother, Dorthea, who was glaring at him. He kept his eyes fixed on his calf-high, military-style black boots. He rubbed at his bony knees, which protruded through the frayed slits he had made in his jeans.

Dorthea leaned into him. "You hear this man talking to you?"

"Yeah," Jared grunted.

Jared was already fed up with hearing about the fight. He had explained to his P.E. teacher, who had pulled him off of the kid, that it wasn't his fault. Once his mother arrived...she having to leave work early...he'd told both her and principal Allen his version of how Eric, the kid whose nose he broke, had started the fight. He knew they didn't care why it happened, but were more concerned that Eric was now sitting in the nurse's office with an ice pack on his bloody nose.

"And sit up in that chair!" Dorthea barked.

Jared slowly inched up halfway. Even slouched, his six-foot plus frame put him a full head above his mother and Principal Allen.

Principal Allen held up a folder and then dropped it on the desk. "That's yours, son," he said, nodding at the folder. "And there's something seriously wrong, Jared. What's in that folder is not what I see sitting in the chair before me. That folder says that you have an I.Q. of one hundred and fifty. But the Jared I see in front of me says that you've gotten into more fights than you have A's ." He flipped his hands up. "So what's wrong with this picture?"

"You wouldn't think he was that smart just by looking at him," Dorthea snipped. "Despite what you may think, Mr. Allen, Jared does have decent clothes *and* shoes to wear. The pants he's wearing are brand new, and look at them—torn up! And that *was* a Sunday shirt he's wearing *when* it had a collar on it. *And* he didn't have my permission to dye his hair orange or red or whatever color that mess is supposed to be. Jared is extremely bright, and I'm not just saying so because he's my son."

Jared ran his hand across his hair and then groaned under his breath. Instead of sporting a soft red Afro, he had left the dye in too long, which turned his hair coarse and crayon orange. He wasn't feeling so awesomely intelligent about that at the moment either.

"You're right, Ms. Tripkin," Principal Allen responded, scratching his milky-white, bald head. "I should have said he has a stellar I.Q." He looked to Dorthea for approval, who replied with a sharp and proud lift of the chin. "Son...you skipped ahead a grade in elementary school and again one in middle school, so I know you have the brains. Now you're a junior and you've earned nothing but Cs and Ds? So, let's not even talk about all the fights you've been in for a second, OK? Explain to me how we're supposed to let a gifted fifteen-year-old graduate early with these grades?"

"I'm passing," Jared offered weakly.

"You call Cs and Ds passing?" Dorthea asked. "That's passing for stupid."

"I got As in Spanish and French."

"True—true," Principal Allen admitted. "Which goes back to the point I was just making. You should be acing every class." He paused and looked at Dorthea for a moment, then looked back at Jared. "At the very least, I should suspending you today."

Jared sat up. "So, I'm supposed to let Eric and his idiot friends just mess with me? Eric and his boys screw with everybody and the teachers ignore it. But I get in trouble because I do something about it?"

"You still can't go around fighting just because somebody called you a name," Principal Allen explained. "We have conflict resolution groups that our social worker runs. We can bring you and Eric, or whoever is bothering you together and work it out with words, not fists."

Jared slumped in his chair again. "Yeah, because that works every time," he griped, and then rolled his eyes. He didn't realize how bad his little display had went over until he glanced at his mother. Her lips were pursed in that way, he knew, that if there weren't a witness present, she would have already slapped the back of his head several times.

Principal Allen placed his elbows on the desk and folded his hands. "What did breaking Eric's nose accomp...." He stopped and looked up toward the door behind Jared and Dorthea and waved his hand. Jared turned around just as Mr. Pierceman, his World History teacher, opened the door.

"Afternoon Mrs....?" Mr. Pierceman said, as he stepped in front of Jared's mother and extended his hand to her.

"*Ms.* Tripkin."

"Taylor Pierceman—history teacher." He smiled. "Nice to finally meet you. I wish it were under better circumstances of course, but a pleasure nonetheless."

Principal Allen resumed. "I asked Mr. Pierceman to join us, because—well, he actually has an idea of how we could handle this whole matter. But it's going to take your full and absolute cooperation, Jared," Principal Allen said pointedly. "And I do have to say, Ms. Tripkin, it's against my better judgment to do so. By every right, we should not only be expelling him, but arresting him for assault. You ought to be glad the other boy's parents aren't pressing charges. You can thank Mr. Pierceman for that, too."

Jared gulped. *Expelled* was a word he was used to hearing threatened against him, but not *arrested*, which made him sit up erect in the chair. He swore he could feel his mother's glare burning the side of his face.

"But since Mr. Pierceman feels that you can turn this around," Principal Allen waved his hand over the folder on the desk, "and since you were supposed to graduate early—which remains to be seen now—we're going to give you one last and final chance. Mess this up, son, and you are out of here. I'm not going to have this school turned into a free-for-all."

Dorthea lowered her head at Jared. "You hear that?"

"Yes, ma'am."

Mr. Pierceman moved next to Jared and put a hand on his shoulder. "Jared, listen a second."

Jared focused his gaze on Mr. Pierceman's brown eyes and mousy-brown hair that was always neatly parted on the right. He then gazed down at the black buttons on Mr. Pierceman's grey cardigan...the lapels of his black shirt...anything to keep him from looking at his mother. He knew her patience with him was all but sapped and he didn't want to face her when it was completely gone. He already accepted the fact that he was going to be grounded and severely so. And any thought of her lessening the punishment after a few days wasn't even worth considering. Puppy dog eyes had never worked on her before and surely wouldn't now.

"We've spoken many times about your performance in class, which we both know is not near your best. When you complete in-class assignments, I see something special in your work. You really get it! But you don't turn in homework. You don't show up for tests either. I have no choice but to give you the grade you've earned."

Dorthea crossed arms. "Now you don't turn in homework either? Skipping class? I'll fix all of that—*tonight!*"

Jared shuddered.

"You've said that the work here at Chapman is baby work," Mr. Pierceman continued. He glanced at Principal Allen and Dorthea. "And it probably is for Jared. It's not all that unusual for bright students who aren't challenged enough to act out."

"You can stop right there," Dorthea piped up. "I'm not sending him to that prep school over in Bankston, if that's what you're talking about." She shook her head, bouncing her black curls about her shoulders. "I went through this at the grade school and when I enrolled him here at Chapman High. The answer is still no! It's too far for one...and two...he can learn the same..."

"No—no—no," Mr. Pierceman gently interrupted. "I uh—already heard about that from Principal Allen. I understand that you don't want to send him there, Ms. Tripkin."

"Absolutely not. Period!"

"Which is why I wanted to propose something that may help all of us," Mr. Pierceman said. "I taught at a prep school out east before working at Chapman High. Jared has said he wants to go to college, but there's no way with his grades the way they are now. Colleges want stellar grades from a student his age before they will even consider looking at him. They won't care that he's brilliant. Right now, all they'll see is that he doesn't have the drive to be successful."

"That's absolutely right, Ms. Tripkin," Principal Allen added.

"So here's the deal." Mr. Pierceman held up his index finger. "You can go to summer school and *I* will instruct you in two different courses—accelerated courses—not just honors level, but college level Physics and Biology. Either you earn an 'A' in both of them or no grade at all."

Jared stared at him in disbelief.

"And," Mr. Pierceman continued. "There are five weeks left in this school year, so that gives you time to complete and turn in every assignment due and those that will be coming. Instead of a suspension, you'll tutor. One hour after school tutoring and another studying college level English Lit until the end of the school year."

"And not one more fight," Principal Allen added. "We didn't have a chance to run this by you, Ms. Tripkin, so please don't think we had decided this without your input purposefully. But just so that you know, it's either this—which from what Mr. Pierceman has said, Jared has wanted all along—or expulsion."

"Sounds like there's not much of a choice," Dorthea said flatly.

"I'll do it," Jared mumbled.

"What's that, son?" Principal Allen asked.

"I said I'll do it," he repeated. "Can I, Mom?"

She faced him. "Can you? You're going to. So just get watching any and all TV out of your head right now. But I don't see how you can work at the Rec center and do this, too."

"Mom, I swear I'll do everything Mr. Pierceman says," he begged, hoping for a small bit of mercy. "I—I won't have any money if I can't work."

"You see how these men are giving you *one* more chance?" she told, more than asked. "That's what you have with me. You even look like you're not doing right and I'll call Mr. Robinette myself and tell him you quit. Understand me?"

"Yes, ma'am," he replied, though wondered if the on-again-off-again relationship between his mother and Mr. Robinette played a role in her accepting his plea deal. If it did, he couldn't tell by her stone-eyed glare.

Before anyone could speak again, the last bell of the day sounded off. Mr. Pierceman looked up at the clock on the wall behind him and then at Jared. "Study hall starts in twenty minutes in the library," he told him, over the sound of students moving through the hall outside like cattle being herded.

"And you be home right after work," Dorthea added. "I'm going to talk to Mr. Robinette and have him call me as soon as you're done working. The center is five blocks away...hear? You got twenty minutes to make it home."

Jared uttered a meek thanks to Mr. Pierceman on his way out, and then sighed long as he shut the door. He turned and peeked back in the office and could see them still talking. Mr. Pierceman looked over and nodded at him. Jared forced a slight smile in reply. He then began the slow push against the mass of student bodies fleeing the school as he went in the opposite direction to his locker.

"So, you get kicked out or what?"

"No!" he snapped, already knowing who it was talking behind him. Jared grabbed his backpack and slammed his locker shut. He turned around and had to look down at him. "I almost got my skinny butt expelled and arrested," he said to Chris Knopfitter, or Chris-Rub-your-knob-fitter' as the other kids often teased him.

Though Chris' inch-thick lenses of his horn-rimmed glasses tripled the size of his green eyes, it was the least difference between them. Chris was almost five feet tall—and nearly as wide—whereas Jared had a foot and two inches on him without shoes. The mere mention of the words sugary and salty got Chris salivating. To Jared, junk food was simply fuel that evaporated as soon as he put it in his mouth.

Jared knew the first time he saw Chris, that like him, he would never be welcomed into any clique at Chapman High. Chris didn't have the smarts to join the nerds, the good looks to be a prep or athleticism to hang with the jocks. And though he'd transferred in freshmen year from California and was the only son of two pseudo-hippie wannabes—as Jared called them—Chris certainly hadn't inherited their free-spirited genes. Yet, he was determined to conform and be a prep...designer jeans, polo shirts and moccasins as an attire staple. If the preps were wearing it, Chris was going to buy it. Jared, on the other hand, wanted no part of any group, clique or gang but his own.

"You busted the hell out of Eric's nose," Chris crowed, and then grinned. "There was blood from the locker room all the way up to the nurse's office. He needed the living crap beat outta him anyway."

"You outta be glad!" Jared snapped.

"Did I say thanks?" Chris asked sheepishly.

Jared rubbed his chin and rolled his dark, nearly black eyes. "Let me think a second. Oh yeah." He leaned even further down until he was inches from Chris' glasses. "I think *you* gave me the thumbs up as they hauled my butt down to the office!" He glared at Chris for a moment before flinging his backpack over his shoulder and walking off.

"Jared, wait up, dude," Chris called as he ran to catch up with him.

Jared stopped and waited. "For what? So I can get in trouble for you again?"

Chris was huffing from the short jog. "Hey c'mon. I didn't ask you to break his nose."

"Why in the hell did you tell me what he did to ya?" Jared waited for a moment while Chris stood mute. "You knew I wasn't going to let him get away with it. *Especially Eric.* You know I can't stand him."

Chris looked around. They were near the main hall, though only a few students and a couple of teachers were still around. Chris whispered. "He whizzed all over my gym clothes."

"Because you thought, Eric—Mr. I'm-so-popular—wanted to share a gym locker with you?" Jared stared at him.

"So it's my fault, huh?"

"Look, Chris," Jared said, lowering his voice, "they don't like you. OK? Eric and his butt-buddies and those fake, stupid valley girls don't...they don't...awww forget it." Jared threw up his hands and started walking again.

"Forget what?"

Jared kept walking. "News flash, man. You're not one of them, alright?"

Chris had to fast walk to keep pace with Jared's long stride. "I never said I wanna be one of them."

Jared looked down at him and smirked.

"Well...just a little." Chris shrugged his shoulders and hung his head.

"Whatever, man," Jared said. "Just leave me outta of it next time. Or else, I'll beat your sorry butt, too." Jared shook his head and then turned and headed for the stairs.

"Hey! Where you goin'? The buses are gonna split."

Jared started up the stairs. "I'm going to the same place you are."

"You're going to tutoring?"

"Yeah. Part one of my never ending punishment, thanks to you," Jared replied sourly. "But *I* have to tutor."

Chris beamed. "Sweet, dude!"

Jared snapped his head back and stared at the ceiling. "*Arrrrgh!*"

"O.k.—not so sweet," Chris replied, quickly erasing his smile.

"Then I have to take a course with Mr. Pierceman after I'm done helping all the dummies figure out that r—e—d—spells *red.*"

"Screw you," Chris quipped.

"I didn't mean you," Jared added quickly, not catching Chris' levity, but realizing it was the wrong thing to say to the wrong person. He knew Chris was more than familiar with the term *remedial* and *special* attached to all of his course subjects.

"First Eric spits in my face and now you." He pushed up his glasses and wiped at his eyes.

"Hey, dude...sorry. Ok?" Jared looked Chris over and saw that his polo shirt had—as usual—come un-tucked from his dark blue jeans. Though Chris was so round, he probably had no idea that his shirttail was flopping about, Jared figured. He never understood Chris' obsession with trying to fit in when he avoided anything that was in at the moment. Black boys and wannabe-black white boys were into fake leather or parachute pants and star endorsed tennis shoes. He preferred punk music, but abhorred the punk's cookie-cutter style...studded bracelets and collars...and took pride in creating his own look, much to the chagrin of his mother.

"I'll just jump off the roof after tutoring," Chris offered, and then smirked.

"I said I'm sorr..." Jared stopped and stared at him, and then realized he'd been duped.

"I thought you were some Einstein," Chris said. "It sure took you long enough to catch up."

"Well, that's what happens when you get in a fight. You can't think straight for a while after it," Jared joked, and then became serious. "I can't keep fighting for you, dude. You're gonna have to stop taking crap from everybody." They reached the top of the stairs and headed toward the library.

"That's easy for you to say. Nobody screws with you."

"Not anymore they don't," Jared boasted. "I used to take their crap in middle school—especially from, Eric. So I started swinging back."

"*And* you're a freakin' giant. That helps."

"So?" Jared puffed. "Don't fight fair, Chris...just fight. Kick'em in the balls if you can."

"Fight like a girl?"

"No," Jared whispered, as he opened the library door for Chris and spotted Mr. Pierceman talking to a student seated next to him. "Win like a dude."

"But I can't get all *black* on them like you did."

Jared shook his head in dismay.

"You were all up in Eric's face like...*Bam! Bam! Kapow!*" Chris crowed, as he pretended to punch Jared.

Jared pushed him away. "Knock it off. You look retarded."

"You don't," Chris replied. "I act like that and it makes them wanna kick my fat butt even more. I gotta get more ghetto, dude."

"We don't even have a ghetto in Homer—but we do have a couple of trailer parks. You can get all *white trailer-trash* on them."

"I gotta lose some teeth and get my cousin pregnant first, don't I?"

* * *

Jared was surprised and relieved to discover his punishment was easier to swallow than he had first thought. The first few weeks, he was quick to become impatient tutoring the five to sometimes ten freshmen students who showed up. Most students that came were already in grave danger of failing. Stacy Willows—or as the other kids called her, Spacey—needed everything explained at least three times before the wheels of comprehension began to turn. George Allenson, who'd been far too ambitious when he signed up for honors Chemistry, was now thoroughly lost in its concepts.

Soon, Jared was able to spot where each student's gap between understanding and confusion began and ended. For the first time, he actually realized how much he took for granted his ability to passively understand and master math, science and language concepts. The students—some average and some who were actually bright—were completely baffled by them.

He particularly enjoyed the one-on-one sessions with Mr. Pierceman. After the rest of the students had left, Jared was allowed to call him by his first name—Taylor—and could literally put his legs up. He liked Taylor as a teacher, but had figured his personality was as stiff as the neatly pressed slacks and shirts he always wore. He realized he had it all wrong.

"Try again, carrot top," Taylor had admonished him during one of their tutoring sessions. "Rome didn't fall solely because of corrupt rulers, as much as it did because of a disparity of wealth between the populace."

Jared gawked at him. "Did you just call me carrot top?"

Taylor looked around and then focused back on Jared and smirked. "Do you see someone else here who looks like they have an eraser stuck on their head?"

"It's red, Taylor. My hair is red," Jared insisted. "Well...kind of."

"If that's the story you're selling," Taylor said, and then shrugged. "But I would get my money back from whoever did it to ya."

"*I* colored it," Jared snipped.

"Ooooh-boy." Taylor grimaced. "We can work on colors after Shakespeare, OK? And if you need it, we can work on your shapes, too...circles...squares...triangles."

"A-ha-ha," Jared groaned. "So funny, I'll laugh about it later... *Taylor.*"

The next Thursday after tutoring had ended, Jared went about putting all of the library chairs back in their rightful place. Taylor had gone to the restroom, and all of the other students, except Chris, had already departed. "Why don't you come over tonight?" Chris asked, while stuffing his notebook into his backpack. "My parents keep asking about you anyway. They think you're such a rebel, ya know?"

"Dude—that's because your parents are freakin' cool," Jared said. "They're not so uptight about stuff, like my mom is."

"Well, that's what happens when you're stoned all the time," Chris explained. "I could dance on the roof naked, and my folks would applaud. They're trying to relive their hippie days." Chris flashed the two-finger peace sign at him. "And dragging me along with them."

Jared chuckled. "I guess the eighties is the best thing that's ever happened to them."

"For real," Chris agreed. "Everybody's smoking weed. Punk rockers rule, like you..."

"I'm not a punk rocker!"

Chris rolled his eyes. "Sure you're not. You just dress like one."

"I dress like *me*, alright?"

"Whatever," Chris relented. "Anyway, you're the flower-child son they really wanted. I'm just some cool prep living with them at the moment." He raised his narrow nose in the air and flicked the lapels of his neon-yellow polo shirt.

Jared sat down as Chris stood up. "Just kill me if you ever see me dressed like you."

"Sure will," Chris chirped. "Or you can just take my place at camp this summer. My folks aren't happy until I'm miserable."

"Join the club," Jared groaned. "I have to go down to Mississippi during the only week I have off before summer school begins."

"Your Aunt huh?"

Jared stared off. "She wants to go back down and stay with my grandmother, so we're driving her down."

"They can't do anything else for her?"

"Her cancer has already metastasized...spread all over," he re-phrased, knowing the word had two too many syllables for Chris to understand.

"Sorry, man," Chris uttered. "Isn't Mississippi where your dad lives? You gonna try—"

"What's up with this camp?" Jared quickly interrupted.

"Um...um, oh yeah. But I wouldn't call it a real camp," Chris said. "It's a healthy eating camp."

"Youch! Now that's punishment."

"It's even worse than that." Chris shook his head slowly. "On the handout are all of these fat, ugly kids smiling like they actually like being there. And they got some lame logo like, *'go lean being green'.*"

"Well—maybe you're folks *aren't* so cool."

"Duh!" Chris snapped. "I know I'm fat. So why do I want to hang out with a bunch of other fat people? So we can talk about how fat we are?"

"Well, have fun at fat camp then?" Jared joked.

"A day of finals then off to fat camp, and then back for summer school. I'm so screwed."

As the door to the library squeaked open, both boys turned around to see Taylor walking in. "Hey...you coming over or what?" Chris asked as he walked backward from the table, facing Jared, but with his back to Taylor.

"Can't tonight. I gotta work after I'm done here. This weekend?"

"Cool, dude."

"Hey! Tell your mom to save me some." Jared winked.

Chris put his fingers to his lips like he had a joint. He quickly lowered his hand and turned around before Taylor could see. "Have a great evening, Mr. Pierceman," he cooed.

"You too, Chris," Taylor replied.

Jared fished his book report from his backpack and laid it on the table. Taylor sat down in the chair Chris had occupied just moments before. Taylor crossed his legs and folded his arms across his chest.

"I've written a synopsis of Dante's circles of hell," Jared volunteered proudly. He pushed the neatly printed papers in front of Taylor. "It sure beats reading *To Kill a Mocking Bird* for the gazillionth time. Dante Alighieri was way—way out there with this book."

"What if it was all true?" Taylor asked.

"I would definitely start paying more attention at church. But—"

"But what? You don't think it can be real?"

Jared sat back and settled in for another juicy debate. "Its just some Italian guy with his own perception of what he thinks heaven, hell and purgatory is all about."

"Uh-huh," Taylor grunted. He looked over Jared toward the rows of books behind them. He stood and walked over to them, and then disappeared down a row.

Jared turned completely around. "Taylor? Mr. Pierceman?"

"Calm down, son," Taylor called back. He walked out of the last row carrying a small black book. He sat back down and laid it on the table.

"What's this?" Jared asked, looking at the black book with no title, name or any marking on it for that matter.

Taylor tapped the book with his fingertips. "A little something for you to read."

"I thought we were working on Dante?"

"We were. But something else has come up."

"It's a week before finals," Jared moaned. "C'mon, Taylor—I can't start another report now. The deal was that I would ace my finals— so I'm gonna try, plus take English Lit. with you *and tutor*."

"You don't have to report on this book," Taylor said, and began tapping the book again. "In fact, all you have to do is read it."

Jared lowered his head at him. "Just read it? What about my grade for English?"

"I've already given you an 'A'. And in the next two days, your mother will receive an excellent letter of recommendation from me for your college applications."

"Really?"

Taylor pushed the black book toward Jared.

"So all I have to do is read it—right?"

"Tell me, Jared. What's real."

"Real? You mean reality?"

"Yes."

"Well, you see and touch things and it's converted to electrical impulses that your brain translates into a sensation."

"Do you believe in God?"

Jared grinned, figuring Taylor was weaving a web to catch him in. "Yes—but that has to do with faith."

"But you can't see him or touch him. You believe in God because you were taught to believe without any evidence to corroborate his existence, hmm?"

"Yes," Jared replied reluctantly.

"But if you were raised, say Buddhist or Hindu, or your family believed in Zoroastrianism, you would most likely believe in their gods and teachings, but again without any verifiable proof."

Jared thought for a moment. "But, I have free will, too! I can change my mind and my religion if I want, no matter what I've been taught."

"That still requires that you believe without proof, unlike this book right here."

"This?" Jared asked. "Wait a sec. Are you saying this book proves the existence of—"

"Whatever your brain translates those electrical impulses into," Taylor said. "You've heard the phrase, 'oh ye of little faith'?"

Jared nodded.

Taylor winked. "You won't need faith with this book."

Jared scooted his chair closer to the table. He looked up at Taylor, as if expecting him to suddenly let him in on the joke. But there was nothing humorous about Taylor whose eyes were now shadowed by a heavy brow.

"Before you open it," Taylor told him. "You must promise me one thing."

"OK."

"You speak to no one about it—not one sentence," he said in a tone that had changed from flat to deep in pitch. "Not even about this conversation we're having right now."

"Gotcha. So what is this book?"

"A memoir."

"Whose?"

Taylor shook his head. "Wrong question. You should have asked *what*."

Jared looked at the book. It was no more than ten inches long and no thicker than his thumb. There wasn't a mar or telltale sign of spilled pop or crusted food that usually decorated books from the school library. When he opened it, its stiff spine cracked. But what he found on the first page, and then turning to the next, and then quickly picking it up and flipping all the way through it, was not what he expected. He chuckled and tossed the book back on the table. "You got me. I guess I'm not getting whatever point you're trying to make."

"You haven't read it yet."

"It's blaaaaank," Jared sang, leaving his mouth open for effect.

"Is it?"

Jared grabbed the book and opened it up facing Taylor. "See. There's nothing there."

Taylor poked his head around the book. "Oh, I see. But blank it's not."

Jared turned the book around and quickly pulled it to within inches of his face. "What the—" What had at first been blank white pages were now filled with calligraphic handwritten text. He looked at Taylor and then back at the book. He began flipping through it and saw that each and every page...front and back...was full of words written with the same swooshy strokes of a fountain pen. "There was nothing here before," he uttered.

"Yes, there was." Taylor placed his elbows on the table and clasped his hands below his narrow chin. "Perhaps it was just your *perception*. Maybe your mind interpreted the signals incorrectly."

"Bull!" Jared knew what he had seen, and it was nothing.

"Maybe you do need faith after all."

"A psychiatrist maybe."

"Why don't you just read it, and then decide which one you need...one or both...*or neither.*"

Jared gave Taylor the most sinister look he could muster. He opened the book and glanced at the title page that read simply...

"Gods of Egypt," Jared whispered. He turned to the next page and began reading.

I tell you now that magic is as real as the air you breathe. It is as real as the water that flows up the Nile...the sand upon which I stand and as mighty as my voice, which wields a force that is beyond mortal comprehension. So say I—Horus—god of Egypt.

Jared looked up. "What is this?"

"A memoir, I told you. Keep reading and see."

Jared continued.

My every word became holy law, which was obeyed by my sons— the Pharaohs of Egypt. Yearly I loosed the waters of the Nile to enrich the lands and nourish my people.

"It's just Egyptian mythology," Jared explained. He looked up to hear Taylor's response, but he was gone. Jared stood up and spun around. "Taylor! Taylor?" He walked around the library and checked each aisle, and even behind the librarian's desk, but saw no sign of him. He went back to the table and picked up the book. He looked around once more and sat before deciding to read a bit more.

I gave my people knowledge to create monuments of such grandeur, not even the fury of time has destroyed them. I am he who judged the world of the living and the dead. The fate of a man's ba— their living spirit—rested in my holy, sovereign hands. I brought life to the weak, death to the wicked and salvation to the honorable.

I was that which resideth in the horizon.

I am the god of kings.

I am Horus.

Jared stopped. He realized that even though he was looking at the words, it was if someone else was speaking them directly into his mind. But just as soon as he realized this, the room began to darken, as though the lights in the library and even the sunlight from the windows were being dimmed. Within moments, he was enveloped in a sea of complete darkness and felt as though he was being flung around in a void that had no up or down...front or back.

The air around him began to warm. He began sweating all over as his body tried to cool down. When he touched himself, attempting to give his mind a sense of orientation, he discovered his pants and shirt were both gone. All he felt was a strip of cloth covering his groin and another one behind that barely covered his rear.

Without warning, a white light flashed in his eyes. And then, as quick as the light came, it was gone. He looked around and realized he was no longer in the library, or Homer, Illinois for that matter. The oil lamp lit hall he stood in was fashioned out of stone that gleamed in the low light and cast dancing shadows on floor. A few feet away, a dark-skinned man wearing a white shenti-skirt stood with his back to him. And in front of the man was a human-sized statue with the head of a hawk—gold and blue plumes cascading down its shoulders.

Jared looked down at his own body. His Sam Mosley—the British soul singer—T-shirt, his black combat boots and camouflage army pants he'd had on earlier were gone. In their place was a loincloth that barely covered his bits. He touched the loincloth; his fingers sent signals to his brain and told him it was really cloth. He touched his skin; it was warm and moist with sweat. When he touched his head, his dried-out, red-orange hair was gone—completely, as though it had just been shaven off with a razor.

He dared a step toward the man, who then turned around and looked at him with eyes as black as soot. "I am that which is in the horizon, Jared...I am Horus—god of Egypt," the man said. It was the last thing Jared remembered before everything went dark again and he was falling once more in the void.

Jared opened his eyes and gasped. He was back in the library with his same clothes on and hair back on his head. Though now, every muscle from neck to feet ached, as though he had just run a twenty-mile marathon. Taylor Pierceman was still nowhere to be seen and neither was the book that had started it all.

Jared grunted as he rose from his chair and limped out of the library. He painstakingly made it down to the ground floor, where Mrs. Cedars, the school secretary, was just leaving the main office. "Mrs. Cedars! Wait a second—please." He walked to her as fast as his aching muscles allowed.

"You alright, honey?" she asked.

"Yeah," he grunted.

"You don't look alright."

"I'm fine, thanks," he lied. "Have you seen Taylor...I mean Mr. Pierceman. Taylor Pierceman."

"About an hour ago, honey."

"An hour?" Jared looked at his watch and saw that only ten minutes had elapsed since he had last seen Taylor. His lessons with Taylor always started at four-thirty, right after tutoring ended. But it wasn't even a quarter to five yet by his watch. "What time do you have, Mrs. Cedars?"

She looked down at her watch. "Almost four forty-five."

"And Mr. Pierceman left an hour ago?"

"Mmm-hmm," she replied. "He came into the office, grabbed his school-mail, and then left. But...come to think of it, honey, he usually tutors some boy after school. I thought it was strange that he left early, too. Maybe that boy didn't show up today or something."

"Oh...he showed up all right," Jared muttered.

CHAPTER 6

Tamen hated having to pull the illusions from Jared's mind so abruptly and leaving him bewildered. But just as he was beginning the tale—the one Jared had to hear and learn from for him to have any chance against Shazadeh and Lord Yikan—he had sensed a foul and powerful chant being sung. It was yet another chant he'd heard in just a few week's time. This particular chant had come from hundreds of miles away from Homer, but far too close for his liking, and far too close to Jared.

Had it been another time, he would have done what he always did when sensing Shazadeh and Lord Yikan nearby, which was to flee to another continent and assume another identity. There he would stay for fifty, a hundred or two hundred years, until he heard them closing in on him once more, and then run again. But the time for running was over. He had found Jared—Shazadeh's counterbalance—but knew Jared was nowhere close to understanding that he would be the one to alter the fate of man, demons and angels.

With his body safely hidden and his spirit—*his ba*—freed from its fleshly constraints, he willed his spirit aloft into the dusky afternoon sky. Once the brick school building was no more than a dot on the landscape below, he listened for what was beyond the detection of mortal hearing. The chant he had heard was still echoing, but fading quickly. He followed the echo southwest at the speed of thought, which led him to the most southern portion of the state, New Mexico.

The chant led him away from the clusters of homes and businesses and out into the rocky desert. Brush and cacti with dainty pink and yellow flowers were sprinkled throughout the arid land. He sensed a coyote who was waiting patiently for a rabbit that had no idea it was about to become dinner. A colony of bats were stirring in their sleep and thirsting for gnats and mosquitoes. The scraping of a snake's belly on the desert ground caught his senses as it wound its way about looking for a meal. But as he moved his spirit further on, the hunters and hunted of the desert sudden could no longer be heard, which meant he was in the right spot. Even they, he knew, had enough sense to stay away from evil...unlike humans.

To his right, off the road a few hundred yards, Tamen caught sight of a building with a few cars and a minivan parked by it. He moved closer to the structure and saw that it was a church built of adobe. The ginger-colored façade of the single-story church was cracked in several places along its sidewalls, and in the front, pieces of it were threatening to fall off in child-sized chunks. On the ground, next to the pale red, double doors that looked as though they had been ripped from their hinges, lay the church bell broken apart in three jagged pieces. Despite all of the vehicles in front of the church, where the resonance of the chant went cold, he was certain those who had came in them were already dead.

He looked down as he entered, and was not in the least surprised to see a man's shriveled corpse lying in the aisle and devoid of every ounce of fluid it once had. Every time he saw the remains of Shazadeh's victims, they reminded him of the shrunken, leather skinned-mummies of ancient Egypt that was often displayed in museum exhibits. Whereas time had dried out the skin and sucked every bit of moisture from actual mummies, Shazadeh's victims were unwillingly parted from theirs.

Moving down the center aisle, he discovered even more of the prematurely mummified-looking bodies...men and women...young and old. Some, like the man by the entrance, had almost made it out—though he still likely wouldn't have gotten far—but most had been drained of their spirit-essence by the front of the church. So far, he had counted over twelve of the dry skinned shrink-wrapped corpses. But the more he looked about, the more bodies he saw and added to the tally.

Ah...*her altar*, Tamen thought, as he hovered to the front of the church and came upon an overturned wood stand with Shazadeh's statue laying next to it. The stone statue was of her nude, with her arms raised and her legs intertwined. Like her true form, the skin was as black as tar and finger thin braids extending all the way to her backside. Tamen figured she had never looked like that until Duke Astaroth—Regent of Hell—remade her as a demon.

"You fools," he said to the corpses. "She promised you beauty and perfection, and all those lovely things you thought would come with it. So you chanted. She heard and came, and then took your essence instead. And now all of you have paid with your lives."

Or had they?

His immortal eyes caught movement. He looked at the pew near the altar and the wizened leg sticking out from under it. Almost as if it had waited for him to see it again, it twitched. He moved closer and passed his spirit form through the seat of the pew. It was a woman's face staring straight up that he saw, but one that still contained life, albeit barely. Her eyes were sunken in her skull. Her shallow breaths came like pants from a ghost. The outline of every curve and jut of her skull was visible beneath the paper-thin skin over it. Unlike the others around her, not all of her fluids and spirit-essence had been drained, as though the process had been started and then abruptly ended.

Tamen knew all of this was just a prelude of what was to come if he failed to do as the Christ commanded. Without balance—without Jared becoming what he was destined to be—the world fall into the hands of Shazadeh, the famed Whore of Babylon herself made flesh, who's rule had long since been prophesized in the book of Revelations.

And the woman was arrayed in purple and scarlet color, and decked with gold and precious stones and pearls, having a golden cup in her hand full of abominations and filthiness of her fornication: And upon her forehead was a name written...mystery, Babylon the Great, the mother of harlots and abominations of the earth.

Tamen raised his spirit through the roof and soared high above the church. He stretched his senses out and sought human life. Miles south of the church, he sensed the thoughts of a man who was exactly the type that he needed. He knew the mind of the woman in the church was beyond repair, but felt at least her family would have someone—some thing—to cling onto.

Tamen followed the man's erratic thoughts, which led him to a sheriff's outpost just outside the nearby town. As he passed his spirit through the wall and into the room, he understood why the man's thoughts were so jumbled. Kevin Walker was the name he sneaked from the man's mind, and he was fast asleep dreaming about fixing the roof above his kitchen. Despite going up and down the ladder and applying glob after glob of tar and layers of shingles, it still leaked profusely. Tamen watched as Kevin came down the ladder once more and looked in the kitchen.

'Son'bitch!' Kevin spat. He looked at the bucket in his hand, which was already filled with more bubbling tar, and from nowhere, a set of shingles appeared under his arm. But instead of just one leak, there were now two dripping on the white linoleum floor. After spewing a string of curses, he climbed back up the ladder and started patching the roof all over again.

Tamen slipped out of the dream and positioned his spirit in front of the desk where Kevin was using his hands as pillows to rest his head. *Wake up, Kevin,* Tamen called, projecting his voice into Kevin's thoughts. Kevin's eyes fluttered open for a moment and then shut. *Get up!* Tamen yelled.

Kevin jumped out of his chair and scrambled for his gun. He jerkily aimed the revolver in all directions. After a moment, seemingly confident he was truly alone in the office, he sat down and sighed. He rubbed his forehead and ran his hand over the few black and gray hairs left on his fifty-year old head. "Whoa," he whispered. "Christ, that sounded real."

I am not the Christ.

Kevin's jaw slowly unhinged and his mouth began pooling with saliva.

Close your mouth, Kevin.

Kevin jumped out of his chair. "Where da hell are you?" Kevin demanded. He pointed the gun from one end of the room to the other. He then leaned back and looked out the window behind him.

I am right here, Kevin Walker, Tamen replied. *Do you not know with whom you speak?*

"I'm—I—I'm...?"

You are not dreaming this. The roof of your home is not leaking. Pinch yourself. Kevin quickly pinched his arm. *Did you feel it?*

"Y—yes?"

Then you are not dreaming—are you?

Kevin looked up, and then bent down and slowly stuck his head under the desk. He straightened up and looked around the room again. "*God?* Are you...God?"

Yes, Kevin.

"The God?"

The one and only.

"Oh God!" Kevin muttered. He dropped the gun on the desk and began grinding his knuckles into his temples. "I'm goin' nuts! Oh God—oh God! Not...*not you, God*...ohhh God!"

On your knees, Kevin! Tamen commanded. Kevin dropped to the floor and clasped his hands together. *You are not crazy.*

"I'm—I'm not?"

No. I have come because I have need of you tonight. Do as I say and I might forgive your sins.

Kevin hesitated. "Uh...yes Lord?"

Tamen searched Kevin's thoughts and found exactly what he needed. *You are an adulterer, Kevin Walker. You and that woman, Missy Adler, from the county clerk's office have sinned greatly. You shame your wife and your daughters.*

Kevin squeezed his eyelids shut and groaned.

You thought I did not know?

"Uh...?" Kevin clasped his hands tight until they were bloodless and bone white.

I see everything!

Kevin raised his hands in the air and bowed his head. "Have mercy, God. I swear I'll leave Missy alone. I swear to God. I—I mean I swear to you."

If you even think about touching Missy Adler again, I will make your you-know-what fall off! Do you hear me?

Kevin started shaking. "Yes, God...oh yes! I swear!"

Good then. Now listen, Kevin Walker. Something terrible has transpired at the deserted church north of here—the one out in the desert. Send many officers and an ambulance to meet you there. There is a woman under the front pew on the left side of the aisle who needs your help.

"Yes, God!"

Tamen waited as Kevin picked-up the radio's handset and called for an officer.

"The old church off of route eight? Over," the officer replied through the radio's speaker.

"Roger that, Bobby," Kevin replied. "Meet me there in ten, over."

"All the way out there? What happened? Over."

"Somethin'! I don't know, Bobby!" Kevin yelled into the handset. "Just get your bony butt out there like I said—got me?"

An irritated response came back through the speaker. *"Ten-four."*

Kevin ran to his cruiser. He flipped on the red lights and sirens as he pulled out onto the road. He then radioed for additional officers to meet him at the old church and ran into the same resistance as he had before with his deputy, Bobby. He assured them that help was indeed needed, but stopped short of explaining how he knew. He looked through the windshield and up at the sky turned amber by the setting sun. "God—you still there?"

Yes, Tamen replied. He had positioned his spirit in the passenger's seat.

"If—if you don't mind me asking, Lord.... Why do you need *my* help? You're all powerful and everything...aint'cha?"

Do you want to go to hell, Kevin Walker?

"No, Lord!"

Then never question my ways, for they are mysterious. Now be quiet and do as I told you.

"Yes, God! Please don't send me to hell...I was just asking."

As Kevin drove up the road leading to the church, Tamen left the car and began following from above. Deputy Bobby had already made it to the church and was on the side of it puking, adding another layer to his uniform top that was already drenched in chunky yellow vomit. He looked up slightly as Kevin parked and came running toward him.

"Christ sake, Kev!" Bobby growled at him, with an inch of yellow vomit dangling from his lower lip. His already white face was the color of fresh milk. "Why didn't you warn me? Holy Christ!" He heaved, and then turned away and puked again.

Kevin readied his gun and shakily moved toward the entrance and peeked inside. He gasped and dropped his gun. He stumbled back and joined Bobby in decorating the sand and gravel with vomit. Tamen wondered how often this same scene was playing itself out all over the world. Each week it seemed there were ten more groups such as these that Shazadeh and Lord Yikan were using to recruit mortals in order to find the one who could balance her. Only, he thought with some relief, he had already found Jared —her counterbalance. But he knew how quickly his and Jared's fortune could change with just one misstep.

Kevin, Tamen said.

"Y—yes, God?" Kevin wiped his mouth and looked up to the sky. Bobby looked over and stared at him.

Be brave. Go in and find the woman.

"Th—th—those dead bodies in there been...something happened to them. There all over the place!" he cried.

I know, Tamen replied. *But there is still one alive and she needs you now. I will give you strength, Kevin. Believe in your God for once in your life.*

Kevin shook his head.

Bobby straightened up. "Who the hell you talking to, Kev?"

Do not mind him. Go rescue the woman and you will be a hero, Tamen promised.

Kevin did not disappoint.

Tamen rose into the sky and began heading back north. Below, he saw ambulance lights flashing a few miles away en route to the church. *Help is already coming, Kevin.*

"Yes, Lord!"

And Kevin?

"Yes?"

Stay away from Missy Adler!

CHAPTER 7

Nicholas was already gone, Eric Lightner realized. And the man with the swirling blue eyes standing next to him scoffed and turned away when he begged for help. Eric was on his hands and knees and couldn't move—could barely even breathe—with her foot pressing into his back with the weight of what felt like three men standing on one of his vertebrae. But she wasn't really female, Eric knew that much now. For that matter, he was positive she wasn't even human. But regardless of what she was, he still found her beautiful...alluring...intoxicatingly irresistible. But she—or whatever she really was—was most definitely a killer above all. He'd watched helplessly as she drained the life from his girlfriend, Cheryl, at the abandoned church, before going after everyone else. Though despite her murdering the others, he wanted nothing more than to be near her.

* * *

Beauty is only skin deep.

That was the lie Eric had always held onto.

It was a lovely delusion that helped he and his girlfriend, Cheryl, cope with the stares from others whenever they left the safety of their college apartment. Together, they had convinced themselves that what really mattered resided inside the person, not the skin covering them. He wanted desperately to believe that. He knew Cheryl—all two hundred and fifty pounds of her—wanted to also. But no matter where they went...no matter how hard they tried to pretend they didn't see people unabashedly gawking at them and even feeling pity for them...they couldn't escape the fact that they were unsightly to look at.

Smarts they both had in abundance. Cheryl was on track to graduate sum cum laude, and Eric not far behind with only two B's amidst all A's to mar his three years at the university they attended. Possessing a genial personality was a quality they had both worked hard to develop and it had even gained them a few friends. If invited to a party or a gathering—which was rare indeed—Cheryl was always the first one in the kitchen to help and the last one to leave after every dish and cup was washed and put back in its place. Eric, meanwhile, would busy himself laughing the loudest and the longest, making sure ever pun, joke and witty sarcastic remark someone made was overly appreciated.

But Eric knew the mirror didn't lie when he looked in it, nor did his wide-set eyes when he looked at Cheryl's pockmarked face. Children, who pointed at them in grocery stores and malls, were the most truthful of all. Their parents, who snatched at their little ones for staring and whispered admonishments to them through fake smiles, where the real liars, Eric knew.

Though his brown eyes had a mind of their own...the right one preferring to look straight on, while the left wandered where it wanted most of the time...he hoped Cheryl could see some beauty in them, even though he couldn't. He felt that if he pretended to see past her hook of a nose and her baby-sized teeth in her adult wide mouth, then she could do the same for his wayward eye, stick thick build and his too large lower jaw. He hoped he could. He hoped she could. But in the back of his mind, he knew she was as hideous to behold as he was, and it disgusted him to think it and know it to be true.

He didn't want to be handsome or even average looking. At this point, he was willing to settle for just ugly. He knew if the stares stopped, then friendships—people who could feel comfortable around people who looked like he and Cheryl—would then follow. If he was just ugly, he figured he could be part of a group. He would even have friends to call-up, hang out with and even get to complain about how Cheryl thinks he's spending too much time with them.

But realizing miracles didn't happened, Eric uncomfortably settled into complacency with Cheryl. And it was that very reason that the infomercials for the *Institute of Perceptual Minds* took so long to finally become appealing to him. Using the TV for white noise as he studied well past the midnight hour, he'd simply ignored the infomercials the institute ran continuously. But as the summer was winding down and fall semester approached, he began giving the infomercials a glance...then a momentary look...and then his undivided attention.

The infomercial had been filmed at a park with rows upon rows of food-laden picnic tables. Those present were young and old, and of every shape, size and color. They rose wine glasses and toasted frequently as music made for skipping played in the background. And just as it seemed life could get no better for this multicultural mash of folks, a woman's voice eased in over the raucous celebration of life and diversity.

"How wonderful it would be if we were all judged on who we are on the inside. The world would be such a better place for all of us," the woman said. *"But we all know the truth, don't we? People still judge us by what they see, not by who we really are,"* she stressed softly, as though it hurt to say the words.

As her voice trailed off, the picture of the utopian picnic scene became shaded in a blood-red hue. It was replaced with a montage of beautiful celebrities walking the red carpet in neck plunging sequined gowns that only the über-rich could afford. Bleach blond starlets on red carpets turned and spun, and then flipped their salon coiffed blond hair. The chiseled-jawed men with smoldering bedroom eyes were practically Greek gods.

"*Stop!*" she begged, just as the film devolved into a montage of washboard stomach men and size zero young women in stilettos drinking and dancing poolside. The scene faded to black before switching back to the picnic scene.

"*Mankind has struggled so hard to survive through the ages, and this is all that we've become?*" she asked, with a thread of condemnation echoing through her voice. "*We're more concerned about having youthful skin, than feeding our youth? We're no one if we don't have the perfect hair, perfect smile, the right clothes and the right friends? This is unconditional love?*" She grumbled lightly.

"*Here at the Institute of Perceptual Minds, we show you how to break free of those negative thoughts and destructive relationships that hold us back from becoming who we truly are. And once we know who we are, we learn to love who we are. What you look like... how much money you have...who you choose to love isn't important when you see that our true destiny is to be one great, loving family. That's where peace, happiness and unconditional love comes from.*" Headshots of each of those at the picnic took turns being flashed on the screen. They smiled at the camera. Some laughed. Others giggled. Everyone looked happy.

"*When you feel a need for change within yourself...when you're ready to really love yourself and others around you...when you are ready to make this world a truly better place, one loving heart at a time...then come see us—your brothers and sisters at the Institute of Perceptual Minds. We love you, because you deserve to be loved, so you can love others.*"

Each week it seemed as though there was a new commercial touting the institute's vision of a new life. And each week, Eric grew more curious about it. They even began showcasing testimonials of doctors, teachers, janitors and politicians who had come into the organization and been awakened to their true selves. All across the United States, and in almost every country around the world, people swore they had found their path to connecting with the harmony of the universe—which was love.

At the college's student union, he noticed flyers for the institute showing up on tables and bulletin boards and outside on telephone and light poles. Convincing Cheryl to check out one of the institute's meetings was easier than he thought it would be. Her eagerness to go comforted and reassured him that he wasn't alone in feeling shunned and thrown away by society. He wanted was to be a part of some thing or some group as much as anyone else...but just a whole lot more.

* * *

Eric found those at the social were as warm and welcoming as the institute had promised. But those attending, save a few who were almost as unattractive as he and Cheryl, looked nothing like he thought they would. He expected the room to be full of people from the infomercial having a gay time at the picnic, not anorexic girls who looked like Parisian models and centerfold-ready guys prowling about.

He and Cheryl didn't even have a chance to finish smoothing their nametags down on their shirts before a couple greeted them. Alena was a slim, busty black girl with short hair and a round rear, and her boyfriend, Tim—a thin-waist Korean guy with perfectly cut hair that draped his narrow face.

Alena and Tim chatted them up, but as more members came over to greet them, they were soon off chatting away separately with newfound friends. After hours of conversations with guy after girl after guy, and then couples here and there, Eric spotted Cheryl rolling her head back in laughter with a handsome Latino guy. He ended his own conversation and was about to head over and find out what Cheryl was finding so hilarious, when someone grabbed his arm. He turned to face a black guy with dark brown eyes who was as tall as he was.

"Don't worry about Cheryl, man," the guy said. "She's in good hands with Alehandro. You're Eric, right?"

"Yeah, it is," Eric said, dropping his voice an octave as he shook the man's hand.

"You wanted to make sure she's alright? I know. Just be cool, man." He patted Eric on the shoulder. "The name's Nicholas—but Nick is fine."

Eric looked Nick over and smiled nervously. Beneath Nick's snug white shirt and even tighter gray slacks, it was plainly visible he was a workout fanatic. His broad shoulders looked more like a beam of wood in comparison to his adolescent-sized waist.

"I was just talkin' to Cheryl and she was wondering how you were doing in all this craziness," Nick said. "I told her, don't you worry your pretty little head about it...you're with true friends now."

Eric nearly choked on his own saliva at Nick's compliment of Cheryl. Pretty was a word no one had ever used to describe Cheryl even in her best outfit and covered in makeup. "We just thought we outta check it out. We've been seeing the uh...commercials..."

"Cool man," Nick replied. "I'm executive director of this branch by the way," he said and saluted. He stared at Eric for a moment before letting out a throaty laugh. He slapped Eric on the back. "Which only means I get to organize parties like these. You know, the institute is spreading wide and large, man. Our goal this year is to have a chapter in every university and college in the U.S." He stopped and shook his head. "Wait—wait—wait! I'm not gonna preach and ruin your evening, man."

"S'okay," Eric replied.

"No way, man," Nick said. "You and Cheryl can meet with us every Saturday—right here. Then you can hear me go on and on about how really screwed up the world really is."

* * *

Eric and Cheryl stayed late and then went out to a bar with what remained of the group and chatted away until closing. As the months rolled on and out, they made more friends than either had their entire lives. They began attending the Saturday lectures delivered by Nick and got a chance to meet other institute members from all over the country. Unexpectedly, life finally seemed exciting for Eric, which he attributed also to their study of the book, "Mantras for the Heart"—lines of chants to repeat in times of stress, and to build one's fortitude against it, which all members were instructed to memorize. The institute's infomercials that he had initially ignored were the very ones he and Cheryl touted to their families. A few cousins did join, though most dismissed the institute as nothing more than a cult and warned them about getting involved. But they didn't understand, Eric thought. Couldn't they see how much he had changed on the inside...and more importantly...on the outside? he wondered.

After months of faithfully chanting his mantras three times a day, he noticed that his lazy eye had awoken and straightened up... doing exactly what surgeons had told him was impossible. Energized by the results, he increased his mantras to five times daily and marveled how his lower jaw decreased day-by-day until it aligned with the top. And as he gained weight for the first time in his life and filled out his flat rear end, he still reminded himself of the institute's teachings about vanity, and how unimportant it was. At least that's what he shared at the institute's meetings that he attended in his new tight jeans and shirts that were always unbuttoned at the top.

Cheryl, who consistently chanted her mantras also, had blossomed and then some. As Eric had gained much needed weight upon his frail frame, Cheryl had shed a good deal of hers...a hundred and ten pounds, she was always quick to boast. She even began wearing just enough make-up to bring out her best features, which Eric never thought she had before. And even without it, he had noticed that her once cratered face was all but smooth now.

As the stares stopped whenever they were out in public, and people began smiling at them, he remembered and reminded Cheryl that it wasn't what was on the outside that mattered, but what was on the inside. He wanted to believe that, but he loved what he saw in the mirror more. He wanted it to be true, but his desire for sex with Cheryl—and her new body—overrode those feelings. And deep down, he knew the institute was not what it really seemed to be, but he was infatuated with how he looked now and wasn't willing to give it up no matter the cost.

And besides, he thought, when Nick spoke, it sounded truthful and from the heart.

"The philosophy and practices of the Institute of Perceptual Minds is older than Christianity, Buddhism, Islam and every other religion out there," Nick told the group of fifty or so of them one afternoon.

Eric listened intently as if he'd never heard it, though they were the same words he'd heard months back during private counseling sessions with Nick. It was then that the mystery behind the institute was finally revealed to him and Cheryl. Though before he or Cheryl could even begin to form reservations about the institute, Nick quickly reminded them of all the positive things that had happened to them since joining.

"We worship the true goddess...Shazadeh...not the mother goddess or some earth goddess that Wiccans believe in. And she is very much real," Nick told the crowd. "We don't kill in her name... steal in her name...we don't persecute or judge others do we?"

"NO!" the group spoke as one.

"Go into a church...any church—I dare you." Nick shook his head. "I bet you're hardly in the door before you see a donation box. Or, how about when the person next to you passes the offering plate and gives you *that look*." He cocked his head to the side and raised his brow. "Do we ask for donations?"

"NO!" they cried.

"Do we want you to sell your homes and live in some commune?"

"NO!"

"...eat this or that food?"

"NO!"

"Brothers and sisters...black, white, red, yellow...what do we want?"

"PEACE!!!"

"What do we give?"

"Love!!!"

"Who do we love?"

"My brothers and sisters!"

"And who," his voice was almost a whisper, "do we love above all?"

"The goddess," they whispered back.

Nick folded his hands and placed them on his forehead. "Then by her holy words from the Psalms of Deliverance, let us ask for her blessing."

* * *

As the spring semester wound down into its last few weeks, Nick invited Cheryl and him to a retreat reserved for the most committed. "Not everyone is invited, but you two, man! You guys really know what we're trying to get people to see," Nick complimented. "I can't think of two people who deserve to come more."

They eagerly scrambled into the minivan that evening as it pulled up in front of their apartment. They carpooled to the old church with a few newer members they were partnering with, as part of their advancement inside the real organization that the institute covered for—the Church of the Imperial Goddess—the C.I.G. for short.

In the one room adobe church that looked ready to crumble apart at any moment, Nick gathered them all toward the front, where on a pedestal something was hidden under a white sheet. Nick asked them to kneel. "I present to you...my brothers and sisters...the goddess," he said, and then pulled away the sheet.

Eric finally saw her for the first time. Carved out of a glistening black stone, the goddess was more beautiful than he anticipated. Nick proceeded to open the meeting with his usual thanks and prayers to the goddess, and then asked for her blessing.

"Tonight," Nick began, "is a most special night. You have been chosen above all others to call upon the goddess herself. It may be the song from you...or you...or you," he said as he pointed at them randomly, "whose voice may bring her presence to us...or it may not be any one of you." He paused. "If we are earnest, I have no doubt we will be successful. Marlene, step forward."

A Latino woman in her mid-thirties rose to her feet and let Nick position her in front of the statute. "'The Praise of the Blessed One' is what we shall chant tonight," he told them.

The group rumbled in shock.

"Everyone calm down...calm down," Nick directed. "I know we never say it out loud, and this is the very reason why. It's the only prayer that can draw the goddess forth and so must remain sacred. Marlene, you do remember it don't you?" She shook her head. "Then let's begin."

"Faster!" Nick urged as she chanted.

When it seemed as though Marlene had begun to scramble the words, Nick dismissed her and called upon another. The next was an older white man. After him, a black man who still looked like a teenager. Cheryl followed and quickly screwed up the words like the rest. Eric had his turn next to the last person that tried.

Eric began chanting the words of the mantra, but was determined to find a groove and not start bumbling over the sounds as the others had. The more he repeated the short, two line phrase, the easier it seemed.

"Faster!" Nick snapped.

Eric realized that if he excluded the pauses and blended the sounds, including the last sound with the first of the next, he could say them all quicker and without as much effort.

"Faster!"

The rhythm he found made him start to feel dizzy, like he had a beer buzz. When he looked at the others who were swaying side-to-side in rhythm with his mantra, he knew they were feeling it too. Nick barked for him to chant even faster. And as he did, he swore the room brightened momentarily. Even when the wind picked up and began whistling through the cracks of the windows and double door entrance, he didn't stutter, but kept his rhythm fast and even.

He stopped...and abruptly so, when the doors of the church blew not just open, but apart in a blinding blast. The wind gusted inside and brought desert sand along with it before finally dying out. Eric began coughing as the sandy fog slowly began settling. At first he thought the burst of windblown soot had forced two of the members to run for the outside, though as his vision cleared, he saw that the two figures were actually coming *into* the church.

He recognized one of them who were approaching, but not the other. The light-skinned bald man with weird eyes was unfamiliar. The woman with oil black skin and long braids was not. He turned to the statue of the goddess behind him and back to the bare chest woman approaching him. She wore only a sheer panel of white fabric that barely obscured her privates. *She* was the exact image of her own statue, he saw...oval eyes, puffy black lips and breasts that rose high and looked as firm as those that had been carved for her statue.

Nick gushed. "Goddess...you've come back to me!" He nearly knocked Eric down as he ran to her and kneeled. He kissed both of her feet several times. She rubbed his head with her hand, which was as black on the palm side as on the front.

"Have they all read my watcher?" she asked.

The sound of her husky, gritty voice, made Eric start to feel woozy.

Nick's head was bowed. "Yes, goddess."

She pointed to Eric. "Is he the one that chanted?"

Nick nodded. "Is he the one?"

"Not likely, my watcher," she answered. "Still, you have served your goddess well and will be rewarded."

"May I receive you?"

"We shall see." She smiled at him with teeth the opposite color of her skin. "But it is time for you to leave this place. *The balance* is still out there somewhere, and the creature that calls himself a god may have already found him. But tread carefully. Tamen will not hesitate in taking your life if confronted."

"Yes, goddess," Nick acknowledged. He ran for the exit and off into the night without so much as a fleeting look back.

Eric wondered why Nick's abrupt exit only appeared strange to him. The others were busy muttering prayers to the goddess walking toward them, leaving the strange looking man behind. Cheryl was weeping. Her black-eye eyeliner was running down her cheek and under her jaw. Like the others, she reached out to try and touch the goddess as she approached.

It was growing hotter in the room. But even that, Eric thought, had seemed to go without the others noticing. And who was the old, bald man at the far end of the room? And what did the goddess mean that he wasn't *the balance or the one?* And was that a good or bad thing?

The goddess stopped and looked at him. "Come to me, child," she said. "I have come to love you like no other has before."

Her voice was like an aphrodisiac. He desperately wanted to go to her, but hesitated. The man who came with her didn't look as welcoming, but quite the opposite. In fact, Eric could now see there was something more than just odd with the man's eyes, as they never quite seemed to remain still.

"No," Eric replied.

The goddess turned to the man behind her. "Now that is a word I seldom hear, Lord Yikan."

"What do you expect from mortals, Shazadeh," Lord Yikan groaned.

Eric glanced at Lord Yikan and began shaking his head. He was about to repeat his refusal, when Shazadeh was suddenly upon him, though he hadn't even seen her move. Her hand encircled his throat and began squeezing.

"*Oh*...but you will say *yes* and beg for my love before this night is done," she promised. Eric felt his feet leave the ground right before she tossed him. He crashed against the pew behind Cheryl and the rest of the group. When his head hit it, the wood pew cracked like his head did. With his head bleeding and spinning, he couldn't tell up from down enough to stand up.

Shazadeh pulled one of the men off of his feet by the shoulder and asked..."Do you love your goddess?"

The man nodded furiously.

"Will you die for me?"

The man hesitated and then nodded sheepishly this time.

She brought him closer until their noses nearly touched. "A new world hovers upon the horizon, mortal. This world and the dark realm will soon be forever joined. I shall stand upon this orb as goddess and my father, Duke Astaroth, god and lord of the other."

She stroked his face and then grimaced. "Though not all are worthy of life. Your flesh is repulsive to my eyes. But your soul may serve my father. Will you give it freely?"

The man looked around at the others. But they quickly bowed their heads. As if realizing he was alone, but more importantly, in mortal danger, he grasped Shazadeh's black hand and attempted to pull it off his shoulder.

Shazadeh turned to Lord Yikan. "My Lord...this mortal fights me," she announced, clearly amused. "Have you ever seen such a thing?"

Lord Yikan hovered closer. "What do you expect from such things as they are?"

"Worship!" she replied. "And if not that, then I shall have their life-essence. Duke Astaroth can have their souls to feed to the other demons. I care not."

"Then take it and be done," Lord Yikan grumbled.

"Oh, I shall," she purred, as her deep black eyes suddenly turned white and glowed.

The man in Shazadeh's grasp began shaking and moaning as the skin of his face rippled like still water disturbed by a rock thrown in it. Hundreds of translucent tendrils suddenly burst from his skin and for a moment, hovered in the air before diving into every exposed section of skin on Shazadeh's black body. She gasped in ecstasy as the man's life-essence snaked into her, leaving him nothing but a corpse of dried skin and bones. Without a care, she tossed his carcass behind her.

Shazadeh's skin glimmered like glass. The soft, angled bones of her face were even keener now than before. The almond shape of her eyes sharpened! The texture of her black braided hair became finer and smoother than silk. Her lips were larger now and wet with desire.

She moved her hands along her face and over her breasts like a lover would, and then smiled. "Utter perfection," she gasped, even as some of the members crouched in front of her began screaming.

Cheryl grabbed Eric's hand and pushed herself off the ground. Eric jumped up also. But before Cheryl or Eric were even a step away, Shazadeh caught Cheryl by the back of the neck and brought her back around and began siphoning away her life-essence. Propelled by instinct, Eric turned and swung at Shazadeh but hit nothing but air, as did his second and third tries. When he swung again, she caught his fist and squeezed, snapping his bones and bringing him howling to his knees.

Shazadeh tossed Cheryl away, who flopped about and came to a stop under the front pew. She then turned to Eric. "I save you for thou hath spoken the sacred chant. Though you fear me now, mortal man, know that I see beneath your changed flesh. Without me, you will go back to being that cross-eyed creature you once were."

Shazadeh released him from her grip and turned her attention to the others cowering next to one another. "Alas, not all are meant to live upon the earth to worship me," she told them. "There are demons in hell that hunger for souls. I think they shall feast well tonight."

The horrified group of men and women scattered as best as they could despite tripping over one another. Those lucky few that escaped while Shazadeh was draining someone not quite so lucky, never made it to the back doors. Lord Yikan, who moved with the same mind-bending speed as Shazadeh, swung and cracked the skull of one of the women who tried ducking under him. Two other men who were behind her tried backtracking, but were tossed off their feet when Lord Yikan slammed his foot on the stone floor and ruptured it like a festering boil. He picked up the two men and held them in place by digging his hands straight into the muscle of their shoulders.

Once the rest of the members were drained of their essence, Shazadeh picked up Eric and tossed him over to where Lord Yikan was holding the men. "Do you want these?" Lord Yikan asked, and shook the men in his grasp like rag dolls.

"Partake, my lord," Shazadeh urged.

Lord Yikan glared at her and then slammed the heads of the two men together. Both of them slumped to the floor.

"You have wasted essence?" Shazadeh asked, looking at the men at his feet. "Why?"

"You demons and your quest for absolute perfection grows tiresome," Lord Yikan responded. "I want Tamen dead. That is all I care about."

"And the child of balance," Shazadeh reminded him.

"Of course," Lord Yikan said. "If one falls, so does the other."

"They will both die," Shazadeh assured him. "But remember, my lord, I am a demon...nearly the loveliest. And the essence of mortals makes me lovelier. Who knows, perhaps my beauty will one day rival that of Lucifer's."

Lord Yikan chuckled. "You speak boldly only because Lucifer is bound and sleeping."

"And Lucifer will stay that way if we find the child and kill him," she said. "No balance upon the earth means no rapture or end of days. And without those coming to pass, the Christ can never return to claim earth."

"If...when...maybe," Lord Yikan uttered. "If we do not find the child, then you best run to the end of existence, my dear. For if Lucifer does not slay you and the duke and reclaim his realm for whatever time he may have, then the Christ surely will." He looked down at Eric. "And this one?"

"Make him a watcher," Shazadeh replied. "He has worked so hard to run away from the awful looking man he was. The more he chants, the more handsome he will become...and more faithful to his goddess, yes?"

Eric shook his head up and down. He looked up at Lord Yikan, and saw that the man's eyes were just swirling blue liquid. Eric wobbly rose to his feet and bowed his head. After Shazadeh walked past him, he followed behind her as she and Lord Yikan walked out of the church.

Once out into the night of the desert, Lord Yikan stopped and raised his head back. "Do you hear that? Another chant is on wind."

"Yes," she replied.

Shazadeh and Lord Yikan began chanting. Lord Yikan grabbed Eric about the waist. Before he knew what was happening, his stomach dropped as they hurtled high into the New Mexico sky. When they landed in a dense grouping of trees minutes later, Lord Yikan carelessly dropped him on the ground.

Eric covered his face with his hands and tried to warm it, but it was useless, as his hands were just as icy from the flight in the frigid clouds. The air, wherever they were now, was as warm as the desert. Though the thick grouping of trees all around them assured him they were far from New Mexico now. On the ground, he bent to the side and looked around Shazadeh and Lord Yikan and spotted a glimmer of fire off in the distance. He heard a voice coming from there, uttering the same chant he wished he never had—*The Praise of the Blessed One.* When he saw Shazadeh heading off in that direction, he knew that whoever was gathered around that fire would likely never see another morning come again.

"Are you coming, my lord?" she asked.

"It is another false trail," he called to her as she disappeared amongst the trees. "I will wait for Tamen, if you do not mind."

"You will have that pretended god of Egypt soon enough," she said. "You can even tear him limb from limb once we find him. I shall return shortly, my lord," she called back.

"Goddess, come back!" Eric begged, before he even realized what he had said.

"Shut up, you mongrel!" Lord Yikan snapped. "Have some control."

"But—but...I need her."

"Oh, yes you do," Lord Yikan agreed. "You have laid eyes on a goddess. You probably never thought flesh could be so beautiful. And now that you have seen what you can be from what you were, you want more. You want beauty. You want perfection. *You want her.*"

"Yes," Eric whimpered.

Lord Yikan whispered. "You have not smoked, sniffed or injected anything, yet you are drugged. You crave what could be possible now that you've tasted it. You fear turning back into that...that... repulsive looking creature." Eric lowered his head and began crying. "Though it is surprising that someone so pale of skin as you had the skill to even speak the chant well enough to call her. Tamen has spread our magic far and wide. Very ingenious—but it will not save him."

"Tamen?"

"The one I shall kill myself," Lord Yikan stated. "Shazadeh can have the child of balance. But I will have Tamen's head spinning on the tip of my finger for what he has done to me."

"What about me?" Eric asked and begged.

"You have chanted the best since Nicholas, which is not all that impressive really, but maybe..."

Eric looked up. Tears streamed down his face.

"Tell me Eric Lightner...what will you do for complete and unparalleled beauty?" Lord Yikan asked. "No worshipping some would-be goddess. No mantras or chanting. Hmm?"

"Any...anything," Eric mumbled.

Lord Yikan tilted his head up. Just then, a scream rose up from the direction that Shazadeh had gone. And then another, and then a sea of screams began echoing through the woods. He grabbed Eric by the shoulder and pulled him to his feet.

"If you want to be a prince, then stop your damn crying. Look at me!" Lord Yikan demanded. "We must hurry while she is occupied. Show me allegiance and I will make you irresistible. Women will gnash their teeth because they cannot have you. But betray me, and I will incinerate you—teeth and bones included. No one will know Eric Lightner ever existed. Do you understand me, mortal man?"

"Ye—yes."

"Then know this, boy," Lord Yikan said. "Shazadeh seeks the death of the child of balance. I seek Tamen's. But to reclaim my godhood as Aton, the one god of Egypt, and give you your heart's desire, Shazadeh must fall alongside them. But Shazadeh is the spawn of the elder-prince of hell itself—Duke Astaroth. And with that demon on her side, our chance to strike her down is limited to say the least. But if we are clever...I think we shall succeed."

CHAPTER 8

"Why are you limping?" Dorthea asked.

Jared wasn't entirely sure how to answer that, as he still hadn't made sense out of what had occurred in the library at school. Luckily, Thaddeus Robinette—manager at the Rec center—who had given him a ride home, followed him into the house and piped up with a lie.

"I worked him hard today, Dorthea," Thaddeus explained.

"Wha? What's going on?" she demanded, looking from one to the other.

Thaddeus attempted to squeeze past Jared, but instead, nearly squashed him against the doorframe with his two hundred plus pounds, most of which resided in his rear. Even the smallest child at the center knew that if Thaddeus Robinette was coming toward you, it was either back up and get out of the way, or risk being knocked through a wall by a wayward hip.

"We had so much movin' around of thangs to do today," Thaddeus said, as he wiped his brown bald head.

"I'm gonna go study. OK mom?" Jared asked, hoping that would be the end of the inquisition. He wanted nothing more than to collapse on his bed and sleep.

Dorthea eyed him and raised her brow.

"You best be hittin' those books hard, boy!" Thaddeus warned.

"Yes sir."

"You're not even hungry, Jared?" Dorthea asked.

"No ma'am. I'm just gonna do my homework and hit the sack. Finals are next week...remember?"

Thaddeus raised his broad nose and sniffed. His eyes suddenly grew wide. "I smell some fried squash up in here? And don't tell me you got some fried chicken, too?"

Dorthea smiled. "Thaddeus—you hungry?"

He cleared his throat and patted his protruding belly. "Ohhh, just a tidbit."

"Lord have mercy then. Sit your tail on down." Dorthea motioned toward the table. "Seeing that Jared's not going to eat, you can have his I guess."

"Well, I ain't gonna eat much. I'm trying to watch this here waist of mine."

Dorthea put her hands on her hips and laughed. "I see that!"

"What you tryin' to say?" He lifted his head and tapped his second chin. "It shrinking, see?"

While his mother was being distracted by Thaddeus' flirting, Jared slipped by them and into the hallway. But on his way to his room, the scent of sweat and medicine-fouled breath touched his nose. He followed the trail to the entrance of the living room and peeked in. Light from the television danced on the wall in the dark room. The murmuring from the game show playing on it was more like white noise than actual talking. His Aunt Maymee was lying on the sofa under a quilt nodding—eyes fluttering—as she fell in and out of sleep.

The smell of sickness gagged him, but was not enough to prevent him from going over and kissing her cheek. He wanted to curl up beside her like he used to when he was a child. Back then, his mother was always at work during the day, and at night, taking classes at the community college. It was always Aunt Maymee who was the first and last face he saw each day. Even when his mother graduated and began working for an insurance company, the distance between them remained unchanged. In the morning and evening, he still wanted Aunt Maymee to be the first and last... sometimes the only face he saw.

Aunt Maymee's eyes fluttered open at the touch of his lips to her cheek. "Where you been, boy?" she whispered.

"It's not that late, Auntie," he said. "I just got in from work."

"No?" She winced as craned her head up and peered at the television. Jared seized the opportunity to fluff the pillows behind her head. "I done fell asleep and missed Judge...Judge what-her-name."

"You need anything, Auntie?"

Her dry, cracked lips spread into a smile. "Just some sugar, baby," she cooed. Jared complied immediately. She closed her eyes and dozed off for a moment, and then slightly opened her left one. "Is that Mr. Robinette I hear talking?"

"Yes ma'am."

"I didn't know he was comin'. I best say...say...." She paused. "You said it's not late, right?"

"No ma'am." Jared sat on the floor and laid his head next to her stomach.

She began rubbing his head, and he responded by closing his eyes and sighing. "Your hair dry as a bone, Jared-child. What color you got up in it this time? I can't see without my spectacles."

"It was supposed to be red like fire, but I messed it up," he replied, with eyes still shut. He had just begun to drift off when his mother called out for him. "Yeah?"

"Get out of there and let your auntie be!"

He stood up and faced Dorthea who had just marched into the room. "I was just talking to her...*jeez!*"

"Alright now, Jared," Maymee uttered. "Don't let me hear you adding a *sus* to that *jeez.*"

"Yes, ma'am."

"C'mon outta there and let her get some rest," Dorthea said.

"We were just talking. I guess that's against the law now, too!" He brushed past her and walked to his room.

Dorthea followed. "What you say?"

"Nothin'!"

She stopped at the doorway to his room. "It sounded like you were trying to say something smart and sassy."

He plopped down on his neatly made bed next to a stack of jeans, shirts and socks that he had neither stacked, folded nor rolled. He figured she had been checking his drawers, under the bed and between the mattresses again on her never-ending hunt for evidence of wrongdoing.

"We got enough goin' on without you adding to it, Jared."

"Aunt Maymee and I were just talking, and you come in acting like I just kicked her."

"What were ya'll talking about?"

"Stuff."

"What stuff?"

"Private stuff."

She crossed her arms. "Oh excuse me. I didn't know you were old enough to have *secrets.*"

"I don't with you around! You're in my room...my business...my work! But *I'm* not the one with secrets," he muttered just loud enough for her to hear.

She walked in and leaned her back on the dresser by the wall. "Jared...I told you all of this before, but it's just not enough for you, is it? Being mad at me isn't going to change how your father is."

"It doesn't make it fair."

"You don't think I know that?"

"I don't know what you think, because you never say," he replied. "Why can't I decide if I like my own father? All you ever say is that he doesn't want to be bothered with me. Or is it he doesn't want to be bothered with you?"

"Alright. Fine!" she shot back, her voice wavering. "When we get down south in a few weeks, go see him. See for yourself what he's like. But don't say I didn't tell you. So you can just run over to the church he's preachin' at and hear what kind of man he is from his own mouth."

Jared's mouth popped open just before his eyes bulged nearly out of his head. *"Preaching?"*

She cocked her head to the side. "You wanted to know so bad, so now you do. They say he's a righteous preacher...maybe now he is...but not when I knew him. Folks say he walks with the Holy Ghost and people from all over come to see him. Maybe once you talk to him, you'll find someone you can hate more than me." She walked out and slammed the door behind her.

Before Jared could even begin to sort out, let alone comprehend that his father was a preacher in addition to being a deadbeat dad... according to his mother...a knock came to his door. Thaddeus peeked his head in and then squeezed the rest of his body through the doorway. "You OK, son?"

Jared looked down at his boots and rubbed the soles of them together.

Thaddeus smiled at him. "Your momma didn't mean for that to come out like that."

"So she said," Jared muttered.

"Why don't you just tell me what's on your mind, son...huh? You come to the center limping and won't say why. Then you got me lyin' to your momma about it. You know what you say is always just between me and you, right?"

"Yes, sir."

"I told the Lord I keep an eye on this family best I could when your uncle passed away, and I meant it." He shook his head. "He was a good Christian man. So what's up? Just between me and you. Man-to-man."

"She—she—"

"Go on, son."

"She keeps riding me about every little thing I do. She always has," he insisted. "And after I've asked her about my father...since forever...she just drops it that he's a preacher, like that?"

"She's in there cryin' about that right now. She didn't mean to hurt you, son."

"Sure," Jared sighed.

"Now you know it's true," he argued. "Even when you got in that mess at school, she was more worried about you being alright than mad about you fighting."

"It wasn't even my fault."

"Didn't you throw the punches?"

A moment passed before Jared eventually nodded. "You remember my friend, Chris?"

Thaddeus nodded. "Chubby little white boy...uh-huh."

"That kid I punched, Eric, and his friends tricked Chris into sharing a gym locker with them. Then they pissed...I mean peed all over his clothes while he was out in gym class."

"What?"

"So I told Eric to back off of Chris." Jared shrugged. "He swung on me. So I swung back...a few times," he added.

"And he deserved it!" Thaddeus exclaimed, and then quickly looked up to the ceiling. "Lord, forgive me for that one."

"They're always messin' with him, Mr. Robinette."

"Does your momma and the folks at school know this?"

"No! So please don't say anything," Jared pleaded. "Mom will make me stop hanging around Chris if she knew."

Thaddeus waved his hand. "You know I won't. But she might feel different about it if she knew what really happened. I know I do."

Jared sighed. "It's over with now. School is almost out anyway."

"Don't be keepin' stuff like that from me now...alright?"

"Yes, sir."

"You like my own flesh and blood. You know I used to change your pampers."

"Why does everyone who has ever changed my diaper have to remind me that they did?" he asked, slightly embarrassed.

"'Cause it's true." Thaddeus grinned. "Every mother and father of the church did, but me more so because I was around here with your momma off and on. Don't mean a thang other than you got a whole lot of folk who love you." Thaddeus walked over and gave Jared a hug, though to Jared, it seemed as if he was being suffocated in rolls of fat more than anything. "Now you get to studying now," Thaddeus directed. "And give your momma a little break, too. Alright Golden Gloves?"

Jared couldn't resist smiling. "Yes, sir."

* * *

The following day, Jared convinced his mother to drop him off at school early instead of him having to take the bus. Foremost in his mind was to find Taylor Pierceman and get some answers about what happened the day before. With a quick wave goodbye to his mother, which she replied to with a rare smile, he ran inside the school and headed for Taylor's classroom.

"Mr. Pierceman!" he called out as he ran into the room.

The man writing on the blackboard with his back to Jared turned around. "Can I help you?"

"Who...who are you?" Jared demanded.

The young man grimaced. "I'm the sub. And you are?"

"Where's Mr. Pierceman?"

"I don't know. They just called me...wait a minute," the man said, changing his tone from defense to offense. "Do you even have this class first period?"

"I have it sixth hour. I just have uh...a paper to turn in," he lied.

"You can give it to me," the man said. "I'll be taking over Mr. Pierceman's class for the rest of the year."

Jared backed out of the classroom and made for the stairs, ignoring calls from the substitute to wait. Once on the main floor, he had to push past the throngs of students now streaming into the school en masse. He wound his way past them to the main office where Mrs. Cedars, the secretary, was sitting at her desk talking on the phone. She winked at him and held up a finger as she continued listening to the voice on the other end. When she finished, she looked up at him. "Alright now, honey. What can I do for you?"

"There's a sub in Mr. Pierceman's room," Jared charged.

"Oh yeah, sweetie. Mr. Pierceman had a family emergency," Mrs. Cedars replied. "Weren't you looking for him yesterday, too?"

"He left—just like that?"

"He called in this morning," she answered. "Everyone likes him so much. We're all just hoping everything is alright."

"What happened?"

She shook her head. "We aren't allowed to say—I'm sorry. We have to respect his privacy, you know."

"This isn't fair," Jared mumbled.

She bobbed her head. "Life sure isn't, is it?"

* * *

By the time lunch period rolled around, Jared had already cycled through anger, disappointment and even more confusion than he had started off the day with. Between Taylor sending him on a mind-trip yesterday and then disappearing for the remainder of the year, and his mother dropping the *'your deadbeat dad's a preacher'* bomb on him, he was ready to give the entire world the finger.

After accepting his portions of overcooked burritos and greasy tater tots, he spotted Chris at one of the tables at the far end of the cafeteria. "What's up?" Chris asked through a mouthful of pizza as Jared approached and then sat beside him.

"Hey, dude. There's plenty of room over there." Chris pointed across the table. On the other half of the table—down from where Chris and Jared sat—were the students the others called geeks and Principal Allen referred to as the brightest.

Jared looked at them and saw they were staring at him and Chris. "One of you got a problem?" Each one quickly looked away. "Forget them," Jared said to Chris.

Chris wiped the orange grease oozing from the corner of his mouth with the back of his hand. "They're gonna think we're homos with you practically sitting in my lap."

"Why can't you ever say screw what people think?" Jared asked. He looked down at Chris' tray, which was covered with a slice of pizza, two burritos and tater tots treading for their lives in a sea of ketchup. "Is there a famine coming I don't know about?"

"Just filling up," he replied. "I'll be starving at fat camp this time next week, so I figure I better enjoy myself while I can."

"If you think that's gonna help." He saw Chris had already dribbled a glob of orange grease onto his gray polo shirt. "We still on for me sleeping over tonight?"

"Only if you get your butt on the other side...*freak!*"

Jared playfully slapped him on the back and went to the other side and sat.

"My parents are going out for the night anyway," Chris said. "They got another class on how to cure yourself *all natural* and all that crap." Jared nodded, but only half-listened as Chris went on. "Now she's forcing me to drink some aloe or seaweed juice that's supposed to make me lose weight."

Not in the mood to eat, combined with watching Chris stuff himself on food that was more grease than anything, Jared felt his stomach start to rumble. He pushed his tray over to Chris, who happily accepted it. "Did you hear Mr. Pierceman isn't here anymore?" Jared asked.

"Yeah," Chris replied. "Some jack-off was in there third period and didn't know what the hell he was talking about. Every time we asked him about a question that might be on the final, he was like...'*duh! I don't know,*" Chris said in a lazy drawl. "We finally convinced him to put on a movie like he should have in the first place."

*　*　*

Jared sat in the rear of the school bus, which was parked and waiting for the last of the students to board. With only a few days of final exams separating them from three months of freedom, and it being Friday, too, the students were practically shaking the bus with their laughing, dancing and jumping from seat-to-seat. Jared didn't share their enthusiasm.

Jared looked up at the middle windows of the third floor where the library was. The inside was still dark like it had been when he stopped by at the last bell. By some miracle, he had hoped to find some clue as to what had happened to Taylor, but instead found a note taped to the locked doors saying that tutoring was cancelled and good luck on finals.

Screw you Taylor, he thought. He began turning to the side so that he could stretch his spindly legs out on the green bench-seat, when a glimmer caught his eye from the side. He turned back around and looked up. The library lights were on. But even stranger was that a figure was standing at one of the windows and seemed to be looking right down at him. He fumbled for his backpack and sprinted for the front of the bus. He pushed on the accordion doors, but they failed to give.

"Hey, dude...whoa!" Jared's eyes widened as he realized that the bus driver wasn't a *he* but was actually a *she*. "Ma'am, I mean—I gotta get off," he told her.

"We're about to leave...dude," she sneered. "If you forgot something, you better just wait 'til Monday or else you're gonna have to walk home."

"I don't care. Just let me off—alright?" She huffed, and then pulled the lever and swung the door open. Jared had barely set both feet on the ground before she slammed the door shut and gunned the engine, setting the bus in motion.

Jared's lungs were burning by the time he reached the library. The sign that tutoring was cancelled for the day was still taped on the doors, but the doors which were locked before, opened freely as he pulled on them. Not seeing anyone as he ran in, he called out. "Taylor!" He dropped his backpack and sprinted for the window where he had seen the figure while on the bus. "Mr. Pierceman? Taylor...you here?"

"I'm over here, Jared," a voice called from the front of the library.

Recognizing Taylor's voice, he ran back and found Taylor sitting at the same table they were at yesterday as though he had never left it. In front of Taylor, on the table, was the same black book that sometimes had and at other times didn't have words. At first, Jared wanted to yell at him, but then...suddenly...he didn't want to. The anger and frustration he had been building all day toward Taylor suddenly began to wane as his nose detected something sweet in the air...something he hadn't noticed until just now.

Strangely, Jared felt calmer than he had all day. He walked over and sat down opposite from Taylor who was dressed in ever-creased slacks and a crisp starched shirt. Jared looked at him. "You gonna tell me what's going on?"

Taylor folded his hands and placed them on the table. "You're thoroughly confused, yes? I would be too."

"Confused? Uh-uh." Jared shook his head. "What did you do to me yesterday? And what's that?" he asked, pointing at the book.

Taylor glanced at the book. "It's my *and your* final lesson, but written specifically for you."

"You gotta do better than that," Jared demanded. "This is like—like—I don't know. It's like taking acid or something."

"You drop acid, first of all. And two...you've never taken acid."

Jared leaned over the table and smirked. "How do you know?"

"The same way I know that last year you bought cigarettes at Wilson's gas station after leaving the Rec center. You took two puffs and couldn't stop coughing. You threw them away and wondered why people would smoke something that tastes like crap."

Jared's mouth gaped open. He remembered that day and eerily recalled having thought those exact words, *tastes like crap.* "This is crazy," Jared whispered. "How did you know that? I—I was down at the railroad tracks behind a caboose when I did that. And I was alone."

"You didn't even tell your best friend, Chris."

"No."

"Strange how I knew all of that, hmm?"

Jared stared off into space. "I think I'm gonna puke."

Taylor closed his eyes for a moment. "All those questions you want answers to are right here in this book."

"This book?" Jared asked suspiciously. "You're doing a lot of talking, but you haven't answered one thing yet, Taylor. How about, where have you been? And why was I hallucinating yesterday?"

"If I were to just tell you, you would probably do one of two things," Taylor replied. "You would believe what I say or go running out of here like a madman. This book is the second most important book you will ever read in your life."

"Every question that I want answered is in this book?" Jared asked, not quite convinced.

"That and more," Taylor assured. "Men have killed to learn what's inside this book. The truths contained in it will change the world as you and I know it to be...maybe for the better, but knowing mankind, likely for the worst." Taylor shrugged.

Jared stared into Taylor's brown eyes, looking for some sign of deceit that was opposite of his stony face and stiff posture. To the right of Taylor's head, he suddenly spotted movement by the library doors. It was Stacy Willows, one of the students he tutored and had more than a thing for, but still hadn't built up the nerve to ask her out. He waved to her, but she didn't return it.

Spacey-Stacy, he thought and waved again, but this time with more vigor. Even though they were only fifteen feet from the doors, and she seemed to be looking directly at them, she still didn't respond.

"Put down your arm, Jared. Stacy can't see you."

Jared ignored him. "Hey, Stacy! No tutoring today. We're just... we're ju—" Jared stopped and lowered his hand, as he realized Taylor had never turned around to see who was at the door. "How did you know it was Stacy?"

Taylor tapped the book in reply.

Jared looked down at the book. "Everything is all in here?"

Taylor crossed his legs and nodded.

Jared opened the book. To his relief, there were words written upon the pages this time. He started reading from the beginning again, but this time he wasn't as afraid when his vision began to dim and the library became shadowed in darkness.

Before fully leaving reality, he heard Taylor say to him. "Farewell Jared. You now go to a land lost to time. When you return, you'll never look at your own world the same way again."

Jared began spiraling up into darkness.

CHAPTER 9

"Welcome to the holy temple of Horus, Jared," a voice said to him. Jared looked up and around, and saw that he was back in the stone hall. In front of him—but facing him this time—was the same bald black guy wearing a white shenti. And like before, behind the black man was the statue of the hawk-headed figure with blue and gold plumes.

Oil lamps hung from one end of the ceiling to the other. Lazy smoke from incense snaked out of brass braziers positioned on each side of the statue of the god, sweetly and heavily perfuming the still air. Jared looked at himself and saw he was clothed as be-fore—*or* rather barely clothed. This time, against the sweltering heat in the room, he welcomed the immodest loincloth wrapped around his waist and draped over his privates.

"I don't think I'm dreaming—*am I?*" Jared finally responded. "I must be hallucinating because—because this can't be real. You can't be real."

"True...oh so very true," the black man replied. He looked around and held up his hands. "Nothing here is real, Jared. You are not here and neither am I actually. All I have done is made the words of the book you were reading real in your mind. Is that not what happens when you read anyway? Is that not why one reads in the first place...to be delivered from where you are to another place and time?"

"Yeah, but..."

"That is all that has happened."

Nothing about the black man's smooth mahogany skin or deep brown eyes hinted to Jared that he wasn't real. Jared held up a hand and rubbed the index and thumb together. He then touched his arms, his bare chest and face, and they too felt the same as they had when he'd showered earlier—*only, his crispy, overly-dyed orange hair was now gone.*

"For most of your youth, you have excelled in learning, like me. Languages—your ability to decipher sounds and words that compose them—has been nothing less than exceptional," the man said. "But now, young Jared, it is time for *my* words to absorb *you*. It is time for you to see my tale...the tale of Tamen. It is much easier to show you rather than tell you, for there are things in this world there are not yet words for—but must be seen."

"Your name is Tamen?"

"Yes," Tamen replied. "I was named after the creator god, Amon-Ra, like many other children my age. It was a very common name in its day, like John or Matthew or Peter."

"But you said you were the god Horus last time."

Tamen nodded and walked toward him.

"Which means you're Egyptian and I'm in...Egypt?"

Tamen stopped in front of him and looked down at him. "Everything you see, smell, taste and touch here is but a trick of the mind. You are still in the school library in Homer, Illinois. Whether here in this illusion, or in your world, nothing your senses encounter is made real until—"

"Until my mind makes it real," Jared finished.

"Precisely. I am simply feeding your brain stimuli...telling it that this is real. And in my illusion of Egypt, you shall witness true magic."

Jared's eyes widened. "Gods are real?"

"The gods are dead," Tamen droned. He walked past Jared, looked back and then beckoned him to follow. He led Jared up a short flight of stairs and out of the temple hall. They walked down a narrow corridor lit with oil lamps and then up once more and out of the building itself. "Remember, everything here is an illusion, Jared."

Jared wiped the sweat from his head and squinted until his eyes adjusted to the bright light of the sun beating down on him. Only a span of twenty feet separated the building they had walked out of and the series of homes across from them. Some were free standing —two and three stories tall—while the other pale, cinnamon-colored homes were connected.

A petite elderly woman carrying a reed woven basket on her back was walking toward them. She looked up at Tamen and immediately stuttered in her steps, kicking up a puff of dust as she did. "Priest Tamen—the blessed one," she professed, and then bowed before him.

"Blessings of Amon-Ra be upon you, mother-sister," Tamen replied, and laid a hand upon her scarf-covered head. The woman quickly touched the palm of her hand to the deep-creased wrinkles of her forehead and then scuttled along.

Tamen and Jared resumed walking down the dusty cobblestone street. They didn't make it far before a brown-skinned young man in a loincloth, equally as short as the old woman approached and kneeled before Tamen. "Great priest...may I have your blessing?" the man asked. Tamen touched the young man's bald head. But before going about his way, the man took hold of Tamen's hand and placed it on his cheek. "You are favored by Amon-Ra above all others."

As Tamen and Jared walked on, even more people, young and old...men and women stopped and kneeled for Tamen's blessings, and with some even coming out of their homes to receive it. And once having had Tamen's hand lain upon their head, they went about their day. Women swept sand off of their doorsteps while keeping a watchful eye on their children running about. Loincloth clad men and boys pulled pallets of mud-brick, or were in the midst of arranging them into walls and structures, while even more were busily painting the facade of their homes.

Jared looked up at Tamen. "I feel short standing next to you. But compared to everybody else, I feel like a giant."

Tamen chuckled. "It is called evolution, my boy. There was no reason for people to be tall in this year of 1425 before the Christ... or simply, B.C. In this age, Pharaoh Amenhotep has been on the throne for three years and presides over a great empire."

The bazaar they were approaching was crowded with scores of tents and hundreds of people milling through them. Voices waxed and waned, filling the air with a constant buzz as people shopped, bargained and counter-bargained for goods. Many of the women—alabaster white to midnight black skin and every shade between—with children on their hips and jugs in their arms, wore sheer linen dresses that hugged their every curve. Their black or henna-hued hair was styled into dangling braids or cornrows. The ones with wigs wore their hair straight and bluntly cut at the shoulders. Men and young boys—all hairless—wore nothing but shentis or loin-cloths.

Tamen tugged at Jared, and drew his attention away from the bustling bazaar in front of them. He pointed high in the air. "Look up, Jared!"

Jared did so and gasped as he stumbled back a step.

Two, five-story tall orange obelisks stood on either side of an equally large statue of a hawk-headed man. Its head—covered with a headdress of gleaming red and blue feathers—was turned to the right. In its right hand it held a golden ankh by its chest. And from the back of its shenti, a lion's tail snaked out and hung just above the ground.

Tamen guided Jared through the monolith's agape legs toward a city-block sized building with red, blue and gold pennants streaming down from its flat roof. Five spear carrying beefy guards, who seemed eager to use them, manned its two roof high wood doors. And beyond the doors—amidst wide-leafed plants—palm, lotus and sycamore trees crowded together and gave shade to those crouched under them as they worked.

"This never existed, did it?" Jared asked dubiously.

"But it did," Tamen replied. He pointed to the reliefs of a man holding a spear on each side of the temple's painted limestone walls. "There is just no record of the many wonders that were once here."

"No record of any of this?"

"Do you really believe *everything* you read?" Tamen stared at him for a moment. "What Egyptologist's of your time have discovered in the ruins of my time pales to what once was. How vain they are to think they know my people because they have unearthed a few temples or stumbled onto a pittance of a treasure from a boy-king," Tamen sneered.

"There is a reason why no one has ever heard of the great statue of Amon-Ra at Karnak, or other monuments even greater than this one. In less than twenty years from now, that statue of Amon-Ra will be nothing but rubble. And as you will discover, Amon-Ra was the first god to die," Tamen said as his voice trailed off to a whisper. "But now, let us pay homage to the king of the gods while he still lives?"

They walked into the garden courtyard, which in addition to its hearty trees and plants, it contained a maze of blue and red painted columns and hieroglyphs carved up and down on them. Some of the men and teenage boys about carried scrolls and clay jars. Other workers were applying fresh coats of paint to walls and columns that had lost their luster. Farther on, past the courtyard, was a passageway separated by two rows of pylons with statues of pharaohs seated in front of each.

"Before my father died, he was a Lector priest—as am I—of the god, Amon-Ra, here in Karnak. Every city and village, and for that matter, every household had at least one altar to a god or goddess. But it was the main temple of the city one lived in that was most important. Here in Karnak, the god Amon-Ra's temple was the most sacred above all. We fed and offered sacrifices to the gods, who in turn gave us magic to vanquish evil spirits, especially *'Those Who Walked at night with Their Heads Backward'*—the demons from the nether realm," he uttered.

"When the local physician could not heal your malady, you sought a priest. When your luck was tainted, you begged the priests to appeal to the gods to bless you. When you died, we were the ones who prepared the body and the *ka*, or what you call a spirit, for the afterlife. There were some illnesses the priests could not vanquish. Of those who were incurable, we would say it was simply the will of the gods. And who would dare question those who spoke to the gods themselves?"

"But you said there were no more gods," Jared countered.

"I said the gods were *dead*. There is a substantial distinction between the two," Tamen corrected, and then pointed toward the temple opening between the pylons. "Here is where I started my training as a boy. And like you, Jared, I was soon discovered to have quite a gift at learning. But unlike you, there was never a moment that I did not use my ability to absorb as much knowledge as I could."

Jared stopped and cocked his head at Tamen. "Is that supposed to be a dig at me?"

"Take it as you will," Tamen replied, in a voice as dry as the sand they stood on. "My point being...I quickly rose through the ranks of the priesthood by mastering spells through the power of the chant that not even the master of the temple, Lord Dojan, could perform. Some priests, like Lord Dojan, could conjure fire, water and make objects appear out of nowhere. And I do not mean parlor tricks using slight of hand. I mean *true* magic!" Tamen stressed. "But I saw and heard the chant spells far differently than other priests. I *felt them.* With my voice, I could mold the chants spells to do my bidding in ways that only one other priest had ever accomplished. In my time, I was deemed blessed because of my proficiency at learning. In your time, Jared, they call it being intellectually gifted. I was promoted to teacher at the age of sixteen—the age of a man in those days—and soon after the passing of Lord Dojan, I became the youngest master and lord of the temple."

They walked past another set of stone pylons into a smaller expanse that contained a rectangular reflecting pond surrounded by large-leafed plants. They walked inside the main building and up a flight of stairs and into a room. Sunlight streamed in from the windows positioned high near the ceiling and highlighted every bit of dust hanging in the air. "My world was here, Jared. This is the classroom where I taught the next generation of priests who would protect and carry on Egypt's most sacred tradition—the transition to the afterlife."

The bare stone room began shifting, as though it was a lens trying to find the correct focus—blurry to clear and back again. From nowhere, shapes appeared on the floor before Tamen and Jared, and began shimmering. At first the figures were translucent, but the more the shapes flittered, the more solid they became. Eventually the shapes settled into two distinct rows of loincloth-clad boys, who were sitting on mats made of woven reed.

Tamen looked at Jared and bowed his head. Tamen then walked backwards until he was in the front of the class and then switched his attention to the brown-skinned faces looking up at him. "Blessings of Amon-Ra upon you all," Tamen told the young boys. The boys lowered their bald heads, though each did have a braided lock of hair protruding from each of their napes.

"Who amongst you has practiced the fire chant?" Tamen asked them. All of them raised their hand. Tamen looked at each of them before settling his gaze on a young boy in the front row to his right. "Timmet," he called. "Show me what you have learned."

Timmet stood, but lowered his head. "Lord Tamen...I have practiced the fire-chant—as you have shown us—but fire I cannot make. None of us can, my lord."

"Is this true?" Tamen looked at all of the boys. "Is there not one here who can bring life to fire?" The boys lowered their heads. Some looked away to avoid Tamen's reproachful eyes. Tamen shook his head. "If you have failed, then I have. Let us start again, shall we?"

Tamen closed his eyes and held his hands out palms up. He started chanting slowly before rapidly flicking his tongue and giving the chant a seesaw, up and down rhythm. As the cadence of Tamen's voice increased, the empty space right above his hands began to shimmer, and then without warning, sparked into life. Tamen opened his eyes and looked down at the small flame dancing above his hands.

The boys gasped as one at the birth of the flame, but became silent when Tamen suddenly changed his cadence and the flame rolled into a ball and began growing. Tamen moved his hands up and down alternatively, which in turn made the ball of fire roll side-to-side. "Your chant must be pure," he told the boys. "But you must also feel it! And once you have, you will become master of what you have created," Tamen said as he tossed the flaming ball up in the air and blew at, snuffing it out of existence.

The boy's look of awe quickly changed to toothy smiles in response to Tamen's whimsical display. They turned and excitedly murmured and elbowed each other. Tamen quieted them with a raise of his hand. "Now in pairs," Tamen said, "you will practice the chant, with one instructing and watching the other. I will expect you all to be most proficient before evening comes upon us."

Tamen's body became rock still. The room and the boys in it began to grow hazy, as though a mist had snuck into the room. Soon, the walls began to lose their solidity.

"Wait!" Jared cried. "Wait! Where's everything going?"

"The hour grows late, and the tale must end here for now," Tamen told him.

"But? You can't stop it now! Bring it back, Tamen!"

"Your duties call, remember, young one? Your job at the center where children play and frolic? Come to me tomorrow. I will show you where and then we shall finish what we have started. There is much I must show you, but there is so little time."

"Now wake up, Jared. *Wake up!*"

CHAPTER 10

Chris quickly shook his head at Jared.

"Sure, that sounds good, Angie," Jared replied, feeling as though he couldn't refuse.

Chris' eyes swelled to three times their normal size behind his inch thick glasses.

"You'll never even know the difference," Angie, Chris' mom, told him. She and her husband Mark insisted everyone call them by their first names.

Jared was opposite of Chris at the breakfast table, while Angie was in the kitchen. She had convinced Jared to have breakfast before leaving after spending the night. Chris, who had his back to her, was always vehemently opposed to the idea of eating anything Angie cooked.

"Once I add some tomatoes and cheese to the tofu, you'll wonder why most people don't eat it," Angie remarked. "It's so good for the heart."

"Thanks, bud," Chris whispered snidely.

"I didn't want to say no," Jared replied. "She did save my butt. My mom would've freaked out if she knew I didn't ask to stay over first. What was I supposed to say?"

"How about...*uhhhhh, no?* Now *I* gotta eat it. I could have snuck out and got a burger or something and..."

"Almost ready, boys! You two want toast?"

"Is it real bread?" Chris grumbled.

"Yes, sweetheart. Jared?"

"Sure...please, thank you."

Chris leaned across the table. "Are you still going over there?"

"*Shhh!*" Jared glanced at Angie as she handed them their plates of steaming scrambled tofu. She returned to the kitchen and stood watch over the toaster oven. "Not so loud. And yeah, I am. But remember what I said."

"I'm not an idiot!" Chris snipped. "I was just askin' in case you changed your mind. We could go to the mall or something."

"How about tomorrow?" Jared had no intention of *not* going to 8743 Baxter road, the address he couldn't forget even if he wanted to. Just thinking of Tamen or Egypt or gods brought up the address flashing in his mind's eye like a neon sign.

"Don't you have to go and praise Jesus for dyin' for your sorry butt tomorrow?" Chris asked.

Jared groaned at the reminder. "We can go after I get back from church...cool?"

"Sure!" Chris squawked. "I'll just sit around with my thumb up my butt until you can find time for a friend."

"And the award for best actor in a crappy life goes to...?"

Chris held up his middle finger. "Here...I got an award for ya, too!"

"Don't be vulgar, Christopher," Angie admonished as she returned with their toast.

Chris produced a matching finger with his other hand. "I'm just being myself like you always tell me to be, Angie."

"Not like that, sweetheart." She sauntered away, with her thin paisley skirt billowing behind.

Jared's plan to eat quickly and go was spoiled with his first bite of scrambled tofu, whose consistency reminded him of curdled milk. Chris, who had just taken a bite of toast, spat it out on the plate. He pushed his glasses up, and then used a finger to scoop the rest out of his mouth. "C'mon, Angie! What the heck is this crap?"

Angie looked over her shoulder. "What's wrong, sweetheart?"

Chris curled his lips. "This isn't bread, is what's wrong."

Mark, Chris' father, was just crossing the living room as Chris and Angie began feuding. "What's the fuss?" he asked.

"This isn't real bread," Chris told him.

"It's flaxseed bread," Angie insisted.

"It's the best for your heart," Mark said as he sat down at the table between Chris and Jared. Mark's hair, which was usually in a ponytail, was unbound and strewn over the sides of his head. He leaned over and took a bite out of Chris' toast. "See? Mmm...good." Mark smiled, and then took another bite.

"I'm not five, Mark," Chris droned. "I can tell when I'm being poisoned. If you guys want me dead, just hand me a knife so I can do it quick."

"Jared, what do you think?" Angie asked, ignoring Chris' dramatics.

"Not...eh-hem...not bad," Jared replied as he tried to figure out how he could push the next wad of tofu down his throat without it coming right back up.

"See?" Mark exclaimed. He elbowed Chris who glared back at him. His slender, bearded face became narrower as he took a sip of Chris' soymilk.

"He's only sayin' that to be polite, Angie. It tastes like crap," Chris remarked.

"Your camp is only going to provide nutritious, organic foods," Angie reminded him. "You'll never make it there with that attitude."

"That's what I've been trying to tell you two!" Chris screeched. "I'm gonna die at fat camp."

"Healthy eating..." Mark corrected him at first, then quickly smiled and added, "...*fat camp*."

"*Honey?*" Angie glowered at him.

"Healthy eating camp," Mark revised and winked at the boys.

"You know what?" Chris took on a sullen and dire tone. "Once I escape the fat farm and find the closest mini-mart gas station, I'm gonna pig out, ya know? I'm gonna eat anything filled with cream and wash it down with some fake flavored grape pop. Just want ya to know."

Try as he might, Jared couldn't abide one more bite of tofu or sip of watery soymilk. He was positive he absolutely hated soy of any kind. After claiming he was thoroughly stuffed and graciously declining Mark's offer to drive him home, he left. Though going home was not what he had in mind.

After a half-hour bus ride to the other side of town and walking four more blocks, he finally made it to Baxter road. A sense of déjà vu bubbled over him. The spring flowers half in bloom...lawns that had just been trimmed and those needing to be...restored Victorian homes with wrap-around porches looked exactly as they did in the memory Tamen had given him. 8743—the largest of the newly painted Victorian homes—was no exception. Jared lifted the knocker and banged once, but didn't have a chance to knock twice, as the door was already opening.

"You're here earlier than I thought you would be," Taylor said, as he opened the door wider and motioned for Jared to come in. He led Jared down the hall and into a large room with narrow windows facing the street. "I just woke up a short time ago...long night."

Taylor was in a white t-shirt, jeans and barefoot. His usually coiffed hair was wet and swept back. Jared smiled. "It's weird seeing teachers outside of...*wow!*" Jared stopped mid-sentence as he looked up at the eight-tiered crystal chandelier hanging from the white-coffered ceiling. To his right, there were two high back, red velvet chairs facing a cream colored marble fireplace. "If this is how all teachers live, screw being a doctor."

"There's nothing I can't have," Taylor replied. He motioned to the red chairs.

Jared's heart fluttered as he saw the book that had started it all laying in the chair. He picked it up and sat. "You can have anything you want, huh?" he asked suspiciously.

"Practically." Taylor sat also.

"Who are you...really?"

"Taylor Pierceman," he replied simply.

Jared paused. "Have you *always* been Taylor Pierceman?"

Taylor crossed his legs and leaned into Jared. "I've been a few people over time. Nothing is as it appears. You should be quite used to that by now, hmm?"

"I'm getting there."

"No!" Taylor snapped. "You need to be there right now. If you think you're getting sick on this ride, you've got a big surprise coming. You're just now scaling the first hill before the first plunge. You have no idea what loops and bends are coming."

Jared flipped the book around. "How does it end?"

"Who said it ends? You assume way too much, Jared," Taylor accused.

"I think I've earned the right to assume," Jared replied. "Unless you're gonna start giving me some answers?"

"Why are you talking to someone who isn't here?" Taylor countered, just before fading and then vanishing altogether.

Jared scampered out of his chair.

"You're going to have to be a lot quicker and smarter than *you* think you are," Taylor said with a voice that came from above, below and from the sides of the room all at once.

Jared turned around. "Where are you?"

"I'm still in the chair where I was before. But you should've asked yourself, "Where am *I*?" The solidity of the room began washing away like wet paint hosed down with water. "Hold tight, Jared," Taylor cautioned, "here comes the rise before the fall."

* * *

"I'm back," Jared said, as the form of Tamen appeared like a ghost in front of him and then became solid.

The room ceased warping and settled into a structure of mud-brick walls and a gleaming stone floor. Hanging oil lamps perfumed the air with musky incense. In the center of the room stood the hawk-headed statue of Amon-Ra. The smoke-oozing braziers on either side of the statue were being fed woodchips by two sweat-covered priests in loincloths.

"When I spoke to you last, Jared, I had become master and lord of the temple," Tamen said. "The temple of Amon-Ra continued to flourish, and with my prowess in the art of magic, it became renown throughout the land. It was indeed one of the best times to be an Egyptian, I say. The soil was rich and bountiful. Our lands were expanding after having fought and pushed back the Hittites from the north and the Assyrians and Babylonians from the east. And we celebrated as often as we could.

"Right now, Jared, The Feast of Opet is upon all of Egypt. That is when the crown prince is to escort the statue of Amon-Ra from our temple here in Karnak to Thebes, the capital of Egypt. It is a festival like no other," Tamen boasted. "From slave to commoner... priest to pharaoh...all of Egypt is in celebration as the Nile overflows its banks and replenishes the soil. Once the statue of Amon-Ra passes through Thebes—the city of a thousand gates—the people enjoy bread beer and wine for days on end. But this particular time when Amenhotep, the newly anointed crown prince, came to retrieve Amon-Ra's statue, his own life was thrust into jeopardy."

Just as Tamen finished speaking, the door behind them burst open. Six thick-armed soldiers swarmed in, followed by an even larger dark-skinned one carrying an unconscious man whose white robe was soaked in and dripping blood on the floor. Temple priests followed, as well as their acolytes who frantically wiped at the trail of blood on the floor. Tamen took Jared by the arm and walked him over to the statue of Amon-Ra where the guards laid the injured man on the floor. The priests immediately gathered around the bleeding man.

Another man, older and dressed in an ankle-length white robe and clanging gold bracelets, entered and sidestepped the blood trail and the acolytes cleaning it. He scurried over and knelt next to the priests. One of the priests pulled up the man's robe, exposing a hand-long gash above his belly button oozing blood. The priest wiped away the blood with his hand and studied the wound before more blood pooled up and obscured it again.

"The wound is deep, Chancellor Sefot," the priest said to the man in the white robe. "The skill of our master, Lord Tamen, is required. But Chancellor, he is not here in temple."

Chancellor Sefot's black, make-up covered eyelids lowered. "The lord of the temple absent on the day of transport of the god?"

The priests quickly glanced at each other and then bowed their heads. The closest one to the chancellor again spoke, but haltingly. "He...he...Lord Tamen celebrates the Feast of Opet with the—the village children, great chancellor."

Chancellor Sefot gasped. "Children?"

"The people gather their children to receive his blessings. And then he plays games with them and tells them stories of the gods," the priest explained. "Lord Tamen teaches us that children are the blessed of Amon-Ra. He says they—the children—are to be cherished and—"

"Enough!" Chancellor Sefot barked. "We do not have time, fool! *You* work your magic then. Are you not a priest of almighty Amon-Ra, too?" The priest hesitated and then nodded his bald head. "Then I suggest you work your magic, priest, and work it mightily...or there will be more than the blood of the pharaoh's son spilled in Karnak this day."

The priest clapped his hands and looked at the other priests. "Bring salves and ointments, and as many bandages as can be found...now!" He looked up at the guards. "Go with our apprentices." The young men cleaning blood from the floor stopped and stood at attention. "The apprentices know in which villages Lord Tamen may likely be found. Find him and bring him to temple forthwith."

No guard moved as much as a finger until Chancellor Sefot yelled. *"Go!"*

"Why now Amon-Ra?" the priest uttered, as he turned his attention back to the bleeding prince. "How did this happen anyway?"

"Another senseless slip by the prince," Chancellor Sefot groaned. "Prince Amenhotep was practicing the sword with one of his guards on the barge while we were waiting to disembark. They tell me that the prince moved to cross blades and slipped...*for the second time today*...but this time forward and onto his guard's blade— who is now resting in pieces at the bottom of the Nile, I may add."

The priest began chanting as the other priests returned and set bottles and jars of salves next to him. As the priest chanted on, the blood flowing out of the prince's wound seemed to slow. Chancellor Sefot looked up at the statue of the god hovering over them. "Blessed be, Amon-Ra! It is working."

The priest stopped chanting and shook his head. "No, great chancellor, he is dying. The god of death, Set, has a hand upon him now that I cannot release."

"But the bleeding has slowed," Chancellor Sefot professed.

"Because he has no more to shed," the priest replied.

Chancellor Sefot sighed and placed his hand on the prince's forehead. "The goddess Isis is said to have found the ten hacked off pieces of Osiris, but when you are torn apart, priest, she will never find yours."

The priest shuddered. "But chancellor, we have done..."

"Be silent, priest," Chancellor Sefot groaned. "My body will no doubt join yours at the bottom of the river Nile. The pharaoh entrusted the safety of his heir to me and now he lies dying before me. Rest assured, your fate and mine shall be the same."

Just then, the sound of sandaled feet slapping against stone echoed from the back of the hall to the front of it. The guards and apprentices who had left a short time ago came rushing toward those gathered around the prince. Tamen, who was standing by Jared, walked around and stood in front of the guards and apprentices. Tamen bowed to Chancellor Sefot. "Great chancellor," he said reverently.

"Who are you, boy?" Chancellor Sefot questioned.

"Lord Tamen," Tamen said, and then bowed his head again.

Chancellor Sefot's brow furrowed. "I have heard tell of your prowess in the art of magic, but...but did not know you were so young. You are barely old enough to be a man," he accused.

"I am indeed lord and master of the temple, despite my short years, chancellor," Tamen replied.

"Well, if you do indeed have great healing magic as your priests claim—despite your youth—do not waste your breath on me," Chancellor Sefot replied. He pushed the priest kneeling over prince Amenhotep away.

"He is already gone, my lord," the priest said to Tamen as he stood. "The god, Set, has him in an embrace of death."

"Then let us see if we can pry that embrace open," Tamen replied.

"Impossible, my lord," the priest replied. The other priests mumbled their agreement.

Tamen ignored the doubting priests and kneeled. He put his hand over the wound and another on Amenhotep's forehead. His baritone vibrato filled the room as he began chanting. His pitch rose high and then swung low before repeating the refrain he started with. Chancellor Sefot turned away and closed his eyes. The other priests stared on with open mouths. In that moment, when it seemed as though Tamen's healing chant was in vain, as the prince, for all appearances seemed quite dead, everyone, including Jared, jumped as prince Amenhotep suddenly arched his back, raised his hands toward the ceiling and began gasping for air. Tamen grasped hold of the prince's hands. Slowly, prince Amenhotep relaxed on the floor and closed his eyes. His breaths began flowing in and out rhythmically. Tamen looked up and said to Jared. "You thought I had lost him, no?"

"Uh, yeah!" Jared sighed in relief. He moved closer and peeked over Tamen's shoulder. "I know none of this is real, but it sure feels like it is."

"Glory to the gods!" Chancellor Sefot cried as he looked down at the prince's wound, which was sealing itself back up. Within moments, not even a scar as evidence that the skin had been cut could be seen.

"Yes, chancellor," Tamen said, "glory to the gods." He stood and then helped Chancellor Sefot to his feet.

"And to you, Lord Tamen," Chancellor Sefot added excitedly. "Your magic is truly a gift from the gods themselves. You will be generously rewarded."

"I seek no recompense, my lord. *This* is my duty," Tamen replied.

Chancellor Sefot stood on the tips of his toes and kissed Tamen on both cheeks. "Do you even realize what you have done? Prince Amenhotep shall be pharaoh one day. For this deed of deeds, I shall present you to pharaoh myself."

"No," Prince Amenhotep whispered through painted red lips. His skin had regained much of its mocha hue.

"My prince, rest," Chancellor Sefot implored.

"For a moment I was in the Land of the Dead, Sefot," Amenhotep uttered. "It feels good to speak...*to be alive once more.*"

"Yes, highness," Chancellor Sefot replied and bowed.

Amenhotep focused his glassy, grey eyes on Tamen. "I shall take you before pharaoh myself. After that, you shall forever be by my side. You will be as a prince in pharaoh's court. This I vow on the life you have given back to me." He closed his eyes. "Chancellor?"

"Yes, highness?"

"Take care of this blessed priest."

"It is your will." Chancellor Sefot clapped his hands. "I want the prince's guards—not temple guards—protecting this room. Bring in a bed and any other furnishings you have here that may suit a prince. I want him to stay under the watchful eye of Amon-Ra himself," Chancellor Sefot said, looking up at the statute. He then eyed the guards. "Other than me, cut down any who attempts to enter. *All others out!* But you, Lord Tamen, will remain and attend to our prince."

Tamen looked over at Jared as everything around them, people included, began to blur away. "Prince Amenhotep recovered in the temple for two days with me by his side. When the prince and I finally left for the capital, Thebes, an entourage of servants and a half battalion of soldiers accompanied us.

"There was barely a moment in those two days I spent with the prince that I could move from his side, as he wanted me near at all times. In me...his savior...he found comfort, and for once was brave enough to let down his guard. You see, despite our perceptions of what we think kings and queens are, they are but simple people no different than you and I. Though Amenhotep was crown prince, emotionally he was more of a child of six or seven than a man of seventeen years. And because his father, pharaoh, was in his twilight years, it would not be long before Amenhotep would become Egypt's new god-king—ruler of the greatest empire in the world at that time. That, more than anything frightened him."

"Along with a near death experience, too," Jared added.

"I am sure that had a great deal to do with his candor," Tamen agreed. "Now, Jared, we go to Thebes—the fabled city of a thousand gates. Turn around," Tamen told him as he fully dissolved the illusion of the temple they were in and replaced it with a sea of sand. A structure began forming in front of them, along with the bodies of Amenhotep, Chancellor Sefot, their guards and hundreds of people lined up in two rows on either side of them.

The sprawling palace that formed was more of a city unto itself. It stretched wide and farther than Jared could see on either side. Two massive sphinxes, each three stories tall, guarded the landing leading to a flight of stairs. At the top, two more of the giant sphinxes sat watch on either side of a set of double stone doors, both engraved with mirror images of the pharaoh holding a spear. The crowd cheered as the bodies of Amenhotep and his entourage came to life in front of Tamen and Jared. Amenhotep, in a white shenti-skirt and blue and gold striped headdress, smiled and waved to the crowd on either side as he ascended the stairs. A solemn, gold-robed Chancellor Sefot and bare-chest royal guards in shentis followed behind the prince.

"The lower noble class," Tamen said to Jared, as he pointed to the throngs of women in sheer linen dresses and men in shentis standing on both sides of the stairs. Their gold and silver bracelets tinkled and glinted in the sunlight as they clapped and waved joyously to prince Amenhotep. Their brows were laden with black make-up, though their eyelids were colored in blues, yellows and reds. "They are the sons and daughters and grandchildren of princes, princesses and generals. You see before you direct descendants of Djoser, Sekenere, Ahmose, and other great pharaohs of a time long before I was even born."

The palace doors required six men on either side to open them with ropes. The throne room they entered was easily the size of three amphitheaters and supported by columns carved and painted to resemble lotus plants. The hall was separated into two by a red woven carpet upon which they walked. On either side there were more nobles in attendance, though their higher stature in society than those outside was easily noted by their far ample amount of gold bracelets, rings and multicolored lapis lazuli chest necklaces they wore. Upon the walls...stretching from the floor to the tower-ing ceiling...were engravings and paintings of the hawk-headed Amon-Ra, Isis, Set and various other gods of the Ennead—the grand council of gods.

At the end of the hall and up a short flight of stairs there sat the pharaoh and his queen on gilded thrones. Prince Amenhotep bowed to Pharaoh and his queen—who seemed to be young enough to be his daughter. "Great pharaoh—you who are lord of the upper and lower land," Amenhotep began, "I present to you the creator-father, *Amon-Ra!*"

Four priests—two on either side of a wood pallet covered in gold threaded white linen—carried the statue of Amon-Ra up the stairs and set it on the altar next to the pharaoh. Pharaoh Amenhotep III wobbled as he stood and grasped the arm of his chair for support. Under the white, cone-shaped crown with two black asps side-by-side in front, was a thin, honey-colored man with eyes that were nearly swollen shut.

"Is Pharaoh pleased?" Amenhotep asked.

Pharaoh said nothing for a long moment, before simply stating, "Pharaoh is!"

Amenhotep turned around and faced the audience. His eyeliner was thickly applied, though without it—with his wide, curvy hips—he still could have easily been mistaken for a she. "Pharaoh has spoken his pleasure. Let the royal court be the first to celebrate The Feast of Opet honoring our great god, Amon-Ra. Prince

Mawat—my brother and minister of Thebes, has prepared a celebration and feast for all to partake. With leave from Pharaoh, I bid thee all now celebrate!"

Before dispersing, the noble men and women approached and bowed to Pharaoh and the queen. Afterwards, all that remained in the hall were a few servants and guards who maintained a respectable distance from the immediate royal family.

Tamen leaned over to Jared. "Don't heed Pharaoh's compliments to Amenhotep. He only said such things for the benefit of the nobles present. Pharaoh knew his time was coming to an end, and that the crown would pass to prince Amenhotep, who was not exactly the best choice."

"But he was first born, right?" Jared asked, as he fidgeted with his loincloth.

"No—third born," Tamen replied. "Amenhotep was chosen because he was proposed as being the best for Egypt's interest."

"But I thought you—"

"Amenhotep was not *pharaoh's* first choice—but another's," Tamen interrupted. "One person you did not or could not see in the hall was the one who convinced Pharaoh it should be Amenhotep." Tamen pointed to a man in a white robe standing on the far side of the throne room by a lotus column. "Pharaoh rules with a host of ministers and advisers guiding him on everything from beer and wine production to war. That man you see there is Pharaoh's most trusted adviser of all."

"And he is?"

"He *was* the greatest sorcerer in Egypt," Tamen said. "After Pharaoh, he is the holiest person in the land, which makes him a very powerful man indeed. Remember, Jared, in Egypt, religion is life and death. For us, religion was the only reason for living at all. But he is someone you have never read about. His name is Lord Yikan...a name I promise you, you will never forget."

Jared wiped sweat from his brow and then looked up at Tamen. "I don't like how you said that."

"And you should not," Tamen agreed. "Lord Yikan suggested that prince Amenhotep should be crown prince because he knew Amenhotep was weak and could be controlled. It was not as though Pharaoh had any reason to doubt Lord Yikan's word, for under his counsel, Egypt prospered greatly, ensuring Pharaoh a most grand burial. Remember—"

"Religion is life and life is religion," Jared jumped in. "Got it. So this, Lord Yikan, wanted to have the power of a pharaoh without actually being pharaoh?"

Tamen shook his head. "To become pharaoh or pharaoh-like was the least of his ambitions. He is precisely why you, Jared, are here in this illusion of Egypt witnessing my tale." Tamen turned Jared around and to the conversation at hand behind them.

"My son, to have lost you would have wounded me deeply," Pharaoh said. "Chancellor Sefot has informed me that I have the gods and *one* man in particular to thank for this blessing?"

"Yes, father." Prince Amenhotep swung his hand toward Tamen, who then left Jared's side and kneeled in front of Pharaoh. "I present to you the blessed priest who has brought me back from the Land of the Dead. Pharaoh, I present Lord Tamen of the temple of Amon-Ra in Karnak."

Pharaoh grasped Tamen's chin with his hand that bore two rings on each finger. "Rise, young priest, so that I may look into the eyes of one so blessed by Amon-Ra." Tamen stood and looked down as the pharaoh achingly gazed up. "Amon-Ra!" Pharaoh gasped. "Is there one of my soldiers who stands as tall? And what man, but a pharaoh, has ever been as handsome? Tell me if this is so, my queen."

"His face does beckon the soul, great pharaoh," Queen Tiy replied. "'Tis' a sign of the gods that he is possessed of such beauty and stature."

"Indeed!" Pharaoh remarked.

Amenhotep looked up at Tamen. "I swear father—the god Set had led me into the Land of the Dead when a song like no other came to my ears. But before I was to face Lord Osiris and be judged, I was pulled back. And when I opened my eyes, this man—Lord Tamen—was kneeling over me."

"Then it is even more of a blessing!" Pharaoh declared.

"Lord Tamen's magic is truly beyond compare," Amenhotep added.

"Then I must have failed my prince in some way," a voice from behind them all said. Everyone turned in its direction.

A hum, like a fading spring breeze passing through tree limbs suddenly arose. Lord Yikan, who had spoken, moved toward them —not walking, but gliding a half-foot above the floor. Lord Yikan, who was as fair-skinned, though not nearly as old as the pharaoh, bowed before him, and then lowered his body to the ground. He partially bowed his head at everyone present, and then concentrated his eyes—blue swirling liquid, instead of pupils and irises—on the pharaoh.

"Forgive my offense, my lord," prince Amenhotep said, slightly bowing his head. "Truly there is no greater magic in all of Egypt than yours. I have no doubt had you been there, you yourself would have saved me."

"I would have served you to the best of my abilities, my prince," Lord Yikan replied. "As Pharaoh knows all too well, my affairs of late have kept me absent from the palace. With those vile barbarians at Egypt's doorstep, I must seek the blessings of the gods now more than ever."

"And Egypt is forever in your debt," Pharaoh stated.

Lord Yikan bowed low. "My pharaoh."

"Father—regarding the priest, Tamen," Amenhotep said. "I humbly ask that he be rewarded for his deeds."

"What riches could ever compensate him for the miracle he has performed?" Pharaoh asked rhetorically.

"With the Pharaoh's blessing, I ask that Lord Tamen reside within the palace with us," Amenhotep said. "He will be as a friend and brother to me."

"Is that a proper place for a priest?" Pharaoh asked him.

Prince Amenhotep was silent for a moment. "For a priest who has saved my life—*no*," Amenhotep said. "For a priest blessed by the hand of Amon-Ra himself—*yes!* Lord Tamen tended to my spirit as well as my body. He has come to know me better than anyone else, yet he had never met me until that moment. How can the bonds of brotherhood be stronger than that, father?"

"And if I denied you this?"

"Pharaoh's word is law," Amenhotep quickly replied. "But Pharaoh has just said that all the gold in your treasury could never repay such a debt. But to have Tamen as my brother is such a thing that gold cannot purchase."

Pharaoh nodded and then glanced at Lord Yikan with a semblance of a smile before turning back to Amenhotep. "Your young priest may come to the palace. One such as he belongs here amongst gods and princes, not commoners. I am sure Lord Yikan can find a place in the temple for one so worthy."

Lord Yikan's eyes swirled and darkened to a midnight blue. "Pharaoh's decision is most wise. I sense it is the will of the gods that this young priest has come into the house of Pharaoh."

"What say thee, Lord Tamen?" Pharaoh asked.

Tamen kneeled and bowed his head. "Many thanks I give thee, great one. I have only performed my duty and am not worthy of such a reward. Your kindness is a blessing I most humbly accept."

"I think it shall be a benefit to have one such as you in the company of my son," Pharaoh said softly. "Chancellor Sefot—provide quarters and servants worthy of a nobleman for this handsome lord come into the house of pharaoh. And for his leisure, have built for him a dwelling of his choosing near the holy Nile where the nobles reside. Pharaoh commands it."

"As you wish, Pharaoh. It shall be done without delay," Chancellor Sefot replied.

"And bring me some clothes that do not weigh like a beast upon my back. I feel more like a horse than pharaoh," he added lightly, and removed his crown, which was quickly taken from his hand by a servant.

Pharaoh and Queen Tiy departed amidst a flurry of servants and guards trailing behind them. Lord Yikan and Chancellor Sefot followed suit, walking close together in conversation. Once alone, Amenhotep embraced Tamen. "We are brothers now, you and I. Is this pleasing to you?"

"It is, my prince," Tamen replied.

Amenhotep smiled, causing his cat-like eyes to turn into half-moons. "You shall want for nothing—I swear. In my house, your word will be as mine own and obeyed without question. There are many princes in Egypt who say they are my brother, but only because they seek my father's crown if something...unexpected... should be fall me. I am sure many of them were disappointed to hear of my miraculous recovery at your hands...pity," he added, with a tilt of his head. "Tamen, you are my only brother from this day forward," he said as his image began to fade away, leaving Tamen and Jared alone in the hall.

Tamen rubbed his hairless chin as he stared at the spot where he had conjured and then made Amenhotep's illusion disappear.

"Tamen?" Jared waved his hand in front of Tamen's face. "Tamen? Hey! Are you with me?"

"Yes, Jared," Tamen looked at him. "I hear you, child."

"You OK?"

"Of course. I am an immortal," Tamen droned. "But...Lord Yikan, as I have told you, is a schemer of the highest order. I do not think he became that way, but was born as such. Each time I have told

152 · Orlando Smart-Powell

this tale, I realize that there has never been one word or move he
has ever made that did not place his own interests first."

"Is he as powerful as everyone says?"

"Yes and no," Tamen replied. "Yes—he had knowledge of magic
that no other mortal did. But no—he knew there was more powerful magic out there than he possessed. Let me show you."

Tamen reshaped the illusion so that they stood on a balcony
overlooking a courtyard of sand and dirt. Below were soldiers and
prince Amenhotep with a bow and arrow in hand—cocked, ready
to strike a straw dummy, which was already pierced with several
arrows. The prince released his arrow with a twang and sent it
whistling far off to the side of the target.

"Anubis be cursed!" Amenhotep growled, even as the guards
praised him for coming so much closer this time. A slim, dark-
skinned guard with sinewy muscles spread Amenhotep's legs and
instructed him to move his arms slightly higher. Amenhotep attempted another shot, but was even farther off than the last time.

"He never was any good with weapons," Tamen said. "The bow,
unfortunately, was the one he was actually the best at. When not
being schooled in the art of combat, his days were filled with
learning to read and write, or attending his father as he met with
counselors, advisers and generals, and received foreign dignitaries.
Amenhotep's world as impending king, and now mine as his
brother and confidant, was to learn as much as he could before his
father's death.

Besides being groomed to become pharaoh, there were always
other matters just as important to attend to. First of all, there was
the matter of governing the princes who ruled the cities of Egypt
under the authority of Pharaoh. These princes coveted much more
than just some principality in a nation where being a pharaoh
meant being a god. Even the most honorable pharaohs had enemies within their own court.

"But Egypt was relatively calm at this time. Occupied lands had occasional insurgencies, but our well-armed armies silenced them as quickly as they sprang up. The people were well fed and for the most part, happy and content. There were slaves a plenty to build temples and shrines to gods, and to indulge Pharaoh's narcissism by engraving his image on as many walls and pylons as they could. Besides managing the state, a pharaoh had one more task of utmost importance to attend to...his afterlife. If one did not have a proper resting place, it was thought that their ka-spirit would wander, never finding its way to the Land of The Dead, and from there to the blissful afterlife in the Great Marsh.

"As you can see, being a pharaoh is not just sitting on a throne and ordering servants and ministers about. Being a god-king came with great and daunting responsibilities. Perhaps you can now understand why prince Amenhotep, who was already a weak prince, trembled at the thought of ruling the greatest empire on earth. I have always felt it was why he grew so close to me in such a short time. The prince trusted me fully, but not I he...at least not yet." Tamen's body became ethereal and then disappeared.

Jared turned away from the balcony and saw Tamen rematerializing in a bed behind him. He was on his stomach clad in a loincloth. The illusion that once bathed them in daylight slowly gave way to moonlight, which glimmered off of Tamen's moist, brown skin. Smoking oil lamps from above cast nervous shadows below, and mingled with white smoke of sweet and musky incense from the braziers in the corners of the room.

Just then, Amenhotep entered the bedroom. Though his gait was wide, it contrasted with his heavily painted eyes, narrow waist and broad hips, blurring what was known to be male and female attributes. He ripped the shenti from his waist and dropped it on the floor, leaving himself clothed in only a loincloth. He lay on his side so that he and Tamen gazed at each other.

"What worries you, my prince?" Tamen asked.

Amenhotep's narrow face seemed to elongate even more. "I am neither a warrior nor a leader, my brother. I have not made a decision at court yet that has not had my father shaking his head. And today—today..."

"The bow?"

"Yes!" Amenhotep snarled. "I have been at that damnable thing since I could hold it, and I still do not even come close to nicking the target. Bucharet barely glances at it and can strike the center every time."

"Bucharet's a soldier, *and* Pharaoh's best marksman," Tamen reminded him. "That is why he is your instructor. Being a soldier is Bucharet's life, not yours. You are a prince."

Amenhotep sighed and leaned his head back. "The Hittites and Nubians are probably plotting against my reign even now. They so covet the throne once more."

"The Hittites, Nubians, or even Persians for that matter...if they even dared, they will be defeated bitterly," Tamen boasted. "They exist now only because we allow them to. Egypt is the world and the world is Egypt. In time you will see that everything is not quite as grim as you think."

"You are supposed to say that."

Tamen rested his cheek in his hand. "When I came to live in the House of Pharaoh, you told me to always speak true to you."

"But you lie now."

"It is the truth," Tamen urged. "You know it is such."

"Are you like those bastard brothers of mine who only agree with pharaoh because they have to? You tell me what you *think* I want to hear because someday I will be pharaoh."

"You are mistaken and...*insulting*."

"Am I, brother?" Amenhotep glared at Tamen for a moment before rising and leaving the bed. He walked over to a table where incense smoldered in a brass pot and grabbed a small knife that was lying next to it. He returned to the bed and held up the knife—point down. "Give me your arm."

Tamen sat up, but did not extend his arm. "What game do you play at, Amenhotep?" he asked cautiously.

"A game of truth," Amenhotep replied in a hushed breath. "I am to be obeyed, am I not? I am Egypt's crown prince—god-king in waiting. So brother, give me your arm...*your very life*...if I demand it."

Tamen thrust both of his arms forward—wrists up. "Take it then! Cut my flesh and be done with it," he demanded. "You seek the truth, Amenhotep, then I shall give it to you before I am judged by Lord Osiris in the afterlife. And it is...you are a fool! You seek to please everyone but yourself, and thus have become a shadow of who you are meant to be. Now that the hour of your reign draws near, you know not who you are. If Egypt falls under your rule, it shall not be because of a weak pharaoh, but a hollow one!"

"Damn you!" Amenhotep screamed as he drove the knife down and across Tamen's right wrist.

Tamen and Jared both gasped, though it was Tamen who had his wrist flayed open at the base of his hand. Amenhotep cried out again, but this time in panic. He dropped the knife and clasped his delicate hands over Tamen's wrist, but the blood from the inch deep wound oozed between his fingers and began pooling on the white linen sheets.

"Great Amon-Ra forgive me," Amenhotep cried. "I—I did not mean...I do not know why I—I—"

"Be at...at ease, brother," Tamen warbled, quite shaken at the swift and brutal act. He placed his left hand over Amenhotep's, which were unsuccessful in stemming the flow of blood, and began chanting softly. "Shorra-sei-shorra-mee-tahn-shorra-sei-tah-mali-sahtay...shorra sei-shorra-meetahn."

Tamen peeled Amenhotep's hands away from his wrist like layers of an onion as he continued chanting. When he revealed the wrist that had been cut, Tamen wiped the blood away from where the gash had been. Tamen stopped chanting and then looked up at Amenhotep who gawked at what once was a gushing wound.

"Amon-Ra!" Amenhotep whispered and then covered his mouth with his bloody hands. He lowered his head and began weeping. "I have committed a great wrong against mine own brother and a blessed one of the gods," he muttered. "I am so unworthy of your love, Tamen."

Tamen reached out and stroked Amenhotep's hairless head. "Fear and doubt hath stolen your soul, my brother. But it can be found once more. And I shall I help you."

Amenhotep grasped Tamen's hand and brought it to his lips. Smothering Tamen's hand in kisses, front and back, he then tilted his head and used the palm of it as a cradle for his cheek. He bent forward and rested his head in Tamen's lap and then closed his eyes.

Tamen stroked Amenhotep's head and rubbed his arched back. "Sleep your fears away, brother, and never fear of losing my love. It is yours eternal. I shall, for all your days, be ever by your side so you never walk alone," he promised, as the illusion of Amenhotep wavered and then faded away.

Tamen left the bed and walked over to Jared, conjuring a shimmering blue shenti-skirt about his waist as he did.

"He's like...like in agony over becoming pharaoh," Jared stated, wrinkling his nose. "Tortured really."

"Indeed. It pained me greatly that he was in such a state. I was his brother," he stressed. "Though we did not share the same blood, he is my brother as assuredly as if my mother had given birth to him also. So I stayed even closer to him. With my magic, I guided him in court using the very same trick that I am using with you right now—projecting my thoughts into your mind, but also listening to the ruminations of others. Amenhotep thus had a great advantage with me whispering the secret motivations of other's to his mind's ear. It buoyed his spirit to appear wise and adept at ne-gotiations in front of his father, even if it were only a ruse.

Jared tilted his head back and sighed.

Tamen stared at him for a moment and then smiled weakly. "Ah—your dear friend Christopher," Tamen whispered. "He and Amen-hotep are indeed so similar."

"You read my mind? Just like that?" Jared asked.

"It is far easier than you think once you know how, that is," Tamen replied.

"It's freakin' rude," Jared growled.

"My apologies, Jared," Tamen said softly. "I too know the sacred love shared by brothers of the heart, as you now bear witness to mine."

Jared rubbed his bald head and then scratched at his shoulder. "Just go on, OK?"

"As you wish," Tamen said as he bowed his head at him. "As much as I could, I was in contact—physically or mentally—with Amenhotep. But I had my own matters to attend to in the temple. I was now a priest of the royal family. I commanded the utmost re-spect from all save the pharaoh, the royal court and Lord Yikan. And being a companion of the prince elevated my position even further. I had my own servants and guards who would come run-ning and bow at my feet if I so much as whispered. And too, when I chose to marry, I was expected to choose a wife from a family of the highest noble class.

"It was not long before I was summoned by Lord Yikan," Tamen said as he began altering the illusion from one of a smoky, incense filled bedroom to a cold stone chamber lit by hanging oil lamps. In alcoves that lined the walls on the side were human-sized stone statues of the gods. The room was divided in half by two rows of columns, which created a path down the room's center. At the end of the room was a gilded chair that was more fitting for a pharaoh.

"I had not spoken to him directly since the day I moved into the palace. The priests who brought me to him that night said it was rare for anyone to have an audience with Lord Yikan. In fact, they said they had not seen him for weeks until he told them to bring me to his antechamber that night, which was in the depths of the palace itself.

"Despite my proficiency in magic, mine was but a shadow of Lord Yikan's. The other palace priests professed he could not only fly as an ibis does and raise storms from blue skies, but also that he could be in two places at once if he so chose. It was his swirling liquid eyes that held such power, they whispered.

"As the tale goes, as told by the older priests, brown-eyed Lord Yikan had risen up the ranks of the priesthood quickly—like myself. And then one day, after journeying out into one of Egypt's great deserts, he returned with *those eyes*. Within a week of Lord Yikan's return, the grand vizier, his teacher, was said to have fallen ill and died. No one questioned Lord Yikan's ascension to grand vizier with the untimely—or timely—death of the grand vizier, who was most healthy before succumbing to a mystery illness. Lord Yikan, now elevated to lord and vizier, was revered, but feared more than anything.

"I was in the antechamber behind us for almost an hour before the doors suddenly swung open and released a blast of unnaturally cold air on me. I walked into this room. There were no slaves or guards who had pulled the foot-thick wood doors open...but open they had, though not on their own accord.

"I looked around and thought I was alone. But when I looked back at the throne, Lord Yikan was sitting there motionless. I shivered, knowing that I had not seen anything in that chair just moments before," he said as the image of a black-robed Lord Yikan wavered into existence.

"Priests have trained all their lives to attain what you have in the course of a few years," Lord Yikan said, as his illusion animated. "Is it your intention to succeed me once I have passed into the Land of the Dead, priest Tamen?"

Tamen stepped away from Jared and moved closer to Lord Yikan. He bowed at waist. "No, my lord. I am here only to obey pharaoh's will and serve your needs if I be worthy."

"Pity," Lord Yikan remarked. "From the tales I have heard about your wondrous magic, I would have assumed greater aspirations from one so favored by the pharaoh and the prince. You shame even my best priests with your skills."

"That was not my—"

"Do not dare be humble!" Lord Yikan snipped. "You are far more gifted than any I have seen in my lifetime. You know this is so; do not deny it. If anything, take pleasure in it...revel in it. It should be a shame for a talent like yours to go to waste as simply another priest in the house of Pharaoh."

"Yes, my lord."

"The magic scrolls you study are of no use to you now," he said. "You are far beyond meaningless fire conjuring and making chairs and vases hover about. I see that I must challenge your mind if you are to rise any further."

"My mind?"

"That gray, swirled matter in your head that funerary priests pull through your nose and discard...yes, your mind," he admonished.

"But they say it is of no use, my lord," Tamen countered.

Lord Yikan huffed. "Forget all that you have learned. If you are what I think you may be—and rarely am I wrong—you shall eventually see the truth. You are most proficient in languages."

"Yes, my lord."

"Then I have a task for you. Consider it a challenge." Lord Yikan clasped his hands and leaned forward. "In my possession, I have a book of ancient scriptures whose language is far, far older than even Egypt itself."

"My lord!" Tamen gasped.

Lord Yikan leaned back. "My acolyte, belief that the world began here in Egypt is a lie. There are such things far older than we." He paused. "The language in this tome is no longer spoken. Only a man worthy of attaining the greatest of magic...*such as I*...can unlock these mysteries within the tome."

In front of Jared, a desk and a chair shimmered into existence while Lord Yikan walked over and stood next to Tamen. On the desk, a gold book almost the width of the table, along with writing materials—papyrus, a brush and soot—appeared. Tamen came over and sat in the chair. He opened the book whose pages, though gold, were flexible like paper. The symbols written upon the gold paper were etched in silver and lined up row upon row. There were circles within circles and some with slashes through them, or triangles and squares whose lines never quite connected and others that did. But also, some appeared to be types of letters and numbers. On some of the markings, they swirled at the end or top, and others sideways and so fine it could have been easily missed.

"The tome is more than just an object of beauty, Jared," Tamen explained. "What you cannot feel is that it seemed alive. Lord Yikan was correct when he said that it would challenge my skills."

"Very well then," Lord Yikan said. "I shall leave you to your task. When you believe that you have unlocked the mysteries of the text, transcribe it into our own language so that I may assess your accuracy. But there is one thing that must be resolved before you begin."

Tamen nodded. "Yes?"

"What you write must never be spoken out loud," he cautioned. "Heed this! For should you utter these words, your life will become forfeit."

"Never, my lord!" Tamen declared.

"What is done within the walls of my sanctum shall stay within them. Consider it in the same manner as you do, let us say...what transpires between you and the prince at court. You have fooled the nobles and even Pharaoh himself into thinking the prince has suddenly acquired a mind for politics." Lord Yikan lowered his head at Tamen, though glared at him with his swirling blue eyes. "How naïve of you to think that I did not know," Lord Yikan uttered, as his image faded into nothing.

"When he left, I was overcome with fear," Tamen admitted. "I knew his knowledge of me and the prince could mean my doom and Amenhotep being stripped of his title as crown prince and heir to the throne.

"After steadying myself the best I could, I started at my task. But the symbols were as foreign to me as they are to you right now. I tried to recreate the same sense and feeling I had experienced when learning other languages...letting their letters and arrangement of them flow over and into me until there was a piece I could understand and use as a primer. Though after a few hours of staring at the tome, I saw and felt nothing. I tried twisting the symbols in my mind

...rearranging and intertwining them together as a last resort, but to no success.

"I walked away from the tome wondering if Lord Yikan was still in the room unseen and laughing at my ignorance. But then, as I let that thought go, a more hideous one came to mind. What if I did fail to decipher the symbols? What would happen then? If I failed and Lord Yikan revealed the ruse Amenhotep and I were playing upon the pharaoh and the court, my family's name would become an insult to be used against one's enemies.

"I quickly returned to the tome. Instead of focusing on the beginning of the lines of symbols on the first page, I flipped through the gold pages, scanning it for anything that might be remotely familiar. I was turning the pages so rapidly, that when something did catch my eye, I had already lost its place. It took what seemed like forever to tediously skim each page line by line to find it again. But when I did find the symbols, they still made no sense. I was puzzled as to why it had caught my eye in the first place.

"I traced the symbols with my finger as I searched my mind for why they had stood out so. My tongue, however, seemed to remember why before my mind had...

"...and as my mind did, I remembered something that I was already quite familiar with. I had never seen such symbols before with my true eyes, but the eye of my mind had every time I chanted the healing spell...the same one I used to saved Amenhotep's life. As I studied them and settled on one round symbol with a line drawn through it and curled at the end, I could feel my tongue involuntarily curling just like the circular stroke. In my mind I heard *assi*, such as in the healing chant *assini-sumata alareze-alay*.

"I remembered my vow to Lord Yikan to never utter the words I decoded, and I did not. I just let my mouth and tongue and lips and jaw move without voice. The quicker I mouthed the symbols, the easier the words moved upon my lips...and the more familiar they became.

"To the next set of symbols I went and discovered, that by the will of the gods, I had my primer!

"I saw that the symbols after the ones I had deciphered were different from the ones before them, though now were slightly familiar and recognizable. I returned to the very first page and grabbed a sheet of papyrus and the brush. I began with the first line. This time, however, the symbols did not look as foreign as before."

CHAPTER 11

"Each night thereafter, whatever I had translated from the tome onto the papyrus sheets would be gone when I returned. Know that I only saw Lord Yikan once each night, with him leaving soon after I would arrive. But after years of translating the tome for him, it seemed as though he had warmed a bit toward me. He had servants bring me the most sumptuous foods each night—roasted goose or seared duck, dates and grapes, and sweet red wine. But my greatest fear that he would speak of my aid to Amenhotep in court still remained.

"Lord Yikan taught me magic that only he knew as my reward for such dutiful work. My ability to create and control fire increased so much, that a thought, instead of a chant, was now all it took to make it follow my commands. It was he who showed me how to perfect an illusion in another's mind so much so, I could make anyone see, touch, feel and hear anything I wanted.

"As I neared the end of translating the tome, I saw less and less of Lord Yikan. During his weeklong absences, it was to me that other priests now sought spiritual guidance. You see, Jared, strange events were occurring and being reported to temple priests and then to me. Red, green and orange lights were being seen in the night sky...flocks of geese and schools of fish were found dead on the shoreline from no apparent cause...monstrous sandstorms would arise from nowhere and vanish just as quickly. When I asked Lord Yikan about these bizarre events, I was told that it was simply the workings of the gods and nothing more.

"Egypt, it seemed, was in flux.

Pharaoh was inching ever closer to the Holy Marsh of the after-life by the day, and it was Amenhotep—with my assistance—who began presiding over court. The responsibility of wearing the crown weighed mightily upon him and he relied upon me even more. Egypt was expanding at a rapid pace, which meant there was even more at stake and that which to safeguard. Amenhotep's chosen wife—the next queen—was the legendary beauty, Nefertiti, the daughter of general Ay. And in these same days, prince Amen-hotep and I grew even closer—if that were even indeed possible," Tamen said, as Amenhotep materialized behind him and came and stood beside him.

His face was scrubbed clean of dark make-up around his eyes and red paint over his lips. Still, as he looked up at Tamen, his brown skin was flawless and glowed. "When we pass into the af-terlife, your sarcophagus shall be next to mine, brother," he promised me. "We shall be together in this life and in our next one for all eternity amongst the gods. You have been not only my brother, but also my guiding light in the dark of Egypt's night."

"And you mine," Tamen replied. "But will the gods allow a mor-tal such as I to be buried with you—a pharaoh—a god-king? It is unheard of."

"The gods? Hah!" Amenhotep snorted and then smiled. "*I* will be a god when Father passes. Who among the holy Ennead of gods will deny me such brotherly love as has never been or shall ever be?"

Tamen looked down at him and grinned at first, but then smiled and laughed. "Pharaoh's word is law," he quipped. "If you command it, then I and my wife—if ever I find the time to select one—shall dance with you and Nefertiti in the Great Marsh. And at our feet, our children shall play as brothers and sisters."

"Swear it, Tamen!" Amenhotep begged. He slinked around to the other side of Tamen. "Soon I will be pharaoh and eventually you will be grand vizier. Our duties shall keep us from one another. As I sit on my throne, I will be thinking of you. Will you think of me as you sit in your temple?"

"Of course!"

"Then swear it to me and to the gods."

"I swear it then! Gods of Egypt be damned. In this life and in the next, we shall forever be brothers. I swear it!"

Tamen sighed as the image of Amenhotep vanished like wind-blown smoke. "A few nights later, I was fast asleep when the guards came looking for me. They told me the strange lights that had come again and were now hovering above the city. When I went to the window and looked up, it was as though watching the northern lights...the Aurora Borealis, though of every color and hue between them.

"I dressed quickly and made haste to find Lord Yikan. I forgot his warning to always knock and wait for his permission before entering his temple."

Tamen turned Jared around by the shoulder. As he did, an image of Lord Yikan hovering cross-legged in mid-air wavered into existence. His entire body was enveloped in a tornado of blue, green and red lights. His lips moved furiously as he chanted. And floating in front of him was the golden tome opened halfway through.

Lord Yikan locked his swirling blue eyes upon Tamen and stopped chanting. The circular lights sweeping around him ceased with the last sound of his voice. He extended his legs and lowered himself back to the ground.

"Forgive my intrusion, my lord," Tamen said quickly and kneeled.

Lord Yikan walked to him and laid a hand upon his hairless head. "Rise, Tamen."

Tamen stood, but kept his head lowered. "I only came because—"

"The lights in the sky," Lord Yikan finished for him. "I know. But that is of no importance right now." Lord Yikan waved his hand at the floating tome, which lowered softly to the floor. "Look there," Lord Yikan said as he pointed at the table behind Tamen.

Tamen and Jared both looked and saw another tome—sparkling gold—like the other on the floor. Tamen's mouth gaped open for a moment. "There are two?"

"Yes," Lord Yikan hissed. "Two tomes of unimaginable power they are. The one on the table there—the one you translated so very well—is the simplest one to translate. The other I was just using, far—far unwillingly to release its secrets."

"What are they?" Tamen asked, and then rephrased. "Who wrote them?"

Lord Yikan turned around and walked over to his throne-chair and sat. He spread out his white robes, smoothing them as he did, and beckoned Tamen to come forth. Tamen came and sat on the short flight of stairs leading up to the throne. Jared followed and stood behind him. "Zoe'el—the grand vizier before me—died under the most unusual circumstances. You know of such rumors, no?" Tamen nodded affirmatively. "After he died, he was taken to be embalmed, though his body disappeared when the funerary priests came to prepare him for the afterlife. That is...all I know of it. I swear upon my ka-spirit, I had nothing to do with Zoe'el's demise.

"What I do know," Lord Yikan went on, "is that when I came here to the temple to beseech the god, Amon-Ra, to protect me from those accusing me of murdering Zoe'el, the god himself appeared to me in the flesh."

Tamen gasped.

"I shook in the presence of Amon-Ra—the father of gods," Lord Yikan admitted. "He commanded that I take a cart and beasts to draw it, and go to the desert that parts Egypt from Nubia—and I did. There, in the middle of nowhere, a great sandstorm arose around me, but not one grain of sand ever touched me. And when the winds ceased, there before me were these two golden tomes I now have in my possession.

"As my reward for having followed his command, I was given these." Lord Yikan leaned forward and pointed at his eyes. "And in my mind, Amon-Ra wrote great spells that are now and forever at my disposal with but a thought and chant. But the tomes themselves, Tamen, hold far greater power. So powerful indeed, I had to seek the safety of the desert to perfect these chant-spells and the wonders they wrought!" Lord Yikan closed his eyes for a moment. "I have made the ground itself heave and split asunder. I have drawn liquid fire from down below and burned the sand with it until it was solid and sparkling like water. We have unlocked the secrets of the first tome, but the other..."

"My lord, I will do my best to assist thee," Tamen promised.

Lord Yikan was silent for a moment. "We shall see. But for now, do as you have done and be a comfort to the other priests. When it is time to draw the secrets from the other tome, I shall come for you," Lord Yikan said, and then became completely still like a statue.

Tamen stood and turned to Jared.

"A year passed after Lord Yikan revealed these great secret to me," Tamen said. "Pharaoh was in a coma and Amenhotep, in essence, was ruler. Lord Yikan again became distant. But this time I understood why.

"More bizarre events were being reported. There was talk of people seeing the demons we call *Those Who Walk with their Heads on Backwards*. Gossip and rumor became fear, which spread like a plague throughout the land. No sane Egyptian would walk alone at night during these harrowing times.

"On the rare occasion that I did see Lord Yikan, I never really *saw* him, but just an illusion of him, as though he was spun together with webs from a spider. Rarely did he speak, and if so, only in one-word responses that made no sense at all. I began to think he was going mad. Despite this, I worked on, as there were other matters that now needed my full attention.

"Pharaoh eventually crossed into the afterlife after lying in a coma for weeks. I oversaw his embalming myself, using only the purest salts from our land, Wadi Natrun. After sealing the tomb in secrecy in the dead of night and returning to our chambers, Amenhotep wept in my arms until he had no more tears. I remember lying there in bed as Amenhotep tossed in his sleep as though he were trying to escape from something...*or someone.* I kept his feverish body as cool and dry as I could, though I dared not awaken him from his restless slumber. I knew his first day as pharaoh would no doubt be one of the most challenging days of his life. Only...I was very wrong.

"As I kept watch over Amenhotep, listening to him pant, I heard someone whispering my name. I remained as still as I could. Soon, the waif of a voice returned and lightly kissed my ear. Its voice was female. *'Come to me,'* she said.

"I laid Amenhotep's head on his pillow as gently as I could, and then slipped from the bed and dressed quickly. Using the mind illusion trick Lord Yikan taught me, I cloaked myself from the guards standing watch outside Amenhotep's bedchamber.

Tamen spread his arms wide and slowly turned around. As he did, the temple they were in began to wash away. When the walls became solid again, instead of them standing in a rectangular room lit by oil lamps, the illusion formed into a circular room with candles for illumination. In the center of the room appeared a circular stone pedestal and a foot-high gold figurine of a woman on it. "Her voice guided me to this small commoner's temple for the goddess, Isis, far from the palace.

"Who are you that calls me forth?" Tamen asked, looking up and around the brown mud-brick room, which echoed his words back.

"I am the mother of your pharaohs," a woman's voice answered faintly, seemingly coming from all directions of the room at once.

"Speak your name if you are a queen of Egypt!"

"I am not a queen," she said.

"How have you this magic to come to my thoughts in the midst of the night?"

"You have not listened," she replied. "I am the mother of all pharaohs."

"Mother Isis?" Tamen whispered in shock. "Great mother of the god Horus?"

Just then, the gold statue of Isis began to shimmer as though lights were passing through it. She opened her eyes and wrapped her arms around her chest as though she were cold. Tamen quickly kneeled.

"Run from the god of Evil, for he comes to claim what is not his," the figurine said from its golden lips. "Soon the god of Evil, Set, shall roam the land and great Evil shall follow in his wake."

Tamen looked up and shook his head. "I do not understand, my goddess."

"Your master shall unleash the evil one upon Egypt and none shall be able to stop him. Take the gold tomes from him and bury them for all time," she instructed, before turning back into a lifeless creation of gold.

"Who but Set could cause fear to such a mighty goddess as Isis?" Tamen said to Jared. "And if she, a goddess, was afraid, I knew I should be doubly so! But I did not know what to do, though she was explicit in her command. Isis was instructing me to steal the tomes...the very ones that Amon-Ra—the father of gods, had charged Lord Yikan to decode.

"When I returned to the palace, I went straight to Lord Yikan's chamber. The stone doors leading in were already open and he was sitting on his throne-chair with both golden tomes at his feet. He knew I was coming! His liquid eyes swirled viciously as they bore into me.

"Lord Yikan then clapped and six guards rushed into the room pulling a cart behind them. With three brawny men on either side of each tome, they lifted them into the cart.

"Lord Yikan left with them and was never seen or heard from again. A few weeks thereafter, I was made high priest of all of Egypt. The goddess Isis never came to me again, and Egypt did not burn or sink into the abyss as she said it would, but that was not enough to stay my fears...it only stoked them. This was, as they say, the calm before the storm. And when the storm arrived, it brought the fury of hell itself with it.

"Practically in one day, Amenhotep, now pharaoh, was branded as a heretic. Not only did he turn his back against his people and his land...but against me!

"I had gone to Amenhotep's chamber as I usually did in the evening. Instead of the guards reverently granting me entrance as usual, they crossed their swords and barred my way. They told me my presence was no longer welcomed in the pharaoh's chamber.

"I asked by whose authority and was told...'the pharaoh's!'

"Know, Jared, that as I could heal the sick, I could also kill the healthy. At that moment, I was tempted to voice a chant to stop their hearts and walk over their corpses. It was impossible for me to believe that Amenhotep...the brother of my heart...would ever spurn me.

"Ironically, the Feast of Opet—when I first met Amenhotep—was again drawing near, but Amenhotep had yet to give orders to pre-pare celebrations for it. Instead, he summoned me and the other high priests of each temple in Egypt to the palace. I assumed he had gathered us to discuss the upcoming festival for Egypt's most important god, Amon-Ra.

"I ask you, Jared, what does one say to a pharaoh when he declares the religion that has sustained Egypt shall never again be practiced? Every home had at least one altar to one god or another. Our greatest festivals were in honor of the gods. The gods were in essence Egypt itself! And in one day, the gods of our fathers and our father's fathers were no longer allowed."

The small circular temple of Isis began to waver. As it did, the walls formed into straight lines and moved away from them like giant hands were pushing them. The room finally settled into the form of the massive throne room.

Upon the gilded thrones, the visages of Amenhotep—now pharaoh—and his queen, Nefertiti, appeared. Both wore white cone-shaped crowns with asps affixed to their front. Amenhotep was draped in a white sheer linen robe, and across his chest, a gold breastplate in the shape of a bird with its wings spread. Nefertiti, whose eyelids were painted as heavy as Amenhotep's, wore a light blue dress that hugged her slim frame.

As Tamen and Jared walked toward them, bald priests in shentis and linen robes laced with gold began forming and appearing on either side of the throne room. Hulking guards with swords drawn stood watch not far from them. Tamen led Jared to the bottom of the stairs leading to the thrones. Once there, Tamen proceeded up a few alone.

"*Aton* is now the one and only god of Egypt," Amenhotep declared, as his figure animated. The priests were silent for a moment, before turning toward one another and murmuring. "In a dream the true god, Aton, came to me. Great truths he spoke of all that is in the world. As his loyal servant and intermediary, I deliver to you priests this wonderful news of our new and only god."

"Pharaoh...my lord," Tamen started. "You say there is only one god? That—that cannot be. Amon-Ra is father god, and...and Isis, the mother of gods. And thus they have sired scores of gods, my pharaoh. We know not this god, Aton."

"Oh, but he knows *thee*, Lord Tamen," Amenhotep replied. "The sun-god, Aton, has revealed to me that the gods of Egypt we once worshipped are false. Look up in the sky and bear witness to the great burning orb that gives life to all—that is Aton! He alone is god of Egypt."

"My pharaoh. You said always to speak true to you," Tamen said. "So again, I do. This is blasphemy. The scores of gods that comprise the holy pantheon is everything to everyone. The many gods we worship are Egypt."

Amenhotep grinned. "Dear brother, I promise that no harm shall ever come to you *for your blasphemy*. But what I say is not false. It is the absolute truth. Egypt *will* embrace the sun god, Aton, as I have. I have decreed it so!" he added. "Aton shall be the one and only god of all of Upper and Lower Egypt and its territories. Any man, woman, child or even priest caught worshipping any other god shall be put to death. So says Pharaoh—only son of the all powerful god, Aton."

Tamen stepped back until he was on the ground level with Jared. "You will break Egypt's spine with this...this...this god, Aton. This has all been foretold."

"By whom?"

"By the mother goddess herself...Isis!"

Amenhotep scoffed.

"She saw the evil god, Set, ravaging the land, and now I see it is coming to pass," Tamen said. "I believe this god—Aton—is but a trick of Set's. Do not let Set destroy your father's empire."

"My empire, Lord Tamen. Mine!" Amenhotep barked. "Perhaps you have only dreamed of this pretended goddess. Dismiss it as such. I am afraid you have gone a bit mad like all of Egypt's other high priests before you. At least promise me you will not go wandering off into the desert like Lord Yikan did."

Tamen shook his head. "You will destroy all that your father has passed to you."

"You are not the only one who can speak to a god, Lord Tamen," Amenhotep countered. "The great god Aton came to *me* many days ago in the guise of the purifying sun and cleansed me in his everlasting light. It is through him that Egypt shall prosper, not Isis or Osiris, or the other false gods. Aton is the sole god of Egypt. Eventually, my brother, you must accept that fact."

"Heretic!" Tamen blurted accusingly.

Three guards standing off to the side of the other priests rushed at Tamen after hearing his insult to pharaoh. Tamen spun in their direction, pointed a finger at them and began chanting. The guards, as though remembering what Tamen was capable of, immediately slid to a halt and began backing away.

"Stop!" Amenhotep yelled as he held up his hand. "No one shall do harm to Lord Tamen. But my brother—dear Tamen—you may use your magic and slay a thousand of my guards if you wish, but that will not change what is and what will be. From this day forth, every temple shall be rid of false gods. In their place shall be risen the holy solar disc of life that is Aton."

Tamen turned and faced Jared as the illusions of Amenhotep, Nefertiti and all of the others became translucent and disappeared, leaving them alone in the throne room. Tamen walked up the stairs and beckoned Jared to follow. He sat on Amenhotep's gilded throne and directed Jared to do likewise in Nefertiti's.

Jared looked out across the throne room and then up at it's stories high ceiling. "Wow!" he gasped. "Being Pharaoh would so go to my head."

"Yes, he was drunk with power and self-righteousness, to say it in another way," Tamen commented. "He was so resolute in his devotion to this new god, Aton, he even changed his name to *Akhenaton*. And with his decree that Aton be our only god, the populace, as well as the priests, splintered into three factions. One group vowed to have no part of this new god and was willing to risk death to worship the old ones. Another group did grudgingly bow to Pharaoh's will, and yet others decided to worship the new god in public and the old ones in secrecy, as I did.

"But my faith in the old gods was steadfast. I refused to wait for them to act and save Egypt. Thus, I found a group of young, rogue priests who remained faithful to the old gods. I charged them to seek out Lord Yikan. If there was anyone who could set the pharaoh to reason, I knew it to be him.

"But do not think I had forgotten about the golden tomes, Jared. If the priests found Lord Yikan but could not convince him to return, I commanded them to steal the tomes from him. I assumed that if the tomes were part of Egypt's demise as Isis alluded, then perhaps with them, I could find a way to save the empire. My instructions to the priests were simple enough, but the task daunting indeed.

"During this time, Akhenaton and his queen Nefertiti ruled in Tell el-Armana, where they moved the capital of Egypt and constructed a palace twice the size as the one we sit in now."

"Holy crap!" Jared spat. "Twice as big as this place?"

"Easily," Tamen assured him, and then went on. "Cloistered in his massive palace with Nefertiti and obsessed with worship to Aton, Akhenaton became blind to the fact that Egypt was losing lands to the Hittites, and that famine was afflicting Upper Egypt. In all, Akhenaton and Nefertiti produced four daughters. And with one of his concubines, he sired the celebrated boy-king of your time—Tutankhamen.

"When I did manage to sleep during these troubling times, strange visions always crept into my mind. I dreamt of Isis mostly, but I assumed this was due to my fevered prayers to her that I performed daily without fail. I even began dreaming *of her dreaming*. I dreamt I saw her lying prone in the desert basking her brown skin under the Egyptian sun. Strange though it was, she was only part woman. Sometimes she would have a tail protruding from between her legs, and other times I saw her hands were not hands at all, but paws. Each time I dreamt of her, she whispered my name. *'Come to me,'* she would say.

"From one of these odd dreams I awoke to the night still clinging to the sky. I got up and hung my head out the window to catch my breath. The newly constructed obelisks to the new god, Aton, rose high above all the other structures in Thebes like gleaming fingers pointing skyward. That particular night, the moon was full and white like foam from the sea. Its purity bewitched me.

"I began wondering how some of our oldest structures must have looked in the glow of this sky-illuminating moonlight. I am of course referring to the great pyramids of Giza. In my time, when they were already considered ancient monuments, the polished limestone casing, which has since fallen off, shone like glass. Its top cap was like a flawless diamond and was a beacon in the desert sea that surrounds the Giza Plateau. They were tombs built to last for all eternity, and so far they have endured. And to safeguard the pyramids, the Great Sphinx in the likeness of the former pharaoh, Khufu, sat at their base. But that was it, Jared! The sphinx! It was the sphinx that tied my dreams of Isis to reality.

"In that moment, my mind melded the two forms...Isis of my dreams lying prone with a tail between her legs and the sphinx likewise. A sign perhaps? I thought...*I wished*...I needed it to be true. I had nothing else left to hope for.

"The next day I traveled by ferry up the Nile to Giza. I purchased a camel, food and water at the port, and then waited until night before I made the journey out to the desert. As I drew near the pyramids and spotted the guards, I created a mist in their minds to hide my presence. I then stood before the sphinx not knowing what was supposed to happen. Doubt began creeping into my mind. The outer casing of the sphinx had begun to wear away and crack from hundreds of years of windstorms and unyielding heat. But still, it was awash in dazzling blues and reds on its headdress. Its body of polished limestone gleamed from the glow of the full moon.

"I lay down in the sand beside the sphinx. With my eyes to the stars, a strange, yet welcome sense of tranquility swept over me that I had not felt in years. Soon, I was asleep, soothed by the warm sand beneath me. And in my dreams, Isis came to me again. The sphinx was made of water and through it, in the middle, I saw her looking back at me.

Tamen shifted the illusion of the palace hall he and Jared were in. Beneath their feet, the stone floor became sand. In front of them, the Great Sphinx began to materialize, but it was not of rock, but ceaselessly swirling water as in Tamen's dream. Inside of it was a stone figure of Isis, as the sphinx should have been.

"My voice has been stolen from me," Isis said, though her lips, nor body had moved.

"But you do speak," Tamen replied.

"It is but a thought. It is all that remains of what I was," she whispered. *"My true voice has been stolen from me and that of the father, Amon-Ra, my husband."*

"By whom?"

"The Evil god, Set, who only pretends to be this new god, Aton, so that he may beguile Pharaoh."

"I suspected as much, my goddess," Tamen said.

"He is ever watchful, but not insightful," she said. *"He has become vain and risen himself up on high, yet his pride may fall him yet. Restore my voice! Do this...and I shall lay the world at your feet."*

Tamen kneeled and stretched out his arms. "My goddess, I do not understand what you ask of me. What voice do you speak of?"

"The voice to raise a thousand storms...the voice to fly...one great enough to flood the banks of the Nile itself," she said. *"Restore my voice and I shall fall Set and remove his foot from Egypt's neck. Let my voice rise once more and I shall restore the holy Ennead of gods to its rightful place."*

"But how?"

"In my golden tomes you will find the answer. Therein lies a chant-spell to give you a voice that will restore my own."

"But they are gone."

"No," she countered. *"One is hidden beneath the sands of the great desert, but not well enough. I will guide you to this place."*

"And how will I know which spell—"

"It will burn your eyes, as though you stand in front of the gods themselves," she both informed and warned. *"But beware young one. The eyes and ears of Set are everywhere. If he wills it, he may know your intentions. And if this he discovers, he will slay you."*

"Then how will I succeed?"

"Ah," she sighed. *"You are a mortal, but a formidable one. You have the power to make others see what you wish them to. Think not upon your quest to the point that you have indeed fooled yourself, for if Set should come to you, he will then pass you by. But above all, my child, do not chant until you have found the tomes, for any chant will call him to you. Journey now into the great desert between Egypt and Nubia. Look to their deserted temples and then beyond to the east. A great mound you shall find that was not there before."*

"The tomes are there?"

"Only the greater of the two tomes. The lesser tome is beyond my reach and in Set's possession. Twas Set's folly that when he had the chance, he did not sink them both in the great waters to be lost for all time. It was his vanity to think himself powerful enough to silence me forever."

With the last echo of Isis' last words, the sphinx solidified back to stone. But even that did not last for long as it shimmered out of existence along with the pyramids, and was replaced with high arching dunes of sand as far as Jared could see.

"We are now far away from Egypt proper. Sit with me and listen, Jared," Tamen said as he sat. He waited for Jared to adjust his loincloth—the single flaps in front and back—and sit in the warm sand also, which he sank his fingers into as he listened on.

"I traveled by camel south along the edge of the Nile until I came to the deserted temples and villages of northern Nubia. There I filled my flasks from the well in the center of town with as much water as they could hold. I then traveled east into the desert, which was shunned by all except a few bands of nomads who gave allegiance to neither Egypt nor Nubia. The heat was unmerciful, as you could expect. Within days I was already running out of water. My lips were so dry they began cracking. The wind swept sand felt like a thousand knives poking at my skin.

"All the while, I searched the landscape but found no great mound that seemed out of place as the goddess claimed, but instead exactly what you see right now...rolling sand dunes for hundreds of miles. It was like looking for a proverbial needle in the haystack.

"That first night, I likely switched digging sites ten times before settling on just one, and even then I had serious doubts that I was even on the correct mound. The second, and last night I vowed, I did not search as feverishly. The task I had been given seemed an impossible one. When I slept, the goddess did not come to me, so how was I to find what I needed without her guidance? Too many *what ifs, buts and maybes* about my task made my burning eyes sting all that much more. I did not even have the strength to toss my shovel as I cursed Isis. I just fell to my knees and wept; though I could not even bemoan my quest for fear that Set might hear. So I wept for Egypt and the brother of my heart, Amenhotep. I still could not call him by his new name, Akhenaton.

"Fortunately, yet foolishly, as the wind around me suddenly increased in intensity, I began to enjoy the feel of it against my sunburned skin. When the sporadic blasts of wind became continuous, I realized too late what was happening...or should I say, what was coming.

"When I looked up, there was a wall of wind-driven sand coming straight for me. I barely had time to curl into a ball and wrap my cloak around me before the sandstorm battered down. I heard my camel yelp and knew it had deserted me to my fate, even though it too would not survive this storm. But it was of no matter to me then, as I realized I would soon be next.

"For hours the tempest sought to bury me in a sea of sand. When I could no longer hear the muffled roar of the wind, I began digging myself out of my tomb. And despite my earlier acceptance of impending death, I now struggled for life. I realized that no matter how dreadful my life was at that time, it was better than none at all.

"I made it out just in time to see the sun setting past the horizon. I barely had strength to brush the sand out of my face and shake it out of my robe. But now, to make matters even worse, the storm had altered the entire landscape!

"Whether from insanity or desperation, I ran as quickly as my aching, exhausted legs permitted. I knew I would never make it back to the village. I ran until my feet finally told me...*not one more step!* I collapsed and slept until the next morning.

"I was almost dead, but alive...and ready to accept my fate.

"And then I saw *something* twinkle.

"I thought it was a trick.

"I crawled to my knees with the finesse of a newborn calf. On my hands and knees, I moved toward the glint of light...*this sparkle.* And the brighter it shone, the more of my remaining strength I gathered until I was on my feet and stumbling toward it like a drunken man. The closer I came to this gleam of light, the better I could make out what it was.

"What I saw was the edge of the golden tome.

"I kneeled beside it. I did not care that it had absorbed heat from the sun's rays and burned my hands. On the contrary, I relished the searing pain.

"I cleared away the sand until I was able to open it and flip through its golden pages. The sight of the glorious symbols tickled me so, I laughed out to everyone and no one. I had found it! Finally found it!" Tamen sang. "But also, I had to think of anything but the tome, lest I alert Set. So I thought of water...my mother...even my sandals...anything to quiet my mind from thinking too much about the tome in front of me.

"But it was not the same tome which I had translated years ago. In front of me was the other—the greater of the two. But you see, I already had the primer from the first tome, which was all I needed. I began to do what had always been forbidden of me and chanted out loud. My dry, cracked lips bled when I moved them. But I inadvertently did something with those bloody lips that lessened my suffering.

"The first spell I chanted made the sun glow white and cool my feverish skin. With the next chant, I found the gods' mercy. At first I thought I had wet myself. When I looked under my knees, I saw water bubbling up from the sand itself! I hurried and chanted the phrase again and again, and made the water pool around me. Needless to say, I sang and drank, and sang and drank until I vomited—then sang and drank even more.

"Another chant brought wind down around me, and in the next moment, I felt it lifting my body in the air. When I rose too high to see the symbols I was chanting, I fell back to the ground. But there was not time to be mesmerized with the wonders of the chants, though the rush of power was intoxicating, I must say.

"I turned the pages and studied, deciphered and chanted these new symbols at random. In the process of trying to find what I did not know what I was really trying to find, I caused black clouds to form and rain to fall from them...drew fire from the sky with one chant and shook the ground with yet another. One spell brought small red and blue birds, which then disappeared into nothingness when I stopped chanting. On this page or that page, I read and sung...sung and read...each new line bestowing a new sight to my eyes.

"As I continued my search, I realized Lord Yikan had been so very wrong about this tome being undecipherable. Perhaps it had been to him, but to me there was a rhythm to these chants that were not as chaotic and unpredictable as those in the other tome. The markings on the end of each symbol gave each grouping of sounds a particular cadence the symbols in the other tome lacked.

"As I continued chanting, the sun's heat began to intensify. My skin soon became as hot as the gold leaf pages I was turning. Guessing it to be the work of the chant I was voicing, I stopped. The heat did not diminish, but increased.

Tamen stood and looked up. "I sang furiously now, Jared, hoping the next chant would quell the heat."

Jared looked up likewise. Tamen pointed in the sky—away from the sun—to an orb that was made of roiling fire with crimson, snake-like tendrils extending from it in all directions. But it was not some static ball of gas millions of miles away, but a sentient entity that pulsed, shrank and contracted upon itself that was hanging far too close to the earth's surface. The orb expanded, and from its center, a voice arose in an ear-numbing chant.

Tamen fell to his knees and screamed. Jared scampered away from him and ended up rolling halfway down the dune before coming to a halt. Lying prone, Jared raised his head and looked for Tamen, but heard his screams first.

Tamen's brown skin began to blacken, and then blister and bubble. As quickly, the fringes of his robe began to sear before they burst into flames. Tamen frantically patted at the flames, but they reappeared just as quickly as they were snuffed out. He screamed even more as his burning skin liquefied and began dripping onto the sand.

The orb ceased its screeching, but continued throbbing and spoke. "What has thou done?" it demanded, hovering no more than a few miles above.

"*Aton!*" Tamen whispered through swollen, charred lips. His body was still smoldering. His face and skin was unrecognizable through black crusted skin.

"How have thou come unto this place?" the orb asked, as it pulsed waves of fire that rippled through its circular body.

"The goddess...Isis," Tamen muttered.

The orb's thundering reply shook the ground, causing the entire landscape of sand to shift. "There is only one god and it is *I*...Aton —father of—of...*what is this?*"

A chant was being sung, but not from Tamen or the fire-orb. It was a soprano's voice that pierced the air. Next to Tamen's smoldering body, a figure appeared as a ghost and quickly solidified. She was svelte—her sheer, white dress hung from thin straps at the shoulders and boastfully showed her small breasts. Her hair was a map of pencil thin cornrows that extended past her narrow shoulders. But even more striking than her beauty, was that every inch of her skin appeared to be of solid gold.

"No, my Lord Set...you who pretend to be the god called Aton," she said, from plump golden lips, "you are not alone in your divinity. There are gods that live once more despite your trickery. And I —Isis, mother goddess, am one of them."

The orb swelled and crackled as though it was consuming rotted wood. Then for a brief moment the orb was silent...neither expanding nor contracting. And then without warning, it began chanting, and from its center, spewed a tornado of fire directly at Isis and Tamen.

Isis chanted in reply as the firestorm closed in on them. But whereas the orb's chant rose to a pitch than was humanly possible, hers was far deeper and guttural, like the roar of a lioness. From her mouth, a blizzard of snow and ice shot out and split the cy-

clone of fire into two, and harmlessly away from Tamen and herself. As the orb increased the pitch of its chant, fueling the fire to
grow even wider and hotter, so did Isis do the opposite, matching
her adversary's chant by singing lower and pulling the tempera-
ture down even further.

Both stopped abruptly, as if realizing the stalemate they had
come to.

"You cannot prevail," the orb asserted.

"No...I cannot. Not alone," Isis replied softly at first. "But too,
you cannot stand against us...**traitor!**"

Another chant howled from above the orb.

As it was with Isis, its chant was akin to a roar, bringing with it
ice and frigid winds. As the possessor of the chant grew closer, it
revealed it was far from human. From the neck down it was a
male's body swathed in a shenti-skirt. But its head and large black
eyes were all hawk. Blue, red and gold plumage covered its head
and extended down to its neck—it was a doppelganger of the god,
Amon-Ra.

The orb immediately responded with a chant of fire aimed at
Amon-Ra. But with its attention now diverted from below, Isis began chanting in a higher pitch, sending sand laden gusts of wind
toward the orb. Between sand and ice...one blast cooling the orb
and the other smothering it, the victory of tug of war between hot
and cold was given to the latter. The orb screamed and dropped
from the sky. When it crashed, it shook the desert floor and sizzled. Through the mist created by ice and fire, what had once been
the orb...the being Isis called Set who had been pretending to be
the god, Aton—was ultimately revealed. On his back, in a layer of
foot-thick ice with his arms stretched up to the sky was Lord
Yikan, his mouth frozen open in mid-chant.

"It is over, my son," Isis assured Tamen.

She sat next to him and cradled his charred head against her bo-
som. Amon-Ra—an amalgamation of man and hawk—came and

stood next to them. His black, bird eyes darted side-to-side as if seeking more prey. The feathers on Amon-Ra's face began melting away like wax held too close to a flame. His hawk's head shimmered and shrank, folding in on itself until a hairless, human one replaced it. What had been a beak became nostrils and a mouth. His avian eyes swirled away like water down a drain until they were simply human size, yet still so dark, no pupil was visible. And what was left of the hawk-god was but an old man with the flawless skin of a newborn.

"He will die soon if something is not done," Isis warned.

"Something?" Amon-Ra asked in a hearty baritone.

Isis gently laid Tamen's head on the sand and stood. "You know what I speak of...*Zoe'el.* Or must you shift your body back into the guise of Amon-Ra to understand me?"

Zoe'el motioned with his head at the frozen body of Lord Yikan. "Have we not learned our lesson about trusting humans? Hmm? I do not wish to be imprisoned again. The next time we may not be so fortunate."

"That was your mistake, not mine," she countered. "And you were human once too. We must consider the future and not the moment as we have done before. The tomb of ice will not hold Lord Yikan for long. I sense his mind struggling against our magic as we ourselves did when he imprisoned us in the sphinx. With the magic of another," she said and glanced at Tamen, "we will be assured Lord Yikan will never raise his voice again."

"And what if we create another god who takes the role far too literally again?" Zoe'el asked. "We...*I*...chose Lord Yikan to be the god Set in name only, not imprison us and go off and create an entire new religion for himself as the god Aton. You—Mala as the goddess Isis and I, as Amon-Ra, is plenty gods enough, no?"

"Do you really think Tamen would betray us?" she asked rhetorically. "We have watched him since he was a child...since he first chanted. His skills are beyond anything we have ever seen. Look how easily he deciphered the symbols in both tomes. Remember, Zoe'el, he not only stayed faithful to the old religion, but it is because of him that you are now free of Lord Yikan's prison. Tell me he is not your beloved above all other mortals."

Zoe'el grunted. "As I was yours."

Mala smirked.

"You assume just because you made me that you know me so well," Zoe'el snipped.

"I do!"

"I think not," he replied, and then returned her smile. He knelt on the other side of Tamen. "This gift we shall bestow is more than you have ever or could ever dream of."

Zoe'el began the chant of healing. As his words flowed out, Tamen's bunt skin began falling off in pieces and revealing smooth brown skin beneath. Mala moved her golden hands across his face, his torso and legs and removed the rest of the black crust from his new skin. From his toes to his head, every trace of burn was gone. The only evidence of trauma remaining was the burnt clothes he wore.

Tamen opened his eyes and inhaled sharply. "Praise be to Amon-Ra. I am forever your servant!"

"Let us not be too hasty, young priest," he responded. "You may regret those words yet. I am Zoe'el...that is my true name."

"Zoe'el was the vizier of Egypt," Tamen protested. "You—you are Amon-Ra."

Zoe'el looked at Mala and shook his head.

"My dear child," Mala cooed. "You will know these things very soon."

Zoe'el jutted in. "We offer you a life eternal. Into your hands we shall give you power beyond your imagination."

Mala cupped Tamen's face in her golden hands. "Do you wish to be a god?"

186 · ORLANDO SMART-POWELL

Tamen looked from one to the other. "A god? What do you mean become a god? Gods are born gods—not made."

"But they are made, Lord Tamen," Isis corrected. "Through the magic of the golden tomes we have become as we are...Zoe'el and I...*Amon-Ra and Isis.* There is no easy way to explain such things, for many of these secrets are still hidden from us as well. But I do know this. If ever there was one worthy enough to become a god, it is you."

"I—I would become as you?"

"No," Zoe'el answered. "No one has been able to unlock the secrets of this tome, until now...*until you!* You are gifted, Tamen. And you will become stronger than Mala, Lord Yikan and me."

"You have an innate gift of language as no other has had," Mala said. "But you know this already."

Tamen struggled to rise. Zoe'el reached down and effortlessly pulled him to his feet and steadied him with a hand at his waist. "I wish I could afford you the luxury of pondering this further, Tamen, but our time wanes," he warned. "Lord Yikan has been rendered helpless by my chant of ice, though even now he fights to be free."

"Indeed," Mala added. "We three were to be Egypt's gods. Though Lord Yikan, who we had agreed would take on the persona of the god, Set, had no intention of sharing power once he became immortal. He wanted to rule alone, thus he imprisoned us and created a new persona for himself—Aton—to trick Pharaoh. If freed, he will stop at nothing to become the one and only god of Egypt. If only we could strip him of his immortality."

"Indeed!" Zoe'el replied readily.

"So, my Lord Tamen. Are you ready to become a god?" Mala asked.

"Give up your mortal life for one that shall never end?" Zoe'el added. "We know of your love for Akhenaton, and even know that you refuse to call him by that name. But Egypt's welfare now hangs in the balance. With your added might, we can imprison Lord Yikan forever."

"If you deem me worthy, then I will do as asked," Tamen said to both Zoe'el and Mala.

"Then within the golden tome you shall find that which you need," Zoe'el told him.

"How will I know?"

"In this matter we cannot assist you," Zoe'el told him. "Though we are mighty in ways mortal man will never comprehend, there are limitations. To read the Chant of Changing from the sacred book with the eyes of a god is impossible. Though what chants we possess have been written in our minds and are ours to command except that one."

"All will become known to you," Mala added. She moved away from him. Zoe'el followed, but retreated to where Lord Yikan lay in his frozen tomb. He began chanting again and thickened the ice upon it. "When you begin, no matter what happens, do not stop," she urged, and then looked at Zoe'el.

"You must complete the spell," Zoe'el told him. "Mala and I are powerful. We would have been stronger yet had we completed our spells of changing. Lord Yikan nearly finished it, which gave him dominance over us. But even so, Tamen, we all chanted from the lesser of the two tomes, whereas you shall chant from the greater. And if you succeed where we all have failed—"

"You shall become mightier than us all," Mala added.

"Use your innate gifts, Lord Tamen," Zoe'el instructed. "Deconstruct the language within the tome and complete the spell. *Become a god of unimaginable power!*"

Tamen turned to Jared. "I sat there for hours going through each line of symbols and chanting them, and bringing about even more glorious wonders than I had before. With each wrong chant I voiced, Mala would shake her golden head and dismiss it with a wave of her hand. Zoe'el listened also, but was more focused on his task of keeping Lord Yikan imprisoned in ice.

"As I ventured further into the tome, it became increasingly harder to translate. For many hours I studied. Dusk had arrived when I finally came unto the passage, though I did not know I had at the time. These symbols were unlike any that I had ever seen before. They were far more difficult to pronounce. What I soon realized as I uttered these chants, was that I could feel them. My blood began itching and every cell of my being awakened. Even my tongue seemed to have caught fire.

The golden tome—opened to a page of calligraphic-like symbols and numbers—appeared in front of Tamen, who then sat down in front of it. He looked down at the pages and began chanting, slowly at first, and then quickened his pace. His skin began oozing a cloudy white sweat, which then turned brown and became thick like molasses. From every inch of his skin, including his feet and hands—even out of his ears—the viscous liquid oozed out and dripped on the sand beneath him. Tamen pulled off his burnt clothing as his body began to steam, though he never stuttered in chanting as he did.

"Do not stop, Tamen!" Mala yelled.

Like a fire had been lit inside of him and wanted out at all costs, his body began to glow. Tamen fell forward toward the tome and braced his fall with outstretched arms. His face was mere inches from the golden pages.

He chanted faster and faster until a ray of white light shot out of his skin like a beam of pure sunlight. And then Tamen yelled out in pain.

"Keep chanting!" Zoe'el cried.

Tamen screamed instead as another beam of light burst out from the center of his back. And then came another from the side of his head. His body quickly took the appearance a sieve draining beams of light. Mala and Zoe'el yelled at him to finish. Tamen, even if he heard them, seemed incapable of doing so, as his body suddenly outshined the brightest sun and his cries of pain spiraled higher and higher.

Then like a candle being snuffed out, the light was gone.

Mala walked over to Tamen and helped him rise to his feet. She cupped his face, which was without pores or even the faintest mar, and smoother than newborn flesh. She kissed his soft brown lips and then said, "Welcome to immortality!"

CHAPTER 12

Instead of being surrounded by miles of windswept sand, Tamen and Jared were now on a balcony looking down on thick-trunked, dark-leafed trees. Some of them, heavy with blood-red fruits and pink berries rose as high as the balcony itself. On the ground there were men and women carrying baskets brimming with breads, fish and fruits, while naked children zigzagged between them in play. Whereas the citizens of Egypt were of colors ranging from wool-white to coal-black, everyone in the garden below were either dark or darker-skinned, though were still dressed in traditional Egyptian breast-baring dresses and shenti-skirts.

In the middle of the courtyard, a young woman was filling her clay jar from one of the bubbling circular pools that were scattered throughout the oasis. She brushed back her waist-length braids and looked up at them. "The god has awakened!" she cried, and lost hold of her jar, which sank and disappeared into the water. She kneeled and bowed her head. The others nearby—children also—looked up at Tamen and then quickly did the same. First one voice rose up, followed by many repeating the same words over and over...'*Blessed be Horus—god in the Horizon. Blessed be Horus—god in the Horizon.*"

"They sing to you, my son," Mala said, from behind Tamen and Jared.

"Me? I truly am a..." Tamen began.

"God," she finished. Though no longer encased in gold as the incarnation of Isis, her flawless brown skin shimmered just as vibrantly. "To mortal man and woman...yes! You are a god in the truest sense as they know gods to be. To Zoe'el and me—no."

"Of course, thousands of questions were on my mind," Tamen said to Jared. "Everything I had ever accepted as being true was now teetering on the edge of oblivion." He faced Mala. "What of the true gods? I mean—the other gods of Egypt?"

Mala was silent for a moment, but kept her dark brown eyes on Tamen. "Dead...sleeping...perhaps they never existed at all. I cannot say what I do not know," she said. "I was born a mortal woman long before there was ever an empire known as Egypt, and I have never known a real god in the sense that you speak of."

"You—you are not Egyptian?"

"No," she replied. "I am from an island nation lost to time and a people departed from this earth more than two ages ago."

"Who are you then?"

Mala smiled, but then sighed. "There is so much for you to learn, godling. I will tell you as much as I know, which I fear will not be all that you wish or think you need to know. But first and foremost, you must realize this...we...you, Zoe'el, and I, *are* the gods of Egypt. Egypt's welfare is entrusted to us and us alone."

Mala pointed to the balcony and began chanting softly. As the notes fluttered from her brown lips, a breeze swept up and began flowing into the room, infusing the air with jasmine. "With your chants, you can make the ground move as water does. If you wish, you may fly through the heavens. And here, in the vast desert which is our home, you have the power to nurture the soil to give life where once there could never have been, and shield it from the eyes of those you wish not to see it.

"This," she continued, "is the beginning of your legacy. You are to protect, enrich and assure the survival of our people...*your people*...our Egypt! And when you have served them, they will build monuments in your honor. Kings will bow before you and call you father. Man will call out your name in praise. You shall take on the persona of *Horus*— a god of Egypt!"

Mala chanted again. This time, she brought sand-laden wind into the room and swirled it around Tamen's waist and formed a gold hemmed shenti. Around his ankles and wrists, the miniature sand storm swirled and settled into the form of gold and silver bracelets.

"There is much for you to understand about your new body and power of the chant. Though you did not finish the chant, you completed more of it than Zoe'el and I were able to with the lesser tome. You brim with a power I have never felt before," she told him. "We shall teach you to control it and bend it to your will. But first, there is one matter we must attend to."

"Lord Yikan," Tamen stated.

"Yes," she growled, like the goddess Isis she pretended to be. "Lord Yikan must be put to sleep forever. And once that is done, we must locate the other tome he has hidden from us."

Tamen stripped the illusion of the stone-brick room they were in of its cohesiveness. The walls became transparent and then disappeared all together. When the illusion settled, they were all back at the Giza Plateau in front of the Sphinx. Zoe'el was standing over Lord Yikan and the ice coffin imprisoning him.

Tamen peered into the casket of ice. Jared looked also. Lord Yikan's swirling blue eyes were wide-open. "How did all of this happen?" Tamen asked, daring to touch the ice and quickly pulling his hand back. Lord Yikan's eyes suddenly move to the right and fix squarely on Tamen, as though through two feet of ice, he had felt the touch.

"You thought him vanished into the night and never to be heard from again, no?" Zoe'el asked. Like Tamen, Zoe'el was completely hairless. Unlike Tamen, though, he was a foot shorter, and at least in mortal years, forty years older. "At my bidding, he chanted from your translation of the tome—the Chant of Changing—and became an immortal. He was to assume the persona of the god Set and complete our triad of gods."

"We thought Lord Yikan would wield his power responsibly," Mala said shaking her head.

"Which was a tragic mistake," Zoe'el cut in.

"Ah—so true," Mala agreed.

"He nearly succeeded had it not been for you," Zoe'el said. "We shall now give him what he sought to give us...an eternal prison."

Mala stood at the head of Lord Yikan's ice tomb and directed Tamen to stand opposite of Zoe'el on the other side. She was the first to begin the chant, quickly followed by Zoe'el and Tamen.

Lord Yikan's body began to glow a luminescent blue. His swirling eyes slowed their rotation and then stopped and reverted back to their normal dark-brown shade. Mala, Zoe'el and Tamen then changed their chant and slowed the cadence. Now, instead of looking down on Lord Yikan, this new chant allowed them to look through him, as though it had turned him into a ghost.

While Tamen and Zoe'el continued their chant, Mala changed hers and began rising from the ground, bringing Lord Yikan's blue, ghostly body with her until she reached the mouth of the Sphinx. "May the beast never awaken," she pronounced, and then pushed his translucent body into the Sphinx's mouth. The Sphinx began to shake and the ground along with it. A crack that rang out like thunder created a fissure that stretched from the top of the Sphinx's nose down, and all the way across the left nostril.

"With Lord Yikan imprisoned, Mala now had some godly lessons in store for me," Tamen said to Jared, as the image of Zoe'el faded away. "In those first few months, she taught me about this hairless new body of mine and how to control it. I no longer had organs, blood or any other fluid circulating within me. No knife, spear, fire, or as I later found out once man invented guns...virtually nothing could harm me. I no longer had to breathe if I willed it so, for I had no lungs. My only use for air was to provide a conductor for my voice, and this was made possible by just willing air to flow across my vocal cords.

"And strength!

"I possessed stamina, speed and physical might beyond what you are even capable of comprehending. I could lift boulders as if they were just hollow husks, or with a chant, simply levitate them. By thought alone, I could make my body move so fast, to mortals, it seemed as if I could disappear into thin air. And with my immortal eyes, I could see the smallest of creatures on the desert floor and hear it scrape along from miles away.

"Then of course there was the magic of the chant. Imprinted in my mind at the time of my creation were the symbols of the greater golden book I had deciphered. All I had to do was to think of whatever magic I wished to use and the sacred sounds would come to my mind as quickly as to my lips. As you know, I had already possessed some magic as a mortal...reading thoughts...creating illusions. But after becoming a god, my abilities increased a thousand fold.

"There was nothing, it seemed, I could not do. Fire...wind... earth...lightning...any effect of nature you can think of, I could command. I could reshape solid objects into whatever element I so desired. If I wanted gold, I could transform this sand beneath our feet into bullions. Diamonds? Rubies? Silver? It was never a question of how, but *how many?*

"Above all, flying was my favorite chant-spell. Truly there is nothing to compare to soaring through clouds alongside creatures that were born to fly. The three of us were as children at play when we flew. We chased and raced one another from dune to dune, and from one mountaintop to the next. The sky was our dominion.

"But there were limits to what we could do. Though we possessed the greater golden tome that created me, we could not locate the one Lord Yikan had hidden. But with Lord Yikan imprisoned, we assured ourselves the tome would remain lost to time. More importantly, what set us apart from a real god was that we could not create something from nothing. Therefore, we could not create life.

"I spent the greater portion of that first year at our palace that was hid from mortal sight in the desert between Nubia and Egypt. At the wishes of Zoe'el and Mala, I promised not to go back to Egypt until they had righted the wrongs that Lord Yikan had caused. I complied reluctantly at first. As you have probably guessed, Jared, I desperately wished to see my beloved Amenhotep.

"The time I spent with the three or so hundred mortals that lived with us waned my desire to see Amenhotep somewhat. You see, unlike the Egyptians who worshipped gods through idols, my new people—a sect of Nubians from the south—worshipped us far differently. As their gods, we walked amongst them. Celebrations were held in our honor and incense was burnt at the doorstep of our palace. If they wanted to pray to us, they had but to look up and see us in the flesh. I found out later that it was Mala who had discovered these people...refugees from an island nation long since sank to the bottom of a great ocean. And it was her magic that had created and obscured this magical kingdom of gardens and fresh water springs in this great desert of nowhere.

"While Zoe'el, assuming the persona of Amon-Ra, attended to the armies to reclaim lands lost during Amenhotep's rule, Mala restored the worship of the old gods by assuming the guise of Isis. To the most faithful, she appeared as a ghost or living statue, and instructed the priests in dreams and omens to turn back to the old ways.

Eventually, I could no longer suppress the yearning for my beloved. I think Mala and Zoe'el realized that sooner or later, I would have to return. Our last discussion on that matter is when I learned exactly why they had kept me from Egypt for so long.

"'Your Amenhotep, who calls himself Akhenaton, has gone mad!' Those were Mala's exact words.

"Lord Yikan had poisoned Amenhotep's mind against me and the old religion by casting a chant on him that neither Zoe'el nor Mala were successful in reversing. And with Lord Yikan posing as the god Aton no longer at his side and able to control his thoughts, Amenhotep had sunken into an abyss of despair, for the world no longer made sense to him. They had not even finished telling me such dreadful news before a chant of flight was upon my lips and I was on my way to Egypt. Mala and Zoe'el were airborne and beside me within moments, telling me that Amenhotep's mind was so lost, he did not even recognize his own wife, Nefertiti, or his children. But I rebuked them.

"I flew to the palace in Tell el-Armana. All the while, I could hear Mala in my head pleading with me to turn back. I shut her out, for all I could think about was Amenhotep being strangled by insanity. All that mattered to me in that moment was my beloved brother."

The desert landscape began blurring away. When the illusion stopped warping and became solid again, Tamen was sitting next to Amenhotep, who was strapped down on his bed, and Jared, outside the mosquito netting looking on. The room was thick with the essence myrrh, frankincense and feces.

Jared looked closer at Amenhotep's loincloth clad body, which looked like a skeleton wrapped in papier-mâché. Amenhotep's stomach, which had always been quite round and full, was sunken so much that his ribcage was now the highest point of his torso. His brown skin was an ocean of dark purple and red weeping lesions.

Amenhotep's eyelids fluttered and struggled open. He looked at Tamen and then quickly closed them. "Not you again," Amenhotep whispered.

"You see me?"

"Of course," he groaned. "You come to me every night and haunt my dreams."

"This is no dream," Tamen assured him. "I am real...I am flesh...I am whole...and I am here!"

Amenhotep raised his head as far as the restraints about his arms and legs allowed and looked at him. He flopped back down and laughed. "Spirit...you are most devilish tonight. Why the change of heart? Have you finished with me finally? May I now die in peace?"

"I will not let you die, brother."

"*Ahhh*...that is more like you," he sneered. "Perhaps when I am in the afterlife, I will be beyond your grasp. Torment me while you can, demon."

"My brother." Tamen took hold of Amenhotep's skeletal hand. "Ask of me what you will and I shall give it to you. I *will* prove my love."

"Very well," he uttered, "I will disprove *you*. Take us back to when we were drunk with happiness. I no longer wish to know of this time when I soil myself. Make it like it used to be before I drove you—brother of my heart—away."

"Ahhh..." Tamen bowed his head. "What he asked for brought back such painful memories, Jared. During those long years without him by my side, our past was the only thing keeping me alive. So, I brought back what we once had in an illusion.

"I made the past so real to him, there was no doubt in his mind that he was actually living and breathing in that long ago time. I made the night air moist as it was when I tutored him in the gardens. In the pool, I showed him how we played, bathe and laid about lazily singing songs of the gods. On I went with the illusions —giving him only those that gave him joy and none that hinted of sorrow.

"Believe me, I wanted the illusions to be as real as much as he did. *I still do.*

"When I let the illusion fade away, for a long moment he did not breathe. Finally, after a long sigh, he looked at me and smiled. I knew then, Jared. I knew. In his thoughts, I saw that he was ready and wanted to die. My chants can heal sicknesses, but not the soul. And without a soul, what is left?

"I can feel you in my thoughts," Amenhotep whispered.

"But I cannot do as you ask," Tamen replied.

"Would you have me here only to suffer?" Amenhotep asked. "Priests wipe drool from my mouth and clean my soiled sheets. They pray to gods I forsook for Aton, who has now forsaken me. There is nothing left of me but rot."

"I will love you forever, my brother," Tamen whispered and then kissed him.

"And I you," Amenhotep said. "I promise. I promise I will wait for you in the Great Marsh."

"I could not cry," Tamen whispered, as the vision of Amenhotep faded. "Once I stopped his heart and closed his eyes, I had no more tears left to shed. So I took to the sky, soaring higher than I ever had before. With a chant, I turned the clear midnight heavens in upon themselves and made them weep for me—*but with a fury.* With lighting I drew forth from the sky, I shook the whole of southern Egypt that night. I was mad with grief! And my storm chant was a symphony of pain that still to this day is as raw as it was then.

66666666

"I was so far up, I could no longer see the ground. Unbeknownst to me, as I was consumed with despair, flash floods washed away villages...lighting strikes reduced pylons and obelisks to rubble. Countless grain fields were flattened and market stands flung through the air for miles. The destruction caused by the desert hurricane I conjured was phenomenal to say the least, and it took months thereafter to repair the damage. But still, so very unaware and uncaring of the devastation I was causing, I flew even faster and chanted with reckless abandon, and was unaware that Mala and Zoe'el were approaching me.

"Zoe'el grabbed me from behind. With strength and dexterity I did not realize I possessed, I twisted away from him and sent him hurtling down into the black clouds below us. Mala, however, was not so easily dispatched. Her grip was far stronger than Zoe'el's, yet that proved not to be her greatest weapon. Her voice was warmed honey. She pleaded with me with such warmth that it gave me pause, and with my guard momentarily down, she cast a sleeping chant upon me that was so beautiful, I thought it was my mother's lullaby.

'Sing with me, my child,' she cooed.

"And I did. I wanted the pain gone. I wanted to feel safe.

"As I drifted off to sleep, she held me in her arms and brought her face next to mine. 'Go now, sweet godling,' I remember her saying. 'When you awake, I shall be here waiting for you.'

* * *

"Amenhotep's burial chamber was hastily put together. His hieroglyphs told lies of his successful conversion of the Egyptian religion from many gods to that of Aton. On the other walls of his tomb were portraits of his children and his now despised queen, Nefertiti, who was not long after his death, deposed of. The line of pharaohs of the house Armana eventually went to Smenkhkare, but most importantly and recognizably to Tutankhamen, the last pharaoh of Amenhotep's line.

"I spent days in Amenhotep's burial chamber torturing myself with his memory. Neither Mala nor Zoe'el ever spoke of Amenhotep again to me. It was I who went to Mala after many months of mourning and told her I was now ready to take my place among the Pesedjet...our council of gods.

"With Amenhotep dead and the old gods revived under Tutankhamen, the grandest of all temples once more belonged to Amon-Ra, and it was indeed magnificent...Zoe'el would have his alter-ego worshipped no other way. Fifty, two-story statues of Amon-Ra were constructed around his main temple. Inside, Zoe'el enchanted the gardens to grow alien plants and trees that bore fruits no Egyptian had ever seen.

"At my temple, for the god Horus I impersonated, on either side of the gate was the image of my god-self embodied as a man with the head of a falcon. My priests bathed my statue daily and anointed it with warmed frankincense and jasmine oils before clothing it. I was enthralled at being worshipped. You have no idea what it is like to possess godly powers, Jared, and then to hear them call out your name in prayer.

'With but a word from you and it shall be done,' Mala told me. If my image was not majestic enough, I had but to command it to be so and my priests would fulfill my wishes. If my altar did not have enough jewels, more would be brought at my command.

"In the following months, I learned how to conduct the affairs of my temple by watching Mala in hers. There was a time when there was need to converse with priests in dreams and visions, and other times, for a more lasting and dramatic effect, to animate my stone idol and speak to them directly.

"At our desert place, during all hours of the day and night—as we required no sleep—we debated the politics of Egypt, and agreed and disagreed until we came to a consensus on how much influence was needed and where. Zoe'el, ever the warlord, kept his focus on the royal court and army, which provided wealth for the nation.

"Mala—as Isis, the mother figure of gods and man—nurtured their souls and provided comfort when prayed to. It was not always the beckoning of our priests that deserved our attention, but the thousands upon thousands of simple prayers that needed the most attending to. She showed me how to listen for prayers called out in my name and how to help those I deemed worthy.

"It was truly amazing to hear what people prayed about. Money —not surprisingly was the most appealed for. Others asked for vengeance or power over others, or sickness to afflict their enemies. But to hear the prayers of a child is to hear the sweetest and most unselfish of all sounds ever uttered by mankind.

"But remember what I said before, Jared. There were limitations. It was impossible to know of every single event that occurred or was thought of by the mortal mind. We were far from omnipotent and omnipresent beings. Though we never admitted it to each other, we were still far more human than divine. We made many tragic mistakes, such as that with the boy pharaoh, Tutankhamen.

"While overseeing the royal court, Zoe'el entrusted Tutankhamen's welfare into the hands of one of his advisors, Lord Ay, and bestowed upon him sacred chants. Only now in your present day are you beginning to suspect what we of the past know to be true. Lord Ay was responsible for Tutankhamen's death. Zoe'el had already read Lord Ay's thoughts, but found nothing that raised his suspicion. But Zoe'el, you see, was the weakest of the three of us and failed to detect Lord Ay's true ambition. After Tutankhamen suffered a head injury falling off his horse, Lord Ay used the healing chant Zoe'el gave him in reverse, causing the seemingly minor wound to become infected, thus killing him. Lord Ay thought himself so very clever, though he did not realize that what he had done would eventually become known and raise Zoe'el's wrath.

"In order to maintain peace in the land, Zoe'el allowed Lord Ay to reign as pharaoh and did not molest him even when he took Tutankhamen's widow, Ankhesenamen, for his wife. But once we three gods of Egypt settled on who should replace Lord Ay as pharaoh, Zoe'el unleashed his revenge. In the end, Zoe'el made Lord Ay's bones so brittle, they snapped under his own weight. Zoe'el blinded him for weeks, and then haunted him with visions of the demons—*Those Who Walk with Their Heads on Backwards*—awake and while he dreamt. Lord Ay prayed to Amon-Ra to release him from life, but was denied for months. Even when he attempted to cut his wrists and drink poison, Zoe'el was there to foil each attempt. When Zoe'el finally burst each of his organs one at a time, I do not think Lord Ay's mind was still intact.

"Out of love for Tutankhamen, Zoe'el hid his tomb well, as tomb raiders were so aplenty in the land, even we could not keep track of them. But you know very well what happened anyway...how James Carter stumbled upon Tutankhamen's tomb, and to this day, its riches are still displayed the world over.

"And no, before you even ask. I had nothing to do with the so-called *curse of the mummy* nonsense that befell those who disturbed his tomb. I was many, many miles from Egypt by then and had no care about mortals and their quests to rediscover the past I had already lived. As I have said to you many times, Jared, nothing of this world endures forever...not even Egypt. But that brings me to Egypt's downfall, which occurred after an age of peace and prosperity.

"It all began with the Hebrew slave, Joseph, who was sold into Egyptian bondage by his own brothers. But his brothers sent Egypt not only a boy, but a boy who brought with him the powerful magic of a new and powerful deity...*Yahweh.* Mala, Zoe'el and I were aware of other variations of chant-magic practiced in different countries, and heard rumors of other gods who could grant such gifts to their followers. But the magic of the Hebrew Joseph and his God, Yahweh, was something we were utterly unprepared for.

"Joseph interpreted the dreams of the pharaoh that we could not, and foretold of a time of drought and famine that would last for seven years, but before that, a period of seven bountiful years. I tell you now, as powerful as we were...even with our combined chants, we could not make a drop of rain fall from the sky during that period of drought. The land itself seemed poisoned and resisted our most focused magic to make any vegetation grow upon it.

"It was this indignity by the Hebrew God that angered us, so that after the population of Hebrews swelled after surviving the great famine, and once Joseph, who was then known by his Egyptian name, Zaphenath-Paneah, had died, we enslaved all of the Hebrews. For many years, as the power of our chant returned, we enacted our vengeance upon the Hebrews and their God so as to leave no doubt that the gods of Egypt were all-powerful. The name of Egypt was once more feared throughout the world.

"Ashamed as I am to admit it...at Zoe'el and Mala's urging, I too agreed to the *dark deed*...the slaughter of Hebrew male infants to decimate their resolve and hopes of ever being free. But there was one more reason why I did not object to such a horrid and vile act. It was to slap the face of this Hebrew God, Yahweh, who I loathed most of all.

"But do not think that we were gods without mercy. We did allow one Hebrew child to live.

"Thermuthis, daughter of Pharaoh Seti, had been remiss in her worship to Isis in the eyes of Mala, and by her chants, was rendered barren. But in the months before the slaughter of the Hebrew male infants, Thermuthis paid great homage to the goddess and thus convinced Mala, as Isis, to give her a child. But...

"...Mala had already vowed that Thermuthis shall never give life from her womb and was not willingly to go back on her own holy word. So, when the Hebrew Jochebed sought to save her infant son from the great slaughter and placed him upon waters in a reed basket, Mala saw her chance to answer the prayers of the princess by giving her a child without going back on her promise. She guided the child in that basket along the water to the palace and right into the arms of Thermuthis as she bathed that evening.

"Wait—wait—wait—you've got to be freakin' joking," Jared sputtered. He sat down on the bed that Amenhotep's illusionary body had been tied to. "You can't be saying that..."

Tamen smiled and then sat beside him. "Ah...my child. I said we had the power of gods—not their wisdom. But more importantly, remember—I have lived for thousands of years and have seen and met people you have only read about. This is no different."

Jared stared off unbelieving at the wall of the palace bedroom. "The Exodus? Are you serious?"

Tamen nodded his head. "Mosheh...or Moses as you know him, was always a most conflicted child and even more so as a young man. We gods thought it because of his Hebrew lineage and nothing more. When he killed an Egyptian guard to save the life of a Hebrew slave, we felt that when he went into exile, it was all for the best. There was just something about Hebrew mortals and their undying loyalty to their God that just could not be bred out of them. Mosheh was just another example of such impenetrable fortitude.

"To our surprise...*and despair*...Mosheh returned as Moses, and brought the dreadful magic of the Hebrew God with him. Why... for over four hundred years we held these Hebrews in bondage without this Yahweh using his magic to free them. We even laughed when Moses demanded the release of the Hebrews. How dare this man who we made a prince of Egypt come to us in shepherd's clothing and make demands of our pharaoh, Ramses...and by proxy, of us, the gods of Egypt! The past assault on our empire by this Hebrew God only strengthened our resolve.

"But in our defiance to Yahweh, we drew down upon Egypt the ten fabled plagues and were humbled once more.

"Just as before, our chant-magic was rendered impotent by Yahweh. All of the work done since the death of Amenhotep and Joseph at restoring Egypt to its former greatness began crumbling before our eyes. Our fields were devastated by swarms of locusts, and those that were not, were scorched by fiery hail sent from the sky. Our waters were poisoned with blood and boils were a scourge upon the flesh of man. The most powerful spells we chanted could not bring back light when darkness fell upon us for three days. Only in our desert palace, far from Egypt, did our magic still hold sway.

"In Egypt, our people and priests began to forsake our temples. When they cried out our names, it was no longer in praise, but laced in curses. Ramses was forced to pull most of his troops from occupying foreign lands to keep rioting and looting to a minimum. Reports of anarchy from principalities poured in as public sentiment toward releasing the Hebrews grew louder with each plague.

"I went to see this Moses...this leader of the Hebrews to measure what sort of man we faced who commanded such powerful magic from his God. But I wanted more than that. I wanted to take his life!

"So easy...right, Jared?" Tamen held out his hands. "I have crumbled brick and stone to dust with these. I could take his life easily, no?"

Tamen stood up. Next to him, a figure of a man in a ratted, gray robe began to coalesce as the palace bedroom faded away and was replaced with a sea of sand. Jared hopped to his feet just before the bed he sat on vanished.

"Around this Moses was a force like lightning," Tamen said as the sun above them dropped unnaturally quick behind the horizon and a sliver of a moon appeared in its place. "The closer I came to him, the greater the energy became. To an eternal such as me, to feel this burn upon my skin gave me pause and made me feel *fear*.

"Hidden from mortal sight, I followed him one night as he walked into the desert to pray alone. When done, as he made his way back to the slave village, he turned and began walking toward me. I stepped to the side to let him pass, but again he moved in my direction. I realized that despite my illusion of invisibility, he could see me!

The Moses illusion next to Tamen came alive and looked at him. "Your sorcery cannot hide you from the all seeing light of *I Am*. Why do y-you follow me?"

"I wish to know you, Mosheh," Tamen said to him. "We—the gods of Egypt—made you a prince, but now you are our scourge."

"*I Am's* command is that my people shall walk free from this un-holy land rife with sorcery and idol gods," Moses replied. "Egypt h-has been built with the blood of my people for far too long. Its d-days of greatness are at an end."

"What breed of god is your master?" Tamen asked. "What great magic lays at his disposal to make fools of the gods of Egypt? I wish to see this creature, so that I may speak with him...face-to-face...god-to-god."

Moses looked up to the heavens. "If you wish to speak to *I Am*, speak now, for *I Am* hears every whisper. Or do not speak...*I Am* has already seen what is in your heart of hearts."

"It is my wish to see him in the flesh."

"Then you will surely die, you creature of a-a-bomination," Moses promised. "Be you man or sorcerer, no one may look into the face of the one who is the creator and live. Be gone from me! There is no more to say, and more that is yet to come."

"Then Hebrew blood shall be spilt before all is done...Moses of the Hebrews," Tamen vowed. "You seek to persuade pharaoh to re-lease your people, but you have succeeded only in arousing the wrath of the mighty gods he serves. Yahweh's insults upon our blessed land shall not go unanswered."

Moses pulled his tattered robe up and secured it on his shoulders. "So be it then," he said softly, and began walking away with staff in hand, fading away as he did.

"According to the Bible, Jared, you have learned that Yahweh hardened Ramses' heart," Tamen said. "That is untrue. It was Zoe'el's doing, as well as convincing Ramses to annihilate every firstborn of the Hebrew slaves. But again, as you know now, that did not come to pass.

"That night, a powerful presence came unto the land of Egypt. We gods followed its energy trail like bloodhounds, but it moved so swiftly, we were unable to catch it in the act as it performed its dastardly deed. It stole the lives of every firstborn child in Egypt that night.

"The farther north we went, the stronger the being's presence became to our senses. We flew at speeds that swept up sand from the ground in our wake as we followed this *thief of life*. Below us was a symphony of wailing, our people begging us to return life to their loved ones, which fueled our anger even more. Even gentle Mala quickly acquired a taste for Hebrew blood.

"Our sole objective was to confront and destroy this murderer who moved swifter than the wind.

"We traced this entity's energy trail to the palace. From the skies above, I saw rage and despair turn Thebes into a sea of fire as people took to the streets with torches. Riots soon swept over the entire city.

"We entered from the top of the palace. Mala and I immediately sought out the crown prince, who was still but a child. Zoe'el went in the opposite direction, where the greatest source of energy was emanating to confront the entity head on.

The desert illusion swirled around Tamen and Jared. When the sand blew away, it revealed an expansive bedchamber. Cowering by the open balcony was a small clan of girls and boys, and women with their arms around them. A bare-chested man was in front of them with a sword in one hand and a dagger in the other, both of which shook from his quivering muscles.

"There stands Ramses ready to face death to save his son," Tamen said pointing to the man.

Mala materialized next to Tamen in the guise of the gold-skinned Isis. The children and women screamed at her sudden appearance. "Fear me not," she said to them. "Mother Isis has come unto thee to stay the hand of a great evil come amongst us."

"Say it is the Hebrew God, goddess," Ramses demanded. "Tell me this is so, for I am ready to slay this foul beast."

"Your sword is of no use against what lurks in the palace, Pharaoh," Mala said. She turned and faced the wooden double doors. "Now is a time for gods to battle gods! But know that I shall not fight alone."

Tamen stepped away from Jared. As he walked over and stood by Mala, his bald head began enlarging and sprouting feathers, just as his nose and mouth melded into one and formed a yellow beak. His dark brown eyes tripled in size and became as black as onyx. The women and children again screamed their fright, while Ramses nearly tripped over his own legs to put distance between him and the falcon-headed god he worshipped as Horus.

Tamen looked at Mala for a lingering moment and then faced the door as Zoe'el's voice became audible in the form of a chant. The stone floor suddenly heaved and fell...then swayed from one side to the other before cracking in the center. And then there was silence.

Suddenly, an unnatural scream pierced the momentary calm. The women and children buried their heads in their arms to try and block it out. Ramses dropped his sword and dagger, and covered his ears.

The walls began to shake. And then a howl erupted, right before a brilliant white light shot through the sides, top, bottom and even the smallest crack between the door and its frame. The light stayed for mere seconds and then faded away.

Mala grasped Tamen's hand, but kept her eyes on the door. "Zoe'el," she muttered.

"He is no more," Tamen acknowledged. "I felt it too!"

They did not even have time to come to terms with Zoe'el having been slain when a static charge began floating through the room. Everything made of cloth—sheets, rugs, and even Jared's front and back flap on his loincloth—suddenly adhered together.

Mala rushed to the door and leaned on it with her golden hands. She looked back at Tamen. "Take the crown prince and fly!" she screamed.

Before Tamen could move, the guards outside the room began screaming like children. Swords clanging on the floor were heard next, followed by the muffled sound of their lifeless flesh dropping on the cold stone floor.

Next, a hand the size of a man's chest glowing an incandescent blue passed through the door. Its other hand that followed carried a sword that shone of the same blue-white light. It passed its entire nude and genderless body through the door and stood easily twice the height of Mala who stared incredulously at it. And it looked back at her with its glowing red eyes that were more like two pieces of coal just taken out of a fire.

Tamen ran over to the women and children, and snatched the child-prince from the queen's arms. In the next moment, Mala released a fire chant at the creature that flowed straight out of her golden mouth. The flames split into two before it could even touch the blue-white being.

Mala backed away, though chanted as she looked up at the ceiling. The slabs of rock that were the ceiling began shaking. When the creature took a step forward, Mala screamed at the ceiling, which broke apart and came crashing down. The chariot-sized slabs of stone fell upon the creature, but that was all they did, as the being failed to even flinch as the stones bounced off of it and crashed to the floor.

It charged forward and grabbed Mala by the waist and raised her up to its red eyes. It turned her around and then over, as though stupefied as to what manner of being she was. Mala pounded at it with her fists...the force of her blows rattling the wall and shaking the floor. Still, the creature remained unmoved...even unimpressed.

Jared ran and huddled in a corner away from the women and children. Though as he squeezed his six-foot plus frame into the wedge, he fell back and landed on warm sand. When he looked up, the illusion of the palace chamber was fading and giving way to a night sky. All around him was sand, though in the distance he could see the city of Thebes alight in flames.

"Tamen!" Jared called out. He put his hands to his mouth and shouted again. "Tamen! Where are you?" He turned around, but found only desert. When he spun back to face Thebes, a bright light flashed from the city up into the sky momentarily. And then, closer to him, a figure in the sky caught his eye. He squinted at it, but couldn't quite make out what was speeding in his direction. But then, from a clear night sky, lightning arced out and struck it, and sent it hurtling directly for him. He jumped just as it crashed mere feet from him.

Jared rolled and then turned over. He stood up and hesitantly walked over to where the impact—which created a small smoking crater—had occurred. He waved the white smoke away as he peeked in. "Tamen?" he whispered cautiously.

Tamen stood up in the crater. The crown prince was unconscious and cradled in his arms, seemingly unhurt. Tamen, however, was smoldering. His face was blackened on one side, as well as his arms and legs. "I fled as fast as my chants could speed me away,"

Tamen told him, "but the creature was swifter and attacked me from the sky with lightning."

The electric charge they had felt in the palace began growing around them again. The air sizzled like animal fat in a hot pan. Tamen, still holding the child, and Jared both turned in the direction of Thebes and saw the creature, glowing blue-white, flying directly toward them.

"Run Tamen," Jared cried.

Tamen looked at him. "Dear child...my fight was over. I could barely speak, let alone chant after I was felled from the sky. And if I could have mounted some type of defense against this creature, it would have all been for naught. What the creature demanded that night from the first-born children of Egypt—their lives—it received.

The creature came to halt in front of Tamen. It pointed a blue finger at the child in his arms, who then sighed long...sighed heavily...and then sighed no more. "You may take the child back to Ramses, if you wish. My task this night is over," the creature said, with a voice that was like two...one alto...one baritone...male and female, but spoken as one.

"Murderer!" Tamen cried at it.

It cocked its head to the side as though it didn't understand Tamen's words. "Retribution," it replied.

"The child was innocent," Tamen countered. "You punish the child for sins of his father. I pity your people, for they worship an evil God who is without mercy!"

"I am no more a god than you are," the creature said. "I am but the wielder of the law. This night of so terrible nights, I have been given dominance over man and *creature* that cannot be denied by any. It was by Ramses' own mouth that death has visited the first born of Egypt. Thou cannot fault the Lord thy God, whose name is sacred and *forbidden*."

"Yahweh! I curse the name of Yahweh. He is no God of mine!" Tamen bellowed.

"When Ramses refused to bend his knee, God crushed it," the creature said. "Ramses will release the children of God and they shall flee from this unholy place of bondage."

"Take them then," Tamen spat. "It shall be the greatest blessing to my people that we are rid of you and your filth...*and your God*."

"Such an arrogant creature for one who knows not what you *truly* are!' the creature said as it disappeared.

Tamen walked over to Jared. His blackened face, arms and legs shimmered and regained their smooth brown complexion. "I was prepared to die that night," he said. "Instead, I was carrying this dead child in my arms back to Thebes and realizing how very alone I was now. Inside the palace where Mala and Zoe'el fought so valiantly, there was no sign they had ever existed. They were now but a memory in my eternal mind."

Tamen turned away from Jared and extended his arms, which bore the dead child. As he did so, a stone table appeared before him, which he laid the child on. The desert illusion began to waver. The sun sprang up to the east of them as walls began to form around them and block out some of the light, save that coming through windows at the top of the throne room, which the illusion finally settled into. The figure of Ramses—blood crusted along his temple—appeared on the opposite side of the stone table where his son lay dead.

"For thousands of years the gods have safeguarded Egypt,' Ramses said to Tamen as his figure animated. "Yet before my eyes, the all-powerful gods of Egypt are felled by the God of slaves? Have I not done everything you have ever asked of me? Given you temples filled with jewels...gold...silver? Raised thousands of statues in praise to you throughout the land and beyond? Obeyed all of your laws?"

"This power their God possesses is far greater than ours," Tamen replied remorsefully.

Ramses struck the stone table with his fists. "There are no gods more powerful than those of Egypt!" he cried. "Is that not what you have always told us? Slay the first born of each Hebrew and I shall protect you and rise you up above all is what Amon-Ra himself promised. Now my son, and every first born of Egypt are laid down into the hands of death."

"Then he is in the company of gods, for they too have fallen into death," Tamen informed.

Ramses' mouth gaped open. "A god dead? Impossible!"

"I assure you they are."

"Is this the Hebrew God's final insult?" Ramses bellowed throughout the empty hall. "Our funerary priests are inundated with bodies...the land is scorched and the people starving. Children have been murdered in their bed by a demon god. Now our gods are dying? Has the world gone mad?"

"It is done, Ramses!" Tamen snapped. "The Hebrews will leave our land and take their God with them. The curse shall then be lifted. And in time, Egypt shall rise again."

Ramses' swarthy faced darkened even more. "No! They shall not escape while Egypt lies in ruin."

"You have released them. Already they flee our lands."

"Then they are fleeing into the hands of death," Ramses growled. "I have given the order for what is left of my armies to prepare for our final battle and strike down *every* Hebrew where they stand—man, woman and infant. I have only given the slaves comfort in thinking they have won the war."

"Have you learned nothing?" Tamen roared and shook the walls of the hall. "Call their God whatever you will...a God of the desert or God of slaves—this power he commands is too great."

"The murder of my child demands Hebrew blood be spilt," Ramses countered.

"Then there will be two royal burials."

"God? You are no god!" Ramses spat. "You—Horus in the Horizon—have no fire in his *ka-spirit*. You come with head down bearing my dead child and tell me of the loss of Isis and of the creator father, Amon-Ra. Shall we run off into the desert and find the Hebrews so that we may bow before them also? Shall the great god Horus lick the sandals of Mosheh the—"

Tamen reached over the stone table and grasped Ramses by the neck before he could finish. "You speak as though I could not crush your throat right here and now," Tamen droned.

Ramses smirked. "Oh, my beloved god...there is still a fire within you."

"And one that will consume you, have you not a care."

"Do not punish those who love and worship you," he said. "I and my father, and my father's father have worshipped you with undying loyalty since the world was formed. Avenge them—you who are the god of the setting sun. Be with us in battle, even if *we all* shall die...*be...with...us!*"

Tamen released his hold on Ramses neck. "Send word to your soldiers that we shall fall upon the Hebrews in seven days time. Have them know that they go to sacrifice themselves. But assure them, they will not die in battle alone...for I...Horus in the Horizon, shall be amongst them."

Tamen began chanting. At the ceiling above, dark clouds began gathering from out of the still air. Lightning flashed within the rumbling black cloud before one bolt, shaped like a trident, came straight down upon him.

Jared covered his eyes as the blinding, but benign white light flashed. When he looked up and around, he found a sea of water bordered on his left, and on his right, miles of rock-strewn desert. And in the distance he saw figures of people and carts drawn by beasts of burden...young men and children herding grass grazing sheep and goats wavering into the false reality of the illusion.

"On the seventh day I devised a chant I wagered that the Hebrews, even with the power of their God could not escape from," Tamen said, as he coalesced out of the air next to Jared. "Though I feared the return of the menace that killed Mala and Zoe'el, and knew I would not survive another meeting against it, I needed only two things to satisfy me...two Hebrew deaths...one for Mala and Zoe'el each.

"As the Hebrews approached the waters, I hovered above the bank of the Red Sea behind us. First, I called forth a storm rolling with black clouds and winds strong enough to uproot the heartiest of trees," Tamen said, just as dark clouds began forming above. "Upon the sea, I cast one of my most grand and awe inspiring chants. I created a feat of wonder that would be written, studied and disputed for thousands of years to come. I brought forth a great deluge of water to make the sea impassable except by vessel, and forever changed the structure of the basin itself as I deepened and widened it even further." Tamen moved behind Jared, encircled his waist and looked down at him from the side. "Into the heavens we go," he said, as they began to rise in the air.

Jared closed his eyes at first. When he opened them and looked down, he saw thousands of Hebrews at the sea's swollen embankment below. A few miles behind the Hebrews, a wall of sand stirred up by Pharaoh's chariots announced their impending arrival.

Jared's teeth suddenly began chattering. He tilted his head back and looked up at Tamen. "That thing is back. I can feel it."

"Ah, yes," Tamen said, as the air around them began to crackle with electricity. "I expected at any moment to meet the same fate as Mala and Zoe'el. So I struck at the Hebrews before the creature could strike me."

Tamen raised his head and chanted into the sky. From a black cloud rolling in on itself above, a fire erupted within. In moments, a funnel formed and shot out a pylon-wide tornado of red and black fire toward the Hebrews below. But in the sky above, the heavens opened up, as though the dark clouds were but a piece of fabric that some unseen hand had ripped down the middle. Past the gaping gash of space and time, thousands...hundreds of thousands of creatures—circular in form like chariot wheels—that were both horrifying and beautiful rushed out. Within each was a circle of light upon a circle of light spinning opposite of the one that preceded it. In their center, eyes without lids stared out...four...eight...twenty...some had more than fifty. Though symbolic in form, they were sentient and sang in a sharper, crisper soprano that was possible with a human voice. It was a chant of the purest notes they sung in unison as they swept down upon the fiery tornado—The Pillar of Fire—fully encircling it so that not one flame escaped, and rendered it harmless to the Hebrews it was meant to incinerate.

"And then they came," Tamen announced to Jared, drawing his attention back to the fissure in the sky as thousands of glowing blue-white beings began pouring out and flying toward the sea. They were akin to the one that had taken the lives of the Egyptian firstborns—giant in stature and glowing white blue, hot and cold, male and female all at once. Each of these nude, genderless beings was more beautiful than the one that preceded it.

The creatures dove into the sea. Half of them pushed the waters to the right, and the other half to the left. They were so swift in separating the waters into two, to Jared, it seemed as though the sea was pulled apart from its center.

The creatures stacked themselves upon and in front of one another until they were twenty deep and five thousand high on both sides, and not one drop of water passed between them. With the sea separated and a swath of dry land leading to the other side, the Hebrews began swarming through the seafloor passage. The illusion of Hebrew bodies blurred as they quickly moved from one side of the sea to the safety of the other.

When but a few thousand Hebrews were still left on the sea floor and scurrying toward the shore, the wheel-like beings with eyes swooped back into the cleft in the sky from whence they had come, taking the Pillar of Fire with them. The Egyptian army immediately gave chase and drove their chariots into the gap separating the sea.

Ramses and a thousand or so of his troops did not pursue, but waited...and stared in awe at the great and gaping sea before them. When the last Hebrew made it to the other side, the giant beings holding back the sea began leaving and returning back into the fissure in the sky. As they did, water began pouring over the creatures that had been on the very top of their structure of bodies. And when the others who were in front began to leave also, water started streaming, and then poured out in an inescapable deluge as the dams that had been made on either side were no more. Within moments after the sea crashed back together in a thunderous blow that shook the heavens, bodies—soldiers and horses—could be seen floating in the water before they sank once and for all into the dark waters that was now their graves.

"Perhaps that is the saddest part of this tale—this final blow to Egypt," Tamen said to Jared as he began changing the illusion.

They went from floating upon thin air to standing on a solid stone floor. Walls formed around them and a ceiling the height of a pylon materialized overhead. The stone hall the illusion settled into was narrow and stretched on for hundreds of yards.

"At this point, Jared, the tale becomes no less strange, but even more so," Tamen told him. "I never returned to Egypt after my defeat at the Red Sea. I could not bear to face my people. I was their god who was not a god. And I had failed them miserably.

"I returned to our desert palace. My Nubian people celebrated my return, yet they had no idea what had occurred in Egypt, nor to Mala and Zoe'el. Perhaps you think that I could have stayed in my peaceful utopia forever. I loved my Nubian people and they me.

Here, there were no wars to win and alliances to form. There were no temples to tend to and thousands of priests to instruct and advise. It was just a simple life. Life here was as nearly perfect as life could be.

"Nearly perfect, though not absolutely," Tamen added.

"Try as I might to forget my beloved Egypt and her people, they had not forgotten me. I could still hear them worshipping me with as much fervor as before. Their defeat at the hands of the Hebrews had not diminished the greatness of their gods amongst the faithful.

"Hearing Egypt yearning for their dead gods was just one element that haunted me in those days. I sensed the use of magic everywhere...to the north, south, east and west, well past the borders of Egypt. You see, to an eternal, the use of chant-magic is like a beacon. Though most pulses of energy from chant-magic I felt were so weak, they were not even worth noting. But there were others that stood out. This gave me a sense of hope that I was not the only eternal out there...that is, besides Lord Yikan who was still imprisoned in the Sphinx.

"And though I loved my Nubian people dearly, they were not like me. When you look upon another you see life, whilst with my eternal eyes, I see your flesh aging and rotting. All those I have ever known have long since passed on. And one day, Jared, hopefully I shall too.

"That is why I left my people.

"In the midst of the night, I ripped the stones from the palace floor, and with the power of the chant, buried the golden tome I had in my possession. To my people I gave all the riches of the palace. All of the gold, silver, diamonds, rubies and everything that could be traded were theirs now. I then infused the land with spells to sustain the soil and water for at least two generations before the desert claimed back what belonged to it. To the wisest of women, I taught chants of healing, fire and of levitation, and revealed to them the secret of how to listen to the thoughts of others. Eventually, my Nubian people left their land of paradise, and separated and married into countless other tribes throughout Africa. The name of the god Horus...*my name*...was forgotten, but my gift of the sacred chant continued to be passed down to daughters and sometimes even sons.

"When Europeans enslaved Africans by the millions, still the gift of my magic persevered, though was less potent with each generation. Some did not even realize they possessed these gifts—but they became revered as women of knowledge who possessed the healing touch, or those who were sought out for guidance because of their wisdom of the past and sometimes the future. Others, who knew what power they possessed and practiced their craft, became what you know of as voodooienes, sorceresses, oracles and witches.

"But of course, my magic was not the only magic that existed in the world. I learned of the spirit-demons—Duke Astaroth, Lord Baal, prince Leviathan—but these demons were known to other nations under the guises of the gods Ishtar, Odin, Zeus, Tezcatlipoca and such.

"For thousands of years I wandered from land-to-land...continent-to-continent...assuming the guise of mortal man and living amongst mortals of every nationality and race. By infusing illusions into the minds of mortals, I could appear to be of any age, color or height or sex.

"Still, in all of my journeying, I never found another who was like me.

"But the chronology of my story I know confuses you, Jared. I skip from decade to decade, and this century to that one, as though you understand that those hundreds of years to me is like a month's time to you. Having lived so many years, the sequence of events sometimes become as one, though they are vastly different. Perhaps there may be a day when there is time to tell you of my conversations with Plato and Aristotle or Confucius, amongst the thousands I have known and loved as my own children.

"But let me bring you to the time which is of greatest importance. This part of the tale is what has led me on the path that I walk now with you.

"In the years after my self-imposed exile from Egypt, the bloodline of the pharaoh's had become so muddled that eventually no one of any true royal blood actually sat on the throne again. Egypt's worst nightmare had finally fallen upon her. Libyans, Assyrians and Nubians had conquered Egypt, then been repelled, and then conquered Egypt over and again. In due course, the mighty Persian Empire swept down on a weakened Egypt and claimed it for its own.

"Even though the priests of Egypt still possessed a weakened form of magic, I detected a different type of chant-magic in the land. It was two distinct sources I felt. One, whom I knew to be Lord Yikan, and another...one of even greater power, the likes I have never felt except from those ghastly, bluish beings...*angels you call them*...who serve Yahweh.

"*Oh yes, Jared!* The beast—Lord Yikan, had escaped his prison. He alone was a danger to all mankind, I knew. But this other being whose power-fueled chants rivaled that of the angels invoked a sense of doom within me. I realized at that moment that the world around me had changed for the worse. I did not realize how much so until later.

"Still having never found any who was like I over hundreds of years, I became curious of what I thought I never would be...Yahweh—God of the Hebrews.

"When the Hebrews and their God broke the spine of Egypt, their religion was only one of thousands of others being practiced throughout the world. At that time, Yahweh was but one in a myriad of other gods. For many years, I had heard tales of how this

God of wanderers became that which is the Alpha and Omega—the first and last.

"At first I laughed at Yahweh and his sheepherding prophets. Despite all their lofty morals and values they preached, they proved completely incapable of living together in peace. Nothing has changed even now. Since the rise of Christianity, Islam and Judaism, have not the bloodiest wars been fought over their interpretation of Yahweh's words, or even Yahweh's very existence?

"At first it was simple to dismiss these Hebrews as nothing more than war-thirsty hypocrites—no better or worse than those who worshipped Vishnu, Tannakuturababa or Kali. But there was a distinct difference between this Hebrew God and the gods of others. Yahweh had crushed the mighty Egyptian empire and their living gods when no other nation and their countless false gods could.

"Over time, I began to realize that these Hebrews possessed an unadulterated faith that could not be shaken. There were those who were faithful to the word of their God and lived their lives as such. In the hearts of these true devotees, I found love and compassion, and an undying willingness to serve Yahweh. And if I had any doubt of their favor in the eyes of Yahweh, it was dismissed by the discovery that there were some who were protected from harm by those same angels I encountered in Egypt.

"Angels are the most wondrous creatures, Jared," Tamen swore.

"They can see me as clearly as I see you now, despite my most focused illusions. When I encountered them, either they would ignore me entirely, or would come close and examine me. Sometimes, when there were two or more of them together, they would talk to each other as they stared at me, as though trying to figure out exactly who and what manner of being I was.

"Understandably, I was hesitant of these beings at first. I had more than learned my lesson at the Red Sea. But as I watched...*I learned.* At rest and with the human they protected, they were the gentlest beings. I did not surmise this from their faces, for some had not a face at all, and others too many...or there were those who possessed the head of a lion or a lamb, or a creature that had never walked the earth or flown in the skies above. There were those who were shaped like spinning wheels of light, such as those that I had seen in Egypt. One of the most exotic of their breed were the ones with thousands of tiny hand-sized wings upon their backs, each with its own set of lidless eyes that looked about ceaselessly.

"But when their human charge was in danger, these genteel beings became the fiercest of all creatures that have ever walked the earth. Before my eyes, I have seen them split men into two and engulf others in flames. Their power and control over Earth's elements far surpassed my ability. My fear and apprehension of these beings turned to fascination. Who could not marvel at these giant, grotesquely beautiful beings?

"I had never seen so many of them gathered together as I had on the night the Christ was born. The tales say there was a shining star put into the heavens as his birth neared. Dear boy...that is exactly what is wrong with having mortal man write the words of God. Man's mind is far too limited. There was no star of Bethlehem in the sky, though that is what it must have appeared to be to those mortals who gazed up at it. It was a Seraphim, one of those heavenly spinning wheels of light that actually hung in the heavens and proclaimed the birth of the Christ.

"Truly it must have been a sight to behold when the Christ was born to the virgin. Though I was not there in Bethlehem when this god was born, his birth was celebrated by the Angels, Orders, Seraphim, Powers, Thrones and the other celestial hosts as far as my eternal eyes could see in every corner of the heavens that night. As it was at the Red Sea when they came, the sky split asunder and these beings rushed forth to the very edge of the chasm that separated our world from theirs and peered down like children gazing down from a balcony. I wish I could even guess their number, but like mortal man, I too have my limitations. In every inch of the sky, my eternal eyes saw legions innumerable of these heavenly entities.

"And how they sang!

"Their harmonies were the essence of unadulterated love.

"When next I saw the Christ...the one called Jesus...he had grown into a young man. The energy exuding from him was unlike any energy I have ever witnessed coming from an angel or magic user. But I speak untrue, Jared. The power did not emanate from him, but *was* him...every cell of his being. And he was not alone, but in the company of hundreds of those glowing, bluewhite angelic beings. With every step he took, there was not one angel who was not to the front, side or back of him.

"From that point on, I too followed him, though not once did he ever seem to notice my presence. For me, Jared, to hear him speak was to have truly lived for the first time in my long existence. It was no wonder that he was so loved...*and so hated,* for there were many who were drawn to and despised *the power* of love he spoke of so often.

"There was only one time in which I could not follow this Christ, and I was glad for it, for I felt my life to be in great peril.

The palace Jared and Tamen were standing in disappeared and gave way to a rocky landscape that stretched on for miles. A short distance in front of them, a man in a tattered brown robe was walking away from them and toward this nowhere land of rock and sand.

The dry hot air around them suddenly became thick and then began to crackle. Wavering into existence out of the air were three beings. Though they had the body—from the shoulders down—of a human, human they were not. One possessed the head of a lion. Another had the head of an ox. The third bore the head of a lamb with wool as white as virgin snow. Each was the size of two and a half men.

224 · Orlando Smart-Powell

"You must wait here, Egyptian. Only the *Lamb of God* and the *Beast* may enter yon desert," the lion-headed being commanded, and then growled.

"The Beast? The one called Lucifer?" Tamen asked.

"For eons he has no longer been Lucifer—*the beautiful one*—who *was* the most favored of Yahweh," the lion-headed one purred in reply and then shook its flowing mane.

"Satan he is!" the ox-headed being grunted.

"'Deceiver!" the curly-woolen lamb hissed.

"Woe to those of *this* Earth, for the Beast has usurped all kings and queens. They bow before It and kiss Its feet, for they desire beauty and power," the ox-headed one proclaimed.

"Turn thy heads!" the lamb-headed creature cried. "The Fallen One approaches."

The animal-headed celestial beings, in lock step, turned around.

The buzzing of wings interrupted the silence that had fallen over all present. Flittering up and down...zigzagging as it made its way forward...came a black-hulled locust, the source of the sound. Tamen backed away from it and pulled Jared along with him.

Jared, who had been sweating in the illusionary desert land, wrapped his arms around his chest and shivered. "Holy crap, I'm freezing!" he spat through chattering teeth.

Tamen looked down at him. "Aye. I felt my own energy ebb, as though it was being siphoned off by Lucifer. I was weak and dizzy, which I should not have been since I was no longer mortal.

The locust—*Lucifer*—stopped and hovered before passing by the angels. "Will there be not *ONE* kind word from those who once called me brother and sister? Was I not there at your awakening— when you were called forth from the ether of nothingness? Did I not cradle all of you in my arms when I was ancient and thou were just embers of life? How quickly thou hath forgotten, my kindred!'

"Thou seek to confuse those who cannot be misled," the ox-headed one replied.

"With me, those who are Legion say otherwise,...*Cherub*," Satan replied. "Have you too forgotten the Great War?"

"One that you lost," the one with the lamb's head answered sharply. "Behold your prison which is *this* Earth."

"Not prison, my lovely, Natel of the Seraphim...tis my kingdom!" Satan responded. "My kingdom hath many lands for princes and princesses such as thee...if thou wish it so.'

"And The Satan was cast into the Lake of Fire..." Natel, the lamb-headed seraphim responded, as if he had not heard Satan's offer. "Blessed be the holy name of Yahweh."

"Tis thy folly to put faith in a prophecy that shall never come to pass," Lucifer said. "The laws of what once was hath been broken and changed and bartered long before thou ever knew life."

"Listen not brothers and sisters," the ox-headed cherub advised. "Time grows short for *It*."

"Indeed...I am the Great Deceiver, but it is truth that I speak and thou knowest it to be so. In the time next when you are in the presence of the Father, ask the truth of my words if you believe me not."

"Yahweh has commanded what will be...*will be*," Natel, the lamb-headed one said. "What is done may not be undone."

"Seraphim and Orders and Cherubs and your kindred have been blind to the chasm in that covenant. Thou fail to see the creature that is no longer man, nor Heavenly Host, but is of both, and thus hath broken the covenant thou speak of," Satan replied with a squeak of his locust-legs.

The animal-headed beings all turned and looked at Tamen.

"Wha—why are they looking at you like that?" Jared asked, as he moved slightly behind Tamen. "Tamen?"

"Satan fluttered off into the desert to begin his Temptation of the Christ," Tamen said, ignoring Jared's question. "Satan offered the Christ all of the lands and cities and kingdoms upon the earth. They were Satan's to give, you see. Those pagan gods we spoke of...Odin and Zeus and the like...were no more than Lucifer's demons masquerading as gods as easily as Lord Yikan masqueraded as the god Aton and took control of Egypt.

"I too was perplexed by his words at the time, Jared," Tamen admitted, and then waved his hand, vanishing the illusions of Lucifer and the animal-headed celestial host. "It was not until the crucifixion of the Christ that the cryptic message of Lucifer, and far, far more was made known to me. It was at the foot of the Christ that the meaning of my own long and tortuous life...*and yours*...was made known.

"I have often wondered if I was spared during that time of the Exodus—when Moses led his people from Egypt—because my destiny had already been predetermined. I do know that if I had shown any aggression toward those angels that night, I too would have been destroyed as quickly and easily as Mala and Zoe'el. But I had not and was not.

"Before I begin, just let me say that I hope I have not led you astray by causing you to assume that I have all the answers to the questions you undoubtedly have. I do not! I can only tell you what the Christ said to me as he hung upon his cross.

The sky above them suddenly darkened. In the horizon, rolling black clouds sparked with lightning and rolled toward them, though there was not a hint of wind to be felt. In front of Tamen and Jared, three wood crosses materialized, and upon each were men nailed to them—a stake through each outstretched hand and one through their feet which were laid one upon the other. Roman soldiers in red kilts armed with swords stood guard nearby as two women knelt and cried and hugged one another in front of the man hanging at the cross nearest them—the one wearing the crown of thorns.

But they were not alone.

Seven glowing blue-white angels were standing in a semi-circle around the Christ. They were as still as the air—and seemed benign

—but the glow from their red eyes was as threatening as the black storm rolling toward them.

The Christ struggled and lifted his head skyward, as though he saw something in the heavens that no one, not even the angels could see. And then his head lowered, but did not fall to his bloody chest that was a series of fresh, bloody gashes. His head held steady. His eyes were closed, but then suddenly opened and stared at Tamen.

"For the very first time since I had followed the Christ all those years," Tamen said, "he acknowledged my presence.

"His voice seeped into my mind. The power he commanded was unlike that of any angel who served him and could not...*and still cannot*...be described in any human tongue. So great was the power he commanded, I did not even have to speak, for he already knew what resided in my thoughts.

"And when he spoke, I realized just how insignificant in might the angels and I, and all upon this entire world we call Earth are in his presence.

"It was the closest I have ever come to feeling that which is the beginning of all things: the Alpha...*the source of life*...that which was there before there was a thing called time.

"And he said unto me..."

CHAPTER 13

"I am Alpha and Omega...beginning and the end...

"I know thy many sins against man and against my children of Israel. It shall be that thou must wander *this* Earth, never calling home a place amongst man, for you reside in that place that lieth between Heavenly Host and mortal...part of each, though of neither thou shall ever be. That is my Father's edict, Egyptian.

"The first covenant of the Lord Father hath been broken and a new covenant set forth, for man hath loosed the children of the serpent upon the Earth, who now waits in the storm for thee, though thou must flee from her sight and touch.

"Bend thy knee before the Lord thy God, Egyptian! I reveal to thee that which is unknown to all save the Lamb, the Ghost and the Father...**and** to the *Beautiful One* who was first to rise from the ether of time.

* * *

Thus sayeth the Lamb of God:

In the beginning...before the Lord thy Father created the Heavens and the first Earth...before suns and great orbs were cast into motion, there was nothing save we.

In the darkness, there was only the Lamb, the Lord Father and that which is the Father's living light...the Holy Ghost. We are Alpha and Omega, for we have always been and forever shall always be...amen!

Life we called forth from the darkness, and *It* became the first and most brilliant of all shining stars, for *It* was firstborn. And with its birth came rock and ice, and a fire so great that it shall burn for all eternity and have no end. So perfect it was that the Lord Father commanded that it shall be called *Lucifer*—Morning Star and first life born—so sayeth the Lord Father.

And the Lord Father looked upon what was created by word alone and saw that it was good.

Whilst all that was brought forth from nothingness began to settle, cool and multiply, Lucifer worshipped the Lord Father with a song that is forever beyond compare. And we—all of us—bore witness to time, for never hath there been such a thing as time until the birth of Lucifer—the Morning Star. As *time* aged and came to be called ancient, we saw what we brought out of the ether become new suns and new moons and new orbs of air and mass, which settled throughout what had forever been nothing.

And the Lord Father looked upon these creations and saw that it was good.

At the age Lucifer was no longer a child, but was now as time— ancient to all but I, the Ghost and the Lord Father, Lucifer spoke of loneliness, for Lucifer was not and could never be as *We*, but that which is inimitable unto itself. The Lord Father listened and called forth for Lucifer others such as *It* was. And as they rose from the ether, Lucifer called and named each and every one that were innumerable, and into their truthful place Lucifer put them all.

Dominions...

...Powers...

...Virtues...

...Ophanim...

...Orders...

...Cherubim...

...Seraphim...

...Archangels...

...and Angels...

And thus was born the Hosts of the Heavens of the Lord Father...*amen.*

Since their birth, the Heavenly Host hath sung ceaselessly in marvel at the might of the Father and the living force—the Holy Ghost, for they and I are as one. From nothingness the Heavenly Host came and knoweth no greater force than the Lord Father, whose living Ghost is of horrifying power and unending love.

In awe of the Lord Father's wonders, the angel Metatron went down into the first Earth and gathered precious gold and fashioned it into a tome. With hands of Celestial might, Metatron inscribed each and every song chanted by the Heavenly Host who bore witness to the Lord Father's creation of the first earth.

In this most holy Book of Creation was inscribed songs of everything that hath ever come from the ether. Now sealed with the mark of Metatron, the golden Book of Creation bore the *words* of the Lord Father's force. Though what could not be written or chanted was the Gift of Life, for only the Lord Father and Ghost may give life where there was not life before.

Lucifer, ever faithful and beloved by the Lord Father, knew these chant songs of Metatron could control and form all that had been created. But of all the power and dominion given to Lucifer, to bring forth something from nothing and give life was denied.

And never hath Lucifer been denied.

Lucifer beseeched the Lord Father for the *Words of Life*, so that *It* too may create the holiest of holies. And for the first time since there was a thing such as time, and Lucifer knew life, Lucifer was denied.

Lucifer thus gave birth to *anger* and *malice*, and fled to this first Earth and fashioned *jealousy*. Having borne witness to the rise of the Heavenly Host, Lucifer knew them as a father knows thy sons and mothers know thy daughters, and beguiled Metatron and took the Book of Creation. To those of the Heavenly Host, Lucifer taught them to chant the songs from the book and mold all that was already created.

Lucifer chanted unto the creatures of the first earth and changed them from what the Lord Father had meant them to be. Monsters of great height and savagery they became. The reign of monsters Lucifer had formed held sway for many ages.

Sickened by what they beheld, half of the Holy Host who once called the first earth home, fled to the presence of the Lord Father and told of the abominations that were brought forth and walked the land. Though in the sight of Lucifer, such monsters were of beauty and boastfulness. And again Lucifer came before the throne of the Lord Father, but did not beseech the Creator for knowledge or to worship, but to take pride in what *It* had wrought upon the first earth.

And Lucifer said...

"Are my creatures not beautiful, my Father? I—who am first born and most beloved of all the Heavenly Host hath done that which thou sayeth cannot be done. But look, Father! I have taken that which you gave life and by my own hands fashioned them into images of my own creation. At last Father, I too am as thee."

Lucifer sought to place a throne beside the Almighty. The Lord Father grew angry, for the Lord Father is a jealous Father and the only Lord Father. Lucifer was banished from the presence of the Ghost and Lord Father. The Lord Father's voice thus rose up and above all that ever existed...suns roared and died with great thirst, and into their mouths swallowed many Earths. And all of creation was afraid, for the Holy Ghost had been impugned.

"We alone are Alpha and Omega!"

But Lucifer was not deterred by the Lord Father's mighty wrath. As eons passed, Lucifer grew to despise the Lord Father. The offspring of Lucifer...anger, malice and jealousy sired *pride and evil.*

And Lucifer swayed those of the Heavenly Host who looked upon themselves as gods. Upon the new earth, those Heavenly Host who followed Lucifer became as demons and devils of the land, and fashioned more creatures and abominations upon abominations, until these monsters bred creatures like themselves.

The Lord Father sent the Heavenly Host to do battle with these demons and devils who called themselves gods. And thus ensued the first of the Great Wars...

...and all of creation trembled!

In that first Great War, brothers and sisters of the Heavenly Host fought against one another, so that much suffering afflicted both sides. Lucifer, the eldest...*the most perfect*...the most powerful of the Heavenly Host felled hundreds upon hundreds of thousands with but a single blow of the hand.

Having witnessed that Lucifer was too mighty for the Heavenly Host, the Lord Father brought Michael the archangel from the ether so that Lucifer would find his balance. And thus when the archangel Michael and Lucifer, the first of all created, fought, good and evil formed a balance that could not be broken...neither gained...neither lost.

Lucifer cried out to all that was..."*I am still a god!*"

"So great was the wrath of the Lord Father, that for a time, everything that existed stood upon the verge of falling into a fire without end.

The Lord Father bested Lucifer.

And from the heavens, Lucifer was hurled down to the first earth and rose up dust and dirt for thousands of years, so that every abominable creature made by Lucifer should die by water and fire and wind and ice. And to the demons and devils that called Lucifer father, they too were banished from Heaven for all eternity. Metatron, keeper of knowledge, took back the Book of Creation and hid it deep within the earth from whence it was born.

"In a time when the Great War was ancient, the Lord Father gave life back to the first earth in its seas and oceans and rivers. And too, the Lord Father created man and woman, and set them in his holy garden. But Lucifer, who still resideth upon the first earth, was with bitterness and came into the garden. He beguiled the woman and man into eating of the Tree of Knowledge so that they would know of good and evil.

Thus Lucifer, who was once the Morning Star, became *the Satan* —the One who deceives.

Satan called out to the Lord Father and said...

"Because thou could not claim victory in war, I was cast down low to this new earth...not by the might of your archangel...but by your hands alone. These children of man and woman love thee not because you are Lord Father, but because they fear thee. The Heavenly Host who chant your praise do not love thee because you are Lord Father, but because they fear thee as well. In a balance, the thrones of Heaven shall fall. Of all of that which you have created, mortal man is the most flawed. In a balance, and of their own free will, they shall turn their backs upon thee and shun thy love."

"Thou may not tempt the Lord Father," the Almighty answered. "Over this first Earth thy fallen ones may tempt man and woman. But unto three mortals, I shall always give blessings so that goodness may stay upon this Earth...and thou shall have always three mortals to corrupt man. Of these three of good and three of dark, no harm from heaven or hell may touch them, lest I send forth the Holy Ghost to destroy this new Earth and thy realm with fire without end for all of time. Thou and I shall not molest any, so that the balance remains. The faithful to my word shall walk through the gates of heaven, and the wicked of man shall fall into the realm of darkness that is Hell...*of their own free will.* This final battle shall end this first Earth in fire so that a new Earth may rise from its ashes, and the throne of the Lamb will be placed upon it."

But Satan was not satisfied. Because the Lord Father hath given his word not to intervene, Satan sought to undo the balance.

Satan fashioned from gold his own Book of Creation as Metatron had once done. Into the hands of mortal man Satan gave this tome so that man too could chant and believe he was as a god. In the dark book there lay the power to create those who were neither man nor Heavenly Host, but were of both. Though deeper yet within Satan's own tome, the most powerful of songs could create from man a true demon that could corrupt the balance set forth by the Lord Father.

The angel Metatron discovered Satan's intention and took back from the earth the golden Book of Creation. To a woman who resideth upon the isle in the Great Ocean, Metatron gave it. And within it, Metatron inscribed a chant which had the power to create man into a Heavenly Host that would balance the great demon that would arise from Satan's dark Book of Creation.

For having broken the holy covenant, the Lord Father caused a great sleep to come over Satan and placed The Deceiver on the Isle of Phenox. In slumber Satan shall stay until the last battle of the war, when the balance hath been set and mortal man chooses of his own free will where he shall stand once and for all time...be it in Heaven or in Hell.

Thus the war for the new earth hath begun between man and woman...Heavenly Host and demon...and those—as you, Egyptian—who are neither mortal nor angel, but of both.

CHAPTER 14

"Woe to the Earth, and to the sea, because the devil hath come down unto you, having great wrath, knowing that he hath but a short time." Revelations 12:12

"Turn round, Egyptian, and look upon thy great adversary," the Christ said.

Tamen and Jared both turned. Behind them, standing guard, were the blue-hued angles. Though in front of the angels was Lord Yikan—his blue eyes madly swirling—and focused solely on Tamen. But next to him, walking...creeping...from end-to-end where the angels stood guard was a bare-chest woman whose shimmering skin was blacker than the clouds overhead. Her waist length braids swayed as she slinked from one side to the other.

"Shazadeh—the firstborn daughter of Astaroth, Archduke of Hell hath come for you, Egyptian," the Christ announced. "Her mortal death and rebirth as an unadulterated demon that walks the earth has destroyed the balance of all things. I cannot come back to this earth until good and evil hath equal sway upon men's souls, for man must choose his path free of molestation." The Christ's eyes rolled back in his head as a spool of blood-laden drool escaped from his open mouth. "Find the demon's balance, Egyptian," he uttered. "Seek out the mortal who shall die and be reborn as an angel as pure as any in the Heavenly Host. Do as I command, and balance upon the earth will be struck. And in the hour known only to the Father and the Holy Ghost, I shall return and purify this first earth with fire and nothing upon it shall survive.

"Vengeance is mine, sayeth the Lord Father!

"To the righteous, by the will of the living force—the Holy Ghost —the dead shall live once more and be given everlasting life. The earth will be made whole once more and become my kingdom, and all shall bask in the loving light of the Father and Holy Ghost forever and ever, amen.

"That is the covenant!

"Do as I—the Lamb of God—commands and I shall forgive thee of thy sins against my Hebrew children thou slew in Egypt and I shall give thee death. And in death, thou may once again be with thy brother who was once Pharaoh of Egypt.

"Now go...flee, Egyptian," the Christ commanded. "This mortal form shall soon be no more and my spirit shall go hence forth into the hands of the Father. When I am departed, the demon, Shazadeh, shall no longer be restrained by the angels who now keep her at bay. She will hunt thee, for she knows you seek her balance and thus her death."

"How shall I come to know this mortal who will balance the demon?" Tamen asked.

"To you, the Lord Father shall send his messenger and reveal the birth of the mortal child, as Gabriel revealed mine unto the virgin," the Christ said.

"That was the last time I saw Shazadeh and Lord Yikan," Tamen said to Jared as the illusion of the Christ, Lord Yikan, Shazadeh and everything around them began to dissolve like sand sculptures in the rain. When the illusion once more congealed, it was of the stone Egyptian temple they had started in...when Tamen first introduced himself to Jared as Horus.

"I took to the sky," Tamen went on, "which was the last time I have chanted since, for I knew that if I did, Shazadeh and Lord Yikan would be able to follow the energy trail, and thus find me. Despite my awesome power as a half-angel and half-man, I could not defeat Shazadeh who was entirely demon.

"And so Jared, thus began the second half of my journey and of my life, only this time I had purpose and a reason to live. I had comfort knowing that Amenhotep still existed and waited for me somewhere between purgatory and Hell.

"But now, I was hunted!

"There have been several times when Shazadeh and Lord Yikan have come close to finding me, they knowing I am the one who will find her equal...her balance. The only defenses at my disposal are my eternal body and the innate magic I already possessed. In order to survive the countless centuries that were to come, I used my ability to read and cast thoughts, and my skill to release my soul and travel at the speed of thought.

"We do not have time to go through my endless years of travels during which I roamed the earth in search of *you*, Jared."

Jared's mouth popped open. He took a step back from Tamen. "*Me?*" he gasped, and then shook his head while holding up his hands. "Wait! No way, Tamen! I—I—I..."

Tamen lowered his head and stared directly into Jared's eyes. "I have encountered hundreds of thousands of mortals in search of you," Tamen went on and took a step toward him. "And as Shazadeh and Lord Yikan have chased me, they have founded religions all over the world as a masquerade and a means to entrap you. Now begins *Jared's tale!*"

Jared dropped to the floor as though his legs had been kicked out from under him. Tamen kneeled beside him and pulled his torso upright. He stroked Jared's bald head—front to the nape of his neck—and smiled sorrowfully at him.

"I happened upon your family one night quite by accident...*or did I?*" Tamen asked rhetorically and lowered his eyelids. "The screams of Walter Tripkin, your grandfather, are what made me stray from my path and go into the forest where he was murdered. I slew his murderers, but spared the life of the boy there that refused to participate in the vile act.

"When I brought your grandfather's body to your family that night, it was then that I saw your mother, Dorthea, for the first time. And a beautiful child she was with her large brown eyes and innocent smile. I wanted to protect her. I wanted to protect them all, even your great Aunt Lilly.

"But understand this, Jared, your mother had suffered the loss of her father and then grandmother soon after, and she grew up craving one thing above all...unconditional love. Your father, Reverend Phineas Boremon, had promised to love her always, though that was far from his true intention. Phineas loved and discarded many women, including your mother.

"It was impossible for me to stop Phineas from hurting your mother with his lies of love so that he could fornicate with her. I intended on killing him one night, but was prevented by his angelic protector who was imbued with the power of the Holy Ghost to stop at all costs anyone who tried to harm even a hair on his head.

"Phineas Boremon...your father...was one of the three blessed of God."

"My dad?" Jared uttered. "Why him?"

"I too was baffled why God had chosen this philandering minister to be one of the chosen three," Tamen responded. "The answer to that mystery was solved the moment your father's seed and mother's egg joined. I knew there was life inside your mother, because I could sense you within her at that very moment. I knew then that the child she carried was not just any child.

"And as the Christ had prophesized, an angelic messenger heralded the birth of the one who would become Shazadeh's equal and balance. But somehow, I already knew that before the angel confirmed it for me.

"You...my dear, young boy...are to become the counterbalance to Shazadeh, the daughter of Archduke Astaroth who rules hell in Satan's absence...*that is, if you live long enough.*"

Jared shivered. He opened his mouth to speak, but nothing came out.

"Once heaven and hell are balanced," Tamen continued, "this earth shall come to an end in fire and ice, and the path to heaven or hell shall at last be opened. But unbalanced, the demons will rein upon every throne of power in this world with Shazadeh as their goddess."

"I—I have to become her equal?"

"Indeed," Tamen replied. "You must become her opposite—an angel in the purest form—not a half-breed such as I who could not complete the chant of changing. You must forsake your mortal form for that of a Celestial Host and counter the unbalancing evil Shazadeh has brought upon the earth."

Jared swayed his head from side-to-side. "But if I...if I become this thing—"

"An angel through and through!"

"Yeah," Jared uttered, "an angel. Then the earth is destroyed. That's what you said."

"Aye, child," Tamen replied. "All things must come to an end. But when that time does arrive for the earth's demise, all is not over...it is actually the beginning. Everyone—the faithful—who has ever lived shall be returned to life and reunited with those they love for all eternity should we—*you*—succeed. But heed my words, Jared!" Tamen grasped Jared's chin. "Duke Astaroth, Shazadeh, and the other demons will not relinquish their rule of the Earth without waging war first. They will kill every person on this planet before they go to the Isle of Phenox, a land of unquenchable fire and never-ending torture.

"While you yet remain human, every demon on Earth and in Hell will hunt you until you are dead.

"Your death is their victory!"

CHAPTER 15

Jared was still shivering when he opened his eyes and looked over at Taylor sitting in the chair beside him, realizing he was no longer in Tamen's illusion. "Me?" he whispered, not to Taylor, but to himself, as he recalled Tamen's last words to him. *'Your death is their victory!'*

All of Tamen's talk of gods, God, angels and an impending climatic war between heaven and hell, all lent to the implausible for him. *But I was in Egypt. Well, at least an illusion of it,'* he thought, unable to dissuade his mind that the fading heat from his skin while being in Egypt had been real.

"Not every book has a happy ending, does it?" Taylor asked. "I know all of this hasn't been easy for you. But even if there was time to thoroughly examine everything you've seen and heard— there isn't. You're going to have to find a way to deal with it so you can focus on what's to come."

"You mean that this Shazadeh woman or demon...or whatever the hell she is—wants me dead?" Jared asked as he looked down at the floor. He then looked up and leaned forward. "You're screwing with me, right Taylor? I'll laugh once you let me in on the prank, OK?"

Taylor sat back. "Shazadeh, Yikan and every one of her wacko followers that call her goddess want you six feet under. But it's not *whatever the hell she is*...she is what she is...a demoness, like you were told." Taylor pursed his lips. He held up his hand and began counting on his fingers. "The 'One Heart—One Mind' organiza-tion...'New Generation non-denominational' church...'Five Steps to Peace' self-help program...'The Institute of Perceptual Minds'. Sound familiar? All of those are front organizations created by Shazadeh and Lord Yikan to find you."

Jared sprung out of his chair and began waving his hand. "Just—just hold up a sec. You're saying...really saying that—"

"All of this is real?" Taylor replied before Jared could finish. "Yes!"

"You mean that—"

"What Tamen said and showed you was true? Correct. Every bit of it."

"He actually talked to—"

"Jesus of Nazareth—the Christ? Right again."

"I'm the...this—"

"Balance."

"Hey—knock it off! Stop finishing my thoughts, alright?" Jared blurted. "How did you know what I was going to say anyway?"

Taylor stood and shrugged his shoulders. "Because that's what you were thinking."

It can't be, Jared thought. He slapped his forehead several times and looked down for a moment before eyeing Taylor again. *You're dreaming, man. Yeah...this is just one jacked-up dream. Just waked yourself up and it'll all be gone.* He rubbed his hair and then yanked at it. "Arrgh!" he grunted, as his hair refused to separate from his scalp. *Crap...this is real. Oh crap!*

"Maybe you should just sit," Taylor suggested.

"No!" Jared shot back and then began pacing the floor and mumbling to himself. He stopped in mid-stride and then turned and pointed at Taylor. "Wait a minute. You..." Jared began, but was almost afraid to finish, "...you're not really Mr. Pierceman, are you?"

Taylor smiled. "No."

Jared clenched his fists. "I knew it!"

Taylor cocked his head to the side. "After all you've seen, are you really surprised?"

"Then...if you're not Taylor Pierceman, then you must be..."

Taylor chuckled.

"You're Tamen," Jared said. "Taylor Pierceman is just another illusion."

Taylor raised a finger and slowly beckoned Jared with it. "Let me introduce myself properly."

"I already know who you *really* are."

"Of course you don't," Taylor stated. "I'm not this Taylor Pierceman...you're correct about that. I *am*, as much as I could ever be, the grandson of Tamen and the son of Aria—the witch. I'm that little ragamuffin of a boy Tamen saved that night your grandfather was murdered. I used to be called Henry McCullough Jr., but my true name is *Henrì Bedeau*."

Jared gawked at him. "What? You're not—"

"Tamen," Henrì finished for him. He shook his head side-to-side and grinned.

Jared hesitated to speak. He glanced around the room and then looked back at Henrì.

Henrì held his palms up. "Tamen is where he's been this entire time. Papà—as I know him—has been right beside me whispering everything you've been thinking in my ear."

Where there was nothing on Henrì's shoulder before, a brown-skinned hand began to take shape. Further up the ghostly hand, which was rapidly solidifying, an arm became visible, and then a shoulder and head. Like ocean waves, the image of a young bald

244 · Orlando Smart-Powell

man in dark blue pants and a white shirt became more solid with each illusionary lap. It was the man Jared knew as Tamen, the immortal being who was part mortal and part angel.

Jared inhaled sharply and shook his head. " No—no—no—no—no! If you're really here, then everything you've told me—"

"Is true," Tamen said, before he could finish. "For you to understand what you must do, I had to show you."

Jared closed his eyes. "It doesn't make it any easier to believe, ya know?"

Tamen led Jared by the arm and sat him down in the red chair by the fireplace. He knelt beside him. "What I have told you is only a glimpse of what I have seen during my time on this earth," Tamen said. "I have seen the Persian and Roman empires among many, rise and fall. I have spoken to Joan of Arc, Aristotle, Merlin, and the witch—Morgan Le Fey...Attila and Hannibal. In my time, mortals have gone from horseback to machines that can reach the moon. Yet, for all of mortal man's wondrous discoveries, they pale next to the power of the chants I possess. And even that power pales in comparison to the power *you* will possess. And though you are not quite sure about me or Henri, or of any of this, I already know what you are thinking."

"That you could save my Aunt Maymee," Jared whispered.

"She is dying, child," Tamen assured him.

Jared locked eyes with Tamen. "And you could heal her." He knew he sounded desperate, but it was exactly how he wanted to sound. Though, when Tamen looked away, Jared knew he had the answer he didn't want.

"For me to chant and save one life could bring death to all of us," Tamen said. "I love dear Maymee also. I have known her all her life. But I cannot. Since I fled from Lord Yikan and Shazadeh the night of the Christ's crucifixion, having not cast chant-spells has allowed me to remain hidden from them. This burden you now have is not without sacrifice, Jared."

Jared clenched his fists. "What if I don't want this burden? Huh?"

Tamen got up and walked away.

"First you wanna take away everything in my life with this *balance* crap!" Jared spat. "And now you're sayin' that even though you can save my Aunt Maymee, you won't. I'm supposed to say OK to that? Fine? Sure? Just like that?"

"He never promised it was going to be easy," Henrì added in. "Have you grasped what you are? What you mean to all of us? And when I say all of us, I mean every living person on this planet. If you fall, we all fall...it's that simple."

Jared stared straight ahead into the fireplace. "When do I get to have a say in it?"

"You do not," Tamen droned. "Whether your destiny pleases you or not...whether you choose to become the balance to Shazadeh or not...if they find you before you have transformed your mortal flesh into that of an angel, they *will* kill you. Every person you now come into contact with is in danger by your mere presence, including your family. Believe me when I tell you, child, they will stop at nothing until you are dead."

"Those two, Shazadeh and Lord Yikan, are as much a part of the history of mankind as anything you've ever studied in class," Henrì added. "Just turn on the TV if you don't believe us. These cult members are being found murdered everywhere...gruesomely so! You don't even want me to describe it—believe me! Everyone thinks it's some random, rash of unconnected religious zealots or just another commune of folks that decided to drink the Kool-Aid, ala Jim Jones. Shazadeh and Lord Yikan don't give a damn about leaving a trail of bodies wherever they go. They know you're out there somewhere, and they know they don't have time to screw around, as you would say."

"If they fail to kill you, they are doomed to fall in the last and greatest war between heaven and hell," Tamen said. "But in order for that to come about, you must become the exact opposite of what she is now. From what I have discovered of Shazadeh, in her mortal life she was a princess of the Persian Empire during its occupation of Egypt. She was a formidable witch in her own right, which she was exiled for and sent to Egypt. It was her knowledge of demons and magic, I am sure, that assisted her in weakening the spell that imprisoned Lord Yikan within the Sphinx. And with Lord Yikan free and in possession of Lucifer's golden tome, she unlocked the spell to transform herself from mortal to demon, not a hybrid half-demon, such as Lord Yikan, and far more powerful than I."

"But we have the angel Metatron's tome—the greater of the two," Henrì jutted in. "Well, almost I think."

"And when you have fully completed the Chant of Changing, you will transform from mortal to that which is so much greater," Tamen finished.

Jared left his chair and began pacing the room. His black boots clapped on the wood floor as he looked first at Tamen and then back to Henrì, and then back again to Tamen. "I—I don't know. I can't. This is too unreal."

Henrì nonchalantly waved his hand. "You become used to it after awhile."

"Hey, you know what?" Jared pointed at Henrì and scowled. "You had a choice in leading your life—I don't! And you too, Tamen!"

"I never said it was fair, only that it must be done," Tamen replied. "Your choices are but two. Linger until Lord Yikan and Shazadeh or one of their watchers finds you—be assured, eventually they will—or become what you are destined to be and live. Live and give man his choice of two paths to follow, or doom him to the rule of Shazadeh and her father, Duke Astaroth, for all time."

"Crap!" Jared yelled at the ceiling. "Freakin' crap!"

"Well, Papà, he's actually taking it better than I thought he would," Henrì commented.

"Have compassion, my child," Tamen implored.

Jared started pacing again. "If I become this balance, what then? I mean...will I still be able to see my family? Can I save my Aunt Maymee with this power?" Henrì glanced at Tamen, though the exchange was not lost upon Jared. "What was that look about?"

"When you are transformed, you will no longer be of the mortal world," Tamen answered. "Though you will possess the power to heal, the cancer that has spread throughout your aunt's body will take her life long before that time—*if* we return at all."

"Return? From where?"

"Egypt," Henrì said. "At least at first. Then we go south, right, Papà?"

"To that palace you used to have in the desert?" Jared asked in amazement. "The one Isis...I mean, Mala created?"

Tamen nodded. "Deep within the earth where my palace once stood lays the golden tome of Metatron."

"I know, I know that," Jared sputtered. Above all else, a trip half-way around the world seemed just as unbelievable to him, as it was absolutely wrong. Trekking into a desert was the last thing he wanted to do, and staying by his aunt's side in her last days, the only thing. "But you said the palace was gone."

"Without my magic to sustain it, it is," Tamen said. "The desert has long since reclaimed what belongs to it, but that has kept the tome hidden as I had planned."

"Do you know where it is?"

"I do know where *about* it is," Tamen answered. "Not even my eternal eyes can tell what the desert has covered and reshaped a thousand times over. When we are close enough, I should be able to sense its power."

"And so will Lord Yikan and Shazadeh," Henrì added sourly. "They've had their most loyal watchers searching the desert for it for years. And if what you've told me about where the palace used to be, Papà, well..."

"I can't do this crap!" Jared snapped as he rushed to the door. "I can't go! I can't, Tamen!"

"What?" Henrì yelped. "Papà, say something!"

Jared shook his head, all the while avoiding looking in either one's eyes. "I'm not gonna leave my Aunt Maymee this way. Even if I do what you're asking and become this balance thing or whatever, I can't leave my aunt...*or my mom.*"

"Jared, listen to me," Henrì said softly. "You don't know what you're saying right now. Just—just come back and sit for a moment so we can talk this out."

Jared glared at him. "I do understand, Henrì...Taylor...or whoever the hell you *really* are. I get it, alright? Loud and freakin' clear, OK? Excuse the hell outta me if I don't like it."

"Jared, you have to—" Henrì began.

"Have to what?" Jared snapped. "What I *have* to do is be with my aunt while she's still alive. Oh yeah, Tamen...thanks for just letting her die."

Tamen didn't blink.

"Each day you're mortal you risk your life and everyone else's, including your Aunt Maymee *and* your mother's. You understand *that?*" Henrì questioned, with a tone more akin to that of Taylor Pierceman the teacher.

"No, I don't, Henrì," Jared countered. "You said there would be some hard choices to make so this is one of them. So the answer is no. At—at least until I see to my aunt and straighten all this crap out in my head."

"If you go and they find you, I cannot offer you much protection against Shazadeh," Tamen said.

Jared opened the door, but then stopped. "If they find me with you here or in Egypt, you can't protect me anyway, right? So I'm still jacked-up with or without you!"

"Then go and be with your aunt," Tamen told him. "But promise this. When she has passed into the afterlife, you will come with us."

"Wait!" Henrì cried, and then looked at Tamen. He tilted his head to the side. "Tell him, Papà."

Jared looked up and growled. "There's more? Really? On top of all that you just—"

"They're close, alright?" Henrì blurted. He closed his eyes and rubbed his sandy brown hair. "Lord Yikan and Shazadeh are closing in on you...*fast!*"

Jared turned to Tamen and stared. "T—Tamen?"

"Aye," Tamen said simply.

Jared slammed his fist against the doorframe.

"Papà," Henrì said, "you can't let him go with Shazadeh and Lord Yikan out there, and God knows how many crazy followers they have looking for him."

Tamen remained silent.

"I can't promise anything," Jared said, looking at Tamen and then Henrì. "I'm sorry."

* * *

Tamen was looking out the window watching Jared walk down the street. "I cannot force him. We have to trust that he will come to understand the gravity of the situation before him. Perhaps he will. Even you have said he has a good head on his shoulders."

"He does. He's brilliant! But he has a thick skull," Henrì replied. He sat down in the chair by the fireplace and slumped. "I really don't see how you can be so calm, Papà."

Tamen half-turned and smiled. "Thousands of years of practice."

"And you don't look a day over two thousand!"

Tamen looked outside again. "I have not sensed Shazadeh and Lord Yikan's chant for some time. He should be safe for now."

"That's because they're busy literally sucking the life out of people," Henrì replied. "Every investigative news program is going nuts over these so-called cult murders. Every few weeks they're finding another set of bodies and no one seems to be able to tie them to one of Shazadeh's front religions. The Institute of Perceptual Minds? C'mon on, Papà! People are actually buying into that craziness."

"Like sheep. One right after the other, no?"

"Sheep...lemmings...idiots!" Henrì blurted. "They're all going to end up dead."

"They are just mortals, son."

Henrì huffed. "You mean whackos, right?"

"What transpires in the desert?" Tamen asked.

"Well...they're only sending watchers there right now to oversee the paid diggers," Henrì said. "They're calling it a sabbatical to the Land of the Goddess. That's about all I could piece together from the news shows that have interviewed ex-members who had enough sense to get the hell out."

"I am forever grateful," Tamen said. "You know it is too risky for me to probe the thoughts of their followers, especially these watchers. Who knows what magic Shazadeh has weaved into their minds."

"You don't have to thank me, Papà. You'll never have to."

"Ah—but I do," Tamen whispered. "That is *our* covenant, remember? You owe me nothing other than love for what I have done for you."

"I know, Papà...I know," Henrì murmured. "Do you think we even have a chance of pulling this off?"

Tamen sighed. "She is a powerful sorceress, too. Halesha, the witch of Minns, was adept at summoning demons from the nether regions, but Shazadeh is far more powerful than Halesha ever was. The demon Barbatos, son of Astaroth, counsels Shazadeh. I believe it is he I have felt entering this world as Shazadeh's sorcery thins the portal between the two."

"Can you at least defeat him...this Barbatos? C'mon, Papà," Henrì urged. "We need to have something going for us instead of bad, worse and downright awful."

"I do not know," Tamen replied. "The longer this world remains unbalanced, the greater in strength the demons become.

Henrì laid his head back on the chair. "Now we have hell to contend with. Absolutely beautiful," he snipped. "Well...I've made arrangements for *three* to Egypt whenever we get Jared to get his act together. Everybody that needs to be paid has been paid more than well enough to keep their mouths shut."

Tamen didn't reply.

"Papà?"

"It has nothing to do with Jared," Tamen replied. "My apologies. I already heard you thinking the question. It is just a habit reading other's thoughts. I often think that perhaps if I had completed the spell and been transformed wholly into an angel, I would feel differently about my immortality. Unlike mortal memories that are cut and pieced together and reside as shadows in your mind, from the moment I became half-mortal and half-angel, every memory is as vivid now as it was when it happened. If I were to live for another thousand years, I would still remember this moment here with you in your smudged white socks, jeans and how your t-shirt hangs slightly lower on your right shoulder than your left. I remember all completely. And I am weary of it, Henrì," he whispered.

Henrì looked down. "What do we do now?"

Tamen sat in the other chair. "We listen...we watch...we pray."

"Papà?" Henrì began, "I—I'll be alright. Aria raised me well enough to take care of myself, and...and, no matter what happens, I'm going to be just fine. If *that's* what you really want, then I want it for you too. I love you too much not to." Henrì turned his head and wiped his wet eyes. When he looked back, he realized he had just been talking to no one. Tamen's body was already empty of his spirit. Henrì got up and poured himself a glass of bourbon and raised it. "To the best father that I know of," Henrì said. "Good-night, papà."

* * *

It had been years since Jared could remember his mother touching him so gently. He had no more than entered through the kitchen door, hoping he could slip in undetected, when she came from the living room, taken hold of his hand and led him into her bedroom. She sat down on the bed. She was far too quiet, and he already knew why. Tamen had already told him.

Jared looked at her keloids-scarred hands and saw her childhood story written on them. Despite her perfectly painted nails, her hands spoke of a life of hardship and struggle, a great part of which he had begun to understand he had helped create.

"Your Aunt Maymee wants to go back down home," she said softly. "That's where she wants to be now."

"I know she's dying, mom."

Dorthea's eyes bulged. "She's sick! They've got just as good of doctors...better doctors down home as they do here, if you ask me. You mark me, she'll be fine once she gets around folks that know what they're doing."

Jared looked into her eyes and saw she desperately wanted him to agree with her. But after seeing what Tamen had shown him, and now told him about Maymee, he knew his aunt was never going to get better. "She's not just sick, mom. She's dying."

Dorthea sighed in frustration. "I say one thing and you say the opposite. If its blue, you just gotta say its red."

"I'm not trying to argue," he crowed back and then paused. He took in a deep breath and sighed. "All I'm saying is that *I know* she's dying. *And I know* that the doctors can't do anymore for her."

"Who told you that? Maymee?"

Jared hesitated. "No."

Her eyes narrowed. "Robinette?"

Again he moved his head slowly from side-to-side. "Why were you trying to keep it a secret from me anyway?"

"Jared..." She looked up at the ceiling, as if looking for help. "Look at you! *Just look at you!* You stay in trouble at school, and when you're not there, God only knows where you are. You dress like some...*I don't know what!* You put all that mess in your hair and rip-up your brand new clothes to shreds. Now, how you suppose to handle the truth and you can't even handle you?"

Jared stood up. "That's a sorry excuse as usual." As much as he meant for his words to sting, he regretted having said them as her eyes became glassy and then dripped tears. He wanted to apologize, but knew it was too late for that. His cut was not only deep, but also gaping.

"I know Maymee's your everything," she said, with a squeaky sniffle. "I know that! I know she means more to you than I do. Satisfied?"

Jared's lips quivered. "Mom—no..."

"I tried raising you the best I knew how," she said. "I may not have been there for you all the time, but when I wasn't, whatever I was doing, it was for you. You may not understand me, but I understand you better than you think I do." Dorthea wiped away her tears and dried her hands on her robe. "We're going to strike out tomorrow night and head on down to Nuxta. Well, I guess tonight really, since it's just about fore-day in the morning. You best get some sleep."

"Us? What?" Jared sputtered. "I've got finals next week."

"The us is Thaddeus," Dorthea replied. "He offered to help drive. And that Mr. Pierceman already called while you were gone and said you were all done. He gave you straight A's, so you must have been doing what you were suppose to be doing."

"When?"

"When what?"

"When did he call?"

"Umm...I don't remember exactly when. Three...four...something like that."

"That's all he said?"

She looked at him sideways. "That's all he said. Aren't you glad to hear it?"

Jared rubbed his forehead. "Yeah, great...cool."

"And call that Chris child back tomorrow," Dorthea said. "He's been calling all night"

"I will," Jared promised.

Jared walked to the door and had almost shut it when his mother called out. "I did forget something, baby," she said. "That Mr. Pierceman said you have one more project to hand in, but he already graded you on it? Don't make sense to me how he can grade you on something if you haven't done it yet? Anyway...he said you would know what it is. He said it was about some book? You know what he's talking about?"

"Yeah...I do. It's a tough book to read."

* * *

Lying down on his bed, Jared couldn't force his mind to shut out the voices of Henrì, Tamen or his mother. On the opposite side of the room where his posters were, all he could see were images of Egypt populated with gods and devils. And all around him, unseen but heard, his Aunt Maymee's raspy breaths sneaking into his room from hers next door.

His thoughts turned to the demon Shazadeh and Lord Yikan, who both wanted him dead. Remembering Lord Yikan's swirling liquid eyes was all it took for him to jump out of bed and turn on the light. He searched his bottom drawer of his dresser and found a nightlight he'd buried there. He snapped it into the outlet and made a mental note to hide the *Mogo, the flying purple dog* nightlight his Aunt Maymee gave him as a birthday present years ago, as soon as he woke.

Still, with the lights off and Mogo casting his toothy, canine glow in the corner of the room, he was far from at ease. He pulled the covers up over his eyes. If Maymee wasn't sick, he knew, even though he was a teenage boy, she wouldn't object if he slipped into bed beside her for a reassuring snuggle. But someone else was near.

"Calm your mind, Jared. I am here."

Jared jumped at the sound of Tamen's voice slipping into his head. He pulled the covers down from his face and exhaled loudly. When he looked around the room, there was no one but Mogo glowing back at him. "Where are you?" Jared whispered.

"Shhhh," Tamen thought to him. *"Speak with your mind, not with your mouth, lest you awaken your mother and aunt. To answer your question, I am standing right beside your bed."*

"You are?" Jared thought back.

"My spirit is."

"How long have you been here?"

"Long enough."

"Are you...um, going to stay for a while?" Jared asked, trying and not trying to sound desperate. "I mean...that is...if you have to..."

"I must assist Henrì in finishing preparing for our journey," Tamen told him. *"And then soon, I will be by your side until you no longer have need of my magic, but possess your own. It is a risk that must be taken if we are to have a chance against those that seek us."*

"Its...OK, if you—"

"I will not leave you right this moment," Tamen interrupted. *"Do not fear yet, for that time will come soon enough. For now, just sleep. When you journey to Nuxta, I shall be with you then."*

"You already know what I decided to do?"

"I see your thoughts clearly. You should know this by now. I see what it is you are plotting. I do not agree that it can be done without great risk, but I do not fault you for contemplating such a thing."

"Will you?"

"If you remain true to your word and become who you were born to be, I will do as you wish. I promise on the soul of my beloved Amenhotep."

"Sweet!"

Tamen sighed longingly. *"Still such a child."*

"I'm just a zygote compared to you."

"Rest your mind. Sleep now and I shall watch over you until morning."

"Another story would help," Jared asked sheepishly. "You know... something to doze off to? You don't have to if—"

"Of course, I want to," Tamen replied. *"I have tales enough to fill a thousand books and then a thousand more. Let us see."* Tamen paused for a moment. *"Ahhh! In the year two hundred after the Christ, I was in southern England and had walked into a village that had just been ravaged by marauders. There were heads and legs and arms that had been hacked off with swords everywhere I looked. I—"*

"Tamen?" Jared interrupted.

"Yes."

"You have anything that's not so creepy and doesn't have heads being chopped off? Something happy maybe?"

"Ahh...of course."

The room instantly smelled different than the usual sock and sweat aroma Jared was used to. The sweet smell of lavender tickled his nose and made his eyelids heavy.

"I shall tell you the story told to me by Mala of the life she led before becoming a goddess," Tamen said. *"This, she said to me, happened thousands of years before Egypt was ever thought of, and when mankind was still young. It is about a lost, great isle of legend."*

"Is it true?"

"*Perhaps,*" Tamen replied nonchalantly. "*Who knows? It is a marvelous story nonetheless.*"

Jared pulled the covers to his neck and closed his eyes, as Tamen's smooth, baritone voice washed over him. As he drifted off to sleep, it seemed the words Tamen spoke were no longer merely just words, but moving pictures, like before when he walked beside Tamen in the illusions of ancient Egypt.

"*And it was a marvelous land filled with exotic creatures of lore, never to be seen again by man,*" Tamen thought to him in a whispered voice. "*It was one of these particular creatures, the Zophalian —a gentle creature whose domain was of water and of land, and appeared as both fish and hairless mammal at will—that captured the fascination of Shae-Palappi, princess of Atanteal...or Atlantis, as you mortals have come to call it now. The princess desperately wanted one of these Zophalian for her very own. But to possess one...to cage one of these sacred creatures was forbidden, even for royalty. So, in secret she summoned the court wizard and pleaded that if...*"

CHAPTER 16

"This isn't exactly around town, Jared," Chris commented.

"Sure it is," Jared replied, looking down at him as he balanced walking on the train track. "These tracks go up and cross over the bridge over there, and then make a complete circle around Homer and then out."

"If you look at it that way."

"Technically, it's true!" Jared insisted. "We're around town aren't we?"

Chris shrugged. "Yeah—but only tech-nickle-lee."

"Tech—nick—lee," Jared said slowly.

"Sorry, Einstein!" Chris snapped.

Jared grinned.

Chris stopped. "What the hell's that?"

"What's what?"

"That look!" Chris demanded. "Just 'cause you're some freakin' braniac doesn't mean everyone else is retarded, ya know?"

Jared hopped off the track. "I was kidding."

"Well it always sounds like you're slamming me when you talk like that."

"Talk like—"

"Forget it!" Chris griped, and then walked ahead.

"Hey!" Jared called. He quickstepped to Chris and grabbed his shoulder. "Man, c'mon. I always joke with you like that."

Chris knocked his hand away. "It makes you sound all uppity and phony. You might as well start hangin' around prep-boy, Eric."

"That's jacked-up and you know it!" Jared shot back, more hurt than angry. "Look at me." Jared held up his arms, showing off his deliberately tattered jeans and t-shirt with strategically placed holes. "There's nothing pretentious about me."

"Preten-shoes? Oh yeah...no—no...not you!" Chris mocked. "Just saying the word preten-shoes makes you preten-shoes—whatever that means."

"It means—"

"I don't give a crap what it means—*Jared*."

"Jesus Christ! What's your malfunction?" Jared roared, though the utterance of the Lord's name caused him to shudder. Saying Jesus Christ had always seemed so benign before, but now, it held a whole new meaning for him. He took a deep breath in. "I'm sorry, alright."

"Sure," Chris droned.

"C'mon, Chris, man. I am. I'm sorry."

Chris pushed his glasses back to the top of his nose and rubbed it. "Everyone's got a special somethin'. You're smart and that's yours. I just—haven't found mine yet. But I got one, ya know?"

"I never said you didn't, so don't take it that way—OK?"

"I'm not just some short, fat kid with coke-bottle glasses," Chris protested.

"With bad style," Jared added, with a hopeful wink.

"There's nothing wrong with khakis and a polo," he said, straightening his collar. "It's me. Same as when I find out what my thing is, that'll be all me too. Just me!"

"Alright, alright!" Jared said in faux surrender. "I'm convinced."

"It's not like you're thinking," Chris said. "I'm just sayin', I'm gonna be somebody once I get the hell outta Homer."

Jared groaned. "That's what's got your panties in a bunch? Me leaving?"

"How long are you going to be gone for?" Chris asked.

Jared didn't have an answer to give him. According to Tamen, once transformed, there was no going back or maintaining any connection with those who were still mortal...including Chris. Though he felt saying *so long suckers* to everyone in Homer, Illinois would be sweet; having to say goodbye to Chris was hard to accept. But if the supposed great battle he was in the center of was lost, then Chris having a best friend to pal around with would be the least of his worries. Still, he knew how Chris felt. He could see the hurt on Chris' chubby face and in his magnified eyes, and felt the same way.

"I'm not sure for how long," Jared lied.

"I just wanted to know," Chris said and shrugged. "I'm gonna be at fat camp in a couple of days anyway—*if* I don't convince my mom to spare my life. So I'll just see ya when you get back, right?"

Jared forced a smile. "Sure."

"Things are going to change anyway, huh?" Chris asked. "You're all done with high school and everything now. So what's next? College...job...movin' out?"

Jared added another brick to his façade of lies. "I hadn't really thought about it too much."

"You? That's all you've been talking about since I've known you. *'I'm gettin' the hell out of here!' 'Screw these people!'*" Chris sassed, shaking his head. "You're coming back, right?"

Jared looked him in the eye. "I'm coming back, already!"

Chris studied the ground. "Just make sure you bring your butt back. If you don't, I'm gonna start hanging around with my other friends."

"You don't have any *other* friends."

"I'll make some at fat camp then...fat friends," he added.

"I'll come back. No matter what happens."

Chris stopped and pushed back on Jared's chest. "No matter what happens? You weren't planning on coming back, were you?"

"Yeah...no? No," Jared said, finally giving in. "It's complicated."

Chris' face flushed. "You a freakin' liar!" He set off in a quick walk, causing his butt and fat pockets that hung over his belt to shake and jiggle.

It took Jared only a moment to catch and come around him. Chris tried sidestepping him, but Jared was too tall and far defter. "Just hold on!"

"Why? Got another lie for me?" Chris began walking the other way.

Jared was on him again. "Just listen!"

"Screw off!"

Jared grabbed hold of his wrists and yanked his arms down. Chris struggled momentarily, but the exertion of run-walking seemed to have sapped all the energy he had. He relented finally, much to Jared's relief, as he was now panting too.

"Man, Chris! Just listen to me." He took a moment to catch his breath. "I *will* come back, alright? I promise! It—it just might not be when you expect."

"What's that 'spose to mean?"

Jared squeezed his wrists. "On your life, don't you dare say what I'm going to tell you to anyone. Not your mom or dad. Don't even *think* about it again once I say it—got it?" Chris shook his head. "I mean it, Chris! No one!"

"I got it!" Chris blurted. He tried shaking his wrists free, but Jared squeezed them even tighter.

"Listen," Jared began. "I can't tell you everything...or even most of it. But—but..."

CHAPTER 17

"You did well, Tamen. I give you that much," Lord Yikan muttered, as he sat in his stone chamber in the bowels of the mountain. "But I shall find you. Rest assured, my boy...I will find you."

Thousands of years with watchers scouring through the countless libraries of the world in search of where Tamen had tried hiding had revealed nothing. The only trail left by Tamen was his gift of magic to the Africans, who then spread their gifts of chant magic all over thanks to the slave trade. Now, instead of waiting and listening for just one power surge of chant-magic to trace back to Tamen, there were hundreds and thousands, none of which ever led to Tamen or the child of balance.

But Shazadeh—as cunning as she was lovely, and as lovely as she was deadly—required his sole focus now, Lord Yikan thought.

In the years of her mortal father King Cambyses' abbreviated conquering and ruling of Egypt, she had been more than just a princess of a great empire, but a sorceress of great power and even greater potential. Even without knowledge of true chant-magic, she had mastered the ability to call forth the demon-gods—Tiamat, Upsu and Marduk—and bend their magic to her will. It was this same prowess in those dark arts that had opened her ears to Lord Yikan's calls for help.

'Mala, Zoe'el...Tamen...you fools! To think you could cage me forever was your first mistake,' Lord Yikan seethed.

Only once Shazadeh had weakened the spell enough to allow him to free himself did he realize why the effects of the original spell had waned. To his utter joy, Mala and Zoe'el were no more. When they died, their spells had also, which freed his voice. Though it took hundreds of years of calling out for help, it did finally arrive. And borne from his release was his solemn promise—to make Tamen pay with his life for what he had wrought.

He was weary of the stone temple at the base of the Rocky Mountains, that at least for now he had to consider home. In due time, once he was upon his dais again, and the world under his divine command as the god Aton, he would destroy Shazadeh's mountain refuge and all the mortal slaves within it. That time would undoubtedly come, but patience was needed at the moment.

The temple carved into the mountainside and hidden from prying eyes with an illusion was certainly not the future he had envisioned for himself. To his Egyptian eyes, Shazadeh's Persian influenced art throughout the temple—along with statues of herself as goddess—was crude and lifeless, unlike the more ethereal and vibrant artistry of Egypt that he felt was far superior.

But all was not exactly of Persian influence. Massive generators powered track lighting throughout, as well as ceiling fans in the sacred shrines that housed priceless antiques that were thousands of years old. The office he was sitting in had fallen prey to cold inventions too...computers, fax machines and satellite phones. And all of this, the ancient, the exotic and mechanical fused with the mystical, had all been brought together to find and kill one child and one pretended god...Tamen.

Lord Yikan stopped in mid-thought.

Something was amiss. He could feel it.

Shazadeh was back in the temple. She had left days ago, but had not felt the need to share where she was going, which only added to his theory that he would be disposed of once Tamen and the child of balance were dead. But she was not alone. He sensed waves of energy that were not hers emanating throughout the citadel. Whatever exuded such raw power, he was quite positive, was not of this earthly world.

He willed himself invisible and made for Shazadeh's chamber in the upper most halls of the citadel. He didn't trust the hundreds of human slaves who called the place home and kept the miniaturized city running. Though they feared him and bowed humbly, he knew their allegiance was not with him...*at least most of them.* The mortals were of every ethnicity, background and age. With a glance into their soulless eyes, he could easily identify the ones who had willingly given parts of their life essence to Shazadeh in exchange for outward beauty.

He slowed his pace as he neared the double doors leading to her sanctum. The dual energy—one belonging to Shazadeh, and one from whatever she had called into this world this time—pulsed in waves over him. Like no more than a common snoop, he tilted his head in the direction of the room and listened.

"Why do you doubt me, my daughter?" Lord Yikan heard the voice say to Shazadeh, and knew instantly it was no minor demon she communed with, but the Grand Duke himself...Astaroth. "There are laws which bind even one as great as I. Ask not of me to find the child of balance again, for that knowledge is hidden from my sight. Thou must do this on thy own. And done, it must be."

"Tamen—the Egyptian, has hidden the child," Shazadeh seethed. "What game Tamen plays at I do not know, though I sense he moves quickly, knowing we are close to possessing Metatron's tome which he covets. But he will stumble, Father. And when he does, I shall unleash a fury—"

"Have a care, daughter," Duke Astaroth warned. "Seek out and find the child of balance—kill him and the Egyptian if thou wish—but in thy quest, do not molest the chosen three of Yahweh, or even strike at any Celestial Host or else they will slay thee—that is the Covenant."

"Aye, Father," Shazadeh replied. "I care not about the chosen three of Yahweh. When I have killed the child, the three of Yahweh —chosen or not—will be forced to live under my rule as goddess. The three of Yahweh can pray to him all they want then, but without balance, this world will be mine forever...praise be to thee, grand duke."

"And the rule of Hell solely in my grip whilst Lucifer sleeps," Duke Astaroth added.

"Then it is done? You have reigned in the princes of the lower realms? Asmodeus? Leviathan also?"

"Even mine own father—Beelzebub. *I am* Astaroth, my dear," he boasted. "Until the final war—I rule Hell. Though if you are balanced, then we, all of us are doomed."

"That shall not come to pass, Father."

"Then beseech my presence no more, for I shall not come until the child of balance is dead," Duke Astaroth commanded. "Then I shall bear thy crown and make thee queen and goddess of this first Earth. And by my say, you and you alone shall rule Yahweh's world, as I govern hell."

"Father wait!"

Astaroth continued. "I give thee thy brother Barbatos' ten sacred names and seal of summoning to call upon him and assist thee—but only once."

"Praise to thee, Father," Shazadeh offered graciously.

Feeling Duke Astaroth's essence fade away, Lord Yikan fled back to his chambers convinced now more than ever that once Shazadeh has killed the child of balance, his own demise would soon follow. "You whore!" Lord Yikan spat. He picked up the computer

266 · Orlando Smart-Powell

monitor on his desk and flung it against the stone wall, shattering it into hundreds of pieces.

"Such sweet-nothings you say, my lord," Shazadeh's husky voice piped up from behind him.

It was nearly impossible for anyone to startle him, but it was exactly what happened. Her sudden presence—one moment in her sanctum above and the next in his office—was not an impromptu visit. Spontaneity, he knew, was not her way; her every move...every word...was planned and calculated.

"You have sullied this place with these mortal female and male whores who crave nothing but beauty—like you and your demon ilk. What makes you think I was referring to you?" he asked nonchalantly.

"Why so fiery this evening?" she asked, as if hurt, though she smiled at him. "Do you despise me so much? Hmm?"

"I have no love for anyone, if that is answer enough."

Shazadeh's black braids swayed as she moved toward him. The white silk of her shoulder-strapped gown did nothing to conceal her black breasts. As tall as he was, when she stopped in front of him, they were eye-to-eye with only a wisp of air separating them. "You are a mystery to me, my lord," she whispered.

"I do not have time to share in your frivolity with the humans. As if you did not know, there are more important things that require my attention at the moment—*goddess*," he added, without a hint of reverence.

"Which is precisely why I am here."

Lord Yikan sat down at his desk chair and folded his arms. "Pray tell."

"I have sensed another source of energy that bears our attention."

"When?"

"But only moments ago," she replied. "Strangely, when I felt it, I did not sense the pure essence of the chant."

"Bah!" Lord Yikan huffed, waving his hand as though swatting away a nat. "It is most likely just a channeled spirit."

"But with the child of balance so close, we cannot discount anything," she replied. "Perhaps it is your former apprentice I sensed. He is quite the wily one, is he not? He has evaded you at every turn. You said when he fled from the crucifixion at Golgotha, you would find him within a matter of years—no?"

"He has evaded *both* of us," Lord Yikan corrected her.

"Then how is it I have sensed what you have not just now?" she asked. "Mayhap you were...*preoccupied*...with something else at the moment?"

"Aye," he replied without hesitation. "I have a religion to run. Your dimwitted mortals seem incapable of doing it on their own."

"I see," she acknowledged. Silence lingered a while between them before she broke it. "Accompany me then. I desire to see this one who has called forth magic without the sacred chant. Perhaps we may find some answers to the whereabouts of the child we seek. If not, I am sure I can find other uses for whoever he or she is."

* * *

They flew southeast from their mountain citadel upon the gentle hum of their chants, though there was nothing in Lord Yikan's thoughts of the past that were gentle at the moment. He had loved her when she was still just princess Faridesha of the Persian Empire, that is, until she became Shazadeh, the demon she was now. But then, ever so grateful to the brown-skinned young woman who helped released him from his prison, he didn't have any qualms about tutoring her in the art of chant-magic. Though still a mortal, she quickly impressed him as a fast study. But too, she hadn't come to him ignorant of the unseen world and those in it.

At twenty years of age, she'd been exiled to Egypt from the kingdom of Babylon upon accusations of dark sorcery. From her own mouth she admitted that these charges of demonic sorcery were not based in gossip, but in hard truth. Allegations that she spoke to demons, she claimed proudly. With a slender face, large dark brown eyes, and full lips that begged to be sucked on, it was simple for her to seduce men and women, and then deliver them to the demons she'd called forth, for the dark spirits demanded the taste of human flesh in exchange for their gifts.

During the next few years after being rescued by her, against his better judgment, he fell in love with her—the princess as well as the demon sorceress that she was. He knew she consorted with minor demons and was able to draw power from them. By learning their ten sacred names and being given their seal of summoning from other demons that were in the midst of waging war in hell, she could use them as she wished. What he hadn't known at the time was that she had become the mortal familiar of the mighty demon-lord, Astaroth. And it was Duke Astaroth who gave her the knowledge to completely decipher the chants of the tome. By the time Lord Yikan felt the power of the Creation Chant being sung, and then shaking the lower levels of the palace they lived in, the spell had already stripped her body of blood and bile, and had engulfed her in flames.

But she didn't transform in the same manner as he had.

She sang with such precision, and never once warbled from the pain as her body melted away to nothing but bone. Contrarily, she seemed to enjoy it. With nothing but a skinless skull, she smiled wickedly as she gave voice to new chants that he knew had come not from the tome, but from the duke himself. And when it was over, she was no longer the honey-skinned young woman he loved, but a beautiful full-fledged demon of black, shimmering silken skin.

Her ability to chant was now of utter perfection and precision. Without effort, her chants could outpace his and negate them entirely. This they discovered shortly after her metamorphosis... much to her joy and his chagrin.

What love she had professed to have for him died shortly thereafter, he recalled. The roles shifted—not just teacher becoming pupil, but more akin to pupil now the master and teacher the lap dog. His plans for reclaiming Egypt—and the world—as the god Aton was now in ruins, as a new order arose through Shazadeh. This new destiny was solely hers. And though part of that plan included Tamen's death, which Lord Yikan was glad of, he realized that Tamen and the child of balance would not be the only ones to die in Shazadeh's grand plan. Now, ever so close to the end game, he knew his only choice was to stay close to her and find a weakness in the demon-goddess who appeared to have none. But—if there was a way to kill her, time was running out, and he was no closer to discovering it now than he was over two thousand years ago.

Lord Yikan turned his attention from the past and to the small town below where they flew. Stretching out his senses as he landed on the ground slightly after Shazadeh, he began detecting the fading glimmer of energy she had detected earlier. And for that reason alone, he did not like the vibes the human part of him was now feeling.

They were standing behind a white, wood-frame church in desperate need of painting. Off to the side of it, on the asphalt parking lot, they spotted two black men carrying an unconscious woman from the church and gently placing her in the back of a car.

Lord Yikan slipped into the mortal's minds, starting with the young woman's, and then on to the men who were getting into the front seats. "Do you see him in their thoughts?" Lord Yikan asked, gazing from the woman and men, and then toward the church.

"Yes," Shazadeh replied, as she too gazed at the church decorated with stained-glass windows of flowers, crowns of thorns and crosses.

"The one still in the church—the one they came to see—must be a seer," Lord Yikan stated cautiously. "But there is something odd about him. His thoughts are shielded, though...though he does not even know he hides his thoughts."

"A bit out of practice, my lord," Shazadeh commented, though she too began grimacing as she stared at the church.

"That is not it," he said, wading through the mist clouding the man's mind that was like a jungle of thick, sticky cobwebs. "He is mortal, yet he hides his thoughts like an immortal."

Shazadeh scoffed. "But he *is* human."

"The sort that I have never felt before."

"Then this mortal who clouds his thoughts shall be worthy enough to serve me then," she proclaimed, as she brushed past him.

"Shazadeh, wait!" Lord Yikan cautioned. "We should have a care."

Shazadeh dismissively flipped her hand at him. "He is born of mortal woman and man. What have I—*daughter of a god*—to fear from him?"

"The Christ was born of mortals," Lord Yikan reminded her. He reluctantly followed her toward the church. "You could not stand against him either."

"That was different."

"I see," he quipped.

She paused at the edge of the clearing and looked back at him. "Have you not learned by now that a goddess is denied nothing?"

"At the cost of your life?"

"What life?" she asked incredulously. "I have no life to lose. You, my lord, are simply an immortal in the loosest sense. You should be concerned about such things, not one such as I."

Lord Yikan bowed, though waited until she had turned around before smirking at her.

He expanded his senses ever more and listened as the man inside hummed as he moved about sweeping the floor. He and Shazadeh rose off the ground and glided toward the church like life-size chess pieces. Shazadeh was the first to reach it. Lord Yikan stayed a few yards back.

He rose higher, then used his supernatural vision to peer past the stained glass and spotted the man inside. *Good-looking for a mortal,* Lord Yikan admitted. He guessed when the black man didn't have wrinkles around his eyes or gray in his wavy hair, he had been even more handsome then than now. But other than that, he seemed simply human.

He was a follower of Yahweh; Lord Yikan was able to tell that much from him. He had killed many followers of Yahweh, even as they kneeled and beseeched God's help. So how then, he wondered, could this mortal black man, who was humming an obnoxious tune of glory to his God, unknowingly block his thoughts from others?

Lord Yikan attempted to probe the man's thoughts again, but still came upon screen after screen of haze. That is, until he heard a voice—one that did not belong to the black man, but to a child. He turned and looked toward the wild brush and trees behind the church and spotted the creature, who then spoke to his mind again.

"I believe someone here wants to speak to you," Lord Yikan informed Shazadeh, who was busily stalking her new found prey inside the church.

Shazadeh turned around.

They both concentrated their sights on the waist-tall, white girl beckoning them over. Despite having pigtails and wearing a sun-yellow, summer dress and white knee socks, Lord Yikan knew she was anything but that. Unlike the man in the church, whose mind was shielded, the child that called for them had no such defenses.

Against his probes, the child's outer mind peeled away like an apple raked by razor blades, revealing its true nature.

They glided over to the child. The closer they drew, the greater the child's fear became. But Lord Yikan realized, as he scanned the child's mind, they were not the sole source of the apprehension. When he and Shazadeh were but a few feet from her, the child fell to her ethereal knees without the issuance of a single sound.

"My goddess!" the child said reverently.

Shazadeh smiled. "Why are you here, spirit?"

Her face was pale, though her cheeks looked as though they had been painted with a wet brush dipped in blood. She looked at Lord Yikan and squinted. "Goddess—what kind of creature is he?" the child asked, ignoring Shazadeh's initial inquiry.

"More than you will ever be," Lord Yikan growled back.

The child shook her head slowly and pointed at Shazadeh. "I know who she is. She's the goddess. Yep—she is. Everyone knows the daughter of the duke!"

"You will answer Shazadeh now," Lord Yikan demanded. "Or should I place a circle of binding around you, for I know *thy name!*"

The child's faced shifted from innocence to absolute horror. "*Noooo!* Goddess, don't let him—*please!*"

Lord Yikan's blue-liquid eyes spun as he grinned. Once encircled and captured within the spell, the spirit had only but two choices. One—leave the circle and transcend to one of the two realms... heaven or hell. Or two—stay bound in the circle for all eternity.

"I see you—*Victor Lewis,*" Lord Yikan whispered. "Oh yes, Victor. I see you ever so clearly through this masquerade of yours. Your illusion of a sweet, innocent girl may fool lesser beings, but not us. *We* can see the sick man that you are—the one with a broken neck who was hung from the gallows and castrated for killing the very child you now pretend to be."

The spirit, Victor, swayed his head from one side to the other.

"Hell is a paradise," Shazadeh commented. "Not that you will ever see it, Victor. There are laws that govern such wicked mortals as you. My father and I say who lives or dies, not some maniacal mortal that seeks blood and pleasure in the flesh of a child. Your depravity has reserved you a special place where mad demons reside and await the chance to test the limits of your soul."

"The Isle of Phenox shall be your home," Lord Yikan added.

"But—but I have come to help you," Victor protested.

"In exchange for...?" Lord Yikan posed.

Victor gazed up at Shazadeh. "Ask the duke to have mercy on my soul. I—I did not know what I was doing when I took the child's life. I—I—"

"Liar!" Lord Yikan huffed and looked away from the spirit. He'd already gathered that the child, Elisa Momet, Victor was impersonating was not his first victim, but one of many children he had tortured and murdered during his forty years of life. Elisa just happened to be the one that had transformed the search party who found him into a riotous mob who hung him and cut off his offending parts.

"Let Victor speak," Shazadeh said. She raised her brow as she glided closer to the spirit. "But, my Lord Yikan is correct...you cannot deceive us. So tell me, Victor—what has a damned thing such as you to give that may help one such as I? Speak true now, or I will bind you myself."

Victor kneeled again. "I have lied. Goddess, forgive me," he said, in the voice of the young girl. "But I speak true now, I swear I do! I have nothing left but my soul to give if I don't." Shazadeh nodded. "I—I came to the woman who just left, and had been with her for two whole years. But she called me! She invited me in, so I came."

"You came as a child, not who you truly are," Lord Yikan noted.

"Yes my, lord—I did," Victor admitted. "But she was lonely and craved her child that she had lost, so I did come—but only to soothe her."

"At first," Shazadeh said.

Victor bounced his pigtails as he nodded his head. "Yes, goddess. But then—then I felt her flesh and it had been so long since I've felt my own. So I stood on her spirit and rose my own up within her. Only..."

"Yes, spirit, we know," Lord Yikan said wearily. "When will you imps learn that you are who you are, whether dead or alive? Your taste for child-flesh did not die when you did. You sought to sate your thirst for it by possessing the woman and using her to commit your deeds, no?"

"Yes!" Victor squeaked. "But I was driven out before I could—by him!" Victor pointed to the church.

"Go on!" Shazadeh commanded.

"He has powerful magic, that one," Victor whispered. "Of all the humans I've been in, I've never been cast out of one so hard. It—it was like he grabbed me with his hands. And he bound me from coming near her again, because I tried to, and he threw me back. There was nothing I could do." His ghostly form wavered and almost disappeared before strengthening. "I was running away when I saw you both coming."

"You warn me of a mortal man? That is what you offer a goddess?" Shazadeh asked, obviously insulted. "You are as mad now as you were in life, Victor. You think me some common demon?"

"He is powerful—I swear!"

"Perhaps it is time you just accept your fate, Victor, and go to the isle with the other damned souls," she told him.

He shook his pigtails. "Nooooooo!"

"You cannot escape your fate forever," Shazadeh said with a smile.

"Never there! *Please!*"

"But there you shall go eventually," Lord Yikan assured him. "You may find another mortal to possess for a time. Inevitably, you will wrong a mortal who knows how to bind meaningless spirits such as yourself. Then, my dear Victor, you will have no choice."

"Goddess?" Victor implored.

"Your request for sanctuary in my father's paradise is denied," Shazadeh said offhandedly. "My father's land is for those faithful to the old gods and those who will serve me on this world, but never for the likes of you. Perhaps Phenox will not be as bad as you imagine—cling to that. For now, the reward for your useless warning is to go free from here—that is my decision."

Victor began weeping. He sniffled and looked at both with tear filled eyes. "Y—yes, goddess."

"Go!" Lord Yikan spat. "Enjoy what little time you have left here on Earth."

Victor rose from the ground and gave Lord Yikan and Shazadeh one last glance before running into the woods. "I'll stay here forever! Never to Phenox!" he called and then vanished from sight.

"Victor will get his just rewards soon enough," Shazadeh commented.

"But it will not be as bad as you imagine?" Lord Yikan asked. "Why would you tell him such a thing? In Phenox, he will relive every sin he has ever committed."

Shazadeh chuckled. "And be reborn the following morning, only to experience it again. Being wicked for the sake of being wicked is no cause to be wicked at all. She was already heading back toward the church, but this time toward the front of it. "Hell's paradise will fall into ruin before I declare fear of any mortal."

"And if Victor spoke truth?"

"Have the heart of a warrior, my lord," she challenged.

Patience, Lord Yikan thought, as he guarded his mind from Shazadeh. *Your day shall come demon, but not the one you have envisioned. With your bones I will fashion my throne, and Tamen's corpse shall serve as my footstool.*

"Shall we?" She stated, rather than asked. Already she was pushing open the doors with the force of thought.

Lord Yikan followed, but slowly and farther behind. He didn't discount Victor's warning of the handsome mortal, who was visibly startled by their unexpected presence. That he hadn't heard the black man use chant-magic, yet still had the power to forcefully expel Victor from the woman's body gave him pause and concern, both of which Shazadeh lacked as she continued advancing. The black man let the broom slip from his hands as he stared at her, and then at Lord Yikan.

"Get out!" the man demanded, as he began walking backward, but met resistance from the half-wall situated below the pulpit.

Shazadeh inched closer. "We have come to pray. This is a house of God, is it not?"

The man looked down at their shoes, which were inches above the floor. "Not for *things* like you! Get out! By Jesus' own hand—I say get out!" he yelled.

"You mean, the Christ? The one I myself saw die upon the cross?" she teased. "He cannot help you now, my dear. What you Christian fools have yet to learn is that the Christ has long since forsaken you to we who reside between shadow and light. Tell me —how have you made such magic without the sacred chant?"

"I don't know no chant or no magic. But I know you ain't no woman," he accused, and then pointed at Lord Yikan. "And you ain't no man."

Shazadeh glanced at Lord Yikan. "Well, all praise to Yahweh for that, hmm?"

"I already done sent one spirit to hell tonight, and I'll send you too. Both of you!" the man vowed. "Now git! Ain't nothin' here for you devils."

Instead of an immediate reply from Bazeezk, there was silence.

Silence from Shazadeh, Lord Yikan understood, meant more than just simple irritation on her part. Torture and pleasure were synonymous—he'd never seen her show any difference between the two. But something was amiss and disconcerting with this mortal, he thought. The air felt different to him...as though charged with energy.

He wanted Shazadeh dead—yes, but he also needed her for now. Lord Yikan knew Tamen was too powerful for him to kill alone, but she—a full demoness—could. And once she had killed Tamen and the child of balance was dead, then someway...*somehow*...he could find a way to have her join them in death.

She moved closer to the preacher. Lord Yikan started to also, but stopped.

Shazadeh was mere inches from the man and was slowly reaching for him, even as he fell to his knees and began saying the Lord's Prayer. "Tamen, you are not," she told him.

"Our Father, who art in heaven. Hallowed be thy name..."

"Tamen, that coward, would have already fled from me as he did before."

"...as it is in heav—heaven..."

"And you are not the child of balance either."

"...daily bread..."

"You are but human..."

"...forgive us our trespasses..."

"...just a mortal..."

"...lead us not into temptation..."

"...and soon to be..."

Lord Yikan cried out for her to stop, but it was too late. Shazadeh had her hand around the black man's throat and was raising him up, though even she, he sensed, now realized her folly.

"...deliver us from...," the preacher choked, but his last words were finished with a bellow that was far from strangled, and most definitely inhuman. What flowed from his mouth shook the floor, the walls and the foundation of the church. ***"...EVIL ONE!!!"***

"Get away from it!" Lord Yikan cried.

The air crackled with blue, electric-fire all around them. The man in Shazadeh's grasp was no longer the frightened man he was before, but a being brimming with undeniable confidence. Shazadeh was struggling to snap his throat and even resorted to using both of her hands, though to no avail.

The man's head began to swell. On both sides of the engorged head, it seemed as though unseen hands were pushing and pulling, molding what was once his temples and cheeks into another set of ears, eyes, noses and lips—while yet another invisible hand painted the man's brown skin in a glowing white-blue, like the electrical charge it brought with it. All traces of the human man were gone. Growing, and now towering above Shazadeh, was a creature that possessed a single head, but bore three distinct faces. The left face was female...the one on the right, male. The one in the middle was a blend of both sexes. In unison, the three faces locked their six, blue-white eyes on Shazadeh. She let go, fell to the ground and scrambled away from it. The being was twice the size of the man it morphed from and brimmed with a power Lord Yikan had witnessed only once, which was at the impalement of the Christ— those of the Heavenly Host—*the angels.*

"Thou hath broken the law and thus we have come" the center Order said, echoed by the two others, producing a trembling, tripartite timbre. "Leave this place and take thy mongrel, and thy life, I, he, she—we shall spare."

Shazadeh was already on her feet and posturing at the angel. "You risk your place amongst the stars for this mortal!" Her coal black body began stealing light from the ceiling fixtures and wall sconces.

"Damn you, Shazadeh—do not!" Lord Yikan warned, stepping back to the threshold. "Do you not see the mortal is protected? He is..."

"Dead!" Shazadeh growled.

"We say nay to thee, dark one," the Orders countered. "There shall be a balance amongst all things, alive or spirit. Thou knowest full well there cannot be darkness without light upon this earth. Thou hath three of dark, and we who are of righteousness hath thy equal in number. This blessed mortal belongs to us."

"He is one of the sacred three," Lord Yikan whispered to her. "That is why we could not read his thoughts. We must leave from here. They will protect him unto death—*our death!*"

"Thy mongrel is correct," the three said. "Raise thy hand against our mortal charge and we shall destroy thee, for we of the *Orders*—Oriziel and Nigiel and Palis—hath been given authority from the Holy Ghost thus even Satan must bow to. That is the covenant! It cannot be torn asunder."

Shazadeh spat mucus as black as her skin on the ground in front of the tri-faced Order. "Damn you," she hissed, before starting to chant.

Lord Yikan knew he could not convince her to see reason. The mortal had insulted her, and now the Orders had humbled her. He backed out of the church just as Shazadeh was finishing her chant. He already knew what spell she had sung, so he had no need to look up at the black, rolling clouds suddenly appearing in the sky.

The ground began rumbling as ground-splitting lighting and thunder approached. By the power of her chant, Shazadeh had replicated the black storm outside onto the ceiling of the church itself. The Orders looked up into the dark cloud swirling above them, though there was nothing Lord Yikan saw upon their faces that even resembled concern, let alone fear.

Lord Yikan felt the power of the storm released milliseconds before it struck the Orders. The pure, white bolt of lightning Shazadeh released was so magnificent and devastating, even she stumbled backward when it struck. The sonic boom that followed shattered every window and flung him from the church, rolling him across the road in front. His head throbbed and vision spun in yet another failed test of his invulnerability. He looked back and saw that even Shazadeh had been sent reeling out and onto the ground by the brutal force of her own magic.

In front of her, through a cloud of black smoke, bursts of fire spewed from the shattered windows and roof that had been completely blown away. She turned to Lord Yikan and smiled victoriously. But her smugness only held his attention for a moment, as his eyes were suddenly drawn upward to what was moving behind her.

She did not have a chance to turn around before the Orders, completely unscathed, and all three faces raging in a white fire, snagged her by the neck with its monstrous hand. Without a voice to chant a spell, she struck at the creature with her fists. But the creature would not be denied. It could not. Lord Yikan knew that much of the holy covenant.

With its other hand, the Orders took hold of both of Shazadeh's hands and bound them in a fist. Like the cracking sound of a pickaxe striking a rock, the bones in her wrists and forearms snapped as the creature flexed its hand. Lord Yikan had heard Shazadeh scream in the throes of ecstasy, but never from pain like she did now.

The Orders cocked their arm and threw her toward the forest opposite the church, barely missing Lord Yikan, who ducked moments before Shazadeh whizzed past his head. He turned in the direction she was thrown, and saw two towering trees deep in the forest sway and another shudder, like a meteor had just crashed into it. All three of the Order's faces bore down on him—but only briefly. They looked over at the woods where they had thrown Shazadeh.

He entertained the idea of leaving Shazadeh to the creature's mercy—which it had none. If it caught a hold of her again, he knew it would kill her. But as much as he wanted her dead, he needed her alive...at least for now.

GODS OF EGYPT · 281

With a chant, he flew high above the trees where Shazadeh had been flung. He followed the path of the two large ones she had hit and bent, and landed at the one where she lay unconscious and embedded halfway in its trunk. He slammed his elbow into the tree repeatedly until it splintered and split, and released Shazadeh from its hold. With her in his arms, he took to the sky again, hoping the Orders, who he could see below looking up at them, would not follow.

With a chant, he flew high above the trees where Shazadeh had been flung. He followed the path of the two large ones she had hit and bent, and landed at the one where she lay unconscious and embedded halfway in its trunk. He slammed his elbow into the tree repeatedly until it splintered and split, and released Shazadeh from its hold. With her in his arms, he took to the sky again, hoping the Orders, who he could see below looking up at them, would not follow.

Thankfully for him, they did not.

But all of this—Yahweh and Satan, and the war between angles and demons—he wanted no part of. For all he cared, if they destroyed themselves in the process, then all the better for him.

For a short while, he flew backward with an ever-watchful eye for the tri-faced Order. Shazadeh, cradled in his arms, began to squirm and work her way back to consciousness. It had been hundreds, if not thousands of years since he had felt her skin in such an intimate way, and now with no choice, he was repulsed by having it so close to his own. He refused to look at her face, fearing it would remind him of the young woman he had once loved...his only love. Now, she was only second to Tamen amongst those whom he despised the most.

I—not some demon or pretended goddess, or even the Christ will ever rule this world. On my immortal life, it will never happen, he vowed silently. One by one, he set forth in his mind preparations to lay low every country and state, starting with Egypt, until there was not a nation upon the earth that did not bow to his sacred sun-image and give worship...

...to Aton.

CHAPTER 18

To Jared, the Mississippi sky seemed no different than the one back in Illinois. Though in Illinois, where jacket-worthy spring winds were constant, June in Mississippi felt like the middle of summer back home. Even in the morning hours with the air conditioner running in the van, Jared could feel the heat and humidity already building up outside.

He looked out the van's window and rubbed the crusted sleep matter from his eyes. He'd found trying to sleep sitting up to be nearly impossible, especially during a fifteen-hour ride. His mother and Thaddeus were up front speaking slightly above the radio, which was grinding out yet another soulful, church tune from one of the hundreds of gospel stations Thaddeus turned to while he drove. Maymee was lying down in the back, resting as peacefully as the constant phlegm coming up and choking her would allow.

Jared sensed a change in his mother the moment Thaddeus announced he was *pulling them into home,* when they crossed the Mississippi state line. Her voice still had its husky growl, though he noticed she began stuttering over her words with each mile they put behind them. Her rock, Thaddeus, would sometimes take her hand and squeeze it, Jared saw from the seat behind her.

Jared hadn't brought up the subject of his father since they'd left, and neither had she, though he knew his father was foremost on both of their minds. In daydreams, he envisioned his father embracing him and shedding tears like they did on talk shows where reunions turned out wonderfully. That hope was tainted with the fact that his father hadn't wanted him in his life, according to his mother. But if he really had, where were the phone calls? Jared wondered. A letter? A card? Something? Even a 'screw you'?

With his Aunt Maymee dying, and Tamen and Henrì gone, all Jared wished was for something to make sense. He hadn't seen or heard from Tamen since being lulled to sleep by his tale of Mala and her ancient Atlantic-island home. It was the same with Henrì.

He'd even taken Chris to Henrì's home—first, to see Henrì and Tamen before he left for Mississippi, and two, to prove to an unbelieving Chris, the truth of his condensed tale of God, devils and angels. He knew Tamen was going to be furious at him for having mentioned it to anyone at all. But that became a moot point anyway.

After having to literally pull Chris up the steps of Henrì's front porch and knocking, at first to no reply, then looking in the window, he saw there had been no need to have knocked at all. Through the slivers where the drapes almost met, all he saw was a room barren of furniture and a film of dust on its unfinished wood floors. It was as though no one had lived there for years. Each window he peered through gave him a different view, but the same result.

When an elderly man walking his dog stopped and questioned them, Jared's first impulse was to tell the stooped over white man to *mind his own business*. Though after a few deep breaths, he cooled his temper.

"I said—what are you boys doing around there?" the old man had asked, as he yanked on his dog's leash. The dog looked up at him, chased his butt twice, and then sat.

"We're looking for Hen...Pierceman...Taylor Pierceman?" Jared answered.

The old man raised his gray, stray-haired brows. "Pierceman? I don't know any Pierceman fellow. You boys got the wrong place. Nobody's lived in that house for years."

"Uhhhhh...no one?" Chris squeaked, and slowly angled his head up at Jared. "Wow! Ya hear that? Noooooo one."

Jared growled at Chris.

"Rats and mice maybe," the old man replied. "I've lived across the street here for thirty-one years...be thirty-two come September. I know who lives or don't live around here, and there ain't been no one in this old place for some years."

Chris and the unofficial neighborhood watchman stared at Jared as though he'd gone loony. All in all, he knew Chris didn't believe any part of his tale, even though he smiled politely when he tried to explain what probably happened. Halfway back home, he just gave up trying to convince Chris that their teacher, Taylor Pierceman, was actually a man from New Orleans named Henrì Bedeau, and that Tamen, Henrì's two-thousand year-old-foster father, was really a former god of ancient Egypt.

Seeing Chris' glassy, cow eyes behind his thick glasses begging him not to go still punched at his gut. Chris was the only friend he had—the only person he felt understood what it was like to be a loner—and the only reason he could think of worth going back to Homer, Illinois. Even with all the money Chris' parents had that afforded him the best clothes and the newest Atari and Nintendo systems, he knew Chris was searching for who he really was and where he fit in—just like he felt. He promised that no matter what happened...whether he became the being that Tamen spoke of or not...he would come back to Chris one way or another.

"What's with those ditches in front of everyone's home?' Jared asked.

"They're sewers," Thaddeus replied, as he turned the corner. "See how full they are now? Must have stormed like the devil here last night."

"It cost too much to put in real drain sewers in those days," Dorthea added. "Some of these homes haven't had toilets and running water all that long."

"Another poor southern town," Thaddeus bemoaned.

"Town?" Dorthea scoffed. "Nuxta's just a bunch of old homes and a few stores to get you by with milk and bread. Mama said everyone's moving on out. In a few more years, there won't be anything here."

They passed through the town's center, which was nothing but a long road. Jared bobbed from one side of the van to the other as his mother pointed out each of the red brick buildings that were once stores she used to frequent as a child, not boarded up fire hazards that they were now. "Nuxta may be ran down and fallin' down, but it's home, Jared," Dorthea said proudly. "It's my home and Maymee's home—your home too."

"If you're trying to make me fall in love with the place, you can give it up now," Jared quipped.

Thaddeus laughed. "Boy—you crazy!" Thaddeus pulled the van into the carport of a small house with blue vinyl siding. It was a mansion compared to the rust-covered trailer across the street and the two homes on either side of it which both sat off center on cinder blocks.

Peeking up at his mother, he saw she her lips were pursed as she and Thaddeus got out. He hesitated so that his mother and Thaddeus were the first to make it to the two old women and man waiting on the porch, and pretended to see to Aunt Maymee, who was fast asleep. He took his time unbuckling her seatbelt, all the while sneaking a peek at those his mother was hugging and Thaddeus was shaking hands with.

Though he had never met them in person, but had spoken to Althea, his grandmother, on holidays and birthdays, he knew exactly who each one was. His grandmother was the tallest of the three, though not the grayest; that was his great, aunt Lilly who stood next to her barefoot. The short, stout man talking over everyone wearing a white Kangol hat was no doubt Tobias, his second or third cousin or something like that.

He was glad he'd decided at the last moment to dye his hair to black before meeting his relatives. Though rushing to do so, he'd stained not only the bathroom countertop, but also a good portion of the back of his neck and the tips of his ears. When he got out and came from around the side of the van, everyone stopped speaking and turned in his direction. Instinctively, he sought out his mother's eyes for reassurance, which she gave him with a closed-mouth smile. When he stepped up on the porch, he stood slightly behind her.

Aunt Lilly was the first to approach. Jared had to stoop to see her.

She put her hands on her hips and squinted at him. From a toothless mouth she said, "You down right the spitting image of your daddy. Just a shame what happened over there."

Dorthea sighed. "Not now, Aunt Lilly...*please.*"

"I told ya'll to keep her inside," Tobias grumbled.

Aunt Lilly pointed at him. "Ain't you supposed to be somewhere seeing to those jailbird boys of yours?"

"Look here old woman! My boys..."

"Shush-up! Both of you!" Althea looked each in the eye. "Ya'll get on in before you wake up everyone. It barely even morning, and ya'll crowin' before the rooster done even got a chance to! Ya'll know how Ms. Etta Mae is over yonder." Althea nodded toward the rusted trailer across the street. "She'll have the whole town talkin'."

Aunt Lilly rolled her milky brown eyes. "Shoot! She been peeping out the window ever since they pulled up in the drive. Ain't that right, Ms. Etta?" she hollered across the road. "I heard tell your boy done got picked up for smokin' that wacky mess again. A shame, ain't it, girl? Just a shame!"

This time, everyone scolded Aunt Lilly. But when they all looked over at the front window of the trailer, they saw the curtains fluttering to and fro before coming to a standstill.

Aunt Lilly and Tobias were quickly banished into the house by Althea, though could still be heard bickering even with the door closed. Jared met Althea halfway as she limped on her right hip toward him. Though they didn't really know one another, in her eyes and open arms, he sensed an air of excitement, longing and familiarity. She hugged him tight and looked up at him.

"Dotty...he's so handsome."

"He is, Mama," Dorthea agreed proudly.

"You know you my only grandbaby?" Althea said more than asked. "And a big one, too! You get that from your grandpappy on my side—tall as a tree!" But then, her voice dropped. "Now let me go see my other child."

Dorthea led her by the arm and motioned with her head for Jared and Thaddeus to follow. Althea stretched her head inside the van as far as she could, but began stumbling back, right into Jared's arms. Her mouth began twitching moments before the tears came.

"I know the Lord is goin' to see to my child—I know it...I know it," Althea sputtered.

Dorthea rubbed her shoulders. "It's OK mama. It's going to be just fine. Jared—Jared take Mama inside for me."

He did as asked. Once inside, he helped Althea onto the sofa where Tobias and Aunt Lilly, who immediately suspended their squabbling, tended to her. When he went back out, Dorthea and Thaddeus were sitting on the opening into the side of the van. Dorthea had been crying and quickly wiped her face and cleared her throat as he neared.

Thaddeus looked up at him. "That wheelchair won't roll up over those steps, so I'll just have to carry Maymee in."

"No!" Jared forced his way between Dorthea and Thaddeus. "I will."

Maymee was so weak, Thaddeus and Dorthea had to place her flopping arms in her lap, as Jared cradled her head like an infant's to keep it from falling backward. Aunt Lilly met him at the door and led him to a room down the hall where he laid Maymee in bed. He began pulling the covers over her, but Aunt Lilly stopped him. "Not yet, boy. We need to change her first. You go on out and get her thangs."

The thought of one day becoming so ill and having to rely on others to change, feed and bathe him, made Tamen's offer of immortality a great deal more appealing at the moment. "Aunt Lilly needs you inside," Jared told his mother as he walked outside.

"Baby—bring in my purse," Dorthea told him. "Maymee's going to need her morphine. I don't want that pain getting ahead of her. So why don't you and Thaddeus get something to eat once you're done unloading while I get Maymee settled?"

The incentive of food seemed to have put an extra pep in Thaddeus' step. Jared was able to manage two suitcases at a time, but Thaddeus easily squeezed a third under his arm, though had to set one down to allow room for his generous rear-end to get past the front door. Jared was far more tired than he was hungry, and after getting the luggage in, declined the greasy, pinky sausages Tobias had started frying for them. Thaddeus quickly washed his hands, found the bread and layered butter on it in preparation of the sausages.

With everyone occupied at the moment, Jared kicked off his black army boots, turned on the TV and laid down on the sofa. What seemed like minutes later, someone touched his face and startled him awake. He hadn't even realized he had fallen asleep and that an entire hour, not just moments had already passed. Even before his eyes adjusted and he saw Dorthea leaning over him, her sweet familiar scent gave her away. Her lower lids were swollen and looked as though they had been painted with charcoal. He was about to speak when she stroked his cheek again, gently shushed him and smiled.

"How's Aunt Maymee," he muttered.

"Doing good...sleeping," Dorthea said. "You need some more yourself."

"Naw," he mumbled drowsily and then closed his eyes. "I'm all good."

"I know my baby," she whispered and then chuckled softly. "You go back to sleep now."

And he did.

He awoke just before six o'clock in the evening to the bullish snore he figured was Thaddeus sleeping somewhere nearby. He rose from the sofa. A quick peek inside the living room confirmed his guess. He tiptoed back across the family room and out its patio doors. He sat in one of the black cast-iron chairs next to the patio table and propped his legs up on another. In the quiet that surrounded him, with the exception of two teenage girls who were walking by and unashamedly stared and smiled at him, he began wondering just how close or far away Tamen was at the moment.

He closed his eyes and began calling out with his mind. *'Tamen...are you here? Can you hear me?'* He waited for a reply, but nothing. *'I've thought some more about what you said. It's not that I don't believe you. I—I just...It's confusing, ya know? But—I understand what I need to do. You know what I mean? I'm not going to let my family die. If I got to...I got to! All right? Tamen?"* Jared focused harder. *'Tamen!'*

"Who you talkin' to?" Aunt Lilly was standing in the patio doorway with her hands on her hips.

Jared gawked at her. "Huh?"

Aunt Lilly raised her brow.

"I—I wasn't...wasn't even talking," he sputtered, bewildered as to how she even knew he was thinking to someone.

"Uh-huh," she uttered. She stepped down onto the patio and closed the door behind her. "I think you lying to Aunt Lilly now—ain't you?"

He mustered his biggest, saddest and most innocent eyes. "No, ma'am. I wasn't saying anything to anyone."

"Humph!" she grunted. "I didn't say you was *sayin'* somethin' to someone. I asked *who* you were talkin' to."

Jared looked down to escape her beady, accusing eyes. She pulled her blue and white plaid dress up to her knees and sat in the chair next to his. "Can't even squeak now, huh?" she asked. "Aunt Lilly gonna find out sooner than later. She always do." She looked up and began sniffing at the air. "Mmm-hmm."

"Can I ask you something, Aunt Lilly?"

"You can ask ol' Lilly anything you want," she replied. "I'll tell you—if I know it—if you care to hear it."

Jared peeked behind to make sure no one was near. "Do you know what really happened to my grandfather?"

Aunt Lilly's smirk disappeared. "There be thangs about what happened to him and there be some *other* thangs."

"I already know how he died."

She pushed her lips out. "Humph!"

"What happened after he was killed?"

Aunt Lilly shrugged. "The haint brought Walter back here," she said plainly.

"The who?"

"The haint," she said louder. "The same one that's been hauntin' this family for years. Probably the same one you was *thinking* about when I came out here. Don't take ol' Lilly for some country fool-woman—'cause I ain't. That haint ever talk back to you?"

Jared didn't answer.

She grinned. "Thought so. What that thang want from us?"

"I don't know," Jared lied.

"I wanna know why that thang just don't go back to where it come from," she said. "It just keep on staying around here. Some-times I know when it get close...I can smell it! I can just about taste it in the air. And boy was it thick as weeds last night when that storm hollered through."

"The storm? Now I'm really lost, " Jared admitted. "What does that have to do with anything?"

Aunt Lilly cocked her head toward him. "Cause the weatherman ain't said nothing about no storm coming last night. It was clear as bell right before I went to bed and next thang you know, it storm-ing like the devil.

Jared shook his head. "I still don't..."

"You best get on over there quick to your daddy's church," Aunt Lilly told him. "Quick-like!"

"See who?" Dorthea asked as she stepped out and closed the pa-tio door far noisier than she had opened it.

"Stop actin' ignorant, gal," Aunt Lilly snipped.

"I was going to tell him, Aunt Lilly," Dorthea replied, wiping sleep from her eyes.

"When?" Aunt Lilly demanded.

Dorthea moaned. "Mama could use some help inside, Aunt Lilly. *Please.*"

Aunt Lilly rose. "Humph! You tell him all of it, especially about what done happened last night, too."

Dorthea sat down where Aunt Lilly had been and waited until she had gone inside before speaking. Aunt Lilly tapped on the glass and pointed at her and then at Jared, and then back to Dorthea before walking out of sight. Dorthea combed her shoulder length curls with her fingers.

"It's not easy watching someone die, is it, baby?"

Jared looked down. "No."

"It wasn't for me either," Dorthea admitted. "When daddy died... was killed, I was still too young to know *eight from cat scratch*. All I knew was that my daddy was here that morning...gone that evening...and wasn't coming back. You know how scary that is for a child?"

"It's not fair."

"It sure ain't," Dorthea agreed. "And then after my granny died, I started thinking no one's ever going to stay around. But then you add in some men who promise you the moon and stars...every single thing I wanted to hear, and you got a mess going on. But I didn't know until I met your daddy and got pregnant with you, that I didn't know a dang thing! When your daddy found out I was pregnant, that was the end of us. He was preaching at that point and couldn't claim a child out of wedlock. And I couldn't stay in Nuxta with folks gossiping about it."

Jared began choking up as he began seeing her not as a mother, but just a woman. "Why didn't you tell me all of this before?"

"Baby," she said softly. "Because I didn't want you thinking that just because he didn't want you, that I didn't either, because I did... more than anything in this world. I knew you'd want to know or find out one way or another, but—but I wanted you old enough to know what it meant when you did find out. And what it all means, no matter what happened or—or how it happened is...I wanted you then *and now*."

Jared felt foolish, but more ashamed than anything else. He recalled all the times he'd begged her to be sent away to prep school because he wanted to be away from her, when all she really wanted was to protect and love him the best way she knew how.

Now that it seemed—according to Tamen—that he had no choice but to leave her, he didn't want to.

"I—I..." Jared started.

"Mama said your daddy is probably down at the church cleaning up," Dorthea said. As she was speaking, Aunt Lilly hobbled back out onto the porch. "A storm hit the church pretty hard. They think it was a tornado."

"Is he OK?" Jared asked.

Aunt Lilly smiled. "Oh he doing just fine, I heard. Probably *too fine*, for a tornado dropping right on his head." She tapped his shoulder. "C'mon boy, let's go."

"Where?" Jared and Dorthea asked in chorus.

"Me and the boy taking a walk uptown."

"Now?" Dorthea questioned in alarm.

"Ain't that what I said?" Aunt Lilly crowed. "I suppose to be old and deaf, not ya'll."

"Jared?" Dorthea asked.

Jared stood. "I just want to talk to him. If he doesn't, then there's nothing I can do, huh? I *know* who my family is." Dorthea nodded. "I won't be gone long, alright?"

"Aunt Lilly, you coming back? I got some greens boiling," Dorthea offered.

"I best get back quick, I guess," she answered. "That Tidius—Taddeus man...look like he ain't passed up a drumstick in years."

Dorthea rolled her eyes and moaned.

"See?" Aunt Lilly remarked to Jared. "When you too young or too old, folk got a problem with every thang you say and do." She looked at Dorthea and smiled playfully. "Sorry, sweetie. I meant to say that he a big-boned man. Is that better?"

"And you don't have to get into it every time Tobias is here. You know he's bringing Loretta and..."

"Aw hell!" Aunt Lilly blurted. "Don't tell me he's bringing those lazy, nappy-headed, goin' to jail boys of his, too?"

"Aunt Lilly!"

"Aunt Lilly, what?" she said in kind. "All I'm saying is that everyone of them boys got sticky fingers—steal the black right off your back and sell it."

"His boys aren't coming," Dorthea assured her.

"Ohhh—it's always a good day when prayers are answered. Thank you, Lord," Aunt Lilly said as she touched her chest. "It bad enough I gotta listen to Loretta and her mouth...all painted up like a two-dollah..."

"Aunt...Lilly!"

Aunt Lilly nudged Jared. "Loretta look just like that ol' white lady on TV who always crying with all that black mess around her eyes—the one with the preacher husband. Mmm-hmm, just like her...only Loretta black, but high-yellow, you see, boy?" She pulled him along down the driveway and called back to Dorthea. "He'll be back, gal."

During the walk uptown, Aunt Lilly gave him a quick and biased opinion on the family members he had met and the ones he hadn't yet. She was in the middle of telling him about Tobias's youngest son who had just gotten out of prison, when a plump middle-aged black woman called out to her from across the street and promptly skittered over.

"Hey-hey now, Ms. Lilly," the woman said. "Oh...who's this boy with ya?"

Aunt Lilly crossed her arms. "Betty-Mae...you know good and well who this be."

"Dotty's boy?" Betty-Mae gushed. *"This*...is Dotty's boy?"

"No, gal, he's mine!" Aunt Lilly retorted. "Stop acting like you retarded!"

"Ms. Lilly, now...." Betty-Mae batted her fake inch-long lashes at them. "I just didn't expect to run into him here."

Aunt Lilly smiled and squinted. "Well ain't you lucky as a rabbit's foot. C'mon boy, my feets hurtin'...and now my head is too."

"Tell Ms. Althea I said hey now!" Betty-Mae called, as they walked past her.

"Tell her yourself at church," Aunt Lilly retorted.

"Girl, tornado done tore it up. Didn't you hear?"

"Well, I guess your luck just ran out."

When they reached the end of the block, Aunt Lilly grabbed Jared's shirt and turned him halfway. "This be where I turn around," she told him. "You follow on for a ways and you'll see the church. You can't miss it unless ya blind."

"Can you make it back OK, Aunt Lilly?"

"Oh, I'll be just right on my own. You see about *you* and let Lilly see about Lilly. *You* go see Phineas."

Jared continued on and spotted the small, white church...or what was left of it. He saw a man hammering near the cockeyed front door of the church, which hung only by the hinge at the top. The roof and most of the tops of the walls were gone. What still stood was marred black by the fire that had ravaged it.

For years he had mentally rehearsed hundreds of variations of the conversation that would ensue when he finally met his father. But with each step he took, every sentence of his thoroughly rehearsed script disappeared. He was no more than a few hundred yards to the church, but it seemed like the longest walk of his life. The man, as though having sensed him from behind, stopped and turned around.

"What can I do for ya, boy?"

"Are you...I'm looking for Phineas Boremon," Jared said.

"You lookin' at him." Phineas shielded his eyes from the evening sun with his hand, and then lowered it, along with his jaw. He looked down for a moment, and then walked over to Jared.

"I—I'm..." Jared began, not knowing exactly how to begin talking to the man who was his father and a stranger. Seeing Phineas up close and now knowing what he would look like once his hair thinned and turned grey, he understood why Aunt Lilly had commented that he looked like the image of his father. "I'm..."

"Dorthea's boy," Phineas finished. "My son—Jared. I see that, now."

"How did you know it was me?"

"First off, I can see it," Phineas said. "Second my phone was ringing the moment ya'll drove into Nuxta." Phineas pulled out a handkerchief and wiped his forehead. "The whole town is probably talking about you coming here to see me."

Jared prayed his trembling bottom lip wasn't too noticeable. "You want me to go then?"

"Tell you the truth, I just don't know what you want from me now that you're all grown-up?" Phineas answered. "My wife is already beside herself about the—uh—um—the tornado that ripped through here. When she caught tell of you and Dotty...Dorthea, coming down to Nuxta, that ain't helped none either. We tried having children, but that never worked out. So you, my only son, kinda make her feel...well...she ain't happy about it, put it that way."

"Well, I don't know her, and I don't know how she's suppose to feel," Jared snipped. "I came here to see you, not her." As much as he wanted his mother to be wrong about Phineas, he couldn't contradict her now. Phineas hadn't even offered a handshake, let alone a hug. Jared huffed, and then spun on his combat boots and began walking away. "Thanks, Phineas," he called out.

"Wait a minute, boy. Thanks for what?"

Jared turned and walked backward. "For proving that my mother was right all this time!"

"Right about what?"

Jared chuckled. "*About you!* Have a great life, Reverend!"

"Jared, wait!"

"For what?" Jared snapped. "You know, Phineas,...on second thought, my mom was wrong. You're actually more of a jerk than what she said you were."

"Hey now, boy!" Phineas called.

Jared turned back around and kept walking even as Phineas kept calling for him. He was determined not to let Phineas see the tears coursing down his face. *Sperm-donor,* he thought sourly as he picked up his pace back to his grandmother's house.

* * *

Jared was a few blocks from the church and back in the small downtown of Nuxta within minutes. He wiped his eyes and snotty nose on the end of his t-shirt, and was about to cross the road when the hairs on his arm and back of his neck rose. "Tamen," he whispered instinctively. The hot, dry air of Nuxta suddenly became humid. He stopped and looked around. But as he did so, he caught sight of something that was not Tamen...or even human.

He stumbled backward and nearly fell into the street as he looked up—up—and then further up. A naked and genderless, blue-white being who wasn't there just a moment ago, had materialized right out of thin air before him. The creature—nearly the height of the two-story building it was in front of—had not one, but three faces. The first was straight on, and the other two, on the opposite sides of its head. It swayed its head from one side to the other, giving each face a turn to look at him straight on.

Tamen's last words to him were a jolt up and down his body. *'They—Shazadeh and Lord Yikan—can be anywhere.'* That was all it took for his heart to start thumping, and for him to jam his feet into the ground ready to jettison. Tamen's name was nearly out of his mouth when an icy hand clamped over it, and an arm encircled him, pinning his arms to his sides. *"Quiet! Be still!"* a voice commanded. Jared looked up into a set of familiar and most welcome brown eyes.

"Shhhh," Tamen again directed.

Jared dared a whisper. "What is that thing?"

"That, my child, is one of the Celestial Hosts...one of the Orders," Tamen whispered in his ear.

"It's so..."

"Beautiful? Yes it is," Tamen finished. "But it is quite angry at the moment. It would not be here if it were not." The Order's front face looked away from Jared and settled on Tamen. Its solid body then became ephemeral and faded away into nothing. "If I were to have challenged it—attacked it—it would have killed me. They are imbued with power from the living force of all things...the *Holy Ghost*...which cannot be denied. Even Satan is not bold or foolish enough to challenge the Ghost."

"What did it want from me?"

"Not you," Tamen replied. "Me."

"You? Why?"

"I came too close to something that mattered greatly to it," Tamen explained. "But we have not the time to discuss that right now."

"I know," Jared said. "I was trying to contact you and tell you that...that I ... I'm ready, I guess."

"I heard you. Actually, I was standing right next to you. And that is good, Jared. Our time is drawing very short indeed. I heard them this past night...very close they are."

"Can you sense Shazadeh and Lord Yikan now?"

"No," Tamen replied. "Unless they chant, I cannot find them, nor can they locate me unless I chant. "

"Which is a good thing."

"It is the proverbial sword cutting both ways," Tamen said. "For all I know, they could be thousands of miles away in Asia. Or they could be..."

"A step away," Jared offered softly.

"Precisely," Tamen agreed. "Though rest assured, they are closing in on us. I know it! I can feel it! That remnant of humanity in me...*my intuition*...has not let me rest for days."

They walked until they reached the corner that put them in sight of his grandmother's home. Jared stopped as he spotted people on the front porch. "What do I tell them?"

"The truth," Tamen replied simply.

"You're kidding? They'll think I'm freakin' nuts."

"It will save their lives," Tamen told him. "It will not matter what they think of you as long as they are safe—no?"

Jared looked back and made out his mother, Aunt Lilly and grandmother Althea standing on the porch. "I guess I'm going to... *crap!*" he blurted, as he turned to look at Tamen who was no longer there. "Tamen!"

"Stop yelling, child." Tamen's voice echoed in Jared's head. *"I am right here."*

Jared sighed. "Don't do that. I thought you'd taken off again."

"I will be next to you—always."

"What about Henri? Is he...?"

"Henri is fine. He has business to tend to as do you," Tamen replied. *"Now focus on yours."*

"The look on my face is going to give it away."

"No it will not," Tamen replied. *"But your Aunt Lilly is there with your mother and grandmother. It is she you should worry about."*

"Aunt Lilly?"

"Your mother and grandmother are wondering why you are talking to yourself. But your Aunt Lilly is wondering whom you are talking to. Just speak truthfully like you did with Phineas."

"I had a feeling you were there."

"But far enough away to give you privacy. Though, I did come a bit too close I discovered."

"What do you mean?"

"Enough, Jared," he said in exasperation.

"Jeez—alright!" Jared huffed. *Why the heck was I looking for a dad with you around to jump all over my back,* he fumed.

"I heard that," Tamen replied.

"Sorry," Jared blurted.

"No, you are not. But it does not matter anyway."

Jared walked toward the house. Aunt Lilly stepped off the porch and began walking toward him. "You slick as a weasel you thinking, ain't cha'?" Aunt Lilly said as she stopped in front of him and began tapping her bare foot. "I know you talking to that haint! I can smell *it,* even if I can't see that thang! Maymee-child in there on her last breath, and that haint back here again? *Hummf!* Just like it was when your grandpappy was killed and that thang showed up here with him."

Jared held up his hands. "Aunt Lilly, you got me. You're right."

"I know I'm right! You think I talking 'cause I think I wrong?"

"No, ma'am."

"You know what this haint wants from this family, don't cha?"

"Yes, ma'am."

"Hot damn!" she crowed. "Everybody get inside!"

Dorthea did the opposite and bolted for Jared. "What's wrong? Jared?"

Aunt Lilly grabbed Dorthea by the waist as she approached and used her own momentum to spin her back around. "C'mon, gal. I been telling ya'll about this mess for years. We gonna get us some answers now!"

"Jared, what's going on?" Dorthea asked, as Aunt Lilly pushed her toward the house. "What did Phineas say to you?"

"It's not about him, OK?" he told her. "I'm all done with him. This is about something I need to tell all of you. Let's just go inside. We shouldn't be out here right now."

"Why?" Dorthea asked.

Aunt Lilly stepped up on the porch and stomped her foot. "The haint, dammit!"

"Lord help," Althea groaned, rubbing her forehead.

Jared took Althea by the arm and helped her into the house. Thaddeus was just coming out of the kitchen with a sandwich in hand as Althea and Dorthea sat on the sofa—Aunt Lilly refused to sit. Jared pointed Thaddeus toward a chair behind the women, and then went over and stood in front of the patio doors. "Where's cousin Tobias?" Jared asked.

"Uh-huh," Aunt Lilly grunted. "I want Toby to hear this, too. He think I just talk nonsense, but he gonna find out now."

Thaddeus thumped his chest twice, twisted his neck to the side and swallowed hard. "He told me he was gonna gather up his wife to come see you, Jared, because she didn't want to wait 'til mornin'."

"He gone to get her? Dang!" Aunt Lilly grumbled. "Never mind, boy, just lock that patio door behind you."

"Lilly!" Althea admonished.

"Don't nobody wanna see her sittin' around here sweatin' like a pig!" she protested.

Althea hung her head and groaned.

"Jared," Dorthea said, ignoring the others. "Tell us what's going on, baby."

Jared nodded. "OK. We don't have time to wait for Tobias anyway. I—I..."

"Tell them, Jared. Do not be afraid," Tamen said into Jared's thoughts.

"Hey—hey—hey!" Aunt Lilly skittered to the middle of the room and held up her hand. "Sshhhhh," she whispered. "That haint is here right now, ya'll."

"She's right," Jared told them. "But he's not a haint or anything like that."

"Dear God!" Althea gasped. She and Dorthea scrambled to find each other's hand.

"He's not an *it*. He's a he," Jared continued, as he looked at everyone for a brief moment. "His name is Tamen, and he was born in Egypt thousands of years ago, but he's not human anymore. Well...he is half-human actually. For thousands of years he was called Horus—*He Who Resides in the Horizon.*

"He was a god of Egypt," Jared continued.

CHAPTER 19

"...and so that's all there is—really," Jared finished. He'd watched his mother the closest of all as he repeated what Tamen, who was invisible to them, was whispering in his ear. The moment he mentioned having to leave, Dorthea's head hadn't stopped moving from side-to-side. Everyone, except Aunt Lilly, who was smiling victoriously, seemed in utter shock, and rightly so, he thought. Their initial silence was entirely expected.

"Jared," Dorthea spoke up. "I remember that night that young man came and laid daddy's body on the floor. But he was just a man, baby."

"No *it* wasn't!" Aunt Lilly protested. "You don't remember it all because you was too young, gal." She looked over at Althea, and then lowered her head and her voice. "But you came out of the room later on and saw me passed out, right?"

Althea closed her eyes and slowly nodded.

"Mama?" Dorthea asked.

"But I never saw how it happened to you, Aunt Lilly," Althea said.

"Aunt Lilly was trying to chant at him, and he made her pass out," Jared said, just as Tamen told him to say it.

"Damn right it did!" Aunt Lilly yelped. "He knocked me right out!"

Dorthea stood. "Alright! Everyone stop it, right now! Ya'll sound crazy—every last one of you!"

"Sit down, child," Althea told her.

"No, mama!" Dorthea then glared at Jared. "You aren't going anywhere with anybody, you hear me? Nowhere! Mama and Aunt Lilly...ya'll gonna stop all this crazy talk." Thaddeus stood, resulting in Dorthea pointing at him and snapping. "*You sit down!* I want all this mess stopped right now! Maymee's up in that room dyin', and all of ya'll talking like you—you..."

Knock—knock!

Dorthea shrieked.

"Lord Jesus!" Althea cried. Thaddeus did the same, as if the first call to Jesus had gone unheard.

Jared instinctively jumped in front of his mother. With the light in the room shining against the glass patio doors, all he could see was a mirrored, funhouse reflection of himself gawking back.

"Tamen?" Jared called.

"Who there?" Aunt Lilly demanded.

"It's me, Ms. Althea," the voice replied.

Dorthea exhaled, and then cleared her throat. "Go on and open it, Jared."

Jared slid the patio doors open and let Phineas Boremon enter. He nodded at everyone except Dorthea. He looked at her last and quickly lowered his head. "I'm interrupting something, ain't I?" Phineas asked.

"That just about how you operate anyways," Aunt Lilly grumbled and looked off.

"I know you all don't care for me any...'specially you two." He glanced at Dorthea and Jared. "I just came to say to Jared...*my son*...and to Dotty, that I'm sorry."

"A day late and a dollar short," Aunt Lilly mumbled loud enough for all to hear.

Phineas ran his hand through his hair, then folded his hands in front of his waist and began playing with his thumbs. "I know it ain't much for all I put ya'll through, but it's all I got. Jared...those should've been the first words out of my mouth when you came around. And Dotty...I should've told you that years ago, but I didn't. I was wrong as wrong can be, and the Lord done made sure I knew it too. Ain't nothin' been right for me since, but I—I deserved every lick of it."

"Well now, preacher!" Althea commented with a nod of her head.

Jared hadn't heard Thaddeus get up and move behind him, but knew the feel of his bear-like grip on his shoulder. "I just wanted to see you," Jared said. "I thought maybe you wanted to see me too, I guess. Maybe I even wanted you to be a father. But I don't need you to be my dad, Phineas, because Mom already did your job for you. And Mr. Robinette has always been there for me too. So *I* don't need your apology, but my mom does."

Phineas hung his head like a spanked pup. "You're right, boy," he admitted, and then looked up at Dorthea. "I'm...truly sorry, Dotty. God strike me dead if I ain't."

"Hear that, Lord?" Aunt Lilly peeped.

"I know I did you wrong...*I know*," he croaked. "I'm sure your family done told you how the Lord fixed me since you left. Voices be coming to my head and me passing out and don't know where I been and such. But I done stopped all that mess I used to do and gave it over to the Lord. And I swear, Dotty, I been tryin' to do what's right ever since."

"Folk say he's been actin' goofier than usual," Aunt Lilly admitted.

"I fell again when I saw Jared," Phineas continued. "I ain't gonna do wrong by you again, Jared...or you either, Dorthea. I know you said you don't need a father, but I can at least try and be a friend to you." Jared opened his mouth as if to speak, but nothing came out. "You don't have to answer right now. You can just think about it. I'll leave ya'll to your evening. My apologies, Ms. Althea, for bargin' in on ya'll so late."

"Wait!" Jared piped up. He walked to the kitchen door. "A tornado didn't hit the church last night, did it?"

"What?" Phineas asked.

"Two people came looking for you. One was a man and another a woman, but you knew they weren't really people like us, right?" Jared then looked toward the ceiling and spoke. "What? What do you mean they were here?"

"Boy, who you talkin' to?" Thaddeus asked him.

"How—how—how do you know that?" Phineas' voice warbled.

"I don't," Jared replied. "*He* does."

"Who? *God?*" Phineas asked.

"No...Tamen."

"*Lord Jesus!*" Phineas exclaimed. "I know that name. She was looking for him. Who's this Tamen person?"

"Ask him yourself," Jared told him.

On the other side of the kitchen behind the door, at first the padding of feet on linoleum could be heard. Everyone fell silent as the door opened. When he walked out, Jared didn't recognize the persona Tamen had taken on of a short, portly black man with graying hair...Althea and Dorthea suddenly gasping told him that *they did.*

Dorthea stared wild-eyed at the black man standing next to Jared. She was the first to speak. "Mr. Willie?"

"It can't be," Althea mumbled, mirroring Dorthea's look of be-wilderment and then pointed at the man. "Willie Bell been dead for years now. You left us everything you owned—so—so you can't be..."

"Willie Bell never truly existed," Tamen explained. He walked to-ward her and smiled. "My dear—beautiful Dotty. It has been so very long since you last saw me—has it not, child?"

Dorthea's mouth was still open, but she managed to nod slowly.

"But now it is time that you see me for who I truly am and have always been."

Tamen's illusion of the stout, round-bellied Willie Bell began to heighten and thin out. Like shifting sand, the persona of Willie Bell disappeared and was replaced with Tamen's true, youthful visage. Dorthea's eyes rolled backward as she fainted and fell right into Tamen's arms. He laid her gently on the sofa next to Althea, and then brushed her curly hair back and kissed her cheek.

"Lord help us all," Althea gasped, as she pulled Dorthea close to her.

"I agree," Tamen said. He glanced at Phineas and then looked about the room as though something else had come with him. Tamen quickly moved back toward the kitchen door where Jared stood. "All that young Jared here has told you is true. Unfortu-nately, this is not a benign situation we are all in, but a most pre-carious one indeed."

"The boy ain't goin' nowhere with you!" Thaddeus told him. "I don't know who you are...or what you be...but you ain't takin' Dorthea's boy anywhere while I'm livin'."

"Me either," Phineas huffed.

Jared jumped between Thaddeus and Tamen. "Wait! You don't understand."

"Oh, I do boy," Phineas countered and pointed at Tamen. "You're with them, ain't you...those two devils that tried to kill me last night?"

"No he isn't, Phineas," Jared said. "And yeah, they were going to kill you, but it wasn't you they were looking for. It was me. They want *me* dead."

"You? Why?" Aunt Lilly asked.

"Because..." Jared paused, and then looked at Tamen.

"Because who he will become shall decide the fate of your world," Tamen explained. Everyone turned and stared at Jared. "There is no other way to say such a thing."

Phineas glanced over at Dorthea who was beginning to wake, and then looked at Tamen. "When I told Dotty I changed, I meant it. So say what you want to say, but you're not taking this boy from here," he said and began advancing toward Tamen.

Tamen stepped back. "Jared—stop him."

"You scared of us now...huh, devil?" Thaddeus challenged. He too moved toward Tamen, but then inexplicably stopped. With mouth open and hands reaching for Tamen, he seemed frozen where he stood.

"You!" Tamen growled at Thaddeus, "I can seize control of your mind and actions," he said, and then pointed at Phineas. "But not you. For everyone's sake—you must stay away from me."

"Because God is on my side," Phineas boasted.

"The creature that serves you is," Tamen corrected him. "Other than to give Jared life, I see no other reason why you were chosen as a blessed one. Regardless, what protects you cannot be stopped or killed while it is charged to safeguard you...that is the covenant. But Phineas, if you call upon it...willingly or unwillingly to kill me, there shall be no one to protect Jared. And *when*, not if, those two you encountered last night find him, they will kill him."

"Listen to him, Phineas," Jared begged. "He's not lying. I wish he was, but he's not." He looked at Dorthea who had finally opened her eyes. "Mom, I have to go."

Althea helped Dorthea sit upright. "Where? Going where?" she asked as she slowly shook her head.

"That, my dear Dotty, we cannot say," Tamen answered instead. "We have told all of you too much already."

Jared nudged Tamen. "You can let Thaddeus go now."

Thaddeus, who had been in midstride, dropped to his knees and shook the floor. As though he didn't weigh nearly three hundred pounds, but only three, Tamen effortlessly lifted him to his feet and sat him in the chair by the dining room table. Thaddeus leaned forward on the table by his elbows and looked around at everyone. "Wha—what da hell happened?"

"Nothing, Thaddeus. Everything's OK for now," Jared assured him.

"Baby, you can't just *leave*," Dorthea begged.

"I don't have a choice, Mom," Jared insisted. "I really wanna stay here with all of you. I do! But the longer I stay, the more your lives are in danger. I gotta go."

"He is correct, Dotty," Tamen added. "If it is any consolation, I will protect Jared with my life, as I have yours since you were a child. That is my solemn promise."

"He's my baby," Dorthea pleaded. She looked to Althea. "I can't lose *him*."

"Tamen? Please..." Jared begged.

Tamen looked over toward the hallway. "You understand what this might mean?"

"What ya'll up to now?" Aunt Lilly fumed..

"He can heal Aunt Maymee," Jared told them all. "He can erase every trace of cancer in her body. That's what I want him to do before we leave."

Althea scooted to the edge of the sofa. "You can do what?"

"I ain't buyin' that mess," Aunt Lilly interrupted. "I ain't ever heard of no haint that can heal sick folk."

"That is because I am not a haint," Tamen told her. "It is in my power to heal her, that is true, but...*there is a price to be paid.* The magic of the chant is required to heal Maymee."

"Well...?" Aunt Lilly spat.

"It can signal the ones that attacked Phineas last night," Jared told her. "They can follow the sound of Tamen's chant right to us. But I think if we're quick enough...if we were ready to leave once Tamen is finished, we could be gone by the time they got here."

"Or not." Tamen countered.

"I'll risk *my life* for my niece...any day," Aunt Lilly professed.

"And for my child, ya'll know I'll do it," Althea pledged.

Dorthea was already nodding. "That's my big sister."

"If you can do it, then do it," Phineas added.

Thaddeus wobbled as he stood and leaned on the table for support. "Ya'll know I ain't going nowhere. If Dorthea is willing, so am I. You just do that thing you talkin' about and let us see to the rest...alright?"

"Tamen?" Jared looked at him and waited.

Tamen looked each one of them in the eye, and then said. "Take only what you need. Everyone must be ready to depart the moment the chant is finished. If we are fortunate, we will survive this night. If not...we all die."

* * *

Jared, Aunt Lilly, Dorthea and the others scrambled through the house grabbing provisions and materials to take with them. Several times as Jared ran in and out of the house, he heard Tamen in his mind directing him...*"leave that,"* or *"hurry child." "You can replace that, Jared." "The lighter they are, the faster they will travel. Hurry!"* Thaddeus was the last out of the house with Maymee cradled in his arms.

"Everybody get in!" Jared told them, as he stood by the open van door. One by one, he assisted Althea, Aunt Lilly, and after a protracted embrace accompanied by a face full of tears—Dorthea, who he had to finally push away.

"I've always been proud of you," Thaddeus said, after Jared walked to the back of the van.

Jared smiled. "I know, Mr. Robinette."

"You're like my own son."

Jared spied Phineas watching them, but replied exactly how he felt to Thaddeus. "And you've been a good father, even when I was acting like a knucklehead and didn't want you to be a father to me."

Thaddeus puffed his chest out. "I still am, boy. So don't be talkin' like it's over—hear me now?"

Jared hugged him. Thaddeus squeezed back so tight, Jared began to feel faint for a moment. "Take care of Mom," he whispered to Thaddeus.

"You know I will."

Thaddeus left Jared and Tamen in the back with Maymee and hopped into the driver's seat. "No word from Tobias yet?" he asked the women in back, as he started the engine.

"I called the house, but he didn't answer the phone," Dorthea responded. "I think we're going to have to leave without him."

"That's good though," Jared told her. "The less people involved in this, the better." He turned to Phineas and held out his hand, which Phineas quickly clasped with both of his.

"This is goodbye then," Phineas stated.

"Yeah—goodbye, huh?"

"When you come back from wherever it is you goin', maybe it can be a beginning?" Phineas suggested meekly.

Jared nodded at Phineas more so for his mother, who had turned around and was watching them. He then looked at Tamen. "I think we better start." Tamen placed his hands upon Maymee's chest and closed his eyes. "You still remember the right chant, don't you?"

"Of course I have not forgotten—*I cannot!*" Tamen replied, with eyes closed. "The chants are forever mine. Hopefully in time you will intimately understand this. I have no doubt Lord Yikan and the Shazadeh will hear my chant and come in search of us. I will then chant once more and send us airborne, and then stop and to make cold our trail, and we will fall from the sky. I will wrap you with my body to—" Tamen abruptly stopped.

"What is it?" Jared asked, as Tamen went stone stiff, as though his spirit had left. He reached to touch him, though Tamen was quicker and caught hold of his hand.

"Tobias is coming," Tamen warned.

"Crap! We don't have time, Tamen."

"Tobias' presence is not the problem," Tamen said.

The sound of rubber on the pea gravel road announced the arrival of Tobias' tan sedan. As the car pulled into the driveway, the yellow-tinted headlights blared at the van in front of it. Tamen swiftly lifted Jared off his feet and placed him fully behind the van and out of sight.

"What's going on, Tamen?" Jared asked.

"Quiet!"

"Tell me!"

Tamen again became still. "Tobias is not alone."

"And...?"

"I can sense Tobias, but there is someone else with him whose mind I cannot penetrate."

"Yo, Jared!" A voice called out, as the passenger side door of the sedan opened and the headlights went off.

Jared couldn't believe whom he was hearing. He ignored Tamen's command and stepped away from the van. He squinted for a moment and then raised his brows.

Tobias stepped out of the car. "Why ya'll packed up in that van like sardines?"

"What are you doing here?" Jared asked, but his question was not directed at Tobias, but the other standing next to him.

"That's what took me so long," Tobias answered instead. "I was about to come on over with Loretta and the phone started ringing off the hook—it was some boy from the gas station uptown saying this one here lookin' for you, Jared. All he knew, though, was last names...Tripkin—so they called me. So I just went and got him. And a good thing I did too. He be done started up some mess with his sassy mouth."

Jared shook his head and then pointed to the right of Tobias. "No. What are *you* doing here, Chris?"

"Well, nice to see you too, Jared," Chris said. "I thought you'd be at least a little happy to see me."

"I...am," he replied, though was not entirely sure he still believed he was looking at Chris Knopfitter. "How did you get down here?"

Chris held up a chubby, sausage-like thumb. "Remember that movie *Traders?* It worked pretty good, but there's some freaky people out there too willing to give a little boy a ride." He snickered. "I just couldn't stay at that damn camp another day. I didn't want to go home, so I thought I would find you and go wherever you're going but won't tell me. Remember?"

"I already told you too much," Jared told him. "You gotta go, Chris. You too, Tobias. It's not safe here right now."

Chris' eyes widened and filled every inch of his thick glasses. "Safe? Where you going that's so dangerous?"

"Some place you're not!" Phineas interjected. He jumped out of the passenger's side of the van and positioned himself in front of Jared. He looked back at Tamen. "Go on and do it."

Chris smiled. "Do what?"

"Yeah...what the hell is going on *ya'll?*" Tobias demanded. He crouched and peered at the van. "Lilly! Girl, that you up in there?"

"Shut your ol' mouth, Toby!"

Tobias stood back up. "Yep! That's that ol' witch."

"Tobias," Phineas called. "Come over here."

Chris grabbed Tobias by the arm. "Wait a minute. How's about a last goodbye, Jared?"

Phineas pushed Jared back further, and with his other hand pointed down at the ground by his side. "Tobias...*get over here now!*" he demanded.

Chris held Tobias firm. "Hey, wait a minute. You hear that, Tobias?" Everyone heard what Chris was talking about. What had started as no more than a hum coming from the back of the van became a series of sounds quickly rising in pitch to a rhythmic beat. "Freakin' great, man!" Chris cheered.

"Watch your damn mouth, boy!" Tobias told him.

"Shut your hole, old man!" Chris spat back.

Tobias snatched his arm out of Chris' grasp. "Boy, you don't know—"

Tobias never finished his thought.

As quickly as Tobias pulled his arm away, Chris was faster and grabbed Tobias by the back of the neck and pushed him to his knees. Jared tried to run for him, but Phineas caught him by the shirt and pulled him back. *"Noooooo!"* Phineas cried.

Phineas' cry was not the only one. The women in the van, and Tobias too, began yelling also. Tobias' scream, however, was little more than a croak, as he was furiously batting at Chris' hand gripping his neck.

Jared struggled to get free of Phineas, but was refused. "Let him go, Chris! You're killing him!" Jared yelled.

"Awww man. I can't do that," Chris replied calmly. "You should've just come over like I asked and none of this would've happened. But *nooooo*...your friend back there had to go and start chanting."

"What the hell's wrong with you?" Jared screamed.

Chris chuckled. "Now that's a good one. I tell you what...come on over here and I'll give you the old man. How 'bout that?"

Tamen stepped out from behind the van. "Come to me, Jared."

"Well, looky-looky," Chris remarked. "Never thought I'd get a chance to see *you* in the flesh. Nice chanting for a mutt. You know, I remember when that chant was written," he added proudly.

"All of the oldest of your kind does," Tamen replied.

"What kind?" Jared asked.

"Oh let me, Tamen. Please—please—pretty please," Chris begged and even hopped a little. "You see...Tamen's not the only one who can pull off an illusion. I do have to say it's a bit gross masquerading as this fat slob. But just so that you know, little Chris actually doesn't look so ugly anymore. He's traded up...and traded you in, dear boy."

"Where is he?" Jared demanded.

"With us," the Chris entity replied and then winked. "Safe... happy...much thinner too. You left him...so he said screw you! You didn't want him, but we did. We offered to fix that hideous shell of his and man, he turned on you like that!" the Chris entity crowed and then snapped his fingers.

"Liar!" Jared accused. "If you've hurt him—"

"Come now," Jared heard Tamen say in his mind.

"Come now," the thing that was not Chris, mocked in a girlish voice. "C'mon Tamen, I can hear you—give me a little credit—I am my father's son. That would be Duke Astaroth for all of you mortals who don't know that," he said and waved at those in the van. "Don't think me so weak on this mortal plane, Tamen. You are and have always been nothing! Horus—god of Egypt...*please*," he uttered and rolled his eyes.

"If you are so mighty, then come forward," Tamen dared.

"Uh-uh, my little would-be god. Bring the boy to me and I'll let the old man go. I'll even have Shazadeh release Chris...hmm? I see who is within the preacher. I can smell my own brother's stinking righteousness a thousand leagues away."

"Phineas," Tamen called. "He cannot touch you, that is why he will not come any further."

"Just call me Barbatos—as if you didn't know already," Barbatos said.

"He cannot touch *any* part of you, Phineas," Tamen pressed.

"Any?" Phineas asked.

Barbatos shook Tobias by the neck. "*Phineassss*? Don't you see whom I'm holding here? Be a smart little mortal and just step away—go home. Do as I say and I'll make your wife fertile, and then you can have a son you actually *want* to be around...eh? Want money...you go it, bro! I'll lay gold bars at your feet. Hmm?"

"He can't touch anything of me? You sure?" Phineas asked Tamen again, ignoring Barbatos.

"No—he's not!" Barbatos yelled back.

Phineas looked around in a panic and then at the van. He stooped and jammed his arm under the stainless steel bumper of the van and pulled up swift and hard. He cried out as the sharp edge of the bumper slashed open his arm from elbow to wrist. Blood quickly pooled in the cavern of his splayed flesh. He swung his arm and splattered blood all over the van and the ground in front of it.

"Bad—bad preacher man," Barbatos growled. "Don't think you'll be protected your entire life. Bearing the mantle of a Blessed One is fleeting. Ask Tamen if you don't believe me—he's old enough to know these things. But when the day comes your angelic protector abandons you for another, I will eat your flesh and wash it down with a cup of your blood."

Phineas cradled his bleeding arm to his chest. "Talk all the mess you want, devil, but you ain't comin' near any of us tonight."

"What about this one?" Barbatos looked down at Tobias. "Oh Tobias.... Sorry mortal, but they didn't choose to save you...pity." Barbatos flexed his wrist and snapped Tobias' neck. He let go, letting Tobias' body slump over in the driveway.

Everyone in the van, including Thaddeus, screamed. Jared's yell, however, drowned them all out. The urge to throw-up took hold of him, especially when the already humid air around them began to grow thicker. From above, Jared could hear the sound of someone's voice drawing near, and then a second quickly thereafter. The closer the voices came, the darker the once clear night sky grew with black, undulating clouds.

"We have lost our gamble," Tamen said to Jared. "They are here!"

"You thought I would not hear your pathetic chanting?" Shazadeh called out from above.

Jared stared with open mouth as the man and woman descended from the heavens and set down next to Barbatos. Introductions were not needed, as he'd already seen them before in Tamen's illusions. Shazadeh was as black as Tamen had pictured her to him. Her breasts jutted out between her string-braids covering her chest. Lord Yikan, dressed in a black suit, had liquid-blue eyes only for Tamen.

"Ah...*my sister*," Barbatos said to Shazadeh. "I was wondering how long it would take you to get here."

Jared, this time listened to Tamen's instructions that were spoken into his mind and quickly walked back toward him. Tamen placed an arm across Jared's chest and one around his waist.

Barbatos looked down at his illusionary body of Chris and then turned to Shazadeh. "We should have brought the real boy and bargained with him. Look at the child, Jared, back there. He wants his friend back and badly."

"Let this be done, Tamen," Shazadeh called, ignoring Barbatos. "The preacher can put his blood over whatever he wishes, but it shall cool eventually. I certainly do not think he has enough blood to keep us at bay all night."

Jared felt Tamen's arm squeeze at his waist even tighter. But despite everything happening at the moment, a small spark of hope came to him...his Aunt Maymee was stirring. Her usual grimace of pain she had had for months was now gone. She opened her eyes and looked at him as though she had just woken from a nap.

"Then I'll just be dead," Phineas yelled to Shazadeh. "But you ain't gonna take my boy while I'm alive."

"I, sir," she said, "have all of eternity to wait. You don't."

Jared saw Phineas glance at him and then at Tamen, precisely at the same time he heard Tamen's voice blaring in his ear like a freight train's horn. Unable to move out of Tamen's grasp, he realized, as Phineas ran toward Barbatos, what Tamen's next move was. One moment his feet were planted firmly on the ground and he was reaching for his Aunt Maymee, and then the next he was airborne. Everything below him became a blur as he and Tamen... who was chanting furiously...passed through black clouds and into clear night skies.

And then Tamen stopped chanting...

...they stopped rising...

...and for a brief moment, they were weightless and looking down upon a bed of wispy clouds...

...right before they began falling.

* * *

Shazadeh, obviously having learned her lesson the first time, was the first to call upon the chant of flight and rise up—Lord Yikan was not far behind. Phineas, who'd lunged at Barbatos, had changed from mortal man to the three-faced Order—Oriziel, Nigiel and Palis—moments before catching Barbatos by the throat and raising him aloft. Lord Yikan and Shazadeh hovered a safe distance above as two beings from two separate worlds spoke face-to-face.

"Struggle not brother and I will lay thee low swiftly," Palis, the face on the right said to Barbatos. "Thy soul shall not suffer much if you submit now, for there is no victory for you here," Oriziel, the middle face added. *"Amen,"* Palis and Nigiel said solemnly.

Barbatos—through the eyes of Chris Knopfitter—widened them behind his glasses. He placed his hands on the far larger forearm of the glowing, blue-white Order. "I say to thee nay, my once beloved brother. It is most unfitting for a prince to submit, even in the face of imminent defeat. My father would banish me straight to the Isle of Phenox if I did not at least try."

The Order turned its head left and right to give each of its faces a turn to look upon Barbatos directly. "The sacred covenant protects my charge and with it, the power of the Holy Ghost. None may stand against its will."

"I know this."

"Then struggle, Brother," the Palis face said. "And this time only, until our final battle shall I give thee a quick departure back to thy unholy realm."

Barbatos nodded in agreement. "Until then."

The tri-faced Order pulled its arm back and drove it into the center of Barbatos' chest. Instantly, the illusion of Chris Knopfitter wavered and vanished, and revealed a nude, genderless being with flowing hair and skin as white as chalk. But even that form—with the Order's fist pushed completely through it—was unstable. It began to glow, but suddenly became black like used oil and started dripping onto the ground. Where it dropped it sizzled and melted away dirt, pea gravel, rocks and everything it touched. Nothing but a smoldering steaming black hole was left of Barbatos.

Shazadeh, who was still hovering in the sky with Lord Yikan, called down. "Live what life you have left, mortals—for it shall not be long. Be assured, mother of the boy called Jared...he and his mongrel shall die by my hands. And to you, man of Yahweh...the Orders will not protect you forever. When your Heavenly Host finally abandons you, and you have naught but your faith for sustenance, I shall come unto you and claim you for my very own."

"We should follow the remnants of Tamen's chant before it is too late," Lord Yikan told her.

"It has already grown cold," Shazadeh snipped. "He fled like the coward he is. But he and the boy will surface again. They have no choice now."

* * *

"I can carry you, child. It is not an effort to do so," Tamen offered, but received a resounding *no!* in reply.

"Just back off, OK?" Jared begged as he began dry heaving again. Even though Tamen had cocooned him right before they fell and crashed into a forest...hitting branch after branch of a tree to slow their descent...his head was still spinning like a top. "Are you sure my family is all right? All of them?"

"Yes," Tamen replied. "I sense every one of them—they are alive *and* traveling."

"You told me not to, but I forced you to save my aunt," he said, refusing to look Tamen in the eye. "Everything you told me not to do, I did. I told Chris and now they—they have him somewhere," he muttered, before choking up. "And—and Tobias. He's dead because of me. I screwed up, Tamen."

"Jared, don't..."

"It's my fault!" Jared yelled at him. "I told Chris where we were going, and about you and Henrì, and brought them straight to us."

"More blood will likely be shed," Tamen informed him. "For us to succeed, others may need to be sacrificed along with Tobias. Are you willing to kill?"

"K—kill?"

"Yes," Tamen replied in a hush. "Even more innocents may perish before this is all over. And that is if we succeed. If we do not, one or two, or twenty deaths will be the least of your worries. Hundreds of thousands...millions will perish if Shazadeh prevails. It is time to stop thinking like a boy."

Jared glared at him and then looked away. "Well, I am just a boy," he muttered.

They made their way out of the forest and onto a two-lane road. Jared's head was still throbbing, though now at least was clear enough to sustain a thought for longer than a few seconds. "Where to now, Tamen?"

"For now we go southwest to Texas," Tamen told him. "There is a town not far up the road about twenty miles."

"Twenty?"

"Calm," Tamen urged. "We shall obtain a ride from the approaching car."

Jared looked up and down the dark, rural road, but heard and saw nothing in either direction. "What car?" Tamen turned him around and pointed up the road. A few seconds later, the glow of headlights broke through the darkness.

"The man and his lady friend approaching shall take us to the town," Tamen said. "I may not be able to use chant-magic, but I can still create illusions, remember? They shall give us transport, and by the time they have moved on, I will make sure they have no recollection of what transpired."

"And from there?"

"From there, I shall continue to cloak us from the view of others, for we need to move quickly and stealthily. Shazadeh and Lord Yikan will have every mortal under their control in this area soon...aye." Tamen nodded. "But we will make our trail cold again flying by plane from city-to-city at random until I call on Henri, who even now is finishing preparations for our last voyage."

"To Egypt," Jared stated.

"Yes...to Egypt. My beloved homeland," Tamen confirmed. "We shall recover the holy tome that shall make you an angel and right the balance. It would be a much simpler task if they did not know we were coming."

Chapter 20

Eric Lightner made sure no one, especially Nicholas, was around as he slipped into his tent and retrieved his knapsack. He dug to the bottom of it and felt for the hand-length knife he'd smuggled into the desert camp. He looked around one more time and then closed his eyes and focused on the image of a sun engraved in stone...the sacred image of Aton that was given to him by Lord Yikan.

My god, Aton, he prayed, *protect your faithful servant. Protect us from she...the evil one. And may your benevolence once more calm this world. Times three I say your holy name and ask that your will be done here on Earth. Aton—Aton—Aton!*

He got off his knees and then flopped down on his cot. He tried blocking out the incessant cracking sound of metal against stone outside in the excavation pit. In only a few days, he'd learned to detest the desert. *Sweating like a pig during the day and freezing at night in the middle of nowhere is my reward?* he thought.

The other members of the Church of the Imperial Goddess considered him blessed to be selected to go to Egypt in such a short time in having come into the faith. It usually took years, he was told, in order to be worthy enough to participate in the *Great Search*—the hunt for the golden tome of the angel Metatron. But after all, it was he who had found the fat boy, Chris, which had led to a most valuable secret. Despite his reluctance in coming to the desert, he was not going to disobey Lord Yikan's will, who he came to know as Aton—the sun god of Egypt.

"You, Eric—my most worthy and trusted servant, will be my eyes and ears in the desert," Eric recalled Lord Yikan telling him. "Serve me well and I will raise you above all humans. And I shall give you what you seek most...unparalleled beauty."

To continue the charade of devotion to Shazadeh, he zealously worshipped her like the others in the mountain temple where he had been sent to live. With one word from Lord Yikan to the master of the temple, he was schooled to become a recruiter and watcher, which eventually led to his placement in the Midwest state of Illinois. Originally, small towns such as Homer had been viewed as too small for a mass campaign, but with the C.I.G. membership growing rapidly, low population towns had become perfect starting points for new instructors such as himself.

The masquerade he was taught to use was simple enough. Just present oneself as a God-fearing—God loving motivational speaker bearing hope and peace, and watch them come in droves. No one wanted to go to hell, or even believe in its actual existence. With a few phone inquiries, he was extended invitations to practically every church in Homer. There were so many, he discovered, who wanted to be rich...have perfect, genius children...become connected with their inner being, and were willing to do anything for these things. Everyone wanted their own personal hotline to God, and was always disappointed when calling and asking for their perfect life to find the line busy. Dangling an always available, static-free line to a higher power in their face made recruiting skeptics possible and the weak-willed easy—he knew quite well from firsthand experience.

During the self-esteem seminar he'd given at the camp for over-weight teens, he recalled how Chris Knopfitter had stood out from the rest. It wasn't simply because he was fat, as all the teenagers there were...which he found absolutely disgusting and couldn't wait to get out of there...or because he wore glasses thicker than a lens of a microscope, but because he seemed to be the least inter-ested. Every time he mentioned such clichéd sayings such as *'you have to love yourself before you can love someone else,'...'be your own best friend'...*or *'the good you give out, comes back to you a thousand fold,'* Chris' reply was always a roll of the eyes accompa-nied by an audible groan.

He approached Chris afterwards out of curiosity. With a few kind words about knowing how he felt trapped at camp as a kid also, he quickly created a bond with a child who secretly and des-perately just wanted someone to like him. The teen was ripe with self-hatred and would turn to the goddess without much effort. Though when Chris started ranting about his friend Jared and the fantastical tale he'd been told, Eric nearly cried out in joy right then and there.

All blessings to Aton, Eric had thought at that moment, when he heard the name *'Tamen'* slip from Chris' mouth. "A—A very...*very,* imaginative tale there, Chris," Eric said, as calmly as his trembling muscles would allow. "It sounds like this friend of yours...J—Jared, right?" Chris nodded. "Sounds like he really wanted to get away from you—huh? Ya know...break all ties with his old life and get on with a new one. You think he was really ever your friend?"

"Yeah, he was," Chris squeaked and then looked down momen-tarily. He glanced around the picnic area under the pavilion where Eric had led him to off from the others. "That's what's so screwed up. I don't get it. He was my best friend."

"Maybe he found *new* friends," Eric suggested, baiting his hook for a nice fat catch.

Chris stared at him for a moment and then shook his head. "Naw...not Jared. He's not like that."

"Really?" Eric smiled, displaying a row of perfectly aligned teeth —courtesy of the chant and Lord Yikan. "But he's gone, right? That's what *you* said. Took off...left you alone...*adios muchacho!* That doesn't sound like any kind of friends I know. Friends are there for you when things are good and when things are tough. I gotta tell ya, Chris—*my friend*—I'm reading between the lines here and it's pretty darn clear to me what this Jared kid is really telling you. You know what I mean, little buddy?"

Chris batted his eyes slowly. "Kinda—I guess."

Now reel him in! Eric thought.

As Lord Yikan had instructed, should he ever discover anything of any importance, no matter how insignificant he thought it might be, he was to use the mental link he'd forged with him and apprise him of the situation before uttering a word to anyone. When Chris mentioned Tamen's name, Eric knew he was in the midst of a monumental moment.

"I shall make you a king for this," Lord Yikan told him, after Eric relayed what Chris had said. "Follow the normal chain of command and let them know *who* you have and *what* knowledge he possesses. But see that no harm comes to the child. *I want him.*" And so after speaking with his regional superior, he was commanded to retrieve the child that night by any means necessary. Now new best buds, and with a promise of a greasy, double-cheese, pepperoni and sausage pizza, he had no trouble seducing Chris into sneaking out of camp that late afternoon.

"I knew there was a little rebel in you!" he told Chris and added a *see—I'm your new best bud* wink for good measure. "Forget about that kid, Jared. Screw him, right? I think if you really look back on what you thought was a friendship, you'll see it never really was one. He was just using you because you were convenient. Now that you're not, he's basically telling you, 'so long sucker!'"

After enduring watching Chris eagerly devour nearly the entire large pizza by himself, instead of driving him back to camp, he detoured, and headed out into the country as his supervisor had instructed. He gave Chris credit for suspecting that something wasn't quite right, even though for a short while, he seemed to believe they were going to say *screw fat camp* by smoking a little weed before heading back. When he pulled into the long drive leading up to an abandoned barn hidden from the road, it was then that Chris suddenly changed his mind and asked...demanded to be taken back to the camp.

But it was already too late for either to change their minds.

At Chris' insistence to be let out, Eric stopped the car a hundred yards from the rotted barn. But Chris' grand escape was without success. Eric had been listening to Lord Yikan's voice in his head the entire time, and when Chris bolted from the car, he already knew his master was waiting right outside the door for him. Lord Yikan picked up Chris—who screamed at the sight of him—by his back fat with one hand and carried him to the barn like a suitcase where Shazadeh waited.

"Find the tome for me, your god Aton," Lord Yikan had commanded of him before he departed for the African desert. "Secure it and I shall raise you above kings. I will make thee a demigod. Your flesh will be flawless. Even the demons of hell—who crave beauty and perfection above all—will cry out in jealousy." With that, Lord Yikan placed a knife into his hands. "If thou must kill to secure the tome...then so be it. Kill in my name!"

The only good Eric found with being sent to the desert was having the chance to be close to Nicholas, who had led him and Cheryl into the C.I.G., which had led to her murder. Now, because Shazadeh favored him so, it was Nicholas who was in charge of the excavations in the desert. The promotion from meager watcher to boss had added an extra swing to his already cocky swagger. As much as Eric fantasized about helping Lord Yikan kill Shazadeh, getting rid of Nicholas would be just as satisfying, if not more so.

Eric turned on his side and covered his ears in an attempt to drown out the constant sound of digging outside. *I should be out there anyway,* he thought. The workers had reached the floor of another ancient and undocumented structure. But, as Nicholas informed him when he first arrived, there had been many such false alarms over the years.

"I don't know if you know your history, man, but back in the old days, this area was the end all be all," Nicholas crowed. He was shirtless and displaying his taught brown skin and bulging muscles everywhere muscles could be. "We're talking non-stop warring for centuries—which really screws us up. Sometimes you think you've found the palace, and it turns out to be nothing but an outpost or some stupid temple. I tell you what...the last idiots who called the goddess because they thought they had found Tamen's old palace— well, put it like this man...there not here anymore. You know what I'm saying?"

"I got an idea," Eric replied unmoved.

"That's not going to be my butt!" Nicholas vowed. "Screw that! I'll call her—but only when I got that shiny, golden book right here in these hands of mine—and only then. They sent me here for a reason—get me? They don't want any more screw-ups."

Eric forced himself to smile and shrugged indifferently.

Nicholas elbowed him. "You're not still ticked-off about Cheryl going bye-bye, are ya?"

"No," Eric lied.

"You sure?"

"Why would I be?" Eric asked, as he mentally tallied at least ten reasons why he was. "She didn't get with the program."

"Bingo, man!" Nicholas yelped. "You were freaky looking when you first came. No offense, man." He slapped Eric on the back and chuckled. "Now...your eyes and teeth are straight on. You got the

328 · Orlando Smart-Powell

jaw of a movie star. I've even seen some of the women at the Rocky Mountain citadel winking at ya. Heh? Hmm? You ol' tiger."

"So you think it's here?" Eric asked, changing topics.

"We've reached the floor of something at the B-five site," Nicholas said. "But it's unusual that the stones we've found are just a little too perfect—you get me? Not even the stones of the Great Pyramids were cut and fit this well, and this is just the floor of the place! They didn't build outposts with these kinds of stones back then. Can you imagine what the whole place must have looked like back then?"

"And if there's nothing but dirt underneath?"

"We move on," Nicholas said, wiggling his head. "We *think* the book is here, but goddess only knows if that coward Tamen kept it here or moved it somewhere else. It could be in the Valley of the Kings or in Southeast Asia just as easily—he hid there for a century, the goddess said. That's why the C.I.G. has digs going all over the world. He kept his trail pretty cold, so—"

"We're searching for a needle in a haystack," Eric finished.

"But in style," Nicholas added. "You didn't fly here coach, now did you? Private jet and fine wines the whole ride here...Beluga caviar, if you like that salty crap. Think what it's going to be like when she rules this world. You'll never have to worry about paying bills or having a place to stay. And talk about us being the cream of the crop, baby! We'll have all kinds of sexy little sisters begging at our feet. That's going to be life here soon, man."

Eric too thought life on the earth would soon change, just not quite in the same way Nicholas fantasized. "You know," Eric said, as his mood suddenly lightened. "I can't wait for this new world either."

"Thatta boy!" Nicholas sang.

CHAPTER 21

"Chris Knopfitter?" Henrì gasped. "*Jesus Christ!* The whole town is looking for that kid."

"Then they search in vain," Tamen told him. "Somehow the C.I.G. got their hands on him."

"I'm sorry, Papà, I didn't see that one coming," Henrì apologized. "I really never gave that kid a second thought. He wasn't one of those that stood out as being...someone all that important. Is he alive?"

"I believe so," Tamen replied. "But this is another grim lesson for us that this Church of the Imperial Goddess—C.I.G. organization is more pervasive than we assumed it to be. He was *exactly* who they look to recruit."

"How is...?"

"*Shhhh.*" Jared heard Tamen whisper to Henrì, as he feigned sleep across the aisle from them on the plane and listened in on their conversation. "He is as well as can be expected considering."

"When you two didn't show up in New York, I knew something was wrong," Henrì said. "I thought you were both dead until you came in spirit form to tell me plans had changed because of what happened in Nuxta."

"We had to fly from city-to-city for awhile, so as not to leave a trail," Tamen explained. "I'm afraid flying all over has exhausted Jared somewhat, but it was necessary."

"He'll need a lot of rest anyway."

"Is all prepared then?"

"Yes, Papà."

"The workers will wait?"

"I wouldn't stress the plural of *worker* too much," Henrì said. "I could only find two who seemed trustworthy enough and were willing to go with us. The best ones have already been hired out years ago."

"By the C.I.G.," Tamen stated.

"Exactly," Henrì replied. "Egypt may be an Islamic nation now, but that hasn't stopped the formation of an underground C.I.G. movement. And from what I've heard, they pay them very, very well. It's a good thing you left Aria and me well off, because I used a small fortune to get things set up."

"And supplies?"

"All done," Henrì said. "Our guys will meet us in Luxor first. Then we'll drive to Abu Simbel, right above the ancient, second cataract. From there, it's into Nubia proper, or Sudan as it's called now. Then it's all camelback from there on."

"Well done, child."

"We should wake him up. We're going to be landing soon."

* * *

Jared felt uneasy walking amongst the people at the airport and them unable to see or hear him. It had been that way since Tamen and he had plummeted from the sky and began flying around for hours before meeting up with an anxious Henrì in Chicago for their flight to Egypt. "Do not pay attention to them, but do stay out of their way," Tamen had instructed. "I have shrouded us from their sights, but if you bump into them, they will feel it. We cannot be sure who is with the C.I.G., but we do know they are looking for us. Everyone must be considered an enemy for now."

Once the plane landed at the Luxor International Airport, they waited for everyone to disembark before hurrying out behind them. At the customs screening department, they took turns passing through the metal detectors, following close behind the other passengers who walked through. Outside in the open, after a long, but comfortably climate-controlled flight across the ocean, the midday heat of the desert nation took Jared's breath away.

"Where are we?" Jared asked Tamen, who was standing beside him.

"You know where. Listen to the voices around you," he replied.

"Arabic?"

"You were not sleeping as long as you wanted us to believe you were," Tamen informed, looking past him toward the line of cars and cabs. Men wearing suits or traditional galabeyas and women in burqas and hijaabs with their heads—and some, their entire faces covered—dashed hither and fro from cabs into the airport and vice versa. "How do you feel?"

"Hot as heck."

"This is nothing. Wait until we get to the desert," Henrì added, as he craned his neck in the same direction as Tamen. "You'll know what hot really means once we're in that furnace."

"Do you see them, my child?" Tamen asked.

Henrì put his hand above his brow to block the sun from his eyes. "Awwww...no. They said they would be in an old, brown Mercedes."

Tamen pointed past the taxis lined up at the curb. "Like that one?"

"You know I can't see that far, Papà."

"There is one standing by the car named...Hassan. The other is Wati, the driver."

"Aha! That's them," Henrì confirmed. "Good thing you can still read minds, Papà. I never would've found them way down there."

"Remember, Jared," Tamen said, as they walked toward the car. "They cannot see you or me—only Henrì will I allow them to see."

"So...what if they are with the C.I.G.?" Jared asked.

"I am already sifting through their minds as we speak," Tamen replied. "I cannot detect anything to say they are not with the C.I.G., but remember, Shazadeh is extremely powerful. She could have just as easily cast a spell to hide their thoughts from my probing."

"So if they are?" Jared asked.

"I shall keep a close eye on their every move."

Henrì pulled on Jared's arm and stopped him before they came into earshot of Hassan and Wati. "What Papà is saying is that if they step a hair out of line, they're dead."

Jared turned and faced Tamen. "You'll kill'em just like that? Right here?"

"Instantly and absolutely." Tamen droned. He glanced at Henrì who nodded in agreement.

They walked over to the car. Jared slid into the backseat next to Tamen, while Henrì stood outside the car speaking to the two men who greeted him warmly as they approached. When Henrì got in the back, he handed the younger and lighter brown of the two—Hassan—who was riding shotgun a thick white envelope. Hassan opened it and began counting the hundred dollar bills. He turned around and waved the envelope at Henrì. "Too—too much, sir."

"It's a little extra for you and Wati," Henrì replied. "If you two can continue to keep your lips sealed, I'll double the final payment. And...like I told you before, I'll set you up with my contact in Cairo who makes those pretty little passports and green cards—as many of them as you need."

Hassan gawked at him with eyes that were already too large for his thin face. "Ten-thousand more?"

"Each," Henrì added.

Hassan smacked Wati on the side of the head and spoke to him in Arabic. Wati spun around in his seat and looked at Henrì. "This true, sir?"

"Absolutely!"

Hassan showcased a tobacco-yellow smile on his chubby face. "Any'ting you need, sir, we do...alright? You tell us, sir, and we do right now for you.

"Just get us...me...to Abu Simbel as fast as this car can move, and you and your families will be packing your bags for America, OK?"

"Yes sir! Every'ting is vaiting for us there like you ask," Hassan told him. "But no guide, sir. We go to desert, we need guide, no?"

"No."

"Sir," Wati said, sheepishly, "desert very dangerous place. Quickly one can be lost. Hassan find Bani Rasheed or—Bedouin who know desert well."

"No—we'll be fine. I promise you," Henrì assured them. "We won't even come close to getting lost."

Hassan spoke again in Arabic to Wati—his grayed, mustachioed counterpart—who responded in the same, hurried manner. *"They are concerned about getting lost in the desert,"* Tamen said, having translated the men's conversation and relaying it to Jared. *"But money—the world's most tempting of evils—holds greater sway. Men have done far more, for far less."*

"Are we set then?" Henrì asked the men.

"Yes sir!" Wati and Hassan answered one after the other.

After traveling for a few miles, they entered the bustling and smoky city of Luxor. Tamen was looking straight ahead, but Jared heard him as he slipped into his mind and spoke. *"I want you to close your eyes and relax,"* Tamen instructed. *"We have a few hours travel ahead of us and must utilize what time we have efficiently."*

"For what?"

"It is time for you to truly use that marvelous brain of yours. This will be the final lesson I have to offer you."

Jared closed his eyes and stretched out his legs as far as he could within the confines of the cramped backseat. As Tamen instructed, he tried clearing his mind of all thoughts, but couldn't help reliving the recent past...his mother and Aunt Maymee...Aunt Lilly and his grandmother...Tobias murdered and Chris abducted and in the grasp of Shazadeh and Lord Yikan. Even Phineas, who of all people never gave a damn about him, but was the very one who had saved them all, intruded upon his thoughts. And Thaddeus—God knows how he's handling any of this, Jared thought.

"I said clear your mind, Jared!" Tamen barked.

"I—can't get them out of my head."

"Those who were alive when we left are still alive. You concern yourself about things you cannot change. If you want them to stay alive, you must focus on what is in front of you. The path you travel crumbles and falls away behind you with each step you take forward. There is no going back."

"I'll try."

"No...you will!" Tamen demanded. *"You have a linguistic talent far greater than you know it to be. But unless you hone it, it will be useless to you. The time has come for you to learn the sacred chants."*

"Learn magic," Jared whispered excitedly.

"Yes," Tamen said. *"From the tome, you shall recite the Chant of Changing—that which shall strip you of your mortality. And remember, child,"* Tamen's already husky voice dropped an octave, *"once out of the illusion, you must not utter one word of any chant-spell. Not one!"*

"I know. It'll lead them to us."

"Good then."

Jared was now quite used to the world around him completely changing when Tamen cast illusions. When he opened his eyes, he was sitting next to Tamen on the sandy shore of a beach. When he looked up into what should have been the sky, there was just a black slate of darkness that stretched down to the waters lapping at their feet.

In the dark above, white symbols began popping into existence, and his mind reflexively tried to convert the alien symbols into ones he was already familiar with—decagons, Mobius strips, parallelograms, Reuleaux triangles, trapezoids and others. They were tightly lined up left to right and as far up as he could see. One-by-one, Tamen brought each symbol down from the sky and so close, Jared thought he could almost grasp hold of them. And for each one, Tamen sung it for him.

"Look in the middle of this symbol," Tamen said as he pointed at it. "See that dash at the top? That means the note must be prolonged. But if the dash is on the right side of it, you must make the note short and abrupt...*crisp!* When the dash is only half the length, you must add just a hint of vibrato to your voice, or else it becomes totally ineffective when you blend it with the following note to complete the spell. And if not a dash, but concave, your pitch must spiral upward."

Jared exhaled and closed his eyes, but was soon squinting and raising his brows after a few minutes. "This is too freakin' much," he groaned. "There's no way I can cram all of this in my head this quick. Each one of those chant-symbols has a different rule. If they have a dash or a line the note changes completely...*crap!*" he spat. "And if the one before it or after it isn't sung right, then the spell won't work. But there's thousands of variations for each one!"

Tamen shook his head. "You must not try to remember each one —only feel them. Think of your Spanish, French and Latin courses you excelled at with very little effort. Do not forget, I was there and saw you slacking," Tamen added. "Remember how easy it was for you once you broke each language's code?"

Jared sighed and looked up at the symbols in the sky. "Fine...let's keep going." Tamen flipped his hand and returned the symbol in front of them back to the sky and pulled another down.

To Jared, the hours seemed to pass by like long days of summer in the illusionary world. Tamen placed symbol after symbol in front of him—then came the actual singing of each. He tried mimicking Tamen's flick of the tongue to bend the sounds just so, or keeping it flat for a drone-like quality. Though exhausted, he soon began to realize Tamen was right—it was impossible to memorize them all. But, by letting the notes wash over him, and then trying to recall and sing them as Tamen did, he found they flowed easier.

"We will continue our lesson later, Jared," Tamen said abruptly.

Once back in the real world and now far away from Luxor central, they exited the car and followed Hassan and Wati out to an area that was just miles of sand littered with fist-sized rocks. Off to the side were four camels, each with stuffed supply bags hanging on either side of their bodies. From behind one of them, a young boy of no more than fifteen popped out and called for Wati. Wati and Hassan walked away from them and over to the boy.

"What are they saying?" Jared whispered to Tamen. "Tamen. Tamen?"

Henrì tapped Jared on the shoulder. "The young boy's name is Badu," he said in a hushed voice. "He and Wati are brothers. Just um—leave Papà be for awhile."

Jared glanced at Tamen, who was staring off into the nothingness of the desert before them. "He's not exactly the warmest person, but he isn't usually this distant either," Jared commented.

"Even if he doesn't show it at the moment, he's as worried about you, as you are about him."

"My family is running for their lives out there somewhere," Jared griped, as if Henrì had forgotten. "And that includes Chris, ya know. I've always been there for him—like a big bro. And now I got him right in the middle of a war between demons and angels. You know how sick that makes me?"

"You're not the only one who's lost people they love," Henrì replied, rather smartly. "I have...you have...and Tamen the most." He raised his brow. "Imagine returning home to Homer and everything you've ever known has changed. You see where we are?"

"The middle of nowhere?"

"Remember those four colossal statues of Ramses II at Abu Simbel we talked about in World History class a year or so ago?" Jared nodded. Henrì then turned him by the shoulder and pointed off at nothing but desert. "We skirted Ramses' temple on purpose to avoid the tourists, but over there about fifteen or so miles is where they used to be, but were relocated after they built a dam a few miles away. That's just a speck in how Tamen's entire existence has been altered. That can't be the easiest thing to cope with—immortal or not."

Jared bit down on his lip. "I didn't think of it that way. I'm still trying to figure all of this out, too. Tamen's showing me all of these symbols and teaching me these sounds and I swear I can't make sense out of most of them."

"It's not supposed to be any easier than that," Henrì chided him, but then sighed. "Whether you realize it or not, we're at the end of something that started over two-thousand years ago, Jared. What we do next will decide the fate of a climatic, heaven-versus-hell war. But as melodramatic and crazy as it sounds, that's reality!"

"What about Tamen?"

"Tamen's been taking care of himself for thousands of years. I think he can manage a few more days if we give him a bit of space."

Hassan, Wati and Badu walked over to them. After exchanging words with his brother, Wati, Badu got behind the wheel of the car they came in and drove off. "It getting late, sir. Shall we stay here for the night?" Hassan asked.

"*Tell them no,*" Tamen said to Henrì, projecting his voice to Jared also. "*We cannot delay.*"

"We're going now," Henrì told them.

Hassan gave Wati a disconcerting glance. "Which way, sir?"

"*Southwest,*" Tamen said.

"Southwest, gentlemen," Henrì relayed.

"*Henrì...Jared, come!*" Tamen led them away from the men and over to the camels, which snorted uncomfortably at their approach. Tamen opened one of the bags hanging over the first camel's side and pulled out a white galabeya and a long, ten-inch wide strip of cloth. "Put these on. They will keep you much cooler than what you are wearing."

Henrì started disrobing and suddenly began chuckling as he saw Jared hold up the long strip of fabric like he had just been handed a rotten fish. "It's a loincloth," Henrì explained.

"How in the heck do you put it on?"

Henrì chuckled and looked the other way. "I'm not going to put it on for you. Ask Papà."

Jared didn't have to. Tamen walked over and positioned himself between Henrì and Jared, and then stretched out his long arms. "Remove your clothing," Tamen said.

Even though Wati and Hassan couldn't see him, and Tamen's towering height obscured Henrì's view of him, Jared hesitated removing his underwear. He snatched the cloth back from Tamen, and as quickly as he pulled his underwear down, he placed the strip in front of his genitals. When he looked up, Tamen had also removed his clothing, displaying a shimmering, brown body that was absent of every bit of hair.

"I do not know," Tamen said, as if replying.

"Huh?" Jared asked.

"You were wondering if you will resemble me once you have transformed," Tamen said. "And that I do not know. I do not resemble the other angles or half-angels from history, do I?"

"How would I know," Jared responded. "I've never heard of them."

"But you have!" Tamen stressed. "The Nephilim, such as Thor... Hercules...Perseus...Goliath. All were children of angels and mortals. The old myths suddenly do not seem so farfetched now, do they?" Jared shook his head.

Jared gulped and then closed his eyes as Tamen affixed his loincloth about him. Tamen slipped the white galabeya over Jared—who thought it looked more like a robe—and then dressed himself in a matching outfit, as did Henri and the two other men. Afterwards, Tamen lifted him onto the camel and seated him in the saddle. Wati and Hassan helped Henri onto his and then straddled their own with ease. Tamen then took hold of the reigns of Jared's camel and walked alongside him.

Tamen—inexhaustible and immune from the sweltering heat, walked on as though he were out for a stroll, whereas Jared was certain he was being roasted for dinner under his long, white robe. Still, he was more comfortable than he had been before in his jeans, shirt and boots. Even the strip of loincloth that at first seemed jammed up his rear seemed less of a bother now than before.

As sand riddled with pebbles and rocks gave way to just sand, all that remained were windswept sand locked in static waves rippling toward the horizon. Jared knew, as he watched Tamen stare off into the distance, that he saw much more than just fifty-foot high dunes of sand stretching out for miles. *"Close your eyes and relax,"* Tamen told him.

* * *

It was well into the evening when Tamen finally released Jared from another study session in his illusion. When Jared opened his eyes, he saw Tamen standing right next to where he was laying on the ground. He realized that at some point while he was in the illusion, Tamen had taken him from atop the camel and laid him down.

Rising up on elbows, he saw Hassan and Wati were both stretched out on blankets and fast asleep about one hundred yards away. Henrì came up behind him and tossed a brown, shrink-wrapped package down next to him. "Dinner is served," Henrì proclaimed, as he sat down next to Jared with his own hermetically sealed meal.

Jared had to use his teeth to rip open the thick plastic, and with even more effort, had to tear it down the side to fish out the rations. "This stuff can't be good for you," he commented, holding up a block of rainbow-speckled foam masquerading as dehydrated fruit cocktail.

Henrì shrugged and plopped a spoonful of his own grey-gooey meal in his mouth. "The chicken and gravy isn't all bad."

Jared opened another package and squeezed some of the lumpy, glue-like food in his mouth. He tried not to frown, knowing it would only enhance its repulsive flavor. "Yum! Old chicken in flour water with a cup of salt to hide the taste."

"Hey, Papà?" Henrì looked around. "Cripes!"

Tamen, who had been standing right next to them, was now nowhere to be seen.

They both got up and turned round. They spotted Tamen at the top of the dune they were sitting behind. "Don't you hate it when he does that Houdini disappearing shtick?" Jared asked.

"Yes," Henrì growled. "I think he forgets that his normal speed is like quicksilver to us." Henrì beckoned Jared to follow him up the dune.

Climbing the sand dune proved far more challenging than it looked. Each step up seemed to cause every grain of sand to shift and plant them right back where they started. They slid and grabbed each other's hand for a lift and pull. Tamen had apparently sauntered right up the dune, Jared thought, as there was not the slightest disturbance of sand leading up to where he stood.

"We have been travelling south and slightly west," Tamen told them, as they reached his side. He pointed off in the distance. "Over there, a few more miles away once stood a land of beauty that is no more. Even after thousands of years, the embers of my magic smolder deep within. I sensed it a few hours ago."

"Good for us then?" Henrì asked

"Only..." Tamen began.

"What is it, Papà?"

Tamen looked at them both. "There are already people there."

"Dammit to hell!" Henrì blurted. "Not a chance they're just Bedouins or—or archaeologists?"

"Bedouins? Not likely," Tamen stated. "And it is too far out for archaeologists to have ventured looking for artifacts. If I listen carefully, I can hear them digging and searching for what we must find first."

Henrì took hold of Tamen's elbow. "Can't you just read their thoughts from here and check?"

"It is too risky," Tamen replied. "Now that we are vigorously hunted, I dare not take any more chances. It is only a matter of time before whoever they are discovers what lies beneath their feet —and that cannot be allowed to happen, no matter the cost."

Tamen and Henrì stopped talking—out loud at least. Jared knew that whatever they were saying wasn't good just by the way Henrì's face grew more despondent...Tamen's revealed nothing at all—as usual. He closed his eyes and let go of the sensation of cooling sand under his feet...revenge upon Shazadeh and Barbatos... finding Chris...the ancient symbols...and every errant thought coursing though his mind. He slowly began catching sounds, and then words, which seemed to float in the air around him waiting to be picked like cherries. *"...you come back...why—why now?...we do if you don't?...Papà?"*

"Stay here with Henri," Tamen said aloud to Jared, breaking him from his eavesdropping trance.

"No problem," Jared replied readily. He wasn't sure if Tamen had heard him, as he was already down the sand dune they were on and speeding away. With only a trail of dust blowing up in his wake, he began crossing the desert. Jared looked over to speak to Henri, whose brown eyes were sparkling, though not from starlight striking them. "He said he's coming back, and I believe him," Jared offered, hoping to convince Henri, though he himself wasn't entirely sure. "Like you said, he's survived for thousands of years already—he'll survive now."

Henri tapped the side of his head with his finger. "It's impolite to eavesdrop. I didn't know you had *that* in you."

"I guess—sort of." Jared shrugged. "Tamen taught me while we were studying chants. It's not all that hard...but then again, it kinda is. I just clear my mind of crap and focus."

"A genius I.Q. doesn't hurt either," Henri sassed. "I guess you're a quick study with this stuff, too, hmm?"

"I'd feel better if I was quicker at it," Jared groaned. "I only caught bits and pieces of what you two were saying. He must have made some sort of connection between him and me. Ever since I've been out of his illusion, I've felt him in my head, like I can hear him thinking...feel him, even when he's not around."

"Oh that," Henri replied nonchalantly. "My mother Aria and Tamen tried teaching me how to do it. Only problem was, I didn't have the gift that you do. All I get from trying to read thoughts is static most of the time. Tamen just used whatever magic he uses and forged a link between us since I couldn't do it on my own."

"Do you feel him now?"

Henri closed his eyes for a moment, and then shook his head. "No."

"Me either," Jared said. "What does that mean then?"

"It could mean anything or nothing," Henrì replied. "Maybe he shut his mind out from us. Maybe he's dead."

"Jesus, Henrì!" Jared stared at him. "Maybe he's dead? You say it like...like...it's nothing."

"It's a fact we may have to deal with, like it or not."

"But without him—I mean if he's dead, then we could be next."

"We're dominoes," Henrì stated. "I'm glad you're finally realizing it. If one of us falls, we all fall."

"And if he's dead?"

"We just have to wait and see for now." Henrì studied the yellow-hued landscape of the desert. "It's all we can do. If he returns, then we go from there. If not...? Well, put it like this, kiddo...I hope you can ride a camel. If Papà dies, we have to get the hell out of here and damn quick! Because literally...hell is going to be nipping at our heels."

* * *

"Awake my children. I am back and I am safe. All is well—for now."

Jared was the first to look up and see Tamen. Both he and Henrì had vowed to stay awake until Tamen's return and had failed. He was thrilled and relieved to see Tamen, who was holding a cloth bag in his hands. Jared scrambled to his feet, ran to Tamen and bear-hugged him, though didn't budge him from the ground when he tried lifting him up. Tamen returned the embrace and even smiled briefly. "I am fine, child," Tamen reassured him.

"Don't ever go running off like that!" Jared yelled at him.

Henrì wiped sleep from his eyes and yawned. "Papà." He looked down the dune and searched the perimeter. "Where are Hassan and Wati?"

"Most likely five or so miles on their way back home," Tamen replied. "Right now, they are following an illusion I created that they believe to be you."

"Won't we need their help digging?" Jared asked.

"They have already found the lower floor of my ancient palace and have cleared most of the sand and rubble away from it," Tamen informed them.

"Damn C.I.G.!" Henrì spat.

"There are only a few C.I.G. members there," Tamen told him. "The others are paid laborers who most likely have no idea what they are looking for, but know that the harder they work, the more they will earn."

"So you're saying, Shazadeh and Lord Yikan aren't there," Henrì said, as if it were a prayer.

"Yes," Tamen answered. "But regardless, they are but a thought away should one of their watchers call upon them."

Jared looked from one to the other. "So how are we going to get our hands on the book before they do?"

Tamen reached into the cloth bag he carried and brought out a handful of coffee grounds. He let the black grainy coffee slip through his fingers and back into the bag. "By stealth and deception."

"Coffee...wow!" Henrì mocked.

Tamen grinned. "The coffee is for you, my pale child. Mixed with a bit of water and rubbed into your skin, we shall make you into a most handsome and swarthy Nubian prince."

"OK...so Henrì slips in, and then what? We can't just walk in and out of there with it."

"Stealth," Tamen stated and then disappeared.

Before Jared could even open his mouth in awe, from behind, Tamen picked him up and tossed him well over ten feet away. Moving faster than the human eye could track, Tamen ran toward the exact spot of his throw just in time to catch Jared in midair with one hand. "I'm gonna puke," Jared murmured as Tamen set him down.

"Stealth," Tamen said again, and then patted Jared on the head.

"And the diggers? The ones who aren't with the C.I.G.?" Henri inquired.

"I will knock them unconscious. If I can," Tamen added.

"Even when he pulls a punch, he can knock through a log," Henri told Jared.

Jared rubbed his queasy stomach. "Tossing them around like toothpicks might do the trick also."

"Henri—you must attend to your task," Tamen instructed. "Rub the wet coffee grounds into your skin and bask in the sun. And you, Jared...your ability to feel the chant is still weak. Lie down so that we may continue your studies."

It was indeed the longest and most grueling lesson he'd received so far. The difficulty in deciphering the symbols had increased exponentially, but so had Tamen's frustration with him. Every break in his voice and mispronunciation of a chant caused Tamen to shake the ground of the illusion with thunder.

"Do not say you are focusing, when you are clearly not!" Tamen derided him, after he inadvertently read the flare of a symbol and let his pitch flow up, instead of down. Tamen grasped hold of the glowing symbol before them and slung it off into the sky. "Concentrate like your life depends on it—for it does. This is not one of your videogames that you can press restart if you are killed."

Jared snapped back. "I'm trying, ya know?"

"You try and you will fail. You *do*—and you succeed. There are no more second chances."

When finally released from Tamen's illusion, which felt more like a prison for the last six hours, Jared began to discover that with great concentration, he could recall the chant of healing or the one that caused matter to lose cohesiveness, or the one that released objects from gravity's grip. Though forbidden to speak the chants outside of the illusion, he felt, more than knew, that something unnatural was brewing within him. He followed Tamen and

346 · ORLANDO SMART-POWELL

now a sun-baked, dusky looking Henrì, who seemed more red than brown, up and over the dune that served as their cover.

"I feel like I could lift a mountain," Jared boasted.

"You cannot," Tamen remarked. "Not yet."

Tamen looked to the west, where the sun was still high, but in its final glory for the day. "We shall keep a steady pace southward. By the time we reach the encampment, a dark sky shall be our ally."

Navigating up and down the sand-slippery dunes was a challenge for Jared and Henrì. As they progressed on, it became nearly impossible for them to keep pace with Tamen, who wouldn't allow them to stop. They drank greedily from their flasks in midstride every chance they got. And instead of allowing them even a small respite, Tamen took turns carrying each up the highest of dunes until an hour past nightfall; they were within a few hundred yards of the excavation site. Beyond the scattered tents, the roar of generators and floodlights directed into the excavation pit served as their beacon.

"Stay close to me until we are behind the tents," Tamen whispered to them.

"Can you tell how many are there?" Henrì asked.

Tamen clenched his fists. "About two minute's worth. Once I have gone, two minutes is exactly how long you must wait. Come around to the far side of the pit and I shall bring you the tome."

"Yes, Papà."

"Jared—you must—without the slightest hesitation, locate the Chant of Changing and sing it...*completely*. The only reason you should stop is if you are dead. Had I the power to find the spell for you, I would. But as you know, the Chant of Changing is forever invisible to my immortal eyes. You must be swift. Any questions, my children?" Tamen looked at each one and waited.

Jared and Henrì both nodded their heads.

Tamen grasped each one by the head and kissed both sides of their cheeks. "My love for both of you shall never diminish, whether in this world or in the next...

"The fate of all humankind shall be determined by our success or failure this night.

"Now let us begin."

CHAPTER 22

Nicholas was peering over and into the excavation pit, and then began running along the edge to get a better view. "Hey! What da' hell is going on over there?" he called down to the workers.

"What's happening?" Eric asked. He had just come out of his tent and ran over to where Nicholas was marching to and fro along the edge of the excavation pit. From what he could see from his perch two hundred feet above, was that the workers...one-by-one... and even two at a time...were mysteriously and suddenly passing out and lying motionless on the ground.

Eric stepped back and behind Nicholas, who was still shouting down for one of his translators to respond. He pressed his stomach firmly against Nicholas's back. Nicholas quickly glared at him, but resumed yelling down into the pit to no avail.

"I'm going down there and find out what the hell is going on!" Nicholas roared.

Eric grabbed hold of Nicholas' shoulder with his left hand and held him steady. "Wait! Look...*no—no* listen!"

The sound of pick axes chipping away at rock had stopped, but the cracking of rock continued on. What Eric noticed that Nicholas

failed to, was that the dark-skinned worker that Nicholas had introduced him to earlier...the one who had discovered the ground
floor of the structure...was at one moment running toward the ladder to get out, and in the next, caught up in a blinding whirlwind
of dust and was gone! And he was not the only one this was happening to.

Not even a moment's breath later, strangled screams sang out
from below. Instead of the workers scrambling about in confusion,
they were now fighting one another for position on the ladders on
the side of the pit. Eric didn't understand Arabic, but he knew
what the sound of desperation sounded like in any language.

Nicholas shook his head. "They must have found it. They found
it!" he whispered, as he backed up right into Eric's chest. "C'mon...
move!" He shoved his elbow back and grazed Eric's ribs.

Eric sucked in the pain and quickly placed his right arm on top
of Nicholas' shoulder. "Get off me!" Nicholas demanded. He moved
to twist out of Eric's grasp, but his feet slipped on the edge. He
yelped as his right foot slid off the sand and danced on air.

Eric held Nicholas secure enough to let him teeter precariously
on one foot. He stretched his neck as far forward as he could without losing his balance and gazed into Nicholas' beautiful brown
and frightened eyes. "Cheryl wasn't perfect, but she was mine.
There's gonna be a new world, alright. But not with you in it...you
goddess-lovin' piece of crap!" He pushed Nicholas away and
smiled as he fell into the pit.

Eric dropped to his stomach and crawled over to the edge. He
saw that all of the workers were laying either face up or face down
in the sand, and all unconscious. He even spotted Nicholas, though
his body was prone on the ground, his head was turned in the opposite direction and stared up to the night sky.

He crawled away until he made past the last tent and then
jumped to his feet and began running out into the desert. With no
water or provisions, and miles from the nearest village, Eric hadn't

a care. He knew he had done what he had been called to do and believed in his heart that he would be saved.

"Aton!" he screamed in his mind. *"Come, my lord, and reclaim your throne!"*

No...there was no doubt in his mind that he was Aton's most humble and loyal servant—for the once clear, starry skies above had already begun to grow unnaturally dark and cloudy. With the first flash of lightning and rumble that followed, he knew his god had heard him and was coming.

CHAPTER 23

What the hell! Jared thought. He was already past the point of panicking and was ready to take on hysteria.

The sudden filling of the sky with furious black clouds was the first sign that their plan had gone awry. After crouching and waiting behind the tents with Henrì, Tamen slipped inside each—hitting each work upon their temple to assure they stayed unconscious—and then out. Tamen had then carried them to the opposite side of the pit to hide once more until he had finished what he'd started.

As if by nature's unyielding call of curiosity, he and Henrì peeked over into the pit after Tamen had casually walked over to the edge and jumped down into the midst of the unsuspecting men. Though he couldn't see Tamen, he was able to follow the dust he riled up in his wake as he sped from man to man; inflicting glancing blows upon their temples or to the backs of their heads, rendering them temporarily comatose.

Soon thereafter, the sound of stones in the pit being repeatedly cracked rose up. Henrì, who had continued peeping inside the pit,

352 · Orlando Smart-Powell

verified this. "*My God!* Papà split that damn slab of rock with his bare hands—like—like it was Styrofoam!" Henrì exclaimed.

In the next moment, Henrì's brief moment of awe was overtaken by panic. He rolled over atop of Jared, shoving his face into the ground and filling his mouth with sand. "Watch out!" Henrì sounded the alarm.

Jared felt a wisp of air by his ears right before the golden tome crashed right behind them. Henrì wasted little time rolling off of him and into a kneeling position. He yanked Jared up to his knees. *"Now, Jared! Now!"* he commanded.

Upon opening the golden tome and flipping through its gold leaf pages of ornately scripted symbols, Jared knew *'something was re-ally...really wrong."*

Dread welled up from his stomach in the form of bile. The ancient symbols in the tome shared little, if any similarity to those taught him by Tamen. The ones he'd struggled to learn days before consisted of slashes, circles, curls and stroke marks to signal the rise and fall of the pitch. The ones he stared at now had completely different accents on their geometric-alphabet like shapes. The strokes were shorter, bolder and more deliberate in design. But the more he studied them, using Tamen's symbols as a primer, the clearer the intention of its author started to become.

Slowly, he began to see that they weren't as different from the other symbols as he first assumed, but shared a commonality more in sound, than in their written manner. Though again, the difference was that they were completely different markings. Against Tamen's judgment and following his own gut feeling, he discarded everything Tamen had taught him. He attempted to decipher them again, but this time, with each arcane symbol he saw, he closed his eyes and allowed each one to flow over him—to feel each one as he gave it voice. But there was no tingling upon his skin as he expected there should be.

"Hurry, Jared!" Henrì cried.

Jared dared a look skyward just in time to see the black clouds above them momentarily brighten with lightning before a shock-wave of thunder rattled the ground. He flipped the pages and began chanting another line of symbols. He was distracted again when Tamen leapt out of the pit, and with the grace of a pouncing lion, landed and walked over to him without missing a beat.

"Tamen—I don't feel anything!" Jared cried. "It isn't working."

The clouds trembled again, drawing their attention up. "It must!" Tamen demanded. "It *has* to. You must find the chant now. Our time is already up—for he is here!"

Jared resumed with fiery determination. He knew what Tamen was feeling, for he felt it too—that they were no longer alone.

He flipped to the next page, and this time with his actual and mind's eye, began picking apart the symbols. He raised his voice up and out, which the pit echoed back. He rose and sunk the pitch of his song, stopping and pausing slightly only to flick his tongue to find the right accent for each tone. But except for the ground being shook by thunder, he felt nothing twitching or tingling within him.

A flash of lightning streaked through the sea of black clouds that had now enveloped the sky as far as could be seen. From the sky came a voice that illuminated the clouds with each word uttered. "My pupil. *My jailer!*"

Tamen gazed up. "Show yourself, Lord Yikan!"

"Ah—but I already have, traitor. Look upon me and see that which I am." A series of lightning strikes throughout the clouds made them translucent and briefly revealed a small, brilliant sun that throbbed—expanding and contracting—as though it were about to go supernova at any moment.

"There are no gods of Egypt! There never has been!" Tamen yelled. "Aton is but an illusion."

"Having faith in one such as you has been my only fault," Lord Yikan replied, in the guise of Aton. "Relinquish the child and *my* book to me. I vow on the trust I once had in you as my pupil that I shall not harm him."

"Tamen!" Jared yelled.

"Keep chanting, child," Tamen replied, never once taking his eyes off the sky.

"Nothing is happening. The chant isn't working!" Jared cried.

Lighting flashed again. "I will teach thee what Tamen could not," Lord Yikan offered.

"Go to hell!" Jared screamed back.

"Tamen cannot protect you. Only I can save you and return your...*friend*...back to thee. I—Aton—promise this to you."

Jared's mouth gaped. "*Chris...*"

"Christopher...yes, young one," Lord Yikan whispered, in the form of a gusty wind. "In my possession he resides—unharmed. At least for now."

"Ignore him, Jared," Tamen pressed. "He is filled with lies."

"Nay! It is but truth I speak. Though Shazadeh covets thy dear friend's essence, for she knows he is loved greatly by thee," Lord Yikan added with a cold gust of wind.

"Why does Shazadeh not show herself?" Tamen asked. "Surely she can snuff out our lives as easily as a flame and claim this world for her own."

From the black, cloud-shadowed horizon and beyond, the sky danced with arcs of lightning that shook the earth below. *"This world is mine!"* Lord Yikan shrieked.

"Come and kill us then!" Tamen dared. "Scorch our bones or drown us in a great sea...if you can. Use your mighty chants and succeed in only calling forth Shazadeh to witness your betrayal of her."

"If she comes, then she will join all of you in the Great Marsh!"

"She is demon and nothing more, Yikan. Neither you nor I can stand against her."

"*I am* divine!"

"There is only one God!" Tamen cried out. "The God of Zaphen-ath-Paneah and Abraham and father of the Christ is God and God alone. Can you not bear to see reason after all these years?"

"Blasphemy!" Lord Yikan accused him.

"The chants do not belong to us," Tamen told him. "We stole them. The words of the chant belong only to Lucifer and Metatron who wrote them." Tamen stretched out his arms and cried out. "We are not gods!"

"Word? Of...God?" Jared whispered. Tamen's own admission startled him. He looked at the symbols once more with an entirely new perspective and nearly cried out for joy! In so many ways, he realized suddenly, Tamen had been so right about the nature of the chants, but also had been so very wrong about them.

Henri dropped to his knees beside Jared. "What is it? Keep singing for Christ's sake!"

Jared ignored him. "Tamen! You—you—your own story taught me what you couldn't! I mean...The Christ already gave you the answer, only you didn't see it then!"

"What are you saying?" Tamen asked.

"God...said 'let there be light,' right? He called man from the dust. With the word of God, there came water! *Don't you see?*" Jared cried. "You said the chants were written by Metatron as God created the world and as the angels sang. Those are the chants *you* sing—the source of *your* magic. But when God created the world, he didn't chant...he spoke. The power is his word...*the spoken word*...not chanted."

The spark of realization that flashed in Tamen's eyes was all the validation Jared needed to realize he was right. With his finger pointing back to the first symbol on the page, he started again, but this time read, not chanted, the written word. But even as he greedily absorbed the words and began speaking them with his newfound knowledge, the sky above came alive with light. Unable to resist, he looked up and shielded his eyes with his hands from the unnatural illumination, and saw the glowing disc that was Lord Yikan implode. His orb-like form momentarily sucked in the nearby black clouds before screaming with the voice of a man and plummeting to the earth. The chant-spell that had struck Lord Yikan was still upon the air, but hadn't come from Tamen, who too seemed caught off guard by Lord Yikan's meteoric fall.

Jared followed the sound of the chant, which led his gaze up to the sky and right to Shazadeh. She descended through the black clouds, which rolled up upon themselves and fled from her with a swipe of her arms. Tamen immediately began chanting.

Jared...uttering the first word, felt his blood began to warm within his veins.

"It was never *if* Lord Yikan would betray me, but *when*," Shazadeh offered, as she slowed her descent and hovered above them. "He thought me so blind that I would never discover his deception. He is far more mortal man than he thought he was. But you, my handsome godling...if you will submit, for you know you cannot best me, I will make one so lovely as you a true lord of this world of men—and the consort of a goddess."

Tamen's answer was in the form of a chant. Even as Jared continued speaking the words from the tome, the vortex of wind Tamen propelled at Shazadeh did nothing to cool his skin or his flesh, which seemed ablaze. But Shazadeh had chanted her own spell even as Tamen sent his, and dissipated it into a gentle breeze.

The wind hadn't a chance to even fade when another chant was already forming on Tamen's lips. This time, the ground behind Jared trembled, and from the pit below, slabs of rock the size of small cars rose up and went hurtling skyward. But with a counter-chant from Shazadeh, the limestone and granite slabs exploded and rained down to the earth as pebbles and dust. Even lightning that Tamen sent next, shrieking down upon her like a curtain of pure light and transforming the sand below into solid glass, did nothing more than make her scoff as it passed harmlessly around her.

Henrì moved his body in front of Jared, as if he could protect him from the barrage of elements whipping around them. Jared wasn't sure how long Tamen could keep up the fight or when Shazadeh would tire of toying with him, but what he was certain of was that he had just wet himself...amidst other noxious, thick, gooey fluids pouring out of his ears, nose and even his pores. With each word he spoke, he felt his body dying that much quicker—and painfully, as if he was being eaten from the inside out.

Every word uttered increased the cramps and spasms and finally, his stomach and intestines having had enough, pushed out bile and blood through every opening he had. Inexplicably, the more his body purged itself of fluids, the keener his senses became.

In that moment of dying, he never felt more alive.

The chants both Tamen and Shazadeh exchanged, that had one time sounded so powerful and exact in their articulation, now seemed as though they were broken, and spoken with a lazy tongue. But other voices—clearer, more precise and harmonious— were seeping into the wind—ones that belonged to neither of the two who battled on.

Above Shazadeh, Jared saw—with his newly forming eyes—a rift opening in the very essence of the sky, like a curtain was being drawn back by invisible ropes and revealing another land. In the rapidly expanding chasm, there were innumerable lights as bright as the sun in midday, and their very presence electrified the air. But with his nearly complete angelic eyes, the radiant lights no longer hurt to look at them, but instead allowed him to focus on the bodies in the rift, which were the source of the lights.

He saw thousands upon thousands of blue-white glowing figures standing at the edge of the cleft. Behind them were hundreds of thousands more who sang a haunting, yet very familiar song to him, though he was sure he'd never heard it before. Thousands looked like the Order, Oriziel-Nigiel-Palis, with one, two, three and sometimes four faces. Others were shaped like wheels and spun, emitting a myriad of colors like a kaleidoscope—thousands more had heads of oxen and sheep and lambs, but bodies of humans, lions and wolves standing upright on hind legs.

Though with the light came dark.

Shazadeh propelled herself down to the ground. The force of her landing flung Jared from prone to his back. But Shazadeh's ground shaking impact had done more than just rattle the ground—it had split it! The gaping cavern she created spewed smoky white light from within, and much more.

Creatures twice the size of a man rose up and hovered above the chasm—naked and without genitalia—and in every human hue. Outwardly, their skin was beyond perfection. Their hair—stark white, pitch black and blood red—gleamed like sunlight on glass. Their eyes were large and shadowed by finger-long, black lashes.

Beneath their skin of mortal perfection and exaggeration, Jared's new eyes saw the distorted truth that was their true forms. Some were missing eyes, and others had far too many. Skin that on the surface seemed flawless was actually scaled and riddled with boils that begged to be lanced. Behind white teeth were incisors that seemed sharp enough to mangle metal. And whereas the song of the Heavenly Host from above was harmonious, the creatures below sang one that was disjointed and pained the ears.

"Hurry sister! Kill the child!" A voice from one of the demons demanded. A chorus of demons soon followed the first call.

"The Heavenly Host has come to witness his birth. Take his head and shame them all!"

"Destroy him—he changes even now."

"Annihilate he who is the balance."

"Yes! Kill him and claim thy throne, goddess!"

"Now sister!"

Shazadeh needed no further encouragement.

Jared heard her begin chanting. From the sky, just as quickly as she uttered the chant, a pillar of fire descended upon them and he knew it was too late. Her fire-chant was too quick and powerful for Tamen, who unsuccessfully tried countering it with his own spell.

Though Tamen had deflected some of the conflagration with his chant, his power paled next to hers. The blast ignited the robe Henrì wore seconds before it reached him. The concussive force of the heat sent him hurtling up and over, and into the pit like a Molotov cocktail. Tamen too was lit on fire and blown back for hundreds of yards.

Jared—his skin already melted off exposing muscle and bone by the Chant of Changing—felt as though he'd been ground to dust by the explosion. But as life departed what was left of his body, he could feel a new force already rushing into him.

Tamen got up and cried out. He was smoldering like a branch pulled from a fire. It was the first time Jared had ever heard Tamen give voice to pain. The parts of Tamen's face that were not hanging off his chin, were blackened. The other parts of his skin and robe were still one fire.

Jared's body was rising up in the air. The chant he heard Tamen begin singing was no longer cryptic to his new ears. He knew the spell Tamen was preparing was one of lightning. And then without warning, Tamen flew directly at Shazadeh. She snagged him easily and dug her fingers into his torso up to the last knuckle. As if accepting his fate, he embraced her.

"I do commend you on your fight to the very end, Tamen," she purred. "But as you see now, all that you and the Christ ever hoped for is lost." She looked up at the storm bustling with electricity. "Go ahead, godling—strike us and see who remains and who is turned to ash."

Jared heard Tamen release the chant as she bid. Only...

...he was too late to scream for Tamen not to.

In that moment, Jared realized Tamen's great sacrifice, and that it was too late to even say goodbye.

He knew the moment Tamen's shower of lightning struck not at himself and Shazadeh, but careened into the cleft where the Heavenly Host were looking on, that their retaliation, fueled by the might of the Holy Ghost, would be Tamen's end. And it was exactly, Jared realized, what Tamen wanted to happen.

There was but a brief silence from the hundreds of thousands of celestial creatures who were completely unaffected by the lightning that rolled over and off of them. But below, a riot ensued from the demons that scrambled over one another to get back into the pit.

"*Flee sister!*" A demon cried out in a panic.

"You have failed!" another one said.

"Astaroth...our lord, help us!"

Even Shazadeh knew what now lay in store for her. "Noooooo!" she screamed as she tried to extract her hands from Tamen's torso and wiggle herself out of his embrace. "*Father!*"

In silence, every one of the Heavenly Hosts doubled in brilliance. With their illumination exponentially brightened, they cast down their dazzling, pure light upon both Shazadeh and Tamen. The incineration of both took seconds, if that—first blackening and peeling off their skin to the bone, and then cremating the rest of them—leaving nothing but a rain of ashes lazily floating down to the ground.

Even if Jared had wanted to scream his anguish, he could not... he was no longer Jared...a boy...or a human for that matter. He could literally see the chant-spells being inscribed into his mind's eye, as though someone was carving them with a blade. His body no longer hurt, nor did it crave air to breathe or try to pump blood, as he no longer had lungs or a heart, or any organ at all.

Glowing blue-white skin like the creatures in the heavens began wrapping around densely packed muscle that felt stronger than steel to him. The chants that had been just symbols on gold pages were now written into his mind and begged to be loosed. Jared knew there was no part of him that was human anymore, but that now he was a true immortal being...a celestial creation...an angel...

...the Child of Balance!

From within the heavens he heard two distinct voices calling to him to step into the cleft. Though one did not speak to his ears, its voice flowed through him from head to foot. Though every particle of his new being was drawn to those voices that he could not see, Jared refused and lowered himself back down and into the pit next to Henrì.

Life still lingered within Henrì's body, which had stiffened up like a piece of burnt meat. With angelic eyes, Jared saw the cells of Henrì's body quickly dying, as what life he still clung to had nearly ebbed away. Jared pursed his lips and readied the chant of healing.

He sung the chant as though he had sung it thousands of times before. Power—glowing, snaking tendrils of light—coursed out from him and flowed into Henrì. Like a sculptor, he refashioned burnt skin and fused Henrì's broken spine as though they were both made of clay. Deeper within, Jared renewed the flesh of his charred lungs and made them moist again. What had been Henrì's broken, smoldering body was now slumbering peacefully in his arms, breathing in strong breaths to feed a new, hungry, robust heart.

Henrì stirred after a short while and opened his eyes. *"My God!"* Henrì gasped. "You—you're beautiful, Jared."

"Am I?" Jared replied, with a voice flush with an echoing vibrato.

"Y—Yes! And very blue!" Henrì tried rising up, but slipped back into Jared's arms. He pointed up. "You look like...them. Not like..." Henrì stopped. "Where's..."

"He is no more," Jared said softly. "He sacrificed himself for us."

Henrì's mouth parted and started to quiver. Jared quickly brought Henrì's head to his chest and rocked him back and forth, smothering the cry that eventually barreled out.

"I—I shouldn't be mad. Or cry," Henrì finally sputtered after a short while. "It was what he wanted most. He lived longer than he should have anyway—way too long. And without Amenhotep, too."

"No mortal was meant to have the power of a god," Jared stated.

"But you?"

Jared lifted him to his feet and steadied him until he found firm footing. "Far—far past all of those heavenly beings up there, I hear voices calling to me, but it's not Jared they say, but Mizel—*The One Who Keeps the Holy Balance. Come with us,* they keep telling me."

Henrì stepped forward and stumbled into Jared's blue arms. He tried pushing Jared away, but to no avail. "Are you crazy? Let me go! Go with them, Jared! Or should I call you Mizel?"

"I can't. And Jared will do," he replied.

"What the hell do you mean, you can't?" Henrì barked. "Why not?"

"Because there are matters left undone," Jared replied. "Lord Yikan was struck down, but he still lives and has already fled. And he still has Lucifer's golden tome. I must find it, and then hide both tomes for all time. They can never again be used by mortals."

"You're going after Lord Yikan—"

"And Chris!" Jared interrupted before Henrì could finish. "I promised Chris I would come back for him, and I'll move heaven and earth—*and hell*—to do it." Jared scooped Henrì up in his arms and began rising in the air. "Chris is my brother as much as Amenhotep was Tamen's. And we fight for our family. I'm going to find Chris one way or another. But right now, Henrì...you're going home."

"And you?"

Jared looked up to the cleft in the sky, which was slowly sealing back up. "Me? I'll go home later."

CHAPTER 24

"I still don't know why we standing around this grave and ain't a damn thing in it?"

"Hush, Aunt Lilly," Maymee said, who was standing next to her.

"Don't make no monkey sense at all," Aunt Lilly replied, almost at a whisper, but loud enough to make sure everybody heard her.

"C'mon ya'll and get in. Let them be," Althea said to Aunt Lilly, Maymee and Thaddeus, who were standing around the small gravestone in the back garden of Henri's New Orleans home.

"Hell no!" Aunt Lilly protested. "I ain't goin' in there with all those haints running around. Every time I look, here another of those shadow things moving. I'll be in the car." She marched off, but not before stopping a safe distance from where Jared stood with Dorthea. She pointed at him. "Boy, you *know* you ain't right! I don't know what you be, but it ain't the boy I knew."

Though Jared had assumed the form of his mortal self and had dressed in real clothing, he knew there was no fooling Aunt Lilly. "I love you, too," he professed and then smiled at her.

Aunt Lilly sized him up. "Hmmpf!" she snorted, and then walked off to the front of the house.

"Don't pay her no mind. You know how she is," Dorthea told him.

"I know."

"But...you do come off..."

"Different?"

"Perfect," Dorthea said as she peered at him. "Too perfect is what's a matter. But...you're still you, right?"

"No—not at all," Jared admitted.

"I'm still calling you Jared. That's what I named you."

Jared smiled. "You can call me whatever you want, Mom."

Dorthea looked down at the gravestone. "I think it's beautiful what you and Henri did for him. It doesn't matter if his body is there or not. It's all about how you feel when you see it, right?"

Jared nodded. He looked down at the marker again.

Tamen
Loving Father of Many
Faithful servant of Yahweh

"Henri's going to be alright, isn't he? He's pretty torn up," Dorthea observed.

"In time he will be," Jared replied. "We've been through a lot and...he did lose his father. He's seen things mortals were never meant to see, but he made it. Just give him some time."

"I know you're leaving again."

"I have to find Chris, Mom. I know he's alive and out there somewhere. I'm gonna bring him back," he vowed.

"Lord help you both then," Dorthea said as she took hold of his hand. "I wanted to ask you something, Jared."

"What did I see in the sky when it opened?" Jared asked, having already pulled the question from her mind. "I didn't see who you think I saw."

"Just angels? You didn't see—"

"It was more like a feeling," Jared interrupted. "Close your eyes, Mom.

"Think of how you felt when you first held me in your arms and I opened my eyes and looked at you. Remember how you felt the first time you really ever watched the sun rise on a quiet morning. Imagine you're young again and full of life, and you got that feeling that you can live forever and ever. Dream your most wonderful dream when everything in your life is wonderful and there's not a hint of sorrow in your heart, because everyone you ever loved is with you, and you know they will never again be taken away from you.

"Now make that moment last forever and ever.

"Every time you breathe, that moment washes over and in you. Every time you look around you, and everything you see makes you feel that moment again and again. From now to forever, you feel as if you are swimming in that wonderful, loving and peaceful moment...in a great ocean that stretches on and never ends.

"If you can *feel* that Mom...

"...then you will begin to understand how it was for me...

"...when I felt *God*."

CHAPTER 25

"I knew you would save me," Eric Lightner said, as he followed Lord Yikan down the hall in the Rocky Mountain Citadel. "My god...you shall rise again."

"Aye," Lord Yikan responded. "But not here." He walked up a flight of stairs leading to Shazadeh's sanctum. "The child of balance...Mizel...*now hunts us*. I hear his abominable angelic chants upon the wind. He seeks out and destroys all that Shazadeh and I have built over the centuries. And soon he will come here and set this to ruin."

"Then—then we must go!" Eric sputtered in alarm.

"We shall, my loyal servant. We will flee this place and into hiding we shall go until I am fully recovered." Lord Yikan opened the doors of the sanctum. "Though we shall not leave empty-handed."

In front of him, on a stone pedestal was the golden tome of Lucifer. He walked over to it and placed it under his arms. He turned around and faced Eric. "They have made the child of balance into an angel, but they have not balanced the world as they had hoped, for he remains upon this earthly plane without equal...thus again, unbalancing all that is. And this angel, Mizel, refuses to go to heaven with his kind."

"He wants Lucifer's tome," Eric stated. "He's not gonna leave until he has it."

"Aye," Lord Yikan responded. "But he desires something else even more than that." He looked to his left. Strapped in a chair by his arms and legs, and with his mouth bound sat Christopher Knopfitter.

www.ingramcontent.com/pod-product-compliance
Lightning Source LLC
Chambersburg PA
CBHW071210250626
47159CB00001B/264

* 9 7 8 0 9 8 9 5 7 0 7 0 1 *